In Search of the
ROSE NOTES

by Emily Arsenault

In Search of the Rose Notes
The Broken Teaglass

In Search of the
ROSE NOTES

EMILY ARSENAULT

wm

WILLIAM MORROW
An Imprint of HarperCollins*Publishers*

IN SEARCH OF THE ROSE NOTES. Copyright © 2011 by Emily Arsenault. All rights re-
served. Printed in the United States of America. No part of this book may be used or
reproduced in any manner whatsoever without written permission except in the case
of brief quotations embodied in critical articles and reviews. For information address
HarperCollins Publishers, 10 East 53rd Street, New York, NY 10022.

HarperCollins books may be purchased for educational, business, or sales promo-
tional use. For information please write: Special Markets Department, HarperCollins
Publishers, 10 East 53rd Street, New York, NY 10022.

FIRST EDITION

Designed by Diahann Sturge

Library of Congress Cataloging-in-Publication Data has been applied for.

ISBN 978-0-06-201232-6

11 12 13 14 15   OV/RRD   10 9 8 7 6 5 4 3 2 1

In Search of the
ROSE NOTES

Prologue

Chicago.
A man is about to get on a routine flight.
Suddenly, he pauses. He doesn't know why—
  but he's got to walk away.
An hour later the plane goes down in flames.
It's dismissed as chance. . . .
  —Time-Life Books commercial, circa 1987

When I was a kid, I used to stop cold whenever one of those commercials came on. If I was drowsing to my mother's game shows, I'd jolt awake, sit up straight, and listen. If I was playing with my Spirograph on the floor, I'd stop, stare, and let my colored pen go loose in my hand. If I was getting a snack in the kitchen, I'd run back to the living room to watch. Like the Pied Piper, the spooky synthesizer music drew me in, and the stories told by the priestly sounding narrator gripped me long after the commercial was over—usually past bedtime. I'd lie awake thinking of the woman with the prophetic dream of schoolchildren dying in an avalanche. The matching drawings of aliens produced by abductees who'd never met. The man who points a clover-shaped wire at Stonehenge, feels an inexplicable surge throughout his body, then faints. And I couldn't dismiss any of it.

There are so many hints of a world more remarkable than we ever imagined, and of abilities that we barely suspect. Send for your first volume on a trial basis and see if you can explain these things away. . . .

It wasn't until we were eleven that Charlotte and I learned that her older brother, Paul, had had several of the books in his bedroom for years. All this time we'd been passing his room, holding our noses against the smell of dirty shirts and rotting dregs of milk shakes—and this treasure had been buried there. It was like finding a sacred scroll in the Dumpster behind Denny's. Turns out he'd bought a subscription with some paper-route money but eventually canceled it when he got tired of the books, which weren't actually that great, he said. And now he was cleaning out his bedroom, making space for a stereo he planned to buy, and was going to chuck the books if Charlotte didn't want them.

Charlotte kept her fifteen treasured volumes at the bottom of a cardboard box in her closet, covered with a stack of *Highlights* magazines. The books were beautiful. The textured black covers with the silver lettering made them feel very official and adult, like a high-school yearbook. And the smell of the thick, glossy pages reminded me of new textbooks at school—which confirmed the seriousness of their contents. Besides, it seemed that Paul had barely cracked them. The text was difficult, but Charlotte used her top reading-group skills to decipher a few pages nearly every night. She found the most important and interesting bits for me. Plus, there were lots of pictures. Almost every day after school, we pored over the books, boring Charlotte's beautiful teenage baby-sitter—Rose, with the dirty-blond hair and even dirtier mouth—practically to death.

But then Rose disappeared in November of our sixth-grade year, making the books even more vital to us—no longer a mere source of entertainment but an investigative guide. By then we knew better than the neighbors who whispered "runaway" and the police who let her trail go cold. We knew better than to stop at what people aren't willing to talk about. The commercials had explained that there is much that is unknown but promised that the books would tell us at least "what could be known." And Charlotte and I took them at their word.

Visions and Prophecies:
November 1990

After Rose disappeared, Charlotte's parents never found a replacement baby-sitter. Either they were hoping that Rose would return any day or they'd finally figured out that Charlotte was old enough to take care of herself for a couple of hours each afternoon before Paul arrived home from soccer practice.

"I'm still worried about Rose," Charlotte told me about a week after the disappearance had hit the news. We were sitting cross-legged on her bed, playing a halfhearted round of Rack-O.

"Everybody is," I said.

"Her picture was in the paper again this morning."

"I know," I replied, a little annoyed. Sometimes Charlotte acted like I lived in a cave.

"I don't think we should just be sitting here playing games. I think we should be helping them find her."

I wasn't surprised when Charlotte went to the corner of the closet where she kept her black books. Sighing, I reshuffled the Rack-O cards. I wasn't in the mood for the black books just now. And I wasn't sure I could handle the darkness of their contents without Rose's sarcasm there to lighten it up.

But the picture Charlotte held out to me was a beautiful one, unlike anything she'd ever shown me in the books before. An African woman was sitting in deep orange sand, her shadow extended behind her. Before her were two long rows of flattened sand, each about three feet wide. Within each row was a symmetrical series of boxes, drawn with raised sand borders. Some of the boxes had sand symbols built in them—small spherical mounds, clusters of craters, finger-drawn horseshoes and crosses. Some boxes were left blank. Little sticks stuck out of a few spots on the grid. It looked like a hopscotch court, except more delicate, more beautiful, and far more important.

"It's used to predict things. It's used by a tribe in Africa called the Dogon," Charlotte explained, pronouncing the tribe name like "doggone." "They leave it like that at night and wait for a sand fox to come and walk over it. They read the footprints—which boxes he walks in."

"What if a different animal comes?" I asked, not so much because I cared but because it seemed like something Rose would have said if she were around.

"I'm not sure," Charlotte admitted. "But the sand fox is sort of magical."

I nodded and looked back at the photo. I wished they'd also included a picture of a sand fox.

"I thought we should do one for Rose," Charlotte said. "We should do one to help find out where Rose is."

"Yeah," I agreed. "That sounds good."

"In the backyard, don't you think? There's the spot under the tree where the grass never grows."

"Sure. Wherever."

"Or in your yard, maybe?" Charlotte suggested. "There's lots of patches that don't have grass."

"Mrs. Crowe would kill me, and then my mother would kill me again. Mrs. Crowe's really weird about her yard. She has dreams about dogs in her yard and then wakes up in the morning and goes out to look for the imaginary poops she thinks they left."

"You're so *weird*, Nora."

"*I'm* not. It's *her*." Charlotte didn't understand the politics of living in a two-family house. She knew nothing of grumpy old landladies. "I'm not making that up."

"We'll do it in my yard, then."

"It doesn't say here what the different symbols mean."

"We'll have to think up our own," Charlotte said. "Ones that say stuff about Rose."

"And since we don't have any sand foxes around, what do we do? Wait for a dog to come by?" I asked.

"Funny that our road's called Fox Hill and there are no foxes around."

"Probably there used to be foxes," I said. "Probably they shot them all."

"Who?" Charlotte asked, taking the book from me.

"I don't know. The Pilgrims. The pioneers."

"Oh. Yeah, probably. Well, I was thinking we could try to get Rose's cat over here to walk on it. Wouldn't that make more sense than Brownie, or just any old dog or cat? Rose's cat probably senses things about Rose."

"I don't know if Rose was very close with her cat. She never talked about him."

"Teenagers don't talk about their pets," Charlotte snapped at me, as if this were common knowledge. "It doesn't mean she doesn't love him."

Charlotte and I bundled up and went outside to the grassless patch we'd discussed. Charlotte had brought a sketch pad for practicing symbols. She sat scribbling beneath the big maple tree while I started digging in the dirt with a garden shovel that Charlotte had found in the garage. I scratched at the ground to loosen it and in some places shoveled scoops of dirt around to even out the area.

"You can make it bigger," Charlotte said, erasing something on her pad. "There's hardly any grass on that side, so it doesn't really matter if you dig into it a little."

"Okay."

I cleared a rectangle of about three by five feet and then split it lengthwise with a one-inch ditch. Then I joined Charlotte, sitting on the long root of the maple.

"This is what I have so far," she said. "I think we should use the top box for 'Where,' the bottom one for 'When.' Where she is and when she's coming back."

"Okay."

"And here are some of the symbols we can use." She let me take the sketch pad from her.

I pointed at the first symbol. A rectangle with a small tail on its lower left side.

"Still in Connecticut," Charlotte explained.

I nodded, recognizing the shape of the state. We'd had to draw it about a hundred times in fourth grade. I moved my finger to a crudely drawn airplane.

"Far away," Charlotte said. "In a different state."

A Saturn-like symbol. "Aliens took her. Outer space."

I looked up. "Aliens? That's not funny. That's stupid."

"The way she talked about it, I just thought we should include it."

"Fine."

Four vertical lines: "She's stuck somewhere, and she's trying to get back. The lines are like prison."

I stiffened, trying not to picture Rose in a prison, or worse.

A stick figure with a few lines of hair flying behind, arms out. Smudged on the bottom because Charlotte had erased and redrawn the legs a few times to perfect the angles of legs in a running motion.

"She ran away," Charlotte said.

I nodded and moved down to the "When" symbols.

A moon and sun: "Tonight."

A cross: "Before Sunday."

A Christmas tree: "Before Christmas."

A small grid of squares: "Not for a long time. That's a calendar. Many days."

"That's it?" I said.

"That's all I have so far. You can add some if you want."

I handed the pad back to her. Something was missing. I wasn't sure if it belonged in "Where" or "When." It would be a pretty easy symbol to do. A skull and crossbones or the horseshoe hump of a gravestone.

I stared at Charlotte. I felt nauseous, but her face showed only curiosity.

"What is it?" she said.

"But what about . . . ?"

Charlotte cocked her head, waiting. Maybe we just weren't going to say it. Like when I said something especially gloomy to my mother, about rain on parades or squirrels choking on acorns or whatever it might be, and she'd say, *We're not going to think about that, Nora.* So this was something similar. We weren't going to think about it, and we certainly weren't going to talk about it.

"Nothing," I said, kneeling in the first dirt rectangle. I was grateful to have something to do to take my mind off what we weren't going to think about. I put my hands in the dirt, smoothing it with my fingers, and then set to work. Mashing the soil together with my index fingers, I raised the frames of the first row of boxes.

One

May 18, 2006

Fitting that Charlotte would call while I was doing nothing. When we were kids, she was always saving me from nothing. *What are you doing? Nothing.* And compared to Charlotte's house, with its big brother, its basketball hoop, its VCR, its trampoline, and its pantry full of Oreos, my place really was nothing. *You wanna come over?* Nothing but an apartment with neatly dusted hardwood floors, a grainy television without a cable box, a crotchety old landlady downstairs, and a single mother who prided herself on getting five meals out of a single chicken. Did I want to come over? Back then the answer was always yes.

This time when Charlotte called, I was sitting at my wheel in the garage, staring at a sketch I'd done a week earlier—of a squat teapot with a wide, round handle. I'd nearly sat down twice to make it, and twice I'd found myself distracted by something more pressing—a bill I'd forgotten to pay, the lawn I'd meant to mow.

Now I gazed at the freshly wedged lump of clay in my hands. I hadn't much else to do but throw it down and get started. My grades were submitted, the laundry was done, and this had been my plan all along. Same as last year. Spend the summer throwing like crazy so I'd have lots to sell through Christmas, even if my teaching didn't allow me much time at the wheel in the fall. It had worked beautifully last year. But this year I just wasn't getting into it the way I had. Neil and I no longer really needed my meager profits from the craft fairs and farmers' markets—and maybe I didn't need any more compliments from hemp-skirted ladies and their gentle, bearded husbands. Not to mention that I was a little tired of my quaint teapots and teacups. While I had nothing against quaintness, I wasn't sure I wished to generate it anymore.

I considered ignoring the phone when it rang. Clearly I was having the sort of existential moment a career in ceramics is supposed to protect you from. If I focused, if I made myself stay in the garage, I could work through it. If I simply ignored everything else and got the wheel spinning, I'd probably just forget about it.

After the third ring, I jumped up and ran for the door to the house.

"Hello?"

"Hello? Nora?" I felt oddly relieved by the sound of her voice even before I knew who it was. "It's Charlotte Hemsworth."

"Charlotte?" I repeated. "HEY!"

"Yeah."

"Wow. How *are* you?

Charlotte hesitated. "Not so bad. And you? I heard you and your husband bought a house."

"Umm, yeah."

I looked around the living room skeptically. It had been five months since we'd painted these crisp yellow walls. Neil had assured me that we'd feel better about our color choice once we filled the living room with furniture and hung some pictures on the wall to break it up. But we'd done all that and I still wasn't convinced.

Charlotte was silent on the other end.

"How'd you hear about the house?" I asked.

"I called your mom, and she told me. That's how I got your number. She's easier to find than you are. Your old number didn't work."

"My e-mail's still the same, though."

"I didn't want to e-mail you, Nora. I wanted to talk to you."

"Well, that's nice. I'm glad you—"

"Nora," she interrupted.

"Yeah?"

"They found her."

"Found . . . who?"

"Rose."

I had a flash of Rose walking into the Waverly police station, her dark blond hair still brushing her shoulders, her wide-necked purple sweatshirt still hanging off one shoulder, exposing her exotically black bra strap. Smelling of the Love's drugstore perfume that was supposed to cover up the smell of her cigarettes. That stone-washed jean jacket tied around her waist. Her face about fifteen years older. Or—had it been more than fifteen years?

"Oh, my God," I whispered, my heart now racing. "Is she—"

"They found her body, I mean. Bones."

I leaned against the wall, pushing the phone so hard against my ear that it hurt.

"Nora?" Charlotte said.

I tried to picture what Charlotte might look like at this very moment. Sitting at her parents' old kitchen table, surrounded by that ugly mauve wallpaper with the ribboned clusters of white flowers. Saying my name so gently into the phone, as if coaxing me there for another sleepover, promising no scary movies this time. A promise she never seemed to keep.

"I'm here," I said. Sort of. "How do they know it's her?"

"Something about a bracelet, clothing fibers. . . . Listen, I'm e-mailing you an article. I just didn't want to surprise you with it."

Listening to Charlotte, I could almost smell her mother's Pall Malls. That kitchen was where I was supposed to be when we found Rose—not in this perky little bungalow where Neil and I had accidentally painted every room one shade too bright.

I heard Charlotte take a breath.

"Where, Charlotte?"

"I'm at home," Charlotte said vaguely.

"No. Where did they find her?"

"Near the pond. Adams Pond."

"But . . . didn't they comb that area when we were kids? A few times, even?"

"I'm not sure. But yeah. I thought so."

"Was she buried really deep? I mean, how did they know to dig there?"

"Nobody *knew* anything. Some kids just . . . *found* her. There was something sticking out of the ground, I guess, and . . . well, I'm not sure. My friend Porter's done the first couple of stories for the paper, but the police aren't giving out that many details."

"Your friend Porter?"

"From when I worked at the *Voice*," Charlotte said with a sigh.

"Oh," I said.

"Of course there are all sorts of rumors. I'm not sure how accurate it is, but one scuttlebutt is that the body was moved there. Recently."

I slid down the wall until I was sitting on the floor. "But that's . . . crazy. That's impossible."

"I know."

Now that I was seated, I took a deep breath and tried to get my head around it: Yes, this was real. I was talking to Charlotte again. *About Rose.* But then, what else did we have to talk about except Rose? We'd politely pretended otherwise for years, but Rose was really the only thing we could still have in common.

"Are you all right, Nora?" she asked.

"Yeah," I said.

"Are you near a computer?"

"No. Why?"

"I'm sending you the article just now."

"You want me to read it right now?"

"Well . . . if you want."

Charlotte's sideways insistence was familiar and therefore comforting.

"Give me a few minutes," I said. "I'll call you back."

I opened my laptop and found her e-mail sitting there, dated just one minute before now. The link was to an article in the

Voice. I had no idea my old hometown paper had gone high-tech.

ADAMS POND BODY LIKELY
MISSING YOUNG WOMAN

WAVERLY—The bones found last week near Adams Pond are likely those of Waverly resident Rose Banks, who has been missing since 1990, according to police.

"It's still quite early in the investigation, but we now believe that this could be Rose Banks. We've already spoken to the family, and if it is her, we hope that this will give them some closure in what has been a painful case," Waverly police chief Carl Fisher said during a press conference yesterday.

The skeletal remains, along with Banks's dental records, have been sent to a forensics lab in Hartford for further testing, which could take several weeks. Tolland County coroner Donald Campbell, in a preliminary investigation, identified the skeletal remains as belonging to a female between the ages of fifteen and twenty, which have been decomposing for at least ten years, Chief Fisher said.

The body was found Thursday near Adams Pond by two boys who were fishing there. Local and state police closed off the entire pond area to search for additional clues.

This discovery reopens Banks's sixteen-year-old case, the only missing-person case ever reported in town history. Banks, age sixteen, was last seen on the evening of November 15, 1990, walking home from a baby-sitting job in her Fox Hill neighborhood. Police and town residents searched for weeks but found no clues suggesting her whereabouts.

"With the help of Detective Tracy Vaughan of the state police cold-case unit, we're going over every detail of the case to make sure we didn't miss anything. We'll likely reinterview many of Miss Banks's friends and associates, and we would be grateful to speak to anyone else who might know something about this case," Chief Fisher said.

So it was real. They'd found Rose. After all these years. As I read the article again, I had a feeling that my wheel wouldn't be spinning for another week at least. I knew I needed to see Charlotte, and she needed to see me.

Psychic Powers:
August 1990

It was Charlotte's idea to make the Zener cards. Like all her projects that summer, the idea came out of the Time-Life books. We pronounced them ZEE-ner cards. Rose managed to turn the making of the cards into a two-afternoon affair—one for walking a mile and a half into town to Rite Aid for a pack of three-by-five cards, the other for carefully crayoning thick black circles, squares, crosses, stars, and (the most fun, but also the most difficult) three-lined psychedelic squiggles. Rose rejected our early attempts, insisting that the waves needed to be parallel and that sloppiness might confuse the mind and skew our results.

On the third day of the project, Rose finally shuffled the cards and laid them out for us. She'd been designated for this task since she was, for all intents and purposes, the grown-up. Charlotte and I would take turns guessing the symbols on the overturned cards and recording each other's results. On the first try, I got ten out of twenty-five. Charlotte got four. On my second round, I noticed Rose's face changing before some of my guesses. Her mouth opened round before a circle; her head bobbled lazily before the wavy lines. Once she was certain I'd noticed it, the gestures became subtler—a slight movement of the mouth for a circle, a twitch of the chin for the squiggles. For stars, squares, and crosses, she offered no help, keeping her face motionless and her eyes slanted toward the ceiling in an exaggerated expression of disinterest.

"Wow." Rose raised her eyebrows at Charlotte when my second and third rounds turned out an impressive thirteen and eleven respectively.

Through Rose's facial codes, I noticed a helpful pattern— more often than not, she put squiggly lines on the edges and circles somewhere in the center of the five-card rows. Her hints weren't always discernible, and sometimes Charlotte's intense gaze made it impossible to sneak a look at her. But overall the help made my results significantly higher than Charlotte's. As my psychic superiority became apparent, Charlotte was clearly perplexed. Instead of scrutinizing us, however, she simply focused harder on her own guesses. Frowning and uncharacteristically silent, she was determined to reverse the results. She had apparently been certain that *she'd* be the psychic one. We knew this without ever hearing her say it. Whenever a situation allowed for someone to be the winner, or to be special, Charlotte inevitably—and usually effortlessly—fell into the role.

Rose and I never discussed our cheating or adjusted the methods—even when we could have, when Charlotte was in the bathroom or fetching more graham crackers out of the pantry. I never understood why we were doing it. It wasn't to laugh at Charlotte or to trick her. I wouldn't even say Rose liked me better than she liked Charlotte. She didn't have enough interest in either of us to form a preference.

"Your psi seems stronger for round and wavy lines," Charlotte observed after about three afternoons of repeated testing.

I bit my lip and looked at Rose for help.

"Probably she's using her right brain more," Rose said quickly.

"What does that mean?" Charlotte asked.

"I learned about it in school," Rose explained. "The left brain is more like the science and math part. The right brain is, like, the soft stuff. Art and poetry and stuff. I'm right-brained, I think. My sister's left-brained. Nora's probably right-brained."

"What do you think I am?" Charlotte wanted to know.

"I'm not sure. What do you like better, math or language arts?"

"I like both."

"Well. Then you're neither-brained."

"Or both-brained," Charlotte suggested.

Rose gathered up the cards, looking bored. "Another round?" she asked, shuffling.

"This time with Pepsi," Charlotte suggested, and then she explained to us her latest finding in the black books. Experiments performed by J. B. Rhine in the 1930s indicated that people's

ESP and psychokinetic abilities improved after they'd drunk caffeinated sodas. After hearing this explanation, Rose let us raid Charlotte's dad's impressive Pepsi supply in the pantry.

"If anyone asks, I drank most of it and you guys each just had a glass," Rose called from the living room as Charlotte and I chugged in the kitchen.

I thought I sensed in that statement Rose's desire to have a little Pepsi herself. As Charlotte refilled my glass, I stepped tentatively into the living room to ask her if she wanted any. When I saw her slip a few cigarettes out of Charlotte's mom's coffee-table pack, I crept back into the kitchen for my second glass.

The Pepsi results were inconclusive. Charlotte's performance improved slightly but remained just under chance. Mine stayed the same.

"Nora's looks like a pretty pure power," Rose said. "Kind of a steady, unshakable vision."

Charlotte sucked on a lock of her reddish hair. She looked wounded, but just for a moment. When her eyes met mine, she pulled the hair out of her mouth and gave me an admiring smile.

"Yes," she said, tucking the lock behind her ear. "It looks like it."

Two

May 21, 2006

I drove up to Waverly on Sunday. It would be an ideal evening for me to arrive, Charlotte had said, since she would be around and her mother wouldn't. That same day her mother was leaving to visit her sister in New Jersey for a week.

I'd explained it this way to Neil: that Charlotte had gotten in touch, that someone we both used to know—someone older than us—had died, that it just seemed the right time to reconnect. Neil was aware of Charlotte's existence—remembered snatches of childhood stories that contained her name, had signed Christmas cards I'd addressed to her. And he remembered her from our wedding.

"I didn't think you were that close, though," he'd said.

He was right about that—we weren't close. We hadn't even been close in high school. While I steeped in my own shy gloom for most of those years, Charlotte was relatively popular from all her various clubs and athletics. But Charlotte had made sure we'd never lost touch. We sort of reconnected right around our high-school graduation, had coffee a few times. Then Charlotte had written me letters in college—beautiful letters, her small but sweeping script always in blue felt-tipped pen. I'd been uncertain of what to write back, and I couldn't seem to make my college life sound or look so elegant on paper. I felt guilty for my sporadic response, but also relieved to have my last connection with Waverly dwindle to nearly nothing. Soon after, our relationship became a series of sporadic e-mails and a very occasional coffee in Hartford on the rare occasions I visited my mom in Connecticut.

Neil's eyebrow had also arched at my plans to head to Waverly for a few days. My mother had moved out of town the year after I'd gone to college, and he knew I didn't have much affection for the place. I quickly explained that it was just about getting away, really. I wouldn't be teaching that glaze-chemistry class for another month. My plan, as he knew, was to throw all early summer to build up my stock for the summer and fall markets and shows. But last year I'd gone overboard and made more than I could sell, remember? And a whole month alone in the garage with my wheel? Was that really healthy?

Neil had agreed with that sentiment. Finding him satisfied, I decided not to explain to him about Rose—that she'd been Charlotte's baby-sitter, that she'd disappeared one day on her way home from Charlotte's, that I was probably the last person to see her alive.

As I drove up I-95, I considered why I'd never told Neil about Rose. I'd met him in college, where I always tried to be the op-

posite of whatever I'd been in Waverly. The Last to See Rose Banks Alive was one of my few distinctions in my hometown, so I naturally wanted to forget it. And soon after that, it seemed I'd gone without telling him too long to change my mind.

The drive from D.C. to northern Connecticut took all day. It was overcast by the time I'd made my way over to I-84, and raining by the time I reached the exit that eventually led to Waverly. It was mostly a scenic drive, through the generous-size properties that used to be farms, before coming to the police station, Waverly Elementary, and then downtown. It was Waverly's quaint quality that had made it popular in the eighties, when a few developments went up around the edges of town, giving it its now-suburban feel. That was, coincidentally, when my mother had moved out to Waverly with me when I was five. She wasn't attracted to the expensive new homes—she certainly didn't have the money for that. We were living in the bigger, grittier town of Fairville before then, which I barely remember. She was working as a nurse with Charlotte's mom at Fairville Hospital. It was Charlotte's mom who tipped my mother off about the rare apartment available on Fox Hill Road, upstairs from Mrs. Crowe in her two-family house. My mother often talked about what a stroke of luck that had been and how kind it was of Charlotte's mom to put in a good word for us, because it happened just in time for me to start kindergarten in Waverly's reputably superior school system. Charlotte and I started on the same day—I remember her mother coming home from her night shift in time to snap pictures of us boarding the morning bus.

Waverly's main strip hadn't changed much since I'd last s

it a decade earlier. Its landmarks remained where I remembered them. St. Theresa's, where Charlotte and her family attended church, still looked obnoxiously large and modern a block up from the older Congregational church and its accompanying town green. A few buildings down was the bank. Charlotte's dad still worked there as far as I knew—weathering its many incarnations from Manchester Valley Savings to Fleet to Bank of America. No one in Waverly got a loan unless Mr. Hemsworth said it was okay, my mother told me once.

Farther up, I parked in Waverly Plaza, our glorified strip mall. There were two women's clothing stores now instead of one— one for larger women, one for regular-size ladies. The Stop & Shop where I used to bag groceries was a now a Super Stop & Shop. The mom-and-pop cleaners was a Subway, and the liquor store appeared somehow less derelict than it had in my youth. It had a new sign, a new name—changed from Stompy's Liquor Locker to Waverly Wine and Spirits.

I parked and ran into Super Stop & Shop to pick up something to bring Charlotte. I selected a bouquet of lilies and spent a few minutes considering a brownie mix. Brownie mixes had been an important source of entertainment in our girlhood together. But it seemed a little awkward to hand someone a brownie mix upon entering her home, whatever your history together. I nixed the mix and figured I'd find a nice bottle of wine at the newly gentrified Stompy's.

I went out through the automatic doors to discover that the rain had picked up. A few people were standing under the store's awning. I stood with them for a couple of minutes, listening to their grunts of "Cats and dogs" and their murmurs of

deliberation—"Looks a little better now—should we run for it?" I didn't make eye contact with anyone. If I shared a smile or a look of frustration with these people, I'd be a part of this crowd indefinitely. I'd have to wait for consensus to run to my car or, worse, justify myself if I ran before the rest of them.

I stepped out from under the awning, raced around the largest puddles, and reached my car just in time. A moment after I'd closed my door, the sound of the rain on my roof turned from steady to thunderous. Water came down in heavy sheets that rippled across the parking lot and blurred everything beyond my windshield. I imagined someone in the crowd under the awning remarking, *Wow, she got lucky. It's really coming down now.*

The thought of those other people watching me in the rain made me remember it—walking home from school on a day like this, about thirteen years ago. I was fourteen, a freshman, about a month into high school. I'd stayed after school for help in geometry, which I was already practically flunking. When I'd left the school, it had looked a little drizzly, but nothing terrible. When I was about five minutes along the two-mile walk home, the sky opened up and dumped gallons of water on me. It was the sort of rain you can barely drive in, and walking in it felt absurd—like pushing against a wall of water. But there was nowhere for me to go except home, so I kept trudging along.

My skirt stuck to my legs, and my boots made squishing noises with each step along the flooded sidewalk. I was wearing my favorite of the back-to-school outfits my mother had bought for me—a flowing navy skirt delicately flowered with maroon and cream buds, with cream-colored tights and maroon socks peeking over the edge of soft brown ankle boots. For the last few weeks, though, I'd been starting to think the boots were all wrong. They had pointed toes and flat, balletlike soles. And a lot of the kids were starting to wear heavy black shoes with thick soles and round toes—Doc Martens and the like. Next to them my layered legs and pointy toes had the sad look of imitation eighties rock star.

When I was about halfway home, a black hatchback pulled over next to me. I tried to ignore it. I looked so ridiculous, I just wanted to be left alone.

"Hey!" a young male voice yelled from the car, which accelerated to catch up with me.

I finally turned but said nothing in response. Water dribbled off my nose and chin. The car was filled with a bunch of kids from the boys' and girls' soccer teams. Charlotte was likely the youngest in the car. She was sitting by the backseat window on the side farthest from me, craning her neck to look at me.

"Hey, Nora," she called. It was kind of her to acknowledge me. By then we'd barely spoken in two years.

"Don't you want a ride?" yelled the kid in the driver's seat.

"What?" I said, looking down at my drenched clothes. The car was already packed, and the soccer kids were all dry. If I tried to squeeze in with them, water would pour out of me like a wrenched sponge.

"Do. You. Want. A. RIDE!" the girl behind the driver yelled at me, as if I were retarded.

I shook my head and kept walking, saying, "No thanks," so softly that they likely didn't hear me. I almost stopped to say it again, but I didn't want to extend the encounter.

The car didn't move until I was several paces ahead. Then finally the driver gunned it and sped away.

A couple minutes later, another car stopped for me—this time a brown Chevy Suburban, and its driver didn't give me a choice about a ride.

"Get in," Mrs. Banks ordered.

She always scared the hell out me, Rose's mother. Ever since I was a little kid. She usually wore oversize round sunglasses with brown-tinted lenses—even in the rain. She reminded me of a fly wearing too much lipstick. And when she zoomed up and down Fox Hill with the Suburban's windows open, you could always hear her braying along to her Joan Baez tapes—at least before Rose disappeared.

"What on earth were you thinking?" she demanded as she put her blinker on and pulled back into the flooded road. "You must've seen when you left school that it was about to pour."

I shrugged.

When she turned to me, the stare of her big plastic fly eyes filled me with a self-conscious guilt. "Well? You going to say something?"

"No one could've come to pick me up anyway. My mom's not home."

Mrs. Banks's ketchup-colored lips wrinkled up tight. "I see. And you couldn't have just sat in the library for a while, done some homework, waited it out?"

I said nothing.

Mrs. Banks pulled in to Mrs. Crowe's driveway. "My Rose told me once you were psychic."

"She was joking," I said, but immediately regretted it. Rose was three years gone by then, rendering all her words and intentions sacred and mysterious. It wasn't for me to say what she ever meant. Especially to her mother.

"I guess so." Mrs. Banks scoffed. "Because if you were psychic, you would've known how hard it was going to rain."

When I got home, I peeled off the boots and the new socks to discover they'd bled maroon into the tights. The tights were ruined, as were the boots, soaked and misshapen beyond repair. Not that I cared to wear them anymore. I sat cross-legged on my bed and cried for at least an hour, clutching my clammy feet and trying to keep the sobs low so Mrs. Crowe wouldn't hear them downstairs and ask my mother about it later. The tears weren't for the tights or the boots or the geometry homework I didn't know how to do, but for the four high-school years ahead of me. It still surprises me to think of how hard I cried that day, when I was too young and unimaginative to conceive of how miserable those years would actually turn out to be.

Now, sitting in the grocery store's parking lot, I turned the key. The rain had let up a little.

The Hemsworths' house was the crisp yellow raised ranch at the foot of Fox Hill, squeezed awkwardly between two older, more traditional, farm-style houses. I turned in to the driveway and parked behind a dirty silver Saturn.

It was still raining. I sat in the car for a minute or two, just then remembering that I'd forgotten to stop for wine. The strong, sweet scent of the lilies I'd bought for Charlotte began to relieve the sinking feeling I'd had in the Stop & Shop parking lot. I thought I saw a curtain flutter behind the picture window of the house, but I didn't move.

I didn't much like the house, looking at it now. Oddly, as a kid, I'd envied its wall-to-wall carpeting, its built-in basement bar, its general seventies-style comfort and convenience. It had seemed so much cooler to me at the time than the old mansard-roofed two-family where I lived, farther up the hill. Surely that house would look different to me now, too.

I closed my eyes and waited for the rain to slow a bit. I couldn't quite believe that Charlotte still lived in this neighborhood. She'd spent years away—college, and then a couple of years in an apartment in nearby Fairville when she was working for the newspaper. But then she'd moved back here after she'd quit the paper and started an intensive teaching-certification program—a move that hadn't made complete sense to me when she'd written me about it. I knew that the move back home was largely due to her mother's declining health. Mrs. Hemsworth, who had divorced Charlotte's father while we were in college, had been diagnosed with MS a few years ago. Charlotte wasn't comfortable with her living alone. I think the idea was for Charlotte to help out for a little while and maybe build a nest egg for a nice place of her own once she began teaching—but she'd simply stayed. It wasn't clear to me if her mother truly needed live-in help or if Charlotte was being overly protective.

I wasn't surprised when I heard a thumping on my window. I waited a beat before opening my eyes to see Charlotte's tall, willowy figure looming by my car door.

"Nora! Hi! C'mon!" she shouted through the glass. "What's taking you so long? What, you're *napping?*"

"Of course not," I said into the glass. Charlotte shook her head to indicate that she couldn't hear me. "I'm just . . . thinking."

She had a black umbrella in her hand but was holding it awkwardly to the side so she could stick her face up to the glass. The heavy rain was hitting her right side, and the hair along the side of her face was getting soaked. Her hair was that enviable auburn, gathered into a beautiful mess behind her ears. What surprised me were the lines around her mouth. Laugh lines already. I'd forgotten how much she'd smoked the last time I saw her. It looked like she hadn't ever stopped. Aside from that, her skin still had the perfect alabaster quality it had when we were kids.

Charlotte danced from one foot to the other.

"C'mon, c'mon!" she shouted. "C'mon out of there and give me a hug! I'm getting wet!"

I opened the car door and pushed the lilies into her outstretched arms.

Dreams and Dreaming:
September 1990

"Freud said dreams are the 'royal road to the unconscious,'" Charlotte informed us. She'd marked a page in her book that said so.

"Freud was a jerk," Rose said. She reached into Charlotte's box of animal crackers and pulled out a fistful.

"What makes you say that?" Charlotte wanted to know.

"You'll find out when you're older."

I wanted Charlotte to pursue this, but she didn't.

"This section here gives tips on how to figure out your dreams," she continued, looking at Rose for approval. Rose nodded and popped a buffalo into her mouth.

"The first step is recording your dreams. I think we should all keep a dream log."

"We? All three of us?" Rose examined the hippo-shaped cracker in her hand, then bit its head off.

"Don't you want to understand what your dreams are telling you? What they mean?"

"Where does that come from?" Rose asked. "Where does 'what they mean' come from?"

"What do *you* mean?"

"I mean, if you think that they *mean* something, you believe that it comes from somewhere. Where does the message come from, then?"

Charlotte stared at Rose, openmouthed and breathing through her nose. I could tell she was straining not to roll her eyes.

"It's a mystery," I said softly.

"It's not a *mystery*," Charlotte hissed. "The message comes from your subconscious."

"What is that, exactly? Where does *that* come from?"

"From your brain."

Rose looked at me. "You know what I'm saying, right?"

I hesitated. "Wherever it comes from, it probably helps to record your dreams."

"How's that?" Rose asked.

"Maybe by recording them," I said uncertainly, "you can figure out where they're coming from."

Charlotte nodded her agreement. "That's really what these directions are saying. The more you write them down, the more you remember, the better you'll put the pieces together and learn what they're trying to say."

Rose smiled. "What *who* is trying to say? What *what* is trying to say?"

Charlotte twisted her ponytail into a bun, then let it fall back onto her neck. "Never *mind*," she said.

Rose dusted animal-cracker crumbs off her hands.

"Don't get mad. I'm just asking. Go get some paper, will you?" She grabbed a pen from the middle of the kitchen table. "I actually had a pretty interesting dream last night."

Charlotte dashed off to her bedroom. Rose and I sat in silence. She perched her elbow on the edge of the table, clicking the pen. *Chick-a chick-a. Chick-a chick-a.* Her restless thumb gave her away, clicking maniacally like that. She was actually interested in writing down her dreams—I could tell.

Charlotte returned with a sheet of wide-ruled notebook paper for each of us, but when it came time to start, Rose was the only one writing. I doodled around the middle notebook hole, making it into a fiery sun. Charlotte gazed at Rose. Rose quickly produced a few round-lettered lines, then looked up.

"Done," she said, and pushed her paper across to Charlotte. I looked over Charlotte's shoulder, reading it along with her:

I was in gym class, and Mrs. Powers was making us do endless headstands on those gross old gym mats. When she wasn't looking, when she was spotting someone else, I got off my head and scooched to the end of the mat. I pulled the end of it up like it was one of those curly plastic sleds, and it took off, zipping me around the gymnasium and then, after a little while, into the air. Suddenly my gym mat was a magic carpet, and I was flying up and out of the gym, away from the school. Soon I was flying so high I couldn't see the ground. I'm not sure

where I was, but I knew I was probably pretty far from
Waverly.

"A flying dream!" Charlotte grabbed her book and flipped pages excitedly. "There's a section in the book about those. I've never had one. Have you, Nora?"

"No," I answered. "Only falling."

"Here it is! Let's see . . . hmm . . . well, it says they're common in people who're 'forced to endure unhappy circumstances.' People who want to get free."

Rose wrestled the book from Charlotte. "That's bullshit."

Charlotte frowned. "You shouldn't say that word."

"Sorry. I meant to say 'That's garbage.' Okay?"

"Okay," Charlotte said reluctantly. Then, after a moment's thought, she asked, "Did you crash through the ceiling of the gym?"

The front kitchen door swung open just then, and Charlotte's older brother, Paul, sauntered into the room, looking sweaty. He was home early from soccer practice.

"Hey," he said, sitting with us uninvited, grabbing a banana from the bowl on the table.

"Hey," Rose echoed.

"Hi," I said softly. Charlotte ignored him.

"No," Rose answered Charlotte. "All of a sudden I was above it. You know how sometimes stuff just magically happens like that in dreams?"

"Yeah," Charlotte said. She read over Rose's words again. "So is that all you remember?"

"It got fuzzy after that."

Charlotte nodded knowingly and took her book back.

"What're you guys doing?" Paul asked as he peeled his banana.

"Dream analysis," Charlotte answered, then turned to Rose again.

"You should read this page," she said, flipping back to a bookmarked section. "It tells you how to get better at remembering. You should jot down the dreams right after you wake up. Keep a pen and paper by your bed. And you shouldn't try to make them sound like they make sense. Just write exactly what you remember."

Taking the book back again, Rose raised an eyebrow and glanced at Paul over Charlotte's head. They smiled in mutual amusement at Charlotte's tone. Rose and Paul were friends, sort of. Rose was dating Aaron, a guy from Paul's soccer team. According to Charlotte, Aaron was really handsome. Charlotte was always trying to get Rose to talk about him—to tell us about kissing him.

"I'll take a look," Rose said, glancing at our blank papers. "But you two ought to get to work."

I made my notebook-hole sun larger and stared at the blank lines of my paper, trying to block out the squishy sound of Paul chewing his banana. My most vivid dream in recent memory was something about Play-Doh spaghetti. Ribbons and rainbows of it noodling out of unexpected places, like electrical sockets and air-conditioner vents. Finding little worms of it in the corners of my bedroom and on my pillow, and not knowing if I should feel delighted or disgusted by it.

My mother never let me have store-bought Play-Doh. She thought it was gross and hated its smell. Regardless, I was now too old to be thinking about it, and I therefore probably shouldn't write about it in front of Rose and Charlotte—certainly not in front of Paul. I sighed and peered at Charlotte's paper. She'd written *"Dream Work Log"* across the top in neat, dark letters, and the date below that. Her elbow and forearm hid whatever else she'd started to write.

"Did you read this all the way to the end?" Rose asked Charlotte.

"Yeah."

"'In fact, some authorities believe true dream interpretation should only be pursued with the help of a trained professional.'" Rose scoffed, then continued. "'The messages of the unconscious can be upsetting or frightening, they believe, if revealed too rapidly or without proper guidance.' Woo-hoo. Charlotte, do you know what that means?"

Another glance between Rose and Paul. Paul grinned at her, unaware, probably, of the little banana string stuck to the corner of his mouth. His eager, toothy smile always made me think of an overly enthusiastic camp counselor. I wondered when he'd date someone, too. Probably not for a while. He wasn't nearly as cool as Rose.

"Yeah," Charlotte said.

"Yeah? Pretty serious stuff." Rose clicked her pen rapidly again, holding it loosely next to her ear. "It means it's really dangerous, what we're doing."

"I *know*," Charlotte said, glaring at Rose and then Paul.

Rose ignored Charlotte's snotty tone and clicked her pen once more, smiling just slightly as she gazed down at the paragraph she had written. Seeing her expression, I wondered if the dream had been a joke. She could have made it all up just to make Charlotte and me look silly. Magic carpets, after all, were not what I'd imagined a sixteen-year-old would dream about. Sixteen-year-olds probably dreamed about the things that occupied their lives, like kissing and blue eye shadow and algebra. Maybe her dreams were full of things we were too young to hear about. Or maybe Rose was a little like me. Maybe her dreams, too, were full of things she didn't want other people to understand.

Three

May 21, 2006

We didn't mention Rose at all during dinner, which consisted of pizza and red wine. ("I haven't had time to grocery-shop yet," Charlotte explained. "Sorry.")

Instead we caught up on the most innocuous of topics. Charlotte's job—two years now teaching at Waverly High, where we'd gone as kids—was it still weird? And me—my pottery, the community college, the aging hippies in my night classes. Neil—how he'd finally finished his master's and was really happy to be with U.S. Fish & Wildlife, which he'd always considered a sort of dream job.

As we lingered over our pizza crusts, I gazed around the room, marveling inwardly at finding myself in this kitchen once more. It had been updated somewhat. The ugly mauve wallpaper was gone, replaced with a simple cream paint. Sometime along the way, someone had painted over the dark cabinetry with a dusty-blue shade. Still, that color retained the kitchen's shadowy feel. There was a thick canopy of trees on the kitchen side of the yard, so this room had never gotten any light—and still didn't. The old smell of the Hemsworth house—cigarettes, imitation maple syrup, and dryer sheets—was still there some-where, just discernible under the floral-cinnamon mix of some-one's attempt to cover it with scented candles.

Charlotte sighed, trying to follow my gaze around the room.

"So," I said, sensing that my silence had grown uncomfortable for her. "What made you leave the paper for teaching anyway?"

Charlotte sighed again. "You mind if I have a cigarette?"

"Of course not."

"It wasn't so much that teenagers inspire me." She fished a pack of Camels out of her tote bag and grabbed a lighter off the coffee table. "You don't smoke, do you?"

I shook my head.

"It was that there's only so much you can do with an En-glish background, and things went a little sour between me and the *Voice* management. You know I was the general-assignment reporter for Waverly and Fairville, right? Everything was going pretty well until I had to do this story about the fire depart-ment's radio transmitter. This was years ago, now. Hard to be-lieve. Anyway, there was a new fire chief, and he had this bee in his bonnet about the radio transmitter. The frequency assigned to the fire department is really close to the one assigned to the police department, so apparently for years there's been inter-ference and they're always hearing blurbs of each other's com-munication, sometimes blocking up the line. So this new fire chief started writing to the FCC, asking for a new frequency, but the frequencies are so filled up he had to get the state senate involved. It's a safety issue, he says. They can't be blocking up each other's communication."

"Sounds reasonable."

"Yeah." Charlotte sucked on her cigarette for a moment. "So I'm chatting with the fire chief about this, and he says, 'Just last month one of my guys was putting out a call to verify an address, and he had to wait almost a minute for the PD to finish putting in their coffee orders.' Apparently the police sometimes radio out from the office, giving coffee-and-doughnut requests to whoever was patrolling the streets. The fire department was often getting blips of that."

"Uh-huh. So you quoted that in the article."

"Hell yes. But that was the problem. Everyone was amused except for the police department, especially the chief. But did he get pissed at the fire chief for saying it? No. They're old buddies, they go way back. He gets mad at *me* for quoting it."

"That's dumb."

"Yeah. Well, it gets worse. Everyone was so tickled by that line about the coffee orders that there were a few pranks. Someone built a big pyramid of Styrofoam cups on the front lawn of the Waverly Police Department. Someone else filled up the chief's car with cups. Frankly, I think that one was an inside job. But anyway, the chief got *really* mad then. Writes a couple more letters to the editor. What if he'd been running out to respond to an emergency call? And his car was filled with coffee cups? What then? Someone could have *died*. It's all about *safety*, and it's all *my* fault. Suddenly Charlotte Hemsworth's a public menace. Charlotte Hemsworth's writing her stories in blood."

"Uh-huh," I said, trying not to laugh.

Charlotte picked up the wine bottle, pouring herself more and then poising the bottle over my glass. "You?"

"I still have a lot left."

"Get busy, then. We may as well finish the bottle. This stuff doesn't age well."

I nodded, pushing my glass toward her.

"So my editor, Dave, he ended up having lunch with the police chief to smooth things out." She dumped a generous amount of wine into my glass. "Promised him we'd do a few stories over the next few weeks about all the positive work the WPD does. Blah, blah, blah. Like we'd put them down so then we had to give them a few put-ups, like we're all in kindergarten or something. Such total bullshit.

"Dave even had someone else do those stories, just to give the police chief a chance to cool off on me. Didn't work. Even after that he was tight-lipped with me, and so were most of his guys. It was like pulling teeth trying to do my crime and accident stories. Eventually Dave didn't feel like dealing with it."

"So he fired you? For that?"

"Well, no. He put me on a different beat for a while. But that was the beginning of the end. It was clearly time to start something else."

"And so teaching?"

Charlotte flicked her cigarette into her ashtray and took a sip of wine. "It seemed like a good idea at the time. God, would I like to be on Rose's story."

"I'll bet."

"Porter keeps me posted, but it's not the same."

"Porter was your replacement?"

"Well, he was there when I was there, covering the schools. They gave him my beat when I left. No hard feelings. He thought I got a raw deal."

"So you're friends?"

"Friends." Charlotte blew smoke sideways. "And possibly more."

"What does that mean?" I asked.

"We're sort of dating."

"Oh. That's . . . nice."

"Yeah, I guess," she said unenthusiastically. "Funny thing about the news coverage of the case. They're not saying everything about how her bones were found. They're leaving out some fairly big information."

"Like what?"

"Like that the kids who found it—these two boys, around twelve years old, I heard—found the bones in some wicker trunk. Not just, like, scattered by the pond or in plastic or something."

"*What?* How do *you* know that?"

"One of 'em's older sister is in my study hall. She was telling another girl."

"And you didn't cut in and tell her maybe she shouldn't be spreading that sort of thing around?"

"You kidding me, Nora? Of course not. Then I wouldn't get to hear the whole scoop."

"Wicker?" I repeated. It just sounded very odd to me.

"Yeah. Part of it was sticking out of the ground. The kids started digging it up like it was, you know, a buried treasure or something. Got kind of a surprise, unfortunately."

"Jesus," I said. "That's awful young to be seeing something like that."

"Yeah," Charlotte agreed. "Something like that at that age can really fuck you up."

"Tell me about it," I said.

Charlotte shifted her position, letting her cigarette hang loosely from her fingers.

"Yeah, well," she continued, "I don't think the kids were supposed to be talking about it. I imagine the police didn't want that to get out. Maybe the wicker is secret evidence."

"Or maybe it's just kids talking," I suggested.

"Maybe," Charlotte said before taking another drag. "But there's usually a shred of truth in the shit that kids talk."

"Hard to know what shred you'd find in 'wicker trunk.'"

"Either way, Porter's apparently not gotten wind of it. I mentioned it to him, and he said he hadn't heard anything like that, doesn't want to touch it. Past few days he's been taking the personal side of the story. Trying to talk to a few folks from the neighborhood, getting people's feelings on Rose and the case. So far the only one Porter's really gotten to talk is Mrs. Shepherd, the old gossip."

I nodded. Mrs. Shepherd had paid me to feed her cats when I was a kid. I secretly hated her back then, ever since I was ten and I overheard her telling someone at a block party—in a louder voice than any remotely sensitive person would have used—why she'd chosen me over Charlotte to feed the cats. Sure, everyone knew that Charlotte was smart as a whip, but I seemed like such a gentle little girl, and she wanted to build my confidence. Build my confidence? As if feeding a couple of stinking cats was going to do that for me.

"Tried to chat with the Millers, and Toby Dean, too," Charlotte continued.

"Eyeball?"

"Yeah. Jeez, I forgot we used to call him that." Charlotte flung her hand out backward, again letting the cigarette hang casually between two fingers. "Anyway, no one wanted to say much. Don't want to offend the Bankses, I think. But I think I could've done a pretty good portrait of a neighborhood grieving, questioning what they once thought about this girl. The runaway they should have taken more seriously. People would talk to *me*."

"I don't know how many people *really* thought she ran away," I said. "How *is* Eyeball?"

"Toby's okay. I don't talk to him much. You know he's in charge of the body shop now?"

"What? No. How would I have known that?"

"I wasn't sure if you two kept in touch."

"Why would we?"

"You guys were friends for a little while, right?" Charlotte looked at me coyly, flicking ashes into her brown glass ashtray. "Or . . . dating?"

"Umm. We really just went to the prom. We weren't officially, you know, together."

"Well, he asks about you sometimes. Not as much as Mrs. Shepherd. But once or twice, when I've brought my car into his shop."

"So it's his shop now?"

"Didn't you know his dad died?"

"*What?* No. Jesus."

"I guess I thought you'd know. It was six or seven months ago."

"What happened?"

"Cancer. Colon, I think. They caught it way too late. Once they knew, it happened pretty fast."

."That's really sad. Is Toby married now? Kids?"

"Nope. It's just him and his brother living in the house together."

"Now, why isn't Joe in charge of the shop, then? I'd think
that would go to the older brother."

"You kidding? Not his thing."

"I suppose he was a bit on the artsy side for a mechanic's son.
He still do those weird metal-scrap sculptures?"

Charlotte laughed softly. "Naw. You mean like those wire
wizard people he used to make us? He stopped doing that kind
of thing when we were kids, Nora."

Charlotte's laugh turned into a long cough. I looked away
quickly, trying to hide my surprise. She had an awful smoker's
cough. It sounded just like her mother's.

I was about to ask her more about Toby and Joe, but she
opened her mouth first.

"You know . . ." she said slowly, "the Waverly police might be
interested to hear that you're around. They just might want to
talk to you. Last to see her and all that."

"I know. I did think of that."

"And would you talk to them?" Charlotte studied me for a
moment, looking a little glassy-eyed from the wine and cigarettes. "If they asked?"

"Sure. But I can't tell them anything new. She walked me
home from your house that day like she had a hundred times
before."

"And then kept on walking home."

"Yes. Then kept on walking home," I repeated after a sip of
wine.

Charlotte took a final pull off her cigarette, then let a puff of smoke out the side her mouth. We both watched the smoke linger between us, then disappear above our heads.

"Well. I've got to do some correcting," she said, mashing out the butt. "Now that I'm sufficiently soused. Do you mind?"

"Of course not."

Charlotte picked up her tote bag again and yanked three piles of notebook paper out of it, each clipped with a different-colored paper clip.

"Did I tell you about the time," she asked, "that I spilled a glass of wine on a kid's term paper?"

"I . . . don't think so."

"I made a photocopy of the stained page and threw away the original. The ink was all smudged from when I tried to blot it out, but at least with a photocopy you couldn't ever smell that it was wine or see the color of the stain. And you know what he said when I handed it back to him like that?"

"What?"

"He gets this funny look on his face, and before I even had a chance to apologize—I was going to say it was coffee—he looks horrified, and he says, 'Omigod. Did I hand it in like that?' I guess I got lucky. I wonder what kind of dope that kid was smoking."

Dope. The word always reminded me of my mother, or more generally of people who've never smoked it.

"It kinda reminds me of a story Don likes to tell," Charlotte continued, "about how he was almost finished with his *Diary of Anne Frank* unit once and some kid looks up during a class discussion, all wide-eyed, and says, 'Wait. Anne Frank was *Jewish*?!'"

"Don?" I said.

"Mr. Hauser." Charlotte scanned the page in front of her, then put a big red check-plus at the top.

"Christ," I said, startled to hear Charlotte calling our old high-school English teacher by his first name. "You mean Pizza Nose?"

"Yeah. Don's really nice, actually."

"Pizza Nose?" I'd actually found the guy pretty dismissive, but maybe I'd been overly sensitive at the time. "Nice, huh?"

Charlotte smiled stiffly, turning back to her correcting. "Yeah."

At that, my heart sank a little for Charlotte. It was one thing to be living in the same house all these years and now in a sense attending the same high school. But to think she was now seeking solace from old Pizza Nose, with the pickly breath and the chalk fingerprints around his fly—that really brought it home. And not in a good way.

"That reminds me," Charlotte said after reading through a few more papers. "I've taken over for Don advising the *Looking Glass*."

The *Looking Glass* was Waverly High's lit mag, which Charlotte had edited at one point.

"Cool," I said, "that you'd go back to that."

"Oh, go ahead and say it. It's pathetic. Full circle. A really, really small circle."

"Oh, I wouldn't say that," I protested weakly.

We were silent for a few minutes. Charlotte turned on the TV and handed me the remote, then continued her grading. When she was finished with one full pile, she rummaged in her overstuffed tote once more.

"I wanted to read you something. It's my favorite thing from the *Looking Glass* so far."

"Okay," I said. I tried to arrange my face into a look of interest. Something about this conversation was stranger and sadder for me than the one about Rose's bones.

She didn't look up from her papers but started reading animatedly: "'A giant clothesline in the sky— / so far up you can barely see the ground. / You're hanging on to a thin T-shirt. / It's about to tear, / so you have to pull yourself, hand over hand, / to the next garment— a red terry-cloth robe. / But the wind is blowing, and you flail so hard / that when you snatch it, one of the clothespins snaps off / and the robe nearly throws you into the ether.'"

Charlotte stopped reading and looked up at me, one eyebrow raised, her mouth twisted self-consciously. She was expecting a response.

"That's cute, I guess," I said. "Different."

Charlotte chewed her lower lip. "It's not finished."

"Oh."

"'You're hanging so low now / you're sure you won't be able to reach the next piece— / a sturdy, flesh-colored bra. / You look ahead, and the rest of the clothesline is filled / with your mother's bras, for as far as you can see. / You don't know why, but you laugh to see them. / Your concentration crumbles, / and as you reach for the closest bra, / your giggling makes you miss. / The second pin snaps, / and now you're sailing toward the concrete below.'"

I paused. "And that's the end?"

"Yes."

"I like it. Are they gonna put it in?"

"Who?"

"The kids? Are they going to put that in the magazine?"

Charlotte hesitated. "We'll see."

"You have a pretty fun job, Charlotte."

"It has its moments." She looked glumly at the TV for a moment. "Nora?"

"Yes?"

"Even when we were apart, when I was so . . . busy in high school, I thought about you. I wanted you to do well. I always wanted you to be happy, even though we weren't really in each other's lives anymore. I wished that more people knew who you really were."

I was startled. Why would it occur to her to say this now? Maybe the *Looking Glass* made her think of high school. Maybe, in her line of work, everything made you think of high school.

"I know that," I said. "You wrote something in my yearbook to that effect."

Charlotte sucked in a breath. "Of course," she said. "How silly of me. My students often tell me how I tend to repeat myself."

I ignored the hint of sarcasm in her voice. I hadn't meant to be short with her. I just wasn't quite ready for this subject on my first night back—how we'd been in high school.

I gazed into the corner of the room, where Mrs. Hemsworth's fish tank stood. Impressive that she still kept goldfish after all these years. She always had five or six going. They died regularly, and replacing them had been one of Mr. Hemsworth's regular chores, like clipping the hedges or defrosting the fridge. Charlotte had checked the tank daily for dead ones, always hoping for a weekend trip to the pet store. Now that Mr. Hemsworth was gone, I wondered who replaced the goldfish.

"It's okay," I said. I wanted to do something more—to reach out and touch her on the arm, perhaps, to emphasize the sincerity of my words. But my hands, which so often know what to do before my mind does, wouldn't move.

"It's okay," I said again anyway.

Mind Over Matter:
October 1990

Charlotte and I had fish sticks for dinner, since it was Friday. Charlotte's mother was a pretty devout Catholic. My own mother rarely served me fish sticks. But at Charlotte's—where eating fish sticks on Friday was something one did for God— dipping them in ketchup felt special and ceremonious.

Charlotte's mother wasn't home—she was, as usual, working the night shift at the hospital.

Charlotte's dad had us help clear the table, and when we were finished, she said, "Dad?"

"Yeah?"

"Can we watch a movie?"

"When I'm finished watching the news."

"Thanks, Dad."

For as long as I could remember, Charlotte had always used people's names or titles more often than other kids, as if she'd been born with customer-service training.

"*Jaws* okay, Nora?" she asked as she set up the air popper, plopping about half a stick of butter in the plastic melting cup.

"I guess," I answered sadly.

I hated *Jaws*. We'd watched it several times already, because it was part of her family's relatively small video collection. It really disturbed me, watching people screaming and panicking on the beach, watching swimmers' bloody, dismembered arms and legs float to the bottom of the ocean floor. Charlotte claimed she loved the movie because of her interest in marine biology. This interest was probably sincere—evidenced by the fact that on her birthdays she usually begged her parents to take her to Mystic Aquarium, rather than the roller rink or Chuck E. Cheese—but never seemed to me good enough reason to subject me to two hours of secret terror.

Jaws, like Charlotte's Mysteries of the Unknown books, was something she got away with because she had a much older brother. This sort of thing ended up in Charlotte's house because her brother brought it in with his own money, and because he was too old to have their parents monitoring his reading and viewing anymore.

I endured the movie that night as usual, but I did myself the favor of sneaking down the hall to the bathroom right before the grizzled old shark hunter gets bitten in half by the giant shark, screaming and vomiting blood. This scene always made me feel as if something inside me were being torn to shreds along with the poor man.

In the bathroom I lingered by the sink for a while, first admiring Mrs. Hemsworth's jarful of shell-shaped soaps, then staring at my reflection and listening to Charlotte yelling at the great white, "Haven't you had ENOUGH?"

I sighed and sat on the toilet, yanking down my jeans. And when I did, I discovered, to my horror, a familiar stain. It was only my second period. My first had been three months earlier, and it had been a shock. I was only eleven and a half, after all. But I had started to think, once a month passed without its returning, and then a second, that maybe I'd gotten away with something—that maybe the first had been a fluke and it would just go away and leave me alone for a couple more years.

My heart thudded. Not here. Not at Charlotte's. I breathed in and out. No need to panic. I carried pads with me everywhere, in case something like this happened. My mother had prepared a brown-paper-wrapped package of them for me to keep in my backpack at school, and there were still a couple of pink-wrapped pads crammed into a pocket of my duffel bag from the last time I'd slept over at Charlotte's.

I slipped out of the bathroom and into Charlotte's bedroom, where my duffel sat next to my rolled sleeping bag on her bed. I unzipped the front pocket, shoved one of the pads into my jeans pocket, and raced back into the bathroom.

"Oh, GOD! Gross!" Charlotte was screaming now. I wondered if she could really be grossed out by this scene after watching it so many times already or if she was doing this for my benefit, so I could picture exactly what I was missing.

Of course I couldn't just leave the pad's wrappings in the wastebasket, where Charlotte or her brother might see them. So after I was finished in the bathroom, I ran into the bedroom with the wrapper and the backing from the pad, stuffed it into my duffel bag, and returned to the living room in time to see the shark blow up.

I breathed a sigh of relief.

After the credits began to roll, Charlotte hit "rewind" and turned to me.

"I forgot," she said. "I have something I wanted to show you."

We settled in her bedroom with a tube of Pillsbury cookie dough we'd bought for the occasion, taking turns spooning mouthfuls out of the sticky plastic wrapper.

"Hold on a sec," Charlotte said in a low voice after we'd both had several bites. She left me alone with the plastic sausage. I helped myself to a giant gob and was struggling to get it down when Charlotte returned holding a folded piece of notebook paper.

"I found this on Paul's desk," she whispered. "Rose wrote it."

"Do you think we should be reading something like that?" I asked.

"Well, I already read it. That's why I'm showing it to you."

"Oh." It was pointless to ask Charlotte why she was going through Paul's stuff. She did that sort of thing all the time— although she rarely found anything good.

Charlotte opened it and handed it to me.

Paul,

I really need to talk to you about Friday. I can't talk to Aaron about it. But I'm hoping we could. Remember, it wasn't your fault. If we let people know, I will make sure everyone knows that part. But please please be willing to talk. We need to figure out what the right thing is to do.

Call me, or let's talk tomorrow when you get home.

XO,
Rose

I had to admit this was quite a find.

"Did she just write this today?" I asked.

"No. I found it yesterday. I don't know when she wrote it."

"Oh."

"Do you think this means they're gonna get together?"

"Umm . . ." I looked at Rose's words again. It seemed possible, but I didn't want to give Charlotte any ideas. Then she'd start talking about Rose marrying Paul someday, and her being a bridesmaid or something, and the two of them being like sisters. The very idea might drive me insane with jealousy.

"No," I said firmly.

"What do you think it means?"

"I don't know." I considered some of the sitcoms I'd seen with teenage characters, and the sort of trouble they got into on very special episodes. "Maybe they shoplifted something."

"Paul doesn't *steal*," Charlotte said defensively, taking the note and the cookie dough from me. "I'm gonna put this stuff back before I brush my teeth."

"All right," I said, rummaging distractedly for my own toothbrush.

It wasn't until I came back from brushing my teeth and changing into my pajamas that I saw the slippery pad backing sticking sideways out of my bag, stuck to a sweater. I'd mashed the wrapper down into the duffel bag pretty good, but that slippery little paper backing hadn't stayed put. Now it was poking out like a little flag, announcing my embarrassing menstrual status with *"Always"* written on it sideways, over and over, in light pink.

And of course Charlotte was staring in its direction, looking thoughtful. I folded my jeans on top of it and pretended not to notice it.

"I'm tired," I announced.

Charlotte narrowed her eyes at me. "Now I get it," she said.

"Get what?"

Charlotte slid off her bed and walked over to her closet. I wasn't surprised that she was going straight for her black books. In fact, I felt a little sorry for her. It was starting to feel ridiculous, the way she'd pull out one of those books at every opportunity. Everything reminded her of something in the books—kind of like how everything in Toby Dean's life reminded him of something in those *Police Academy* movies he was always quoting.

I unrolled my sleeping bag and got in. Maybe, I thought, I could get to sleep before Charlotte had a chance to turn my embarrassment into a conversation. She and I never talked about stuff like this, and I certainly didn't want to start now.

Charlotte finally found the book she was looking for and sat next to my sleeping bag on the carpet. She flipped past pictures of Uri Geller, misshapen spoons, fallen-over bookcases, and a half-burned teddy bear.

"See this girl?" she said.

I looked at the page she'd found for me. On it, an older girl in ripped jeans was seated on a recliner, against a dark-wood-paneled living-room wall. There was a surprised expression on her face, and a telephone receiver was leaping across her lap.

"Yeah?"

"She had a poltergeist. She was fourteen."

"That picture looks fake," I said, twisting away from Charlotte.

"Explain how she could have faked that."

I ignored the question and heard Charlotte flipping pages.

"Psychokinetic phenomena," Charlotte explained. "It happens a lot around girls in the early stages of puberty."

I couldn't tell if she was reading or stringing together a bunch of memorized phrases. Either way, I didn't understand what she'd said. But I could feel tears of embarrassment forming in my eyes, mortified that she'd just used the word "puberty."

"Is there anything you want to tell me?" Charlotte asked.

"No!" I said, letting a hot tear fall off the bridge of my nose and onto my pillow.

"Have you ever seen *Carrie*?"

"No." I sniffled.

I knew what she was talking about, though. I'd seen the movie box in the video store, with its picture of that bony, bug-eyed girl covered in blood and surrounded by fire. If Charlotte made me watch that someday, it would surely be even worse than *Jaws*.

"Ever have funny things happening at your house, Nora? Lights flickering or things falling down without anyone touching them?"

"No," I said, wiping my eyes quickly before sitting up. "No, I don't have a poltergeist. Now, let's just shut up about it."

"But you have some telepathic powers," she said.

I was too embarrassed already to argue with that statement.

"That's not the same thing," I said.

"But these things are all connected. People who have telepathy often have telekinetic powers and, if they're lucky, clairvoyance and even precognition."

"Nice big words, Charlotte."

"I'm just saying they're all connected."

"So maybe I'll get a poltergeist?"

"No. I don't know. I understand now, though. That's why you did so much better than me. On the Zener cards."

I stared at Charlotte. I was frustrated with her in a way that I didn't recognize. Not like the anger we had toward each other in third grade, when we'd fight over who cheated at spit or who jumped farther off the swing or who'd bought purple jeans first and therefore who was copying whom. I was angry at her for thinking—and making everyone think—that she was smarter than me, when she was actually incredibly stupid. Too stupid to understand what was so scary about the movies she liked to watch. Too stupid to see I didn't want to talk about *puberty*.

"You're *developing*," Charlotte said.

My cheeks burned furiously at this second uncomfortable word—"develop." It was as bad as "puberty." God, Charlotte was a moron.

"It might be hard to believe, but it's true," Charlotte continued, mistaking my wide-eyed expression for wonderment. "Your psychic powers are probably developing right now, and who knows how strong they'll get?"

I was quiet for a long time.

"Maybe soon," I said, "yours will develop, too."

Charlotte looked wistfully at the girl with the jumping telephone. "I don't think so," she said softly.

"Why not?"

"Because what are the chances of two girls on the same street being gifted psychics?"

I recoiled at the word "gifted." She probably got it from

school—TAG, the Talented And Gifted program she'd recently begun based on some testing we'd had the previous year. I wasn't surprised that I hadn't turned out to be gifted, but I hadn't expected Charlotte to be either.

"I don't know," I admitted.

Charlotte closed the book, put it back in her closet, and went quietly to bed.

"Should I turn the light out?" I asked.

"If you want."

Right before I did, I saw that Charlotte was sucking on a piece of her hair.

"Good night," I said, and ignored the sad tone of her reply as I got back into my sleeping bag.

Just as I started to nod off, I heard her whisper, "Nora? Are you still awake?"

I was awake enough that I should have admitted, *Yeah.* But I didn't. Some small part of me wanted her whisper to go unacknowledged. I wanted her question to go unanswered. Whatever it was, I wanted her to have to wonder about it alone in the dark.

Four

May 22, 2006

I woke up the next morning to the sound of Charlotte bumping her way to the bathroom. I met her at the doorway of Paul's old room.

"Don't even think about it," Charlotte said when she saw me peering out the door. "Go back to sleep."

"I want to see you off."

"Now you've seen me. It's five forty-five. I'm going to get dressed."

"You want me to make you some coffee?"

"I've got it covered, Nora. It's already brewing."

I wandered into the kitchen and fell into one of the chairs. It was the least I could do—keep her company for a few minutes before she headed off to face a bunch of nasty teenagers for seven hours. I nearly dozed off at the table, but a clunk at the front door jolted me awake—the paper boy sticking the *Voice* in the Hemsworths' screen door.

I crossed the kitchen and pulled the paper inside, rummaging through for more Rose news. There was a second-page story that mostly repeated the same information that had been in the article Charlotte had sent me. There were, however, a few additional details about the case. The article mentioned that when she disappeared, Rose had had over eight hundred dollars saved in a bank account that her parents hadn't known about. This had led police at the time to believe that she might have planned to run away—except that no money was ever withdrawn from the account. The article also made mention of Rose's boyfriend—Aaron Dwyer, a star soccer and baseball player at Waverly High, a year older than Rose and a senior at the time of her disappearance.

Next to the article was Rose's picture—the same one they'd always run when we were kids. It startled me to see it. In some ways she didn't look how I remembered her. Her blond hair was blown out dramatically, rather than in her usual ponytail. She seemed to be straining to maintain a toothy, squinty smile. It was a facial expression I associated with cheerleaders.

Charlotte *click-clacked* into the room in thick black heels, a long black skirt, and a snug short-sleeved lilac sweater that showed how trim she still was.

After she had poured herself a cup of coffee, I pushed the Rose article toward her.

"Do you remember much about Rose's ex-boyfriend?"

"Aaron Dwyer?" Charlotte said. "A little. Paul was sort of friends with him. They had soccer together. And I remember always asking her if she liked kissing him. I was such a brat."

"What's the story with him?"

"Well, as I understand it now, mostly from the chitchat in

the teachers' room, they had broken up a few weeks earlier. But he claimed to be as shocked as anyone that she'd disappeared. And he had a very, very solid alibi."

"Which was?"

"The entire soccer team, plus the coach. They had a game in Fairville and had pizza afterward. They were out pretty late together that night. I mean, it at least vouched for the window of time when she'd disappeared."

"Why'd they break up, though? Anyone know that?"

Charlotte shrugged one shoulder slightly. "They were only sixteen . . . did there need to be some big reason? And whatever it was, the rumor was that he was angry at her. That she was maybe interested in someone else, and he didn't like it. But that sounds like the sort of thing people say as an afterthought."

"Has anyone questioned him recently, I wonder?"

"If the police have, we don't know about it. He's still around. He worked in insurance for a while but got laid off. I heard he's been bartending lately, for extra money to support his family. I kind of hinted to Porter that he should find Aaron and talk with him, but Dave told him no. Didn't think it would be appropriate. The *Valley Voice* is still pretty lightweight."

I skimmed over the article again.

"He didn't quote anyone from the neighborhood here," I observed.

"He's still working on *that* story . . . the neighborhood in disbelief. Will probably run tomorrow. I've suggested he come to the high school and chat with some of the teachers. They've had some stuff to say about Rose."

"Like what?"

"Well, Cheryl Griffin claims that Rose came in in September as bright and cheeky as ever, but by November, when she disappeared, she seemed withdrawn. Wasn't herself. Something was up."

"Mrs. Griffin. French teacher, right?"

"Yeah. Of course, something like that could just as easily be like what you were saying with Aaron. Something someone sees after the fact, that might or not be real."

"I think that part might be real."

"What makes you say that?"

"I was only a kid, so I wouldn't have used a word like 'withdrawn.' But I remember thinking that Rose was more fun in the summer than she was during the school year."

"Sorry. Again, maybe projecting. You were a kid. Everything was more fun in the summer. During the school year, she had homework and shit. So did we. And *I* don't remember feeling that way about her at all. But, you know, I think I'm going to do some more digging in the teachers' lounge. They knew her so differently than I did. It's kind of weird, actually."

"Do they know how *you* knew her?"

"Some do, some don't."

The toast popped up—brown on the edges and nearly black in the middle. Charlotte slapped the slices onto a glass plate and carried them to the table.

"I didn't ask you yesterday," I said. "How are your parents doing these days?"

"My mom's okay," Charlotte said before taking a crispy bite of toast. "She has good days and bad days with the MS. Like, right now she feels well enough to take a train out to see her sister. But how will she feel next month? Hard to know. And it's recently started to affect her eyesight, which is scary."

I nodded. Charlotte's mother had stopped working at the hospital a few years ago—when she'd grown too sick to manage it. I was about to ask a little more about her mother's health, but Charlotte continued speaking.

"And my dad's the same. You know he has a condo in West Hartford?"

"Oh, really? West Hartford? I didn't realize."

"Works at the bank branch there now," Charlotte said.

I waited for more, but she didn't add anything.

I buttered my toast in silence, trying to scrape off some of the burned parts discreetly, so as not to appear critical of Charlotte's offerings. She watched me for a moment before continuing.

"How's *your* mom, by the way? Did you see her on your way up yesterday?"

"No. She actually doesn't know I'm up here."

I caught Charlotte's eyebrows twitch ever so slightly as she sipped from her coffee cup.

"You planning on letting her know?" she asked.

"When I feel like it," I mumbled.

She shrugged and got up to stick more bread into the toaster.

After Charlotte left for work, I parked myself on the Hemsworth couch with my coffee cup and turned on the television. The early-morning weather report held my attention for about ten seconds, and then I found myself scanning the contents of the coffee table for objects of interest. There were two wineglasses, still dirty from last night. I made a mental note to wash them. A remote control, an ashtray, and a typed document Charlotte had left there.

"You" was the first word on the page in bold. Below it a poem: "A giant clothesline in the sky— / so far up you can barely see the ground . . ." The poem Charlotte had read me the night before. I was surprised to see it typed on a paper that was starting to yellow with age, with several staple marks in one corner.

Oddly, I'd been under the impression that this year's *Looking Glass* wasn't finished yet, that Charlotte and the kids were still working on it. But here it was all typed up, with the number eleven on the right-hand corner of the page, as if it had already been printed up in a booklet. The torn edge indicated it had been ripped out of something bound already. I skipped to the next piece halfway down the page. "Dandelions" by Jennifer Glass. This poem began with the line "Thick grass tickles my bare feet." Yawn. I turned the page over. A number ten in the upper-right-hand corner and, below that, "Pink-Fingered Heart" by Kelly Sawyer.

Kelly Sawyer. That name was definitely familiar. You never forget the name of the biggest drip in your school. You always remember it pronounced with a mocking whine to it (Kel-*leee* SAW-yerrrr). Years afterward it still sounds like a disease you pray you'll never catch. Kelly was in the same class as Charlotte and me. In high school she was even further down on the social ladder than I was, which was difficult to manage. While I hid behind my hair and my closed mouth, Kelly put herself out there in the most painful and embarrassing ways: singing "Sometimes When We Touch," off-key at the school variety show freshman year, submitting vaguely sensual love poems to the school literary magazine.

I even remembered "Pink-Fingered Heart." How could

I forget a gross title like that? The question was—what was it doing on Charlotte's coffee table a decade later? She'd implied—or at least I thought she'd implied—that the clothesline thing had been written by a current student of hers. But this clearly wasn't the case. This page was probably from an issue of *Looking Glass* from when we were in high school, and maybe Charlotte had written the clothesline piece. Either that or she and the other English teachers kept "Pink-Fingered Heart" on file to use as *Looking Glass* boilerplate—a notion that was only slightly less bizarre than Charlotte's digging up our old school literary magazine to read to me upon our reunion.

I threw the paper back on the table and placed my coffee cup next to it. It was way too early. I headed back to Paul's old room. Maybe it would all make sense after a couple more hours of sleep.

Transformations:
October 1990

Charlotte was busy making a diorama of *The Witch of Blackbird Pond*. I was annoyed with her for picking that book, which she obviously chose only because it was the sort of thing teachers liked—it was long, historical, educational, and it took place in Connecticut. This was our first book report of the year, and we were allowed to read whatever we wanted. I'd picked *Blubber* by Judy Blume and had already finished my diorama of construction-paper girls gathered around Blubber in the bathroom, with little white paper bubbles vomiting out of their mouths, saying cruel things in big, imposing Magic Marker letters. As

I watched Charlotte fashioning cloth Puritans in an elaborate aerial-view court scene in a boot box her father had given her, I was starting to wonder if my own diorama might need some last-minute enhancements.

"Hey. How come we never read this one?" Rose was flipping through one of the black books Charlotte had left scattered on her bedroom carpet.

"Because that one is written for little kids," Charlotte explained, tying a bit of string around a scrap of black cloth to create a waistline for one of her Puritans.

"Are you sure?" Rose licked her finger and turned a page. "It looks like the rest to me. Long, boring articles and gross pictures."

"It's about vampires and werewolves."

"And you're not into that?" Rose asked.

"Not really," Charlotte replied, producing five small wooden spheres. "These are for the heads. Do you think they'll need superglue to stay on?"

"Maybe," I said, watching her begin to pencil-sketch a face onto one of them. "Where did you get those?"

"My dad took me to the craft store in Manchester last night."

"Huh," I said, trying to swallow my frustration. My mother didn't believe in spending lots of money on a school project.

"Do you want to know how to spot a werewolf?" Rose asked from behind her black book.

"Pretty easy," I said. "It's the big, hairy snarly animal that jumps out and eats you."

"No, I mean a werewolf in its *human* form. Let's see. They have bushy eyebrows that are grown into the middle."'

"Like Toby's brother?" Charlotte suggested.

"Joe's got dark eyebrows," Rose pointed out, "and they're thick, but not exactly *bushy*."

Charlotte shrugged and went to work on her second tiny wooden head.

"Their ears are low and far back," Rose continued. "They tend to have a lot of scratches and scabs on their bodies from running around the woods all night. And they're a little hairier than most people."

"Sounds like Joe could be one," Charlotte said.

"Well, Joe's scratches are from when he works with metal."

"So he says," Charlotte replied, dotting a second eye onto the head.

Rose frowned, looking irritated at Charlotte but at a loss for a reply.

"Charlotte's dad is the hairiest man I've seen," I offered.

"Ew!" Charlotte said, looking up. "You're not supposed to say that about someone's *dad*."

"And how many men have you seen without their shirts anyway?" Rose asked.

"Lots," I answered. "At the beach."

"Oh, okay. And you've made a study of it?"

I ignored the question because I wasn't sure what it meant. "Isn't he, though? Isn't Charlotte's dad hairier than your dad?"

Rose hesitated. "Um . . . I don't know. I mean, I've never seen him in a bathing suit or anything."

"You don't need to," I said. "You can see it just from his arms and neck."

Charlotte threw one of her little heads at me. "I *said* you're not supposed to—"

"Charlotte's right, Nora," Rose said.

I was supposed to shut up now because they understood about fathers and I didn't. But I felt I'd hit some nerve, and I wanted to keep pressing it to see what else they would do. So what if there were certain rules about dads? Those were *their* rules, not mine.

"There's even some hairs sticking out of his nose," I observed.

"Okay, Nora, knock it off," Rose said, sighing and turning a page.

"Okay," I said, shrugging.

Charlotte went back to work. I plucked the head she'd thrown at me out of the carpet and slid it quietly into my pocket.

"Werewolves tend to have an appetite for children," Rose informed us.

"Okay," Charlotte replied in a bored singsong. "Whatever you say."

"And they eat people in the most gruesome ways. Devouring their still-beating hearts. Ripping out their throats."

"Really?" I said, feeling the lumpy part of my neck. "How do you rip a throat out? You just bite off the front part of it?"

"Don't ask her stuff like that, Nora. She's only trying to scare us."

"Scare *you*?" Rose replied. "I'm sort of scaring myself. You're not even looking at these pictures."

"Is someone getting their throat ripped out?" I asked, rising to take a look.

"No." Rose closed the book before I reached her. "I shouldn't be reading this stuff."

"I told you it was stupid," Charlotte said.

"It's not that it's stupid. It's really that it'll scare me to death.

I already get scared enough walking on Fox Hill Road at night. There's that spot right after the Cooks' place, you know, where it's all just trees and stuff? Right before the turn for the transfer station. And there's no streetlights or house lights for that whole turn, you know?"

I nodded. I hadn't walked there at night. I'd never had any reason to. But I knew where she was talking about. Charlotte didn't look up or reply.

"Whenever I'm walking there at night, I'm always scared to death for that minute it takes to get past it. The littlest noise in the trees and I take off running. My heart pounds like crazy till I can make it back to my house."

"What're you afraid of anyway?" Charlotte wanted to know.

"Well . . . everything. When I'm walking up that little bit of road, I believe in anything scary, even if it's stupid. Ghosts, vampires, Freddy Krueger . . ."

"Werewolves?" I said.

"Not before," Rose said. "But *now. Now* I'll think about it every time. Now I'll have to hold my throat while I walk by those trees."

"Don't bother," I said. "The werewolf will just rip your arm off anyway."

There was a knock at Charlotte's door.

"Come in," she called.

The door opened, and Paul poked in his head. My face burned red. It was several minutes before that I'd pointed out how hairy his dad was, but maybe he'd heard. I'd die if he'd heard. Having Paul hear it was totally different from having Charlotte and Rose hearing it.

"Rose," he said, "can I talk to you a second?"

"Yeah," Rose replied, leaving the black book on the carpet as she got to her feet.

Paul closed the door behind them. Charlotte smiled to herself as she drew a delicate pair of red lips on one of her wooden heads.

"Maybe we ought to try to see what they're talking about," she whispered.

"Maybe."

"You go," she ordered, still whispering. "You go out to the bathroom and—"

"No," I said. *"You."*

"They'll *notice* me," Charlotte pointed out.

Her reasoning was mean. They'd notice her but not me. Unfortunately, it was also correct. I stormed out of the room to show my annoyance, but as soon as I was out the bedroom door, I realized I'd made a mistake. It would look to her like I was following orders.

I slammed the bathroom door to show her I wasn't doing what she asked—and to ruin any plan she might have to sneak around behind Paul's and Rose's backs. I blew my nose, flushed the toilet, and washed my hands. On my way back to Charlotte's room, I heard Paul and Rose talking in his bedroom.

"But it's better for *us* to say something. If we wait till *he* does—" Rose was saying.

"You aren't thinking of *me,"* Paul interrupted. "Why should I fuck my life up—"

I stiffened at the F-word. I'd never heard Paul say it before—he was just as strict about that stuff as Charlotte. It would have surprised me less if Rose had said it. Rose loved to swear.

I crept quietly by Paul's half-open door. They were sitting

close to each other on Paul's bed. As Charlotte had predicted, they didn't notice me. Or didn't care that I was there.

"It's not about you or me," Rose argued as I moved away from the door.

"Would you like someone to go to jail?" Paul whispered. "Would *that* make you happy?"

"Happy?" Rose said, her voice breaking as if she might cry. "How could *happy* have anything to do with it?"

I returned to Charlotte's room and closed the door hard.

"Whadya find out?" she whispered.

"Nothing," I said. "I just went to the bathroom. I'm not a spy."

"I think they're getting together."

I said nothing.

Rose returned a few minutes later, settled back onto the carpet, and picked up her black book as if nothing had happened.

"What were we talking about?" she asked, in way that seemed to me a little fake-cheerful.

"Werewolves," I reminded her.

"We were talking about how Joe Dean is probably a were-wolf," Charlotte chimed in.

"All guys are werewolves," Rose said, staring into the book.

"My mom sometimes says men are pigs," I said, because it seemed sort of related.

"Hmm," Rose said. "Pigs and wolves are very different."

"So which is right?" I asked.

"Boys aren't pigs *or* werewolves," Charlotte said, curling her lip at us in disgust. "That's *discrimination*."

"Fine, Charlotte," Rose snapped. "*People* are pigs. *People* are werewolves. People in general are awful, disgusting, shitty animals."

Charlotte's mouth hung open for a moment, but she quickly recovered. She seemed too rattled to bother to scold Rose for her language. A moment later she went back to fashioning her little Puritan people.

I bit my nails for a couple of minutes, bored but not wanting to bother Rose or help Charlotte with her A-plus diorama. Then I rummaged through Charlotte's box of black books till I found the one with my favorite picture—of seven fat, squat statues standing in a row on Easter Island. They all had flat, squarish heads and no mouths. I loved this picture, and I loved those statues. They were so mysterious, but so peaceful, too. They surely guarded a very old secret. What was it? I felt I could look at them for a long, long time and not need anything else to keep me busy. Not TV, not music, not Charlotte's chatter about what they might mean. As far as I knew, Charlotte had only flipped through this book once and then tossed it aside in favor of the ones about psychics and ghosts. But I'd spent a little longer on it, and I knew that if you sat with them and stayed as quiet as they were, you could start to feel you might understand them, just a tiny bit. If you stared at them long enough, you started to smile without knowing why. I knew that Charlotte had never looked at them long enough to know this, and I wasn't going to tell her.

Five

May 22, 2006

When I woke up, it was past nine. Charlotte had been gone for several hours. She'd probably discussed the symbolism of *The Scarlet Letter* a few times before I'd even gotten up. I imagined a class full of fourteen-year-olds: some pimply, some obnoxious, some sweet, one with hair in her eyes, and one chewing gum with a self-satisfied smirk. The only unsettling thing about this picture was that I couldn't imagine Charlotte in it.

But that's where she was. And it was just starting to dawn on me that I'd no idea what I was going to do all day—for several days—without her. I'd start with going out for coffee. I threw on some jeans and a peasant top and scuffed into my clogs. Before heading out, I grabbed the typed page off the coffee table, folded it, and shoved it into the back pocket of my jeans. I didn't know what it meant, exactly, but I felt that Charlotte had, in good teacher fashion, left me something to do.

* * *

I parked at the Dunkin' Donuts next to Deans' Auto Body. After I got my coffee, I sat in a booth sipping, watching cars roll through the intersection, wondering if any of them were driven by people I used to know.

It was in this very Dunkin' Donuts that Charlotte and I had last talked right before I left town. I'd been slightly surprised when she'd invited me out for coffee a couple of weeks after we graduated high school.

Charlotte had dumped a few tablespoons of sugar into her cup, but I took my coffee black.

"You really like it that way?" she'd asked, watching me skeptically as I took my first sip.

"Yeah. I like bitter-tasting things, actually," I explained.

"Hmm. So . . . Syracuse, huh? You excited?"

"Yup," I said.

"Kind of a party school. I was surprised when I heard where you were going."

"It also has a pretty good arts program."

Charlotte nodded. She was going to the University of Connecticut—about twenty minutes away from Waverly. She'd gotten a near-full scholarship that was offered statewide to kids with high test scores and grades in the top 10 percent of their class.

"You get good financial aid?" Charlotte wanted to know.

"Really good," I said. My mother and I looked relatively poor on paper.

Before we'd finished our coffees, Charlotte had brought up Rose.

"You sure liked her, didn't you? *And* she liked you. Rose really liked you."

"I never got that sense."

"She did. She liked you better than me."

I wondered how that could possibly matter now.

"Oh, I don't know . . ." I mumbled.

"Why do you think that was, Nora?"

"I . . . don't know. Doesn't matter much now, though, does it?"

"It does to me. You know, Nora, I've been wanting to talk to you about her. I've had a feeling, lately, that maybe we should talk about her."

"Lately?"

"Well, yes. I thought maybe there was something you wanted to say to me about her."

I waited for her to continue, sipping my coffee and trying not to grimace at its strength. But she just gazed at me expectantly.

"What?" I said.

"I thought you'd want a chance to talk about it," she said. "Before you go. Am I wrong?"

"Umm . . ." I said, perplexed. "Maybe."

Apparently this was Charlotte's strange way of saying goodbye. We'd been such close friends as little kids, and now we suddenly wouldn't be near each other anymore. We'd never live on the same street again. There was something sad about that, but maybe this conversation proved that Rose was the only thing we'd had in common for a very long time.

"I don't think about her that much anymore," I admitted. "I try not to."

"You try not to? Why not?"

"Because of what happened to her."

Charlotte narrowed her eyes. "What happened to her?"

"I don't know. But I mean it was probably pretty terrible, whatever it was."

I hesitated, staring into my coffee. I'd drunk only half of it but was already feeling shaky. Coffee in the afternoon didn't agree with me. I was going to have to work on that for college.

"Like I said," I explained, "I really do try not to think about her. It's too . . . sad."

Charlotte nodded, perhaps finally understanding. She avoided my gaze for a moment. I wondered if it embarrassed her, my talking about what made me sad. Of course, I meant "sad" in the regular way, not in the aspirin-overdose, psych-ward-stint way I'd become famous for. But I didn't know how to ensure her of this distinction without making us both even more uncomfortable.

"So . . . are you as crazy to get out of here as I am?" I asked, trying to relieve us both with a change of subject.

Charlotte bit her lip, then smiled. "Almost, I'm sure."

"It's going to be nice to start over with a whole new group of people. I can hardly believe it some days—I'm going to get up in the morning and go to class and look around and *not* see the same faces around me I've seen since I was six."

"It's a little scary, actually," Charlotte said.

"Is it?"

"To me anyway," she added.

"A lot scarier would be sticking around," I pointed out.

"Mmm-hmm," Charlotte said, watching me carefully as I took another sip.

A tiny smile crossed her lips as I failed to suppress a pucker from my black coffee. Then the smile faded, and her light green eyes avoided mine again.

"I'll miss you, though," she said, so softly I wasn't sure I was even supposed to hear it, or to reply.

* * *

As my coffee now grew cold, I found myself squinting into Deans' Auto Body, trying to discern if Toby Dean was one of the men tinkering about in the shadows of the large garage.

It had been a surprise to hear his name come out of Charlotte's mouth yesterday—I'd forgotten to think about him for years. *Toby Dean. That boy with the name like a sausage*, my mother used to call him. Since he was a boy and a whole year older than us, Charlotte and I didn't pay him much attention when we were little kids. On the rare occasions when we did come in contact with him, he was usually doing something that didn't make much sense—like carrying a dead garter snake around in a greasy brown paper bag or whacking at his father's overgrown hedges with a golf club.

When we were really small, everyone called him Eyeball. He had a lazy eye and was always wearing the same crusty disposable eye patch on which his older brother, Joe, had drawn for him a hairy, oozing eyeball. I doubt that patch ever did much corrective work—it was usually loose, allowing Toby to peek out with his good eye.

Toby became more familiar to Charlotte and me when he was left back in the fourth grade and we caught up with him in school. If you were left back, it was generally thought that you were seriously stupid or seriously badass. I wasn't sure which he was, but I wasn't thrilled to be seated next to him. There was a whiff of Frito in his breath and a hint of mothball in his clothes and a low, stupid quality to his laugh. He was much bigger than the other kids, and he was interested in dirt bikes and Axl Rose. And by the end of fourth grade, he would come in from recess with dark pit stains on his shirt and a mysterious, monkeylike odor that always distracted me from my long-division worksheets. I remember trying to pull my nostrils together using just my face muscles—rather than my hands—so as not to tip off the poor stinking Toby. He already had enough problems that he didn't need the girl sitting next to him holding her nose on top of it all.

Sometimes my mother used to stop by and check in on Toby's dad, who occasionally needed help with the care of Toby's grandmother, who lived with them until she died of cancer when we were around ten. I'd usually stay in the yard or the car. If it was really cold, I'd wait for my mother in the Astroturfed mud room of Toby's house. I was afraid if I ever sat at his kitchen table or saw his bedroom, someone might end up calling us friends.

In junior high, Toby started to seem much older than the rest of us—and not just physically. When kids would giggle and squirm in class, he'd check them with a growled, "Hey, guys, c'mon." Or just an exasperated shake of his head as he folded his meaty arms. By then he'd discovered deodorant and even cologne, and kids at least respected him for his size and gruffness, if nothing else. He was never very smart in school, but teachers would promote him for his efforts, his kindness to them, his stoic good sense.

I didn't really think of Toby as a person until late in high school, when I worked down the street from his dad's garage, bagging groceries at the Stop & Shop. The first time Toby offered me a ride home, I declined. I flattered myself that he liked me and I shouldn't lead him on. It didn't dawn on me until much later that he was probably doing it as a favor to my mother, in return for her kindness to his father and grandmother. Toby did stuff like that—extended favors to adults as if he were one of them. I refused those rides for months, until September of senior year, when it occurred to me that no association could damage my status any worse than I'd already done on my own. Whatever devastating social judgments I'd thought I'd been avoiding had already been made long before. I was a senior, I was tired, and there was no reason to walk when Toby would happily drive me.

And it took only a few rides with him for me to realize that I actually liked him better than most of the kids in our class.

I grabbed my coffee cup, left Dunkin' Donuts, and headed for Deans'. I didn't think to be self-conscious until I was already inside the door.

"Can I help you?" said the beefy guy behind the counter.

"Umm," I said, stepping closer. His dark hair was cut closely to his head, almost a crew cut. His eyes were big and brown, the left eye just slightly crossed. Yes, this was Toby Dean.

"Hi," I said, giggling the end of the word like an idiot.

"Hi," he replied, cocking his head with a bewildered smile. "Can I help you?"

"Toby?" I said.

"Yeah."

"You remember me?"

He scowled for a moment, and then his eyebrows went up in surprise.

"Nora," he said.

"How've you been?" I asked.

"Okay." He crossed his arms, hooking his thumbs beneath his upper arms, where his undersize green T-shirt met his thick, pale biceps. "It's been sort of a rough year. I don't know if you've heard."

"Yeah. I was really sorry to hear about your dad, Toby."

"Yeah," he said, nodding just a little.

I felt I should say something more but couldn't think of what. I hadn't known his dad well at all. He'd worked crazy hard at the shop when we were kids, and he always seemed worn out on the rare occasions I'd see him. Kind of like Charlotte's mother.

"You visiting your mom?" Toby asked.

"My mom? No. She lives in Bristol now. Works at a different hospital."

"I know it. She came in here once to get her oil changed. About a year ago. When she came for coffee with some of her old Waverly buddies."

"Oh."

"What are you doing in Connecticut, then, if you're not visiting your mom?"

"I'm . . . visiting Charlotte Hemsworth, actually."

"I didn't realize you guys were still in cahoots."

"Well, it's a recent thing, us getting back in touch."

"That's interesting. I remember you two were like this." He crossed his index and middle fingers. "Back in the day."

"Yeah. Listen, Toby. I didn't want to bother you at work. I just wanted to say hi. I thought maybe sometime we could have coffee or something. Before I go back home."

"How long are you here for?"

"Actually, I don't know. Probably a week."

"You here with your husband?"

Interesting that he knew I was married. I wondered who'd told him—Charlotte or my mom. And I wondered how often my name came up.

"No . . ." I said. "He's . . . um, working."

"Well, today's out. Since you've already had your coffee," he said, looking at my Dunkin' Donuts cup. "Maybe we ought to make it a beer. How's tonight for you?"

"Umm . . . I don't know. I've gotta see what Charlotte's got planned. We haven't actually visited that much yet."

We left it open—we'd meet at Atkins Tavern one of these nights. He gave me his card in case anything came up, and then I started for the door. Once I'd reached it, I turned and looked at Toby again. He was stepping closer to the grease-smudged computer behind the counter and reaching out to click a single button. The slow, determined motion of his arm startled me, reminding me of him pushing my hair out of my face on prom night.

Nora, he'd said.

Be careful, I'd protested. *You'll flatten out the curl.*

You don't need that curl anymore, do you?

Toby looked up just as my face began to burn at the memory.

"Hey," I said, embarrassed to still be in the shop, extending the awkward silence. I tried to recover by saying the first thing that came to mind. "Do you remember the *Looking Glass*?"

"The *Looking Glass*?" Toby squinted at me. "What's that?"

"It was the lit magazine at Waverly High."

"Oh, yeah." He picked up a rag from the counter and started wiping his hands with it. "I forgot it had a name."

"Everybody got a copy every year," I said dumbly.

"And yet almost nobody ever wanted one," he said, grinning.

"I guess that means you didn't keep yours."

Toby twisted his ring and pinkie fingers into the rag. "Umm . . . is that what you *really* came in here to ask me, Nora?"

I looked away, examining my fingernails for a moment. I felt

pretty stupid. Toby had a *real* job, and he had workers and cus-
tomers relying on him. Why was I bothering him with this?
The school *literary* magazine, of all things? Toby had barely
graduated from Waverly High. Who exactly did I think I was?

"You're kidding me," he said, not unkindly.

But his jaw tightened a little, and I wasn't sure if it was annoyance or amusement.

"I'm sorry," I said quickly. "It was a stupid question. It was
just a random thought. I'll see you tomorrow night."

"No, no," Toby rushed to say. "It's not stupid. I just mean, is
there any particular reason you're looking to get your hands on
that? You didn't write for it, did you?"

"No. It's not that. It's . . . well, a long story."

"And isn't Charlotte the person to ask? I remember she was
involved. Wasn't she in charge of it or something?"

"Yeah, but under the circumstances I can't ask her right now.
She might be playing a little trick on me. It's hard to explain. . . ."

Toby balled up his rag and stuck it in his pocket. "You two
haven't changed, I guess. I remember how she liked to screw
with you."

"Oh, well, she's not necessarily—"

"Yeah, *right*, Nora," Toby teased. "Listen, you can tell me the
whole story over a beer."

"Yeah," I said, taking my cue to turn for the door again.
"Good idea."

"And, Nora?" Toby called after me when I was halfway out
the door.

"Yes?"

"I'd try the library."

* * *

Toby was right, of course. I remembered now that the school administration made a big deal of filing the yearbook, the quarterly school newspaper, and the *Looking Glass* in the town library, as if this would motivate us to take all these publications seriously—and to justify censorship of F-bombs and nose-picking candids. *They will represent you as a class, and they will be accessible to everyone in town. Think about how you want to be represented years from now.* As if posterity gave a crap.

I got into my car and hopped back onto Main Street. Just before the library was the high school. I found myself smiling as the long brown building came into view—smiling not for bittersweet memories but to think that Charlotte was in there right now, probably denying a kid a lav pass at this very moment. It made the place seem innocently absurd somehow, rather than menacing, as it had always been in my memory. The semicircle of hedges was neatly trimmed in the front. An outsize American flag flew proudly above the faculty cars, Charlotte's Saturn among them.

At the library I hesitated before approaching the skinny library lady behind the counter. I remembered her. Her frizzy brown hair was now a little gray, but she still had that same odd cone of curly bangs hanging across her forehead, into her right eye.

"Good afternoon," she said, catching me looking at her. She spoke so cheerily that I thought for a moment she recognized me, too. "Can I help you?"

"Hello," I replied, trying not to look at her hair. "Um. I was actually wondering if you still by any chance keep copies of the Waverly High lit magazine? The *Looking Glass*?"

"Of course," the cone lady said, springing from her chair. "Are you a wolverine?"

"A wolverine? No."

"The wolverine is the Waverly mascot," she explained, leading me to a dark corner past the magazines.

"I know," I said. "I graduated from Waverly High, actually. I just never considered myself a wolverine."

She gave me a thin, unsurprised smile. "I understand. Well. Here they are. These green binders. And these tapes below them, they're all the senior musicals on VHS, going back to 1988. With the exception of 2001, which unfortunately melted in someone's car."

"It's okay. I'm mostly interested in the *Looking Glass*."

"I'll leave you to it, then. Let me know if you need anything else."

"Thanks," I said, and she left me in shadows. There was a binder for every five years. I pulled out the binders labeled 1990–1994 and 1995–1999. It didn't take long to flip through the booklets for my years at Waverly High—1993–1996, looking at pages eleven and twelve of each. In the last—1996—I found what I'd expected. The anonymous "You" piece ("A giant clothesline in the sky . . .") and "Dandelions" on page eleven, Kelly Sawyer's poem on page twelve. I opened the rings of the binder and relaxed into the chair with the *Looking Glass, 1996*. Our junior year.

I flipped back to the first page. A few of the names in the editorial section were vaguely familiar, but Charlotte was the only one of them I really knew.

On page five there was something else titled "You," also at-

tributed to Anonymous. An error on Charlotte's part? Or the
layout person's, whoever that had been? But this poem, despite
the identical title, had a completely different text:

You
You are running through a sunlit field.
A red Datsun is chasing you,
revving its engine, plowing through
grass and wildflowers.
You're breathless and sweaty
as you reach the end of the field,
where a round stone entranceway guards a thick wood.
The car nearly reaches you
just before you run through the gate,
but once you're in the woods,
it can't touch you.
It revs and snorts and honks at the gate,
but it can't fit through.
You stand on the other side and cry.
Tears plop loudly off your chin and onto your shirt—
you look down.
These are not tears—
but ants, crunchy and black.
But you don't scream—
you just let them slide out of your eyes and nose
and crawl down your face.
Because you know you're in the forest now—
where anything can happen.

Hmm. Someone playing chicken on an acid trip. Not your typical Waverly High fare. Too bad I didn't really read the *Looking Glass* in high school—apparently I'd been missing out.

Then, on page eight, another piece titled "You":

> **You**
> *In his bedroom,*
> *beneath the blueberry wallpaper,*
> *you kiss till the sun goes down.*
> *You see the darkness fall in the windows.*
> *You have no idea when you'll go home.*
> *And what you'll say when you get there.*
> *You reach up and pull a berry off the wall.*
> *"Are these poison?" you ask.*
> *"Should I eat one?*
> *And sleep forever?"*
> *He shakes his head.*
> *"They're not sweet.*
> *They're not poison.*
> *Sorry, honey.*
> *They're not even real."*

It seemed odd to me that Charlotte and the rest of the magazine staff would have allowed the same anonymous person so much space. But then, submitting to this magazine wasn't exactly considered cool. They probably had to take whatever they could get to fill the pages. (They did, after all, print several poems from Kelly Sawyer.) Perhaps a member of the staff had even written these things for that very purpose—filling space.

There was the clothesline story on page eleven, and the next "You" piece was several pages later:

You

You are knocking on his door this time—
a perfect cabin on a lush green hill
with fruit trees and sunshine
and pinafored children hugging smiling lions.
When he opens the cabin door,
his face is warm and his eyes forgiving,
and he touches you softly on the face.
But then his hand moves up your chin and into your
*   mouth*
and pulls out one of your eyeteeth.
He holds it up for you to see, and you say,
"You can keep it. You can have as many as you want."
He pulls out a front tooth, too,
and drops both teeth on his welcome mat
as if to say,
You can keep your stinking teeth,
and slams his bright red door in your face.

Ick. I kept going. On page thirty-three there was another:

You

The gym mats are a painfully cheerful blue
but hold the sweat from a decade of asses and forearms.
Probably swirled with an invisible ringworm,

which you can almost feel slithering beneath your knees.
You're kneeling at the end of the mat,
and you curl it toward your chest,
swaying and straining until it moves.
Slowly at first—an inch, then another.
But then the mat hits the air and the gym below you
*   disappears.*
Hot Pants waves her arms, yelling for you to come back,
but her voice fades fast, she quickly becomes an ant,
*   and then nothing.*
The blue of the mat suddenly makes sense, now that it's
*   airborne.*
It's a perfect match to the color of the sky.
This was always its purpose, to surf the clear blue sky.
You just never knew it before.

I stifled a gasp as I read, then squeezed my hands into tight fists and held them over my mouth to hide my surprise. I feared that Cone Lady's eyes were probably upon me.

Rose's dream. It was something I might not have remembered if she hadn't disappeared. But her absence anchored that dream in my memory. Long after she'd gone, I'd often remember chewing my pen and gazing at her, wondering what she was thinking. I thought of it most often in high school while stretching—or pretending to stretch—on those same gym mats Rose had probably used. Miserable in purple-and-gold gym shorts, praying not be last in the timed run around the track. Praying not to be humiliated by a volleyball in the face or my inability to yell *Got it!* because who could really be that confident of anything? Too smart, though, to pray to fly away. Rose had already gone and done that, ruining it for the rest of us.

I didn't know what it meant that Charlotte had written this. For a moment it put me back into that afternoon in her parents' kitchen. I hadn't thought of that day much in recent years, but these words made it feel closer, just out of reach—a time before anything much happened. Before wondering about Rose became a terrifying exercise, and then maybe something worse. I ran my hand greedily over the page as if I could grab that afternoon, tear it out, and save it in my pocket.

Apparently that afternoon had meant as much to Charlotte as it had to me. The question was what she'd been trying to communicate about it all those years ago, when she'd anonymously slipped Rose's dream into a poem written for her literary magazine. And was she still trying to say something to me now—bringing it up again but afraid to say that it was hers?

I flipped through the remainder of the booklet. No more "You"s after that. I read each poem once more, then closed the binder and filed it next to its dusty companions.

Alien Encounters:
October 1990

"I got you guys a movie, but I forgot it," Rose said as she rinsed her dinner dish. "I borrowed it from Joe. It's in the VCR at home. My dad wanted to watch it."

It was Sunday night, Columbus Day weekend, and I was sleeping over at Charlotte's. Mr. and Mrs. Hemsworth had gone out to a movie, and Paul was off somewhere with friends. I'd managed to wrangle permission from my mother without her asking if the Hemsworths would actually be home.

"It's about this farmer who was visited by aliens."

"Is it real?" I asked, rinsing my own dish.

"Of course it's real. It's a documentary. I don't mess around."

"Then I'm not sure I want to watch it."

So far Charlotte hadn't chimed in yet. Rose had baked us Banquet chicken in the oven, and Charlotte was picking every last bit of fried crust off her thigh carcass.

"Well, we don't have to watch it. But it won't be any less real if you don't watch it. Only difference will be you'll know what you're up against."

I wasn't sure what she meant, but it sounded like maybe the point was that I was being a wimp.

"Let's at least go get it," I said. "We can read the box and then decide."

Charlotte didn't get up.

"Is it rated R?" she asked, licking her fingers. "I'm not allowed to watch rated R."

"Of course it's not rated R," Rose said. "I don't go baby-sitting, bringing R-rated movies. Come on, Charlotte."

"But you swear in front of us."

I was trying not to stare at Charlotte's glistening fingers, or the way she was gnawing little chicken-skin bits out of her fingernails. My mother would've killed me if I'd eaten like that.

"That's different," Rose said. "Swearing isn't damaging, like sex or violence. Swearing is just a harmless hobby of mine. Let's go."

* * *

It was already dark, so I tried not to worry about my mother or Mrs. Crowe seeing us walk by with Rose. But I was worried that one of them would hear us.

"Shhh," I whispered as we started across the sidewalk in front of Mrs. Crowe's house. "Let's be very, very quiet."

Rose and Charlotte glanced at each other, and Charlotte giggled softly.

"Are we hunting rabbits or something, Nora?" Rose whispered.

I kept my mouth shut till we were way past the house and nearly all the way past Mrs. Shepherd's house. And I fumed the whole rest of the way to Rose's. You're weird if you explain yourself and you're weird if you don't. Why did I have to seem like the weird one just because they needed everything spelled out for them?

This was only the second time I'd actually been in Rose's house. I'd loved the Bankses' house from the outside, though. It was less old-fashioned than Mrs. Crowe's but more than the Hemsworths'. It was a ranch like Charlotte's, but with no garage. The paint job—dark red with bright white trim— always reminded me of an old barn. It seemed like a house where cheerful things happened—where you could imagine kids sprawled on the carpet playing Operation, or snickerdoodles coming out of the oven.

Rose led us up her driveway, up the brick steps, and through the heavy white door.

"Hello," she called as she led us through a dark alcove into the cramped living room. "I'm back."

I was a little surprised myself to see her parents sitting in the living room watching TV. Rose's parents were almost never home, because they were so busy with their restaurant.

"Hey, sweet pea," Rose's dad said from the gliding rocker. It took me a second to realize he was talking to Rose. I'd never have thought of her as sweet, and I wasn't sure I'd want someone calling me a pea, personally.

"Hello, girls." Rose's mom was sitting on a bright love seat, the cream-colored fabric splattered with dark pink flowers and green leaves that looked like watercolors.

"Hello," Charlotte replied as I took in the room. It felt overstuffed with furniture and decoration. Over Rose's dad's head was a painting of a rocking horse, and above that a black-and-white photograph of a desert. Rose's mom sat against a pile of mismatched throw pillows, some of them shiny like prom dresses. And she had a quilt of tie-dyed fabrics pulled over her. Its pinwheels of red and orange could give you a headache if you looked at it too long.

"Hi, Nora," Mrs. Banks prompted.

"Hi," I mumbled.

"Oh, leave her alone, Wanda," Rose said to her. "She *said* hello, you just didn't hear her."

I hadn't, but I was willing to go with this.

"What brings you ladies here?" Mr. Banks asked.

"I'm just getting that movie. How was it, Dad?"

Mr. Banks rubbed his head. I noticed that his brown hair was combed every which way to cover up a golf-ball-size bald spot at the very top of his head.

"Not bad. But I don't have it. I gave it—"

"Okay for underage viewers?" Rose interrupted, pressing a

button on the VCR, then looking at the video that came out. "You're right. It's not here."

"I told you, Rose. Toby came by for it this morning."

"Toby?" Charlotte said, looking slightly offended.

"Well, it's *their* movie," Rose said. "Why didn't you tell me, Dad?"

"I *did*. You just weren't listening. You seem a little forgetful these days, Rosie."

"Rose." Mrs. Banks raised her brown-penciled eyebrows. "You aren't going to show these little girls anything scary, are you?"

"Don't worry, Wanda. This isn't horror. This is science. It's a documentary."

"I see."

"Well, we'll just have to go up there and get it back," Rose said. "Joe probably didn't realize I still needed it."

"You girls can come back and watch it here if you like," Mr. Banks suggested. "I wouldn't mind seeing it again."

"What's this movie about?" Mrs. Banks wanted to know.

"Aliens," Charlotte said.

"Aliens?" Mrs. Banks snorted. "No thanks."

"It was actually sort of interesting," Mr. Banks said. "Wanda, you might like—"

"I think I'll stick with earthlings this evening," Mrs. Banks interrupted. "They're showing that Cher movie on Channel Eight. The one with Cher and the two brothers."

Mr. Banks shrugged and rubbed his bald spot again.

Rose turned her head very slowly and stared at her mother in a creepy way that made me think of something in one of Charlotte's books—the evil eye. Then she stalked into the kitchen, leaving us with her parents.

Mr. Banks turned back to us and asked, "How's school, girls?"

His wife just stared after Rose, into the doorway of the kitchen—even though Rose wasn't visible. And Mrs. Banks's eye seemed about as evil as Rose's.

"Pretty good," Charlotte said. "I got an A-plus on the first book report."

"That's great," Mr. Banks said.

Figuring Charlotte had this conversation covered, I wandered off after Rose. I found her in the kitchen, rummaging through the cabinets.

"What're you doing in there, Rose?" Mrs. Banks called.

"Thinking," Rose called back.

"Oh—Rose?" Mrs. Banks shouted. "I almost forgot. Aaron called again. He said there was some party tonight? He was under the impression you were going with him."

Rose ignored her mother, pulling out a box of microwave popcorn and stuffing one of the packages in her jacket pocket. I examined all the papers and pictures hanging on the Bankses' refrigerator. There was a report Rose had written about beetles when she was in elementary school and a picture her older sister, Cathy, had drawn of a horse. A snapshot of the whole family at Cathy's high-school graduation last year. Half the papers on the fridge were brownish and crinkled and splattered with grease and stuff. The letters-of-the-alphabet magnets were gummed up with dust. Peeking out from a bunch of other drawings was one with purplish paint spattered on yellowed paper. I pushed some of the other papers aside to see that it was children's handprints. *"Cathy"* was written under the purple hand, *"Rose"* under a smaller, bluish hand.

"Well, he's wrong," Rose called back to her mother. "I'm not going anywhere with him. And I *told* him I'm baby-sitting to-night."

Rose returned to the living room, but I stayed and gaped at the old handprints. My mother put my stuff on the refrigerator, too, but she rotated stuff out. The Bankses never seemed to throw anything away.

"Maybe you ought to sit down with Aaron and explain to him—" Mrs. Banks was saying.

"I *have*, Wanda. Jesus. I *dumped* him."

"Well, he doesn't seem to realize that. He keeps calling here, and you keep making *me* make excuses for you."

I surprised myself by thinking of something else in Char-lotte's books. The book said that people sometimes put a hand-print on their door or their house to ward off the evil eye. I rearranged the papers so you could see both of the little hands. I wasn't sure who I was protecting—Rose or her mom. Probably Mr. Banks. He seemed to need it the most.

"Okay, come on, Nora," Rose called to me. And then to her parents: "See you guys later."

"Bye," I said to the Bankses as I crept through the living room—looking Mr. Banks in the eye the way I was supposed to but not managing to do the same for his wife—and followed Rose out the front door.

"Your parents are nice," Charlotte declared as we stepped away from the house and back onto the dark street.

Rose grunted in reply.

"Do they like having a restaurant? Do they ever make you do the dishes?"

"I'm not sure, and no. No on the dishes."

"Do you think you'll run the restaurant when you're older?"

"No."

"Why not?"

"Because the restaurant won't be open."

"Why not?"

"The restaurant probably won't be open in six months, much less when I'm old enough to run it."

"Why not?" Charlotte wanted to know.

Rose sighed. "Just trust me. It's boring stuff. About money."

Charlotte hesitated, then decided to try a different line of questioning. "How come you call your mom Wanda?"

"My sister calls her Mom. I call her Wanda. It's how she tells us apart."

While Charlotte and I puzzled over this response, Rose led us still farther up the hill, past the trees in the no-man's-land between the Cooks' and the Larsons', to the sharp turnoff onto Fox Hill Way, which dipped down slightly, then led up to two more houses, then Toby's house, then the transfer station. One reason kids sometimes made fun of Toby was the proximity of his house to the transfer station. Sometimes kids said he smelled like the dump, which I didn't think was true.

A few steps away from the turnoff, Rose stopped walking and looked upward. Charlotte and I did the same without knowing why.

"See?" Rose said. "All these stars? This movie's gonna get you thinking about this. All these stars, and any one of them could be a sun. There's bound to be lots of other creatures out there, spinning around some of those suns."

"Maybe . . ." Charlotte said skeptically.

Rose didn't seem to hear her. "I just hope the right ones get to us first."

Rose began walking again, and as we followed her, we heard the sound of an engine, and then headlights suddenly appeared.

"Outta the road!" Rose shouted, yanking me by the sleeve as Charlotte jumped from the car's path. There was no sidewalk.

The driver of the car braked and then pulled over slightly ahead of us.

"What the hell are you doing, Rose?" the young man demanded as he got out of the car. "You trying to get these kids killed?"

Rose mumbled something in return, which sounded like, "What do you care?"

"What're you doing? Your mom said you'd just left for Joe's."

"That's right. But I'm baby-sitting tonight, as you can see."

"Doing a real good job of it, too."

"Shut up, Aaron. What do you want?"

I squinted at Aaron. He was tall, with sandy blond hair, fierce eyes, and nice teeth. Charlotte had been right. He was handsome.

"I wanted to know if you'd come later. Paul says his parents just went to a movie. You'll be done by nine-thirty, I'll bet."

"You researched where I'd be all night, you stalker?"

"Do you want me to pick you up when you're done? You can call me at Steve's."

"No. I don't know. I don't feel like it."

Charlotte and I stood by the evergreens, riveted. I couldn't imagine being sixteen, having this handsome guy begging me to come out for a date, and saying no. Rose was a rock star.

"Rose," Aaron said, reaching out for her shoulder, "why won't you at least—"

"Get. Your. Fucking. Hand. Off. Me," Rose snarled. "You make me *sick*."

Charlotte and I looked at each other. This wasn't just hobbyist swearing. Rose really was angry.

"You're such a drama queen, Rose," Aaron said, getting back into his car. "Do you know that?"

"Beats being an asshole," Rose murmured, but I was pretty certain he didn't hear her, because he'd slammed his door shut by then.

He drove past us, spun around at the transfer station, and sped back down the road, turning back onto the main Fox Hill Road, revving his engine as he did so.

"WOW!" Charlotte said as soon as the engine noise had faded. "Why did you yell at him like that?"

"Because he's a jerk."

"Why? What'd he do?"

Rose squinted at Charlotte, and for a moment I thought another evil eye was coming. When we'd nearly reached Toby's driveway, Rose said, "You wouldn't believe me if I told you."

"I would," Charlotte insisted. "I'd believe you."

Rose said nothing. She led us across the Deans' grass.

"I would," Charlotte said again.

Rose paused before heading up the Deans' driveway. She seemed to be looking at the stars again. I gazed across the yard. I loved the Deans' place, with its rickety farmhouse feel and two cool little outbuildings: the dilapidated shed and the root cellar. The shed was where Joe hung out and did his funny sculptures. I wasn't sure what a "root cellar" was, really, but I liked how the tiny building was built into the hill like something a Keebler elf might live in.

"Sometimes," Rose confessed, "I actually wish they'd come soon. I wish they would just come for real already. It's, like, the one thing I can think of happening that *no one* could ignore."

It took me a moment to realize she was talking about aliens again. I shivered. I'd never seen her so serious. The fact that it was so dark around the Deans' house didn't help either.

"So . . ." Charlotte purred. "What'd Aaron do? Kiss some other girl?"

I kicked her in the shin, and she whirled around and stared at me.

"OW! What's *your* problem?"

When I didn't reply, she chased me down the driveway and eventually managed to kick me back after about four tries, clumsily throwing her leg out repeatedly as I dodged it. Her shock at my kick had made her lose her coordination.

Rose caught up with us.

"Knock it off," she murmured as she pushed ahead of us, ran up the steps, and rang the Deans' bell.

"Hey, Toby," she said when he opened the door.

Toby seemed delighted to find the three of us on his steps, and he held the door for us without asking what we wanted. As we stepped inside, the familiar mildewy scent of the old house filled my nostrils. I remembered the smell from when my mom used to help Toby's dad and the elder Mrs. Dean.

"Joe's not home," he said once we were in his living room.

Mr. Dean was snoring on the brown corduroy couch, a bag of Ruffles wedged between his hip and the couch cushions. *Cops* was playing on the TV. He twitched a little, rubbed his nose and mustache, but didn't open his eyes. I was surprised to see the chips. Mr. Dean was so skinny and sickly looking sometimes, you imagined him living on lettuce and chewing gum.

"That's okay," Rose said. "I just came for that alien movie. I wanted to borrow it again and show it to the girls."

"Oh. Okay. I'll go get it," Toby said, hopping eagerly up the stairs.

Mr. Dean snorted softly and then opened his eyes. Startled to see the three of us standing there, he pulled himself up on his elbow.

"What's . . . girls? What's . . . everything all right?" he asked groggily.

"Yeah," Rose said. "We just came by for this video I wanted to borrow. Toby's upstairs getting it for us."

"What's . . . where's Joe? Joe all right?"

"Yeah . . . we're just here for a video," Rose repeated. "There's a party at this kid Steve Hungerford's house tonight. That's probably where Joe is."

"Oh . . ." The Ruffles bag crinkled as Mr. Dean settled back into the couch, looking relieved but still slightly confused. He put his hand through his thick salt-and-pepper hair, mashing flat a cowlick at the top.

Toby bounded down the stairs and handed Rose the video.

"It's due back tomorrow or we have to pay three more dollars," he said.

"I'll return it for you guys," Rose assured him.

"Or," Toby said, "I could come watch it with you guys, and then I could bring it home and Joe and I will return it tomorrow."

"Tobe," Mr. Dean said, opening his eyes. "Don't . . . uh . . . bother this girl. She's already got her hands full tonight."

"You won't be missing anything," Rose assured Toby. "These

girls will be screaming and whimpering the whole time. Really pathetic."

"Yeah, right," Charlotte said, planting her hand on her hip.

"I thought you said it wasn't scary," I protested.

"Well, I'll just walk you guys home, then," Toby said. "Dad, I'm going to walk them home, okay?"

"That's very gentlemanly of you," Rose said, shrugging, ignoring Charlotte's look of pleading disdain.

"Okay," Mr. Dean said, dislodging the Ruffles bag from the couch cushion and peering inside it. "But be real careful on the way back."

"*Yes!*" Toby said, making a fist of victory so enthusiastic that even Charlotte could not protest.

Toby was so weird.

Six

May 22, 2006

Charlotte wasn't home by five, so I tried her cell phone.

"Sorry, I'm having trouble getting out of here," she explained. "There was this parent-teacher conference. This kid's parents finally wake up and realize Brittany's probably not gonna graduate. What are we gonna do to help her, blah, blah, blah. . . . Then I was trying to get these stupid journals graded so I don't have to lug them all home. . . ."

When I mentioned beer with Toby, she said, "You ought to go. I'm swamped tonight. Go ahead."

Atkins Tavern was packed that evening, and it seemed that about half of the clientele was on backslapping terms with Toby. We had a front table by the window. People kept saying hello to him, often coming over to chat for a few minutes. The window at least gave me something to do—gaze across the street to the old town green, which looked pretty under the setting sun. Growing up, I don't think I ever really appreciated how idyllic Waverly would look to someone just passing through. Trees with little white flowers surrounded the wide green lawn, a small stone war memorial at its center. It was completely empty of people, which wasn't a surprise. No one ever walked around the green, even on the most beautiful of days—just drove by it on the way to Stop & Shop.

"How's married life?" Toby asked me between drop-bys.

"Really good, actually," I said.

"How'd you meet your husband again?"

"College."

Toby nodded. "So you're like an old couple now."

"I guess."

"What's he do?"

"He's works for U.S. Fish & Wildlife. He's an . . . environmentalist."

"I think Charlotte did tell me that once. An environmentalist and a potter?" Toby considered this. "Good combination."

I shrugged. "Sure. If you're going for a certain hippie-yuppie balance."

"More hippie than yuppie, I'd say. But that's a good thing. Is that a lucrative business, selling pots?"

I smiled. "I teach ceramics part-time at a community college with a fairly big arts program. Plus, I help run an arts co-op and teach a few noncredit night classes here and there. Between all that, it's a living. Some money comes from the actual pottery, but very little."

I was glad he gave me a chance to explain this. When my mother first heard my intention to study ceramics, I think she started picturing me sitting sadly by a roadside with a Sale sign and a wobbly card table full of lopsided ashtrays. I sometimes wondered if she still pictured my life that way and conveyed this image to others.

"How about you?" I asked. "You seeing anyone right now?"

"Nah. Since I stopped towing, I don't seem to get the girls."

"Since you stopped towing?"

"Yeah. My newest guy does all the towing for me. You meet women when you tow. They're always so damn happy to see you. Women with flat tires, snapped timing belts, whatever it is. You're like the knight in shining armor. They just hop right into your truck and there you go. Instant rapport. Instant conversation."

"I'm sure a lot of women come into the shop."

"Sure, but now I'm just the guy who charges them too much."

"Maybe you should do Match.com or something. Meet somebody who doesn't have car trouble."

"Everyone has car trouble," Toby said. "Just a matter of when. Anyway, I didn't say I was desperate."

"I didn't think you were. I just know some people who've had some fun meeting people that way."

We both sipped our beers in the awkward silence. I deeply regretted mentioning an online dating site. I was becoming one of those obnoxious married people.

"So . . . the police talked to you yet?" Toby wanted to know.

"No," I said, surprised. "They wouldn't know I'm in town."

"Yeah, but they've been making the rounds on Fox Hill."

"They have? Charlotte didn't mention that."

"They talked to my brother a little while."

"Oh, yeah? And you? They talked to you?"

"Not so interested in me, no. Joe was Rose's friend, sort of. But I was only a sixth-grader."

"Me too," I reminded him.

"Yeah, but you're special," he said.

I sipped my beer. "I'm not special, Toby."

"Sure you are. You were the last to see her."

"Right. Well. I still don't have anything to tell them. I'm older now, and Rose is dead for sure, but that doesn't change anything I remember."

"*'The last to see her alive,'*" Toby said, shaking his head. "That was hard on you, wasn't it?"

I took another long swallow of my beer. That designation was already starting to get on my nerves again.

"There are harder things than that, I think," I said, shrugging.

Toby rolled his eyes. "That doesn't mean it wasn't still hard.

"So," he continued, "did you come here thinking you might heal some old wound?"

"What're you, Dr. Phil?"

"No. I'm not Dr. Phil," he said flatly. "I'm just curious."

"I don't know what I was thinking, to be honest. It's starting to feel like there was very little thinking involved, coming back here."

"Well, that's okay," Toby said, then blew a low toot into his beer bottle. "Sometimes thought is overrated."

I giggled at this typical Toby statement, feeling oddly relieved by it. He was apparently letting the topic drop.

"That's true," I said.

"You two are both funny, you know that? Maybe you bring it out in each other."

"Who?"

"You and Charlotte. Remember that day you two bribed me

into kidnapping Rose's cat? You thought he was gonna help you find her or something."

"I don't remember any bribing."

Toby hesitated. "Charlotte gave me a two-liter bottle of Pepsi."

"Well, a bottle of Pepsi was nothing to her. Her dad mainlined the stuff, kept a closet full of it. But I didn't know you two had a deal."

"You don't know how hard that was, getting that nasty little bastard to Charlotte's. I poked around the Bankses' house for a couple of days before I got him. The first time I scooped him up, he scratched my arms and neck to shreds and practically took an eye out."

"Not your good eye, I hope."

"Whichever, he didn't get it. And I got him eventually. 'Cuz I put him in a heavy-duty garbage bag."

"That's terrible!" I said. "You could've suffocated him."

"On my way over, I opened it and gave him some air every minute or so. You girls wanted that cat in your hot little hands. And cats don't follow when you whistle. You had to know it was gonna be rough."

"I never wanted him that badly."

"But Charlotte did."

"If Charlotte knew you were going to risk suffocating him . . ."

"Oh, but Charlotte knew."

"She did?"

"Oh, yeah. She's the one who answered the door when I showed up with the squirming Hefty bag. He'd practically clawed his way out of the bag by the time I got there. We threw him in the bathroom and kept him there till you arrived."

"Charlotte never told me how you caught him."

"Of course she didn't. And she told me not to tell you either. She didn't want you getting upset and screwing up the ceremony."

"Yes, well, my delicate sensibilities often got in Charlotte's way."

"I know," Toby said, rolling his eyes. "Seems if she'd been smarter, she would've used them to her advantage. Another beer?"

"Sure," I said.

Toby waved down our waitress. As we waited for our new beers, I listened to the hum of people chattering at the bar. One of them had a loud, frequent laugh that had occasionally distracted me while I'd talked to Toby. Now that I focused on it, I found its unabashed quality familiar, and I kept staring at the back of the dark-haired head that seemed to be producing it.

"Oh, right, Joe," the bartender was saying. "Like they're not all on 'roids."

Joe. I turned to Toby. "That your brother?"

"Yep."

"This just a coincidence?"

"Nope. He heard where I was going, so he hitched a ride."

"Should I say hello, you think?"

"Sure. You ought to. Hey, Joe!" he called before I could protest. "Come over here a second."

Joe turned, hopped off his stool, and sauntered over to our table, beer in hand. I thought, from his lethargic expression, that he might be a little drunk.

"Hey there, Nora," he said, bumping Toby so he could slide in next to him in our booth. "Toby told me you were back in town."

"Thanks," I said, then blushed. Joe hadn't actually said anything for which I should thank him. I'd always had a crush on Joe. I think, when I finally gave in and went out with Toby, it was probably because he physically resembled Joe. Joe was way too old for me, of course, but Toby was at least like a mini-Joe, minus the brooding intensity or the artistic leanings. I think Toby must have known—I'd always go speechless when we were with his brother.

"What brings you back? Is it your ten-year reunion already? Or did the police haul you in to talk about Rose?"

I looked Joe over before answering. Same intense brown eyes and thick black eyebrows, but he was puffy in the neck, the chiseled quality of his face now cushioned in jowls. His face reminded me—just slightly—of the aged Elvis. Seeing him made me wonder how Rose would've fared—how she'd look now, if she'd made it to her thirties.

"No," I said. "I'm visiting Charlotte Hemsworth."

"That's cool. How long you staying?"

"I'm not sure."

"Where you living now?"

"Northern Virginia."

"Virginia! What the hell are you doing there?"

"I teach pottery at a community college."

"Oh. Pottery." This piece of information seemed to focus Joe's attention somewhat. "That's cool. I haven't done my sculpture for years, but I wish I'd stuck with it."

I hesitated. "I remember you had some interesting pieces."

"Yeah, right," Joe said with a snorting laugh. "*Pieces*. Pieces of crap, you mean?"

I didn't know how to reply to this. I'd liked Joe's wood-and-metal animals the way a kid usually likes everything that has to do with animals. I couldn't tell if I'd been obnoxious to call them "pieces" or if he was obnoxious to call me on it.

"Pretty terrible about Rose, huh?" Joe said after a moment.

"Yeah," I replied.

"Poor thing." He shook his head and stared into his beer glass. "And her poor parents."

"Toby said the police talked to you about her."

Joe's head jerked up, and he glanced at Toby, who remained silent. "Yeah. Yeah, they did."

"What'd they ask you?"

"Oh, just . . . did I see her that day, in the neighborhood . . . did I know of anyone they should talk to. Basically the same stuff they asked sixteen, seventeen years ago. They'd heard we'd hang out sometimes, she and I. . . ."

"Did you? I don't remember that."

"On and off. Weren't exactly in the same crowd, but we were buddies when we were kids. You know, Rose was one of those girls who liked to hang out with guys more than other girls. Plus, girls didn't like her much."

I didn't offer that Charlotte and I had liked her. Being prepubescent at the time, I guess we didn't really count.

"You know," Joe went on, "I was lucky I was bagging groceries all that evening, three till close. Otherwise the police woulda had a *lot* more questions for me. They never liked the look of me, the Waverly PD. They'd already caught me with weed once by the time Rose disappeared."

"Really?" I said. I hadn't a great deal of experience with the Waverly police, but I knew they'd never had quite enough to do. It seemed plausible they'd hound a stoner like Joe just to pass the time. "But it's the state police doing the investigation, right?"

"True," Joe admitted. "Anyway, they didn't ask anything new. Now that she's dead, they gotta cover all the same bases, I guess. Talk to the same old people."

"I guess."

Joe shook his head. "Poor Rose. God, that girl was something. Kind of a nut, but I liked that about her."

"A nut?"

Joe took a sip of Toby's beer, then leaned back in the booth and closed his eyes for a moment. "Yeah. A nut. A good nut, but still a nut."

"Can I ask how you mean?"

"Well, I'll give you an example. Remember the One-Acts?"

"Yeah," I said. Every winter each of the four classes would put on a short one-act play, and a panel of teacher judges would select the best. The winning class would get a small amount of prize money from the PTA, to be put toward their prom or whatever.

"Well, Rose had a bit part at the end of the sophomores' play. I guess that would be the year before she disappeared. She was supposed to wear this jacket—it was part of her costume. But right before she came onstage, she took it off, and she was wearing this black T-shirt with this great big neon middle finger sticking up on the front."

"A T-shirt with a middle finger?" I repeated.

"Oh, the early nineties," said Toby, who'd clearly heard the story before. "The age of Spencer Gifts."

"That's weird," I said. "I didn't think she was that kind of kid."

"Well . . . she wasn't, really," said Joe. "No one would've expected it. That's what made it so goddamned funny."

"Oh," I said, trying—and failing—to cough up a giggle for Joe's story.

Joe frowned, then scratched his head. "Yeah. Listen, I should leave you two to catch up."

"Oh, you don't need to—"

"If you're still around on Memorial Day, maybe you could come by for a burger or something. We might be cooking out."

With that he was gone, headed back to his barstool. His eagerness to leave us kids alone reminded me of the last time I'd seen him—the night of Toby's and my senior prom. Toby had brought me to his house in the middle of the night, after the prom and after a few swigs of vodka on the Waverly Elementary playground had rendered me loudmouthed and silly. We'd tried to sneak quietly into Toby's house but found Joe up and watching *Goodfellas* on the VCR. His dark eyes sparkled with amusement at our shiny prom garb and our clumsy attempts to explain that we were just looking to watch a little TV.

"I was just leaving," he'd said good-naturedly, turning off the movie and grabbing his keys as if he had somewhere to be at 1:30 A.M. But then he'd hesitated in the doorway, making us squirm for a few seconds more. "I know you two aren't stupid," he said. He didn't say it in a scolding way, but rather matter-of-factly. Still, I'd wished I could disappear. The guy might as well have handed each of us a condom and patted us both on the head. And seeing him had made the prospect of fooling around with Toby seem like a sad sort of consolation prize.

Now that sentiment felt foolish. Seeing them next to each

other in the booth, it struck me that they didn't have much in common besides dark hair and dark eyes. And Toby seemed to have come out the more together of the two brothers. Maybe I'd feel differently if I saw Joe on a better day.

"Eyeball," I said. "Listen."

Toby tugged at his ear. "Been a while since I heard that name."

"I'm really sorry about that one night. Remember, the night of the prom?"

Toby shook his head and took a long sip of beer. "Don't do that, Nora. It's been, what, ten years?"

"Nine."

"Okay. Nine years. Sometimes time fixes some things so you don't have to talk about them. Even if I didn't really understand then, I understand now."

"Okay. I'm sorry I brought it up."

"Don't be sorry. You know what I think your problem is? You haven't been back here at all. Maybe somewhere in your head you think the whole place has been in a holding pattern since you left. You think everybody's still driving the same car, radio tuned to the same station. . . . You think I'm still *Eyeball*. And that I've still got blue balls from that night . . ."

I blushed again and stared at my beer.

"Laugh," Toby said. "That was a joke. It's all supposed to be funny now."

"Thanks," I said. "I know it is. I'm just a little slow."

Toby shrugged and finished his beer.

"How are the Bankses taking all this?" I asked, changing the subject back to Rose. "How do you think they've been doing?"

"Up till now they haven't changed much. Mr. Banks is kinda sad, but his gardening seems to make him happy since he retired. Mrs. Banks—she keeps busy. You know she sells cars for the Honda dealership now?"

"No, didn't know that."

"She's their top salesperson. Not a big surprise. She's good at that sort of thing. Schmoozing."

I nodded. Back when the Bankses ran their restaurant, Mrs. Banks had played the role of bubbly restaurateur—visiting everyone's table, making new people feel like regulars. The place was called Popovers, and it was slightly cuter and significantly more expensive than most of the old American-fare joints in town. The Bankses closed it about a year after Rose disappeared.

"You talk to them much?" I asked.

"Mr. Banks, sort of. I helped him with his Christmas lights. He's kind of a quiet guy, though. And Mrs. Banks is never around much. Or out in the yard anyway. And I haven't talked to them since this latest thing with Rose, if that's what you're asking. And I wouldn't really know what to say if I did."

"Yeah, I can imagine."

Another guffaw came from the direction of Joe's barstool. And again I thought of the later Elvis. Joe's laugh reminded me of that recording where Elvis can't get through the lines of "Love Me Tender"—the one where he keeps making jokes and laughing because he's all high on something.

"Is he okay?" I asked Toby.

"Yeah," Toby answered, shaking his head a little. "This has just been a hard couple of weeks for him. Broke up with his girlfriend, which is why he's camping out at my house. And this thing with Rose . . . You know, they were friends—at least when they were little. It's kind of rough."

"And so soon after your dad . . ." I added sympathetically.

Toby nodded, then shifted his gaze slowly from his beer to me. I was startled by his eyes—I'd forgotten what it was like to look at them. Back when I was in high school and had trouble looking most people in the eye, I'd never had any trouble with him. Since one of his eyes was slightly askew, it was a softer stare than most, as though part of him wasn't looking at you anyway. I had liked that about him.

"What're you thinking about?" I said.

"Rose," he said, a little sadly. "I had a little crush on her. I thought she was so cool."

"Me, too," I said.

"Do you remember when I had to stay back in fourth grade?"

"Yeah."

"It was partly because of my grandmother dying and partly 'cuz I missed so much school that year, when I got pneumonia, I don't know if you remember. But let's call a spade a spade—I was kind of a little bonehead, too."

"Oh, now, let's not—" I began, suddenly sounding like my mother. My mere geographical proximity to her was changing my speech patterns, apparently.

"But she didn't make fun of me for it, like almost everyone else did."

I was silent. I was probably included in the "almost everyone else." At least I certainly never came to Toby's defense.

"But I remember her and my brother talking to me about it, trying to make me feel better. She kept trying to make it sound like it was a good thing, going on and on like, 'This is a harder thing to go through than those kids know anything about. And once you get through this year, you'll have something they don't have, something they don't even understand—you'll be better than them, tougher than them, because you'll know you can get through it.' I'm paraphrasing here. But she made it sound like staying back was like getting a badge of honor. And I bought it. Because I wasn't very bright."

"But it made you feel better, right?"

"Yeah," Toby said. "Rose was actually full of shit sometimes."

I nodded vaguely at this, even though I'd never really thought of Rose that way. But it sounded like she had a different side to her when she was around boys. I was so busy puzzling over this that I didn't notice the waitress dropping our check on the table. Toby grabbed it before I could stop him.

Mystic Places:
October 1990

Mystic Places was, in general, my favorite of Charlotte's black books. I didn't care all that much about Atlantis, but I liked the pictures in the other sections—of the Egyptian pyramids and Stonehenge. Especially Stonehenge. The pyramids were impressive but somewhat explainable, thanks to social-studies lessons we'd had on Egypt in the fourth grade. Stonehenge and the Druids were another thing entirely. There was something forbidden about them, as they were never mentioned in school. I'd noticed that while the pyramids were always pictured drenched in desert sunlight, Stonehenge was almost always pictured under a darkening sky. And while illustrated Egyptians wore next to nothing, the Druids wore mysterious-looking hoods. I respected the Egyptians but feared and loved the Druids.

Charlotte didn't really like *Mystic Places*, but she always let me take it out when we were planning our trip—the around-the-world trip we'd go on when we were eighteen, just after we graduated. Rose would be twenty-three, which was unfathomable, but she would come with us if she didn't have kids by then. Charlotte had made a shadowy, stapled-together copy of a large world map on the library photocopier weeks before. Now it hung on her bulletin board with little red construction-paper flags on our planned destinations. Stonehenge was marked on my insistence. It worked well for us to go there, as there were a number of haunted castles Charlotte wanted to investigate in Ireland and Scotland.

As we finished marking all our British destinations, checking and rechecking their locations as best we could, Rose had grown bored, slipped *Alien Encounters* out of Charlotte's stash, and started flipping through it.

"Could we go to the Bermuda Triangle?" Charlotte asked when we'd finished.

Rose gazed at the page in front of her, skimming.

"COULD WE GO TO THE BERMUDA TRIANGLE?" Charlotte repeated.

"Don't be rude, Charlotte. I heard you the first time."

"Then why didn't you answer?"

"Because I was thinking."

"No you weren't. You were reading."

Rose defiantly read a few more lines before giving Charlotte her full attention. I stared at the two-page photo in *Mystic Places* of "modern Druids" gathered at Stonehenge for the summer solstice. A few of them were dressed in white robes and head scarves. More of them had on regular clothes—sweaters and jackets. A few sat on top of the high horizontal slabs. I'd often wondered how one went about becoming a modern Druid, whether my American birth and Unitarian mother automatically excluded me as a candidate.

"I was *thinking*," Rose said, "that that might have to be a separate trip. That's in a totally different direction."

"Well, I *know* that. I guess I was just asking if you'd wanna go there, too. Not just Europe and Egypt."

"Sure," Rose said with a shrug, lowering her gaze back to her book. "We could get bikinis and—"

"I don't like bikinis," I protested.

"We could spend a few days on the beach before sailing out to the triangle," Rose continued, without looking up. "Get a little sunbathing in. Make a real nice trip of it. It doesn't need to be all business."

"My mom doesn't even let me wear a bikini," I explained. "She makes me get a one-piece."

"You'll be way older by then," Rose said. "She can't tell you what to do."

I scoffed at this weird notion, this mystical time and place— age eighteen—in which I'd wear a bikini and my mother could not tell me what to do. Atlantis seemed more probable and more reachable.

Rose was reading again.

"Maybe we should do a separate map for that trip," Charlotte said.

"Maybe," Rose murmured. "I guess you're going to need to photocopy some more maps."

"How about just one big around-the-world trip?" I asked.

"If we do, can we add Easter Island. I've been meaning to add Easter Island. I love those big stone statues on Easter Island, in that other book—"

"Jeez, Nora," Charlotte said. "What's with you and the megaliths anyway?"

Charlotte probably just said that to use a big word, so I ignored the question.

"Man," Rose said, gaping at her book. "Your parents really let you read this stuff?"

"What?" Charlotte snatched at the corner of the book, tilting it down so we could both see it. "I haven't read much of the alien one yet."

On the page was a drawing of a very weird-looking child, its whole huge head visible under gossamer hair. It appeared to be wearing eyeliner.

"It's a half-human, half-alien baby," Rose said.

"How'd *that* happen?" I asked.

"Oh, think about it, Nora," Charlotte said, rolling her eyes for Rose's benefit. "How do you *think* it happened? That is *gross*."

Rose didn't react. I stared at the drawing. Aside from its head, the shape of its body wasn't visible. It was clothed in a long, shiftlike dress with a wide, low-slung belt.

"She looks kind of like Kelly Sawyer," I replied.

Charlotte giggled. Kelly Sawyer had big, creepy blue eyes and a funny bowl cut that made her look like a character from one of Paul's seventies movies.

"But she dresses kind of like Sally Pilkington," I added.

Charlotte frowned. "Probably you shouldn't make fun of Sally," she said.

I bit my lip, chastened. Usually Sally was an easy laugh, because everyone thought she dressed weird—not to mention she was a Jehovah's Witness. But her older brother had been in a car accident recently and was still in the hospital. Apparently we weren't allowed to make fun of her again until her brother recovered.

"I'm going to read that book next, I think," Charlotte said, keeping her hand possessively on the book's page.

Rose gazed silently at Charlotte's hand for a moment before acknowledging her.

"Well, add Roswell, New Mexico, to one of your maps," Rose said slowly. "That's where I'd like to go."

"What'll we do there?"

Rose gently pushed Charlotte's hand away and turned the page. "We'll drive around in the desert." She sounded frustrated with us. "Looking for human-alien bastards."

Then, ignoring Charlotte's gasp at "bastards," Rose slammed the book closed. "Let's do something else, okay, girls? I'm not in the mood for this shit anymore."

Somehow we ended up watching *Jaws* again late that afternoon. Rose hadn't noticed my pleading glance when Charlotte suggested it. She'd simply popped in the tape and then settled at the kitchen table with her homework, leaving me in the living room with Charlotte and the shark. Charlotte's dad was no help either. When he came home from work about twenty minutes into the movie, he didn't seem to notice what was on the screen.

"You want a ride up the hill, Nora?" he asked.

"Up the hill?"

"A ride home. Would you like a ride home? I'm going in that direction, to the transfer station, so I can take you and Rose."

"Okay," I said with a shrug. Every so often, on garbage day, Mr. Hemsworth offered to drop me and Rose on his way. The walk was so short that it seemed silly, but it always felt impolite to say no.

"She doesn't have to go now if she doesn't want to, though," Charlotte said. "If she wants to walk, she can stay, right?"

"Charlotte." There was a sharp quality to Mr. Hemsworth's voice that I didn't understand.

Maybe he wanted to get rid of me and he didn't like Charlotte's lip getting in the way. Maybe it was something else entirely. Dads were a mystery to me, with their gruff moods and unpredictable preferences. Charlotte's dad in particular was an enigma, with his arms so hairy and gray they reminded me of a dryer lint trap and his tyrannical interest in things like lawns, car washing, football. In a way he didn't seem real, but rather like just another dad I watched on television. He was tall and chinless, with a paunch that pressed robustly against the buttons of his white work shirts. His face was always red, but his anger always seemed halfhearted.

"I'll be ready to go in just a few minutes," he said. "Got to pack up the garbage in the van first. You and Charlotte can watch your movie for a few minutes, and I'll give you a holler when I'm going."

"Okay."

I rocked enthusiastically in the Hemsworths' rocking chair, now relieved that I wouldn't need to stay for the movie's final scenes. By the time the fisherman got eaten before Charlotte's eyes, I'd be having a quiet dinner with my mother, eating salmon patties and white rice at the card table, telling her about school during the commercials of the *CBS Evening News*.

But before I knew it, fifteen minutes had passed and one of the other dreaded parts of the movie was approaching—the part where the kid on the raft gets eaten, his blood squirting up and out like a fountain, the other swimmers running and screaming while his poor mother looks for him frantically on the beach.

After the sleepover I felt I'd paid my dues and I shouldn't have to watch this scene again so soon. As the scene drew near, I began to make clicking noises with my tongue against my teeth, to distract myself from the movie, to remind myself that I was real and it was not.

"Shh," Charlotte said.

I narrowed my gaze on the plush aqua-green upholstery behind her head and the sunken aqua buttons that made the sofa look like a giant pincushion. Whenever I sat on that couch, I had a strong urge to twist and yank at those buttons, which is why I'd lately been sitting in the rocking chair instead.

"What?" Charlotte said sharply. "What are you staring at?"

I hated how people were always accusing me of *staring* when I was only *looking*.

"Nothing," I said, glancing back toward the kitchen. "But maybe your dad forgot about me?"

Charlotte didn't take her eyes off the screen. "I didn't hear the car pull out."

"Maybe he changed his mind. Maybe I'm supposed to walk."

"Maybe."

I stood up and walked through the kitchen, then opened the door to the garage.

Rose and Mr. Hemsworth were tucked down low against the wall of the garage, huddled close in conversation. Mr. Hemsworth was seated bowlegged on Charlotte's old red hop ball, his hand on the handle and his belly resting heavily on his thighs. Rose was sitting next to him in a lawn chair. Both were facing slightly outward, as if the minivan were a third party in their conversation. My first thought, when I saw them that way, was that Mr. Hemsworth's seat would surely pop. My second thought was that one of us—Charlotte or I—was getting a bad report.

"Hey, Nora," Rose called to me.

Mr. Hemsworth jumped up off the hop ball, snatching at his lower back as he did so.

"Getting antsy?" Rose asked.

"No," I said, feeling like a wimp for running to the adults in the middle of a scary movie.

"You okay?" Mr. Hemsworth wanted to know.

"Yeah . . . I just thought you'd left," I said. "Even though—I guess—I didn't hear your car."

Mr. Hemsworth jingled the coins in his pocket for a moment. Rose shivered and rubbed her hands together, then blew on her knuckles.

"Two minutes, okay?" Mr. Hemsworth said.

"Okay."

It took me a moment to figure out that this was my cue to step back into the kitchen and close the door behind me.

Just after I did, I heard Mr. Hemsworth say, "She's an odd one, that kid, huh?"

I strained to hear Rose's quiet response. There was a "just shy" somewhere in there, but I didn't hear the rest.

I stepped away from the door, afraid of the next lines of conversation—afraid that they might be about me and that they might be even worse than what I'd already heard. For five minutes I stood in the dark kitchen, glad to have a room to myself. I leaned against the Hemsworths' dark cabinets, trying to ignore the screams from the living room and the murmurs from the garage.

Seven

May 22, 2006

I parked on the street, since there was another car in the driveway besides Charlotte's. Maybe she and Porter were hanging
out. I took my time opening the front door and threw my stuff
noisily on the kitchen chair so as not to surprise them in the
living room.

"Hey, Nora," Charlotte called.

When I stepped into her living room, I found her curled up
on her couch, still in her work clothes. A bottle of wine sat
open on the coffee table, next to a stack of papers and com-
position books. Across from her, in the old rocking chair, was
her brother, Paul. I was a little surprised to see him. I knew he
lived just outside Hartford—not far from here—but Charlotte
hadn't mentioned he'd be dropping by.

Paul looked exactly the same as I remembered him. The
last I'd seen him was Charlotte's and my high-school graduation. He was about twenty-four at the time. Then, as now, he

looked like he could still be in high school. He was pale, freckled, and round-faced, with a wave of reddish blond hair dipping across his forehead. My mother used to refer to him privately as "Opie."

"Hey, Paul," I said.

"Hi," he replied. "Great to see you."

"You, too."

He shuffled his feet as I sat next to Nora on the couch. His ultrawhite sneakers made me grin. He was in his thirties, married, with two school-age kids and his own physical-therapy practice, but still the big dopey sneakers.

"How was Toby?" he asked.

I looked up, surprised. "Good. It's been a while. But he seems to be doing well."

"He mention how his brother's doing?"

"Joe was there, too, actually."

"Really?" Paul shrugged with mild surprise. I wondered how he felt about Joe. They were close as kids, just like Charlotte and me. But they'd grown apart around high school, for similar reasons—Paul was a scholar-athlete golden boy, Joe a bit of a freak.

I decided against mentioning that Joe was a little drunk. Us freaks had to look out for each other's reps.

"Paul was just getting ready to leave, unfortunately," Charlotte chimed in. "Got to help put the kids to bed."

"That's right," Paul agreed.

"Will I see you again?" I asked as he went toward the kitchen.

"Yeah, maybe we can visit," he said, "before you head back home."

His lack of enthusiasm didn't bother me. Paul and I never

had much to say to each other. When he was seventeen and I was eleven, his entering a room made me want to leave it, and I suspected that the feeling was mutual. I always got a general feeling of discomfort from him, as if he could not for the life of him remember what a person six years younger might want to talk about.

After he'd gone, Charlotte picked up a pile of papers from the coffee table. "Back to these stupid vocabulary sentences. Listen to this: 'She tried to cover the zit with her bangs, but it was still really *palpable.*'"

"Ick," I said, sitting next to Charlotte on the couch. "Good one."

"I believe one of the book's definitions was 'noticeable.'"

"Yeah, I caught that."

"Yep," Charlotte said, reaching for her glass. "I'm doing a bang-up job educatin' those kids. You want some wine?"

"Nah, thanks. I already had two beers tonight."

"Crazy, Nora. Well, I need it for these vocabulary sentences. I had to pour myself a glass when I came across 'The teacher has *malevolent* coffee breath.'"

"For real?"

"Yup." She leaned back against the arm of the couch and took a long drink of wine. "Little fuckers think they can break me with shit like that. It's hilarious."

I watched her put a neat line of red checkmarks down the page in front of her, then a big red check at the top. She flipped to the next page.

"Hey, I know this is boring," she said after reading through another paper. Then she kicked at a box under the coffee table. "Listen, I pulled our old favorites out of the basement. Thought it would be fun."

I yanked the box out. It was torn and musty and full of our old Time-Life Mysteries of the Unknown books. The top book pictured a human hand reaching out from a celestial blue background, with a star of light exploding from its palm. *Powers of Healing* was written across the top of the black book, in a familiar silver lettering.

"That's awesome," I said, grabbing a few books and stacking them on the table. "You kept them."

"Of course I kept them, Nora." Charlotte pulled her feet up onto the couch and hugged her knees. "I keep everything. Now, there's some good shit in those books. Stuff I don't even remember. Like there's the one called *Phantom Encounters*. I looked at it when I first brought the box down. Most of it seems to be about ghosts, but I saw this one chapter called 'Apparitions of the Living,' thinking, what the hell is that? Ghosts of the living? I couldn't have read this when I was a kid, because I would've remembered it. It starts right in with a story about this woman, this *teacher*—"

Her shoulders shook. She was giggling at the very memory of it. Her pantyhosed feet pressed against the side of my leg. I remembered, for a moment, her writhing on her parents' couch when we were kids, when her father would sometimes sit with us, grab her foot, and start tickling it. *Stop, oh, GOD, stop!* she'd squeal while I sat quietly on the other side of her, enduring the bumps of her flailing head and sharp elbows.

"This teacher in Latvia," Charlotte tried again, "in the 1800s. She'd be teaching in front of the classroom sometimes, and the darnedest thing would happen. Her students would look out the window and see her also hanging around in the school garden, sniffing flowers."

"She had a double? A flower-sniffing double?"

"Yes. She couldn't see it, but everyone else could. All the students vouched for it. She got fired for it. It freaked the kids out too much."

Charlotte's tittering grew into loud laughter and ended in a painful-sounding coughing fit.

"You know, I wish I had one, too. I'm teaching in front of the classroom, then they look through the window and I'm also smoking a cigarette in the parking lot. Better yet, *I'll* step out for a smoke and my double could teach the class."

Charlotte returned to her correcting. I picked up a few of the books and started to flip through them.

"A few of these have your old notes in them," I observed.

"I know, isn't that crazy?"

"Purple pen. Very cute. Is this the first time you've taken them out since then?"

"Um . . . no. I think I've looked at them once or twice before this. When I've had a hankering for the paranormal."

Charlotte's red pen whipped through another page, then another. I rummaged through the box, looking at all the old, vaguely familiar titles: *Cosmic Connections*, *Psychic Voyages*, *Mind Over Matter*.

"Goddamn it," Charlotte snapped at her pile of papers, making me jump. "These kids are driving me crazy."

"Who? What? More bad-breath sentences?"

"No. This girl's got a sentence about setting her mom's bed on fire."

"Oh. I take it that's worse?"

"She's always pulling stuff like this. A couple of weeks ago, she had some sentences about cutting her toes off or something like that. She's screwing with me. Either I have to be the lame teacher who reports her to the guidance office on the fractional chance she's psychotic or I have to risk feeling responsible if she does in fact set her mother's bed on fire."

"You could throw it away, give her credit for it, then tell her you spilled something on it. Then at least you've gotten rid of the evidence."

"You're sick," Charlotte mumbled. "Why aren't you an English teacher?"

"So what are you gonna do?"

"I don't know. It's a freaky situation with this girl. Give me a suicide threat in a journal any day. That's at least straightforward. Everybody knows the rules about that."

Charlotte's statement took me by surprise, tongue-tying me just for a moment.

"Well—" I began, trying to think of a quick, casual response. But Charlotte had already noticed.

"I'm sorry. I wasn't thinking. I didn't mean to be glib. I only meant that with that, you kind of know what to do. It's not like with this girl, who's just *intentionally* pushing my buttons."

"Well, the situations are actually probably pretty similar. In either case the kid probably doesn't quite know what she's doing or why she's doing it."

"Sure. I get that." Charlotte threw her pen and the stack of papers on the coffee table, then folded her arms. "But that never helps me figure out what to do."

She frowned and then peered at me, looking a little sheepish. I ignored her for a moment, pushed her glass toward me, and poured a splash of wine into it.

"Are you asking my advice?" I said.

"Yeah. I hope that doesn't offend you, but I guess I am."

I took a sip and tried not to grimace. Seven-dollar headache wine.

"I think you should trust your instincts," I said. "If you know for sure this kid's just a rat-lipped little brat, then don't do anything. But when in doubt, I'd say it's better to show the kid you care than let her see how cool you are."

Charlotte tapped a cigarette out of her pack. "Can I ask you a personal question?"

"Shoot," I said, emptying the glass.

"You didn't think anyone cared?"

"You know, this is going to sound like I'm ducking the question, but I can't really remember what I thought. I guess I just wasn't thinking at all. For a really long time—and I mean since before we even graduated—I felt like that wasn't *me*. That was some whacked-out version of me, indulging in a vacation from reality for a month or two."

"Uh-uh. I think I know what you mean. Some of my sophomores—well, never mind. Let's just say I know that vacation pretty well."

Charlotte hesitated. "I've kind of wanted to ask you. Why the girls' room, of all places? And *that* girls' room . . ."

"Pretty simple. It had the most traffic during lunch. I did it just before lunch."

"You wanted to make sure someone would find you."

"If it came to that. But, really, I didn't take enough to . . . to really even . . ."

"I'd heard you'd taken a whole bottle of aspirin."

"No," I answered. "I took a few handfuls. But I was too scared to finish. I'm pretty certain I never planned to take the whole thing."

I paused for a moment. "Who told you that I'd taken the whole bottle?"

"I don't remember. I'm sorry, but . . ." Charlotte's white cheeks turned just a little pink—embarrassed for me still. "*Every*body heard about it. How could they not?"

"Ashley and Karen told everyone I was out with mono."

Charlotte snorted. "Umm. Yeah. And what a great couple of actresses those two were. They said it with such fake righteousness that you knew they were quietly telling everyone the biggest secret a couple of drips like them could ever imagine having. Just a couple of hens sitting on an enormous egg.

"And besides, how could they keep it a secret when it was Robin Greenbaum who actually came in and found you doubled over. Before she ran and fetched Philippa."

"Philippa?"

"I mean, Mrs. Norris. She says hi, by the way."

"Awesome."

"Robin told a couple of her friends before those two got around to damage control. I don't think she meant to be gossipy about it. I think she was just surprised."

"Well, that's fine," I said. "I wanted everyone to know about it anyway."

Charlotte looked surprised. "I know you did."

"I guess I can say that now," I said.

Charlotte puffed on her cigarette so intensely it made me want to have a coughing fit.

"One reason I ask why that bathroom," Charlotte explained,

"is that I think of it almost every time I go in there. When I have to go in there and chase the smoker girls out."

"Well, I apologize."

"Thank you."

"Do you think about it much?" she asked.

"Not really. Not anymore."

She blew an aggressive puff of smoke out her mouth, not taking care to keep it away from my face.

"The main thing about it that still bothers me," I said, turning from the smoke, "when I *do* think about it—I mean, aside from my mother, how it upset my mother—is that in all of high school that was the loudest, most obnoxious thing I ever did."

"If you could have been louder," she asked, "what would you have said?"

"Irrelevant now. I chose for that to be my biggest statement. It's no one's fault but my own."

"I'm not denying that." Charlotte yawned. "Excuse me. But I'm still asking. What would you have said?"

"Back then it felt like a million different things. Now I can't remember a single one of importance."

"Did any of them have to do with Rose?" Charlotte asked.

"Of course not," I answered, surprised. "Why do you ask?"

"Sometimes I wondered if you'd had some dark vision and that was part of what made you . . . you know . . . depressed."

"No, there was nothing like that. You'd read too many of these books. A *'dark vision'*? No, just dull misery mixed with stupidity."

"You shouldn't be so hard on yourself. Almost all the girls I teach have some crazy impulse or other. Even if it takes a very different form. Sluttiness. Shoplifting. Cheerleading. That age

for girls, it's like . . ." Charlotte twisted her cigarette in her ashtray and glanced down at one of the books on the coffee table.
"It's like the Bermuda Triangle. Smooth sailing, then something
goes haywire. Nobody understands exactly what happens. And
it's totally random, who makes it out the same, who gets lost,
who comes back okay."

"How about the boys?"

"Oh, God. The *boys.* Sure. They turn into lunatics, too. It's
different for them, though. More outwardly destructive than
inwardly destructive, but . . . basically the same thing."

"Oh, I don't know . . ." I said. "The boys' stuff seems different somehow . . . funnier. I mean, Neil tells me these stories
about smoking a joint with his friends before chemistry lab and
being fascinated with the Bunsen burner and practically setting
himself on fire. Or crashing into the annuals driving too fast
through the Home Depot parking lot. But that stuff basically
just sounds fun. Not pathetic. How come I don't have stories
like that? Remembering that time for him is crazy, but not sad."

"Well," Charlotte said, glancing down at her papers, "what
does he think of your girls'-room story?"

I hesitated, picking up *Alien Encounters* out of the musty box.
I wondered if my face changed color as easily as Charlotte's did.

"Well . . ." I said, trying to recover, "he, uh . . ."

Charlotte twirled her red pen, waiting for me to continue. I
just shook my head, letting my sentence go unfinished.

"I see," she said slowly. "Jesus, Nora. I'm sure he'd understand. I'm sure someone who got stoned for a chem lab would
understand a little lapse of—"

"It's not about that," I said. "It's not about what he'd understand. Of course he'd understand. I wouldn't *marry* someone who wouldn't understand. It's just never seemed relevant. It was so random it's not relevant to anything."

"Okay," Charlotte said, shrugging. "I guess I know what you mean."

I wondered if she needed further convincing, but a moment later it didn't appear to matter. She'd started in on a new batch of sentences and seemed content to drop the subject.

I opened *Alien Encounters* and perused the first few pages.

"Have You Been Abducted?" asked a gray breakout box. *"The Signs to Look For."*

I smiled at this, remembering how Rose would often make us answer all the questions whenever there was a quiz section like this one. I silently took the quiz as Charlotte tore through a few more of her papers.

"Missing time?" Nope.

"Confused memory?" Sometimes.

"Irrational terror?" Well, that depends on what you consider irrational.

"Nighttime disorders?" Only very occasional insomnia.

"Finding blood on your pillow?" No.

I flipped through the next few pages, looking at pictures drawn by abductees. A line of blue-suited spacemen standing in a pretty yellow kitchen. A stick-drawing woman strapped to a table, humanoid figures removing her eggs. A big glass portal in outer space, guarded by a creature resembling the Pillsbury Doughboy.

"Sorry about my brother," Charlotte said suddenly. "He wasn't in the friendliest of moods."

"Does he come over often?"

"No," Charlotte said. "He helps with the yard work when he can, but he's usually pretty busy with his kids."

"Oh."

"But he's been having a hard time lately. Keeps coming over to talk."

I didn't ask what the "hard time" was about, since it wasn't any of my business. Charlotte looked up from her correcting and cocked her head. It seemed almost as if she were waiting for me to ask, but I wasn't sure. I studied a photo of a crop circle and waited, too.

"Paul thinks it's possible that Aaron could have done something to Rose," Charlotte said, setting her papers aside.

"Are you serious?" I said, closing the black book. "When did he first start saying this?"

"Tonight's the first time he said it outright. He says he put it out of his mind at the time but that Aaron really *was* very angry at Rose. Says it was getting pretty bad. I guess he suspected she was seeing someone else, and he wasn't taking it well."

"Then why didn't Paul say something about it at the time?"

"Well, *lots* of kids told the police that things had been tense between them. But I guess that little tidbit didn't lead anywhere. And remember, Paul and Aaron were *together* the evening Rose disappeared. The whole soccer team, they were together."

"Yes. You mentioned that." I remembered Joe telling me he'd been working that night. It seemed all of Rose's old male classmates were eager to remind everyone of their alibis. "So how—"

"And, you know, in the end everyone thought it must've been some random psycho kidnapping. That's what it seems like. Aside from her running away, that always seemed the most likely possibility. Paul says he focused on those two possibilities and tried not to think about Aaron."

"But that's changed now that they've found her?"

"The theory that she'd run away is now proven wrong, obviously. I guess after a few years passed and there was never any sign of her, that possibility was eliminated. Not that anyone ever talked about it. And a random psycho . . . well, would a random psycho come back with her body and bury her in Waverly a couple of decades later?"

"How sure is anyone that the body was moved? Why can't a random psycho be local?"

"Why can't the random psycho be *Aaron*? Aaron's parents retired and moved out of Waverly just a couple of years ago. Think about it."

"So you think when they made him come and take all his old Star Wars figurines and baseball pennants, he figured he'd go ahead and move his old girlfriend's body, too?"

"That's not funny."

"I'm just trying to understand your reasoning. You don't think the police have thought this all over again?"

Charlotte shrugged. "I didn't say anything about the police. I was just telling you what Paul thinks. He and Aaron weren't great friends, but they knew each other fairly well from playing sports together. He says Aaron had a temper and maybe not much of conscience."

"Are you sure Paul's not just getting paranoid, now that she's been found? I mean, these are scary times for everyone, with her body turning up like that," I reasoned. "Maybe it's just kind of a knee-jerk fear. And it's natural to start doubting what you remember when—"

"There's something Paul's not telling me," she interrupted.

"What makes you say that?"

"I can just tell. I always thought there was something between him and Rose. When I was a kid, I liked to think they secretly liked each other. Remember?"

"Why don't you just ask him?"

Charlotte shook her head and had a weary, halfhearted sip of wine.

"Don't take this the wrong way, Nora. But you don't have siblings. That's not how we communicate. By *just asking.*"

"Well, do you *want* to know?" I asked her, ignoring the correction. "Do you want to know what he's not telling you?"

"I don't know," she admitted.

Magical Arts:
October 1990

It was my idea to make the runes, but Charlotte took over the operation. While I'd thought we could find flat stones outside and scratch the symbols into them, she wanted to do something quicker. She found a big piece of corrugated cardboard and set to work cutting jagged little ovals out of it with a tiny pair of craft scissors.

Charlotte's scissors gnawed away at the cardboard for at least an hour. She stopped every so often to count her runes and to shake her sore hand, but never to ask us for help. Rose and I lounged on the couch, flipping through *Magical Arts*. I had to look away for a moment as she paused at the page with a picture of a sheep's heart stuck full of nails.

"Yeah, there's a lot of gross things in this book," Charlotte said when she saw what we were looking at. "In a different chapter, there's this thing called a love pie. It's when a lady gets all sweaty and then dries herself with flour and then saves the flour and mixes in a few of her fingernail and toe clippings all ground up and then makes a pie out of all that stuff and gives it to a man she likes, and then he eats it and he's supposed to fall in love with her."

"Ew!" I cried. "Can't he taste the toenails?"

Rose's reaction wasn't as spirited as Charlotte was probably hoping for.

"I could've gone my whole life without knowing that," she said, not looking up from the book. "Thanks."

"There's love potions, too," Charlotte offered. "Near the end of the book. If you're looking for something less gross."

"I'll have to look at those later."

"Yeah, you might need them," Charlotte said. "Since you broke up with Aaron, I guess you'll be looking for a new guy."

"You think so, do you?" Rose murmured.

"Why'd you break up with him anyhow?" Charlotte wanted to know.

"Because . . ." Rose hesitated, turning a page of the black book. "Well, I already told you. He's a jerk."

"No he's *not*. I met him at Paul's pizza party. For his birthday. He seemed nice to *me*."

"When was that, Charlotte?"

"Like three years ago."

"Uh-huh. Well, that was three years ago."

Charlotte reluctantly started cutting her cardboard again. "So . . . *are* you gonna get a new boyfriend?" she asked.

"I don't know. Maybe."

"You will," Charlotte assured her. "I bet you."

"I don't really care right now, actually."

"Are you sad you broke up?"

Rose and I both looked up from the book. I thought Charlotte should quit bugging Rose, but I was interested in her answer. Because Rose *did* seem a little sad.

"No," she replied.

"Did you used to kiss Aaron?"

Rose ignored the question. "Hey," she said, pushing the book over so it sat half in her lap, half in mine. "Look, it's that same circle stone you liked from the other book."

The picture was of a huge, perfectly round stone with a hole in it, sitting in the grass. It was put there by the Druids.

"Oh, yeah," I said. "I keep wondering how they made the hole in it."

"It's big enough to walk through," Rose observed. "It says people walked through it to be healed. Kids would walk through it nine times."

"Did you used to—" Charlotte began again.

"I heard you the first time." Rose interrupted. "Charlotte, aren't you finished with those things yet?"

"With the cutting, pretty much," Charlotte answered.

Rose suggested we use pencil for the actual symbols, pressing hard to imitate the relief look of the runes pictured in Charlotte's book. Rose finally flipped back to that page, and we all started drawing, each taking a row of seven runes. When they were almost finished, Charlotte disappeared into her bedroom for a few minutes.

"Look at this!" she said when she returned. She held out a small red velveteen pouch with a silver pull ribbon. "I wasn't sure I'd be able to find it, but it's perfect."

"Where'd you get that?" I asked, only a little bit jealous.

"It came with lip glosses in it. I got it in my stocking last year."

"I'm not sure if the Druids had velvet," I pointed out.

"I think it's a nice bag," Rose offered. "And you want to keep your runes safely in one place."

The book had suggested that you could toss all your runes at once for a detailed reading or pick out just one for a quick insight. We decided to do just one for now, since the book didn't really detail how to go about giving a full reading.

I pulled first and got a relatively simple-looking rune. A single vertical line with a short tail hooking off it in a slant. I laid it on the coffee table so Charlotte and Rose could see it.

"The Laguz," Rose said, and read its description to herself. "Let's see. Hmm. *Very* interesting pull for Nora."

"Just read it," Charlotte said.

"All right," Rose said. "It says, 'A rune of initiation, Laguz, the lake, signifies water. It was originally associated with the pagan baptism of newborns. The rune also suggests emotion, intuition, and dreams, and the inquirer who draws it should pay special attention to the messages of the unconscious mind.'"

"Wow!" Charlotte said. "That *is* interesting for Nora. The messages of Nora's unconscious mind . . ."

"I want to try again," I said.

"You can't go again," Rose said. "It's like a fortune cookie. You listen to what it says and take it or leave it, but you don't get another one."

I opened the bag to Charlotte, who fluttered the runes around annoyingly before finally pulling one out. Hers looked like a pair of chopsticks.

"The Naudhiz," Rose announced. " 'This symbol represents human struggle in the face of adversity. Naudhiz, meaning need, indicates an overwhelming compulsion to achieve something. The inquirer who draws the rune is invited to examine his or her motivations and to separate true needs from desires. Trust fate, Naudhiz counsels, for it will ultimately guide you to what you need.' "

Charlotte looked thoughtful. Her eyes met mine. "I think we should try again," she said firmly.

"So do I," I said, grabbing the bag and shoving my rune back in.

Charlotte tried to do the same, but Rose stood up, leaned over her, and snatched the little red bag out of my hand.

"Oh, no you don't. You don't just keep putting them back till you get one you like. Then it doesn't mean anything. Charlotte, that one's perfect for you. And, Nora—I remember what yours looked like. I'm going to find it for you."

She dumped out the runes on the sofa cushion and plucked my Laguz from them.

"What about *you*?" Charlotte asked.

"I'm going to pick mine right now."

I slid the black book away from Rose so I could do her reading. She jammed her fist into the red bag and pulled out what I identified as the Tiwaz.

" 'Tiwaz,' " I read. " 'Rune of the Norse god Tyr, Tiwaz stands for his qualities of bravery, truth, and justice. According to myth, Tyr once sacrificed his own hand to the jaws of a wolf in order to save another god from destruction. Drawing this rune signifies that sacrifice and courage may now be required in the name of justice.' "

Again we considered the words for a moment.

"I'm glad I didn't get that one at least," Charlotte said.

"You don't know what you're talking about," Rose replied, taking the book from me to reread the explanation. "This one is awesome," she murmured unconvincingly.

"The jaws of a wolf?" Charlotte repeated. "You don't want that. Come on. Let's *all* pick again."

"No," Rose said, pulling away abruptly as Charlotte tried to reach for her rune. "We keep them. In fact, we should wear them. I think we should make them into jewelry."

"What do you mean? You can't *wear* this rune."

"Why not? I'm gonna make a bracelet. We all should."

Charlotte looked uncertain. "You can't."

"Why not?"

"We need to have a full set."

"So make a new one. You've got plenty of cardboard left. You got any yarn or anything?"

"Those are the originals," Charlotte insisted. "You should make your own to wear."

"Come on, now. Don't be like that. *I'll* make the replacements, okay? But we should wear the ones we actually pulled, right? The ones we pulled are the ones that mean something."

Charlotte sucked air through her teeth. I wasn't sure if Rose was right, but at least she was taking this seriously.

"Can you find something to string them with?" Rose continued. "We'll put a little hole in the top and—"

Charlotte stomped back to her bedroom.

"Does your rune scare you, Nora?" Rose asked me when Charlotte was gone.

"Huh? No. Why?"

Rose turned her piece of cardboard over in her fingers. "No reason. I thought for a second there you looked a little scared."

"Nah, I'm okay," I said, hoping Rose would think me cool for it.

"Good for you," she said, staring at her rune.

To my surprise, Charlotte came back with some pink gimp from her jewelry-making set.

"You haven't made the replacements yet," she observed, practically throwing the gimp at Rose.

"I will," Rose assured her, sounding a little tired.

And then we set to making our simple jewelry, reluctantly tying to our wrists these awkward fates that Rose had imposed upon us.

Eight

May 23, 2006

I awoke on Tuesday to my cell phone ringing. It was Neil.

"What's up?" I asked.

"I just wanted to say hi, since I didn't call yesterday. You having fun?"

"I'm not sure, actually."

"Then come home. I miss you. And Stanley misses you, I think. He was barking for no apparent reason last night, and this morning he was sniffing around your chair. Probably he was wondering where you went."

"I think he's just still smelling that bacon grease I spilled last week. Probably there are still a couple of tiny drops on the floor."

"Oh. I forgot about that. Never mind, then. Don't come home."

"I miss you," I said.

"I miss you, too. What've you been up to up there?"

"Not much. Visiting old landmarks, grocery stores. I saw this guy Toby last night, someone else from the neighborhood. I went to prom with him."

"Oh, really? Is he handsome?"

"I can't tell. I've known him too long."

"Right. One of those. Well, when are you coming home, did you say?"

"Soon, I think. Charlotte's been a little swamped. We should maybe try to have one more nice dinner together and leave it at that. I guess I should have come with more of an exit strategy, or just come for the weekend."

"Have you seen your mom yet?" Neil wanted to know.

"Oh . . . no, not yet. You know, Bristol's like a half hour from Waverly."

"Half hour south, though, right?"

"Um. Sort of. Basically."

"Well, then you'll at least see her on your way out. I'd think she'd want you to stay for a night, huh?"

"Probably."

"So tell her I said hi when you see her. I should probably let you go. This traffic's getting a little hairy."

"Okay. I'll call tonight," I promised.

Not half a minute after I'd hung up, the phone rang again—this time showing a Connecticut number.

"Hi, my name is Tracy Vaughan," a woman said after I'd picked up. "I'm investigating a case in Waverly, Connecticut. . . ."

I recognized her name from the newspaper articles—Detective Tracy Vaughan of the Connecticut State Police—but let her explain. About Rose, about the newly opened case. About how they were questioning many of Rose's old neighbors and friends. About how my name came up in the file as the child who'd been walking with Rose on the afternoon she disappeared, so they just wanted to touch base with me. And she'd gotten my cell number from my home voice-mail message.

When she was finished, I said, "I happen to be in Waverly, actually."

"Oh." There was a long pause. "I thought you lived in Virginia."

"I do. I'm . . . um, coincidentally visiting someone here in Waverly."

"Well, then. How about that? In that case would you mind coming in to chat with us? We just had a couple of questions for you."

"How's this afternoon?" I asked.

"That's perfect. I'll be at the Waverly station all day."

Perfect, I told myself. Might as well get that out of the way sooner rather than later—the depressing exercise of explaining again—officially, once and for all—how unremarkable that day, and that walk home, had been.

I stretched and then wandered into the living room.

Several Time-Life books were scattered across the couch cushions, the coffee table, and the floor. I searched through the books and made a small stack of the ones that had papers stuck in them. I wanted to check out Charlotte's old notes from when we were kids. For entertainment value, it probably beat *Good Morning America*.

After the coffee was brewed, I settled on the Hemsworths' front steps with a mug and a few of the books. In the first one, *Mind Over Matter*, there were several slips of small, notepad-size paper stapled to a piece of purple construction paper.

"After several minutes of dillydally," read the first note, *"the subject now finally appears to be under. She is describing the missing person's outfit on the day of the disappearance. Purple sweatshirt. Jeans."*

Leave it to Charlotte to secretly refer to me as "the subject." I closed that book and moved on to *Psychic Voyages*. It said, *"Not sure if the subject has the capacity for astral projection. Must have a sleepover to experiment with this possibility."*

I snorted, then folded up the faded pink paper and set it on the step next to me. I was definitely going to call Charlotte on that one. I flipped through the rest of the book. No further notes. Apparently the young Charlotte had no interest in near-death experiences or reincarnation. Probably for the best.

I sipped my coffee and picked up *Dreams and Dreaming*, which was so stuffed with papers that the binding of the book had come loose. When I opened the front cover, one of several paper-clipped piles of notebook paper fell into my lap.

I recognized my own eleven-year-old handwriting on the top pile—awkward cursive slanted to the left. *"Nora* Nora *NORA"* was scribbled across the top—in cursive, then bubble letters, then an odd lettering than I think was supposed to resemble leaves, with a freaky-looking owl peeking out of the *O.*

Under that:

> *Last night I dreamed that a huge McDonald's hamburger floated down into my room. I tried to bite it, but when I did, it made the sun come up, and I woke up before I could taste it.*

A few blank lines skipped. Then in pencil:

> *I dreamed a witch was chasing all of us with a bull-*
> *dozer. We all ran and hid under Charlotte's trampoline.*
> *She got off the bulldozer and chased us but didn't see*
> *us under there. She started jumping on the trampoline.*
> *The trampoline kept poking down at us whenever she*
> *landed. We could all hear her cackling up there while*
> *she was bouncing up and down. We were scared, but*
> *she never caught us.*

I remembered that dream. I'd had it a few times, actually. But I'd had it when I was about seven or eight. I'd probably written it here to avoid having to supply a more recent dream. My dreams went on for a number of pages after that. An inordinate number of them were about junk food. We'd recorded our dreams for a couple of weeks but hadn't discussed it much, as Charlotte had lost interest.

I put my dreams aside and picked up the next stack. It didn't have a name on it, but I could tell from the maturity of the handwriting that it was probably Rose's. It was round and girlish, with delicately curved tails coming off the lowercase *a*'s and *d*'s. Sure enough, the first paragraph began:

> *I was in gym class, and Mrs. Powers was making us do*
> *endless headstands on those gross old gym mats. When*
> *she wasn't looking, when she was spotting someone else,*
> *I got off my head and scooched to the end of the mat. I*
> *pulled the end of it up like it was one of those curly plas-*
> *tic sleds, and it took off, zipping me around the gymna-*
> *sium and then, after a little while, into the air. Suddenly*
> *my gym mat was a magic carpet, and I was flying up*

and out of the gym, away from the school. Soon I was flying so high I couldn't see the ground. I'm not sure where I was, but I knew I was probably pretty far from Waverly.

A few lines down, another paragraph:

I was running through a field of flowers, and a car was chasing me. I got away just in time. I ran into the woods that came after the field. They were guarded by a round stone, sort of like Nora's favorite megalith. The car couldn't get through it. I stood right at the entrance of the woods for a while, watching the car try to get through. It never would. Then I started crying, because even though I'd gotten away from the car, now I was in the forest and I couldn't ever get out.

My mug crashed on the second step of the Hemsworths' stoop, shattering and sending coffee splattering onto my feet and down the cement steps. I yelped and hopped up, knocking two of the black books down the steps. I swung the screen door open and stepped back into the kitchen for a rag. Then I picked up the shards of the mug and mopped up the coffee from the yellowed pages and the cement steps, feeling foolish. What had spooked me so badly? If Charlotte was going to write a poem about one of Rose's dreams, it wasn't such a big jump that she'd write about another.

I settled back on the steps with the stack of papers. Below the car dream, dated a few days later, was this:

I was hanging on clothesline somewhere up high. It was so high I couldn't see the ground. It was sort of fun at first. Until I realized I was hanging from only my mother's underwear and a dinky clothespin. I tried to get to the end of it. Hand over hand, rushing from this piece of clothing to that, but there was no end in sight. This clothesline went on forever. I stopped and laughed at how ridiculous it all was. I couldn't believe this was happening, and I started to suspect that I was dreaming. That's when the shirt I was hanging on snapped off the line, and I fell. I woke up just before I hit the ground.

Okay, so this was the inspiration for that poem Charlotte had read to me the first night. Why had she chosen to tease me with that one? I wondered. Was that dream of Rose's supposed to be memorable to me for some reason? I flipped to the next page and found a couple of familiar-looking typed pages attached to it:

You
*The gym mats are a painfully cheerful blue
but hold the sweat from a decade of asses and forearms.
Probably swirled with an invisible ringworm. . . .*

It was one of the poems from the *Looking Glass*, apparently photocopied. It was the 1996 *Looking Glass*, same as I'd seen yesterday—same type, same layout, and with the name of another girl in our class on the poem below Charlotte's.

And after that, another:

You
You are running through a sunlit field.
A red Datsun is chasing you,
revving its engine, plowing through
grass and wildflowers. . . .

And then, clipped behind that:

You
A giant clothesline in the sky—
so far up you can barely see the ground.
You're hanging on to a thin T-shirt.
It's about to tear . . .

In each case the 1996 *Looking Glass* content was essentially the same as one of Rose's recorded dreams, pimped out with line breaks and slightly more flowery language.

Charlotte had gone in and attached her *Looking Glass* passages to Rose's corresponding dreams. Recently? Or just after she'd written them, when we were in high school? A little creepy, perhaps, but not out of sync with Charlotte's obsessive attitude toward Rose when we were kids. Maybe that attitude had extended into high school. I certainly couldn't begrudge anyone a little unhealthy teenage behavior.

I riffled through the remaining papers. The next page was another notebook page, with Rose's handwriting—this time scrawled relatively sloppily:

Last night I dreamed I was in a room where the wallpa-
per came to life for a moment. But then it went back to

*being paper. And then everything was dull again. And
I was alone again.*

Then, after that, pulled from the *Looking Glass:*

You
*In his bedroom,
beneath the blueberry wallpaper,
you kiss till the sun goes down . . .*

The final page, behind that, was also from the *Looking Glass:*

*You are knocking on his door this time—
a perfect cabin on a lush green hill
with fruit trees and sunshine
and pinafored children hugging smiling lions . . .*

On top of that page, Charlotte had drawn a thin, light question mark in pencil. So nearly all of Charlotte's writings were based on Rose's dreams. But this last one—with the question mark on it—apparently wasn't. Either that or Charlotte had simply lost the corresponding dream.

That was the last page in the stack of Rose's dreams. The last set of papers was Charlotte's. Her neat, round, eleven-year-old handwriting confessed:

*In my dream last night, I knew how to play the violin.
But no one except Nora could hear it. Whenever I tried
to play, Mom and Dad and Rose just kept saying,
"There's nothing coming out." But Nora could hear it.*

After a while she couldn't hear it anymore either. But then Brownie could hear it, and Mr. Cook's dog could, too. All these dogs came running, barking at our door. And Dad finally said, quit playing that stupid thing! We'll never get these dogs out of here!

And then:

I had five backpacks that were five different colors: turquoise, purple, pink, blue, and I think the other one was yellow. One for each day of the school week. I had matching notebooks and pens each color, one for each day of the week. And in the dream it was Tuesday, purple day. But when I got to school, someone had switched everything. The pink notebook was in there. And the blue pen. I walked out of the class and started walking all the way home. When I got home, Paul was there, and I knew he did it. I said, Why did you switch everything? And Paul was like, Yeah, I switched your notebooks. So what? Was it really worth cutting school for? Now you're in big trouble. In the dream I got very upset about that and didn't even think about why Paul was home from school, too, which was pretty weird.

I set the dreams aside. Part of me missed the young Charlotte of those dreams. That Charlotte was sometimes annoying but always direct.

I sighed and stretched my legs down to the lowest step on the stoop. My foot hit *Psychic Voyages*, which had tumbled down the front steps when I'd spilled my coffee. The book was open to a series of photographs of a thin, naked man lying on a bed. His shadow appeared to be getting up and walking away from his body. I smiled as I picked it up, remembering how Charlotte and I had giggled over the sideways view the photos offered of his genitals. I turned the page.

The drawing on the next page was all done in silver. It was a forest path made up of tall, leafy trees that arched inward, forming a sort of sylvan tunnel. Two rows of trees with a narrow path between them, blanketed with delicate oval leaves. The branches closed in on one another at the top; the roots swirled downward and nearly met one another in the middle. The trees went on and on, getting smaller and smaller as the path twisted slightly, disappearing into infinity.

I remembered now how beautiful I'd thought this drawing was. It was one of my many second-favorites after the line of statues on Easter Island. It had apparently been created to illustrate what an out-of-body experience felt like. I had to admit it was pretty, but I couldn't remember what exactly I'd found so captivating about it as a kid.

I closed the book, feeling unsettled. This thing with Charlotte and the dreams and the *Looking Glass*—I couldn't avoid it again tonight. She'd apparently been trying to get my attention that first night, and I was going to have to give in and ask her about it.

Detective Tracy Vaughan was older than she'd sounded on the phone. As I followed her gray, helmetlike bob down the corridor, I mused that this was the first time I'd ever actually been in the Waverly police station. I glanced into each of the offices we passed, hoping to catch sight of the chief slurping on a cappuccino so I could report it back to Charlotte.

Detective Vaughan led me into a surprisingly cheerful room—painted sky blue, with a long table, lots of windows, and a soda machine. A uniformed male officer was sitting there waiting for us. As I sat in the chair Detective Vaughan pulled out for me, I studied the other officer. There was something familiar about the longish quality to his face, the crooked nose, the deep-set eyes.

"Since this is a joint investigation, Officer Borello will be joining us while we talk."

"All right," I said.

That name was familiar. *Officer Borello.* He certainly wasn't the officer who'd chatted with my mom and me all those years ago. That officer had been round in body and face, with a thick gray mustache. And if I recalled correctly, he had been older than this guy was now.

"Thanks for coming in for us, Ms. Reed," he said, putting out his hand.

As I shook his hand, I remembered. Officer Borello. Of course. How could I have forgotten? He'd been the Waverly youth officer. He would come to school once a year and tell us about Saying No. He'd tell us about PCP/angel dust and quaaludes, about people who jump out of windows when they're tripping. I remember thinking that "angel dust" sounded so pretty.

"I'm sorry," I said. "Didn't you used to be the youth officer? Did you visit the schools a lot?"

A craggy little smile came across his face. "Yes. But I haven't been the youth officer for six—no, seven years."

"I remember how you'd come in to teach us about stranger danger. And then, right in the middle of this speech you were giving about strangers, this pretty lady would come in and tell us she'd just lost her puppy and could we come help her look for it?"

Officer Borello chewed the side of his lip for a moment before responding, as if considering whether he should engage in this conversation. I felt like a fool. Being in the presence of two police officers had made me nervous. My attempt to cover it up with casual friendliness was apparently falling flat.

"That was my wife," he said.

"I liked her," I mumbled. "She was surprisingly convincing, under the circumstances."

Detective Vaughan cleared her throat.

"So . . ." she said, touching her lips with her fingertips. "Let's get to the matter of Ms. Banks, if you don't mind? We don't want to take too much of your time."

"All right," I said, unsure if the burning sensation in my cheeks was producing a visible red.

"So we have the statement from you and your mother from 1990," Officer Vaughan continued. "We just wanted to touch base and go over it with you. Why don't you go ahead and tell us what you remember about the day Ms. Banks disappeared."

"Sure," I said. "I never saw anything unusual. She walked me home from my friend Charlotte's—"

"From the Hemsworth residence?" Detective Vaughan asked.

"Yeah."

"Sorry. Go on."

"Well, it was still light out, but just barely. I remember that. Rose walked me home, since it was on her way home, too. She did it all the time. We chatted most of the way. We didn't see anyone else walking. She dropped me there in front of my house and kept walking up the street."

"Any cars that you noticed?"

"It's hard for me to remember. I think there were probably a couple. There usually were, since it was the end of the workday. But I don't remember any specific cars from that day, unfortunately."

"Did you go straight inside after she dropped you?" Detective Vaughan wanted to know.

"No." I glanced at Officer Borello, who looked bored. "I played outside for a little while, which I often did in those days."

"And did you see or hear anything unusual after Rose walked up the hill?"

"No."

"And it was your understanding she was going straight home?"

"I think so. Yeah."

After a few similar questions, Detective Vaughan turned to Officer Borello and asked if he had any other questions. He shook his head.

"I'm going to take this from a different angle, then, Ms. Reed," Detective Vaughan said. "What did you think when you heard she'd been found?"

"Well . . . I was shocked."

"I mean, did it make you reconsider anything you'd seen? Any of her relationships you knew of?"

"I didn't know a great deal about her relationships. Since I was only eleven."

Officer Borello nodded sleepily. Detective Vaughan put her hand out, gesturing for me to continue. "Did you ever meet her boyfriend?"

"Only once. They did have a little fight, but it didn't seem like anything serious."

"Uh-huh. And her family?"

"They were nice. Her dad was a real sweet man. Her mom maybe a little stricter, but . . ." I had the distinct feeling I was just going through the motions here. "But . . . um, nothing more than mother–teenage daughter stuff, from the little I saw."

Officer Vaughan nodded vaguely. "And how was her relationship with the Hemsworths?"

I hesitated, unsure which Hemsworth I should speak about first.

"Well, she and Paul had some of the same friends. She was a little more popular than he was, but they seemed to respect each other. They knew each other since they were little. They were nice to each other, I think."

Detective Vaughan seemed to be waiting for me to say something more.

"Charlotte was a little bratty. But Rose was pretty casual about that. And she was paid to deal with her, so, you know, that wasn't a real problem. . . ."

I trailed off, feeling I'd betrayed Charlotte by speaking ill of her in the police station, where she'd already been unfairly maligned during her *Valley Voice* days.

Both officers looked at me as if they expected something more. I shrugged.

"Just typical baby-sitting kind of stuff," I said, if only to fill the silence.

"Well, we really do appreciate you coming in and talking to us," Detective Vaughan said, glancing at Officer Borello. "I hope this isn't too difficult for you."

"It's not difficult. I'm just sorry I don't have more to tell you."

"Well, it's good to touch base with you. Will you be at that same cell number if we need to reach you again?"

"Yeah."

"And how long will you be in town?" Officer Borello asked. "You're visiting family, you said?"

"No. A friend."

"Oh. Where are you staying? Not the Maplewoo, I hope."

The Maplewood Motel was Waverly's only motel, on Route 5 on the way out of town. Everyone made fun of its icky mint green siding and its outdoor sign with the oft-missing acrylic letters. People were always stealing the *d*. Though they mocked it, I think the Waverly High kids were the ones who kept it open. It was a popular spot for losing one's virginity.

"No," I said. "I'm staying with my friend on Fox Hill. Charlotte Hemsworth, actually."

Detective Vaughan looked startled and glanced at Officer Borello. "Oh," she chirped.

"An *old* friend, then," Officer Borello said with a knowing nod.

"Yes," I replied.

"You girls are still friends?" Detective Vaughan said. "You're staying with the Hemsworths?"

"Yeah. Well, just Charlotte. Her mom is away. And Mr. Hemsworth—he doesn't live—"

"Yes, I know," Officer Vaughan said. "They're divorced."

"Have a good one," Officer Borello said as Detective Vaughan led me out of the room.

She thanked me in the front lobby and let me go.

Mysterious Lands and Peoples:
November 1990

There had been no mention of the black books for a week. A Nintendo system had recently come into the Hemsworth home on account of Charlotte's birthday. Charlotte was now spending hours each afternoon entering and exiting the endless, layered worlds of Super Mario Brothers—leaving the realms of prophecy and untapped psychic energies suddenly abandoned. Rose and I took an occasional, casual turn at the game, missing all the secret troves of coins and dying early. I couldn't get into it knowing how strongly my mother objected to my playing video games. I don't know what Rose's problem was.

On this particular night, Paul had a soccer game and Mr. Hemsworth got home a little late. It was nearly dark by the time Rose and I left the Hemsworths'. As we stepped out of Charlotte's driveway and onto the sidewalk, Rose brought up the Nintendo.

"I don't like it very much," she said. "That song it plays is really annoying. That's why I've been bringing my Walkman. So I can listen to something else while I'm not playing. So it won't drive me crazy."

"I don't mind the song," I admitted. "But I'm really not supposed to play video games."

"I wonder if this is the end of the Mysteries of the Unknown. I was wondering when Charlotte was gonna lay off that. Maybe she's finally outgrown it."

"Maybe," I said, proud to be talking to Rose like this—as if we were both older than Charlotte. As if we both knew better.

"I never thought I'd say this, but I'm going to miss it. I mean, if Super Mario Brothers is the only other choice."

"I'm not going to miss those books," I declared. "The only thing I liked about them was the Druids. Well, the Druids and Easter Island."

"My favorite was the aliens," Rose confessed. "Why the Druids for you?"

"Well, lots of reasons," I said, although none were actually coming to mind. "Umm. Maybe one thing is that they were *real*. Like, Charlotte spends all this time talking about psychic powers, and they might not even be real."

"Well, sure. The Druids were real. The magic that people think they had, though . . . *that* might not have been real. And we'll probably never find out if it was."

"They had to have some kind of special power to move those stones," I pointed out.

"I'm not going to say there was no magic involved. But all they needed to move them was a hell of a lot of people."

I shrugged. "And I liked the doughnut stone. I want to go there someday. And walk through it. And see what happens. See if I felt different."

"The doughnut stone?" Rose stopped walking for a moment. The wind blew her dirty-blond hair across her face, and she didn't bother to push it away. "Oh, yeah. I remember what you mean. I was just thinking about that the other day, actually. That was interesting. The big rock with a hole in it? That heals the kids?"

I nodded.

"So you really believe it could heal people. You think that was real?"

I shrugged again. "Maybe. I think it had to have some kind of power. Otherwise they wouldn't have bothered to put that hole in that rock. That was probably a lot of work. You wouldn't do that for nothing."

"Well, I guess I'd like to see it sometime," Rose admitted. "Whether it works or not."

"We should put it on the map," I said. "Charlotte's map. I haven't told Charlotte to add that yet."

"You don't need to put it on Charlotte's little map to remember you want to see it. Maybe someday you'll just go see it on your own."

This statement seemed a sort of betrayal. It sounded as if Rose definitely had something against Charlotte's trip.

"Charlotte and I have planned this trip for a while," I said defensively. "There's a lot of stuff on the map we *both* want to see."

"But if Charlotte's already losing interest because of Nintendo, how likely is it she'll want to do the trip when you guys are eighteen?"

"Well, do *you* still want to do the trip?" I asked.

"You know, it was really nice of you girls to include me. But I don't know if I'll be around then."

"Where will you be?"

"Not here, I hope."

"What will you be doing?"

"Well, that I don't know. I haven't figured it out yet."

"Charlotte already wants to be a marine biologist."

"Right." Rose rolled her eyes. "Good for Charlotte. She can

study all the great white sharks you guys see on your way to the Bermuda Triangle. Make sure you take a good sturdy boat."

I was quiet again as we walked toward my house. I felt stung by her revelation that she wouldn't be taking the around-the-world investigative trip with us. Of course, it made perfect sense, now that I really thought about it. She'd be much older than us, and she couldn't wait around.

But it still hurt—the way the last week of school hurts, when you look at your lovely teacher writing on the board and realize that you're never in your life going to see her every day or every week or maybe ever again. That she'll forget your name in a few months and it will be like you'd never even met. You spend a day or two considering writing her letters over the summer— letters so sweet and charming that she won't be able to resist writing you back, and you'll stay friends once you've grown up, and she'll come to your wedding and maybe meet you for lunch when you're twenty-five and sophisticated.

But after a day or two of trying to figure out what you could possibly write in these letters to make this all happen, reality sets in—there will be no letters and no fancy lunch. You will have to learn to see your whole life without her. It hurts for days, but by the last day of school you're pretending to yourself that you've accepted it.

Our world trip was ambitious, sure, and maybe a little unrealistic. But the idea that Rose would come along was just plain dumb. I saw that now. Even dumber than the idea that my fourth-grade teacher would come to my wedding. We couldn't keep Rose forever. It came to me like a kick in the stomach. She wasn't our friend—she was only our baby-sitter. She spent time with us because Mr. Hemsworth paid her money. He paid her a lot, in fact—last time we walked home together, I'd seen her counting the bills. Soon she'd go away to college, and then the wide world would swallow her up. And we'd never see her again. I hated to start thinking of it, but I was going to have to.

"So you really believe in miracles, then, Nora?"

"What?" I said, too sad to really hear what she was asking.

"You believe that that doughnut rock could heal someone. You believe in miracles, then."

"Maybe," I admitted.

"I don't think I can even say maybe," Rose said. "I'd like to, but I don't think I can anymore."

"Yes you can. You'll believe in anything," I pointed out.

"I will?" Rose looked puzzled. "What makes you say that?'

"Well, you believe in aliens. Plus, you said it when you were reading about the werewolves. You said that when you walk up the street at night, you'll believe anything."

"A werewolf is hardly a miracle," Rose said, sighing, looking up Fox Hill. She seemed a little anxious, or at least bored with this conversation.

"I think maybe it is, though. If you saw one, you'd think so."

Rose finally smiled—just barely.

"I don't know about that. You'd probably be too scared to stop and think about it being a miracle. And what I think I meant was that when it's dark and you're scared, it's easier to believe in stupid stuff like ghosts and werewolves. But I don't *usually* believe in that stuff."

"Do you right now?"

"No. Do you?"

"No," I said firmly, lying.

"Only the Druids, then?"

I wasn't sure if she was teasing. Her serious expression indicated she wasn't.

"The Druids and Easter Island," I corrected her, trying to sound certain.

"Well, those are good choices. See ya, Nora."

"Okay," I said. "Bye."

I stood in my yard for a moment, cold but reluctant to go in and attempt small talk with Mrs. Crowe while I waited for my mother to get home. I watched Rose for a moment, her jeans moving in that swingy way some teenage girls had, unafraid of making their butts look big. She adjusted the strap of her backpack, then slung it over one shoulder again before disappearing where the sidewalk turned up the hill. Then I bent down to pick up one of the stray red leaves that hadn't been raked the week before. Joe Dean had raked Mrs. Crowe's leaves for her, although she'd grumbled that he'd done a bad job, saying she should've docked his pay. But I was glad he'd left a few leaves scattered across the lawn. I hated that winter was coming, that the trees were now bare, and that most of the yard's color had disappeared so quickly somehow, while I wasn't paying attention.

Nine

May 23, 2006

"I'm showing a movie to my sophomores tomorrow," Charlotte announced as she came in the front door, tossing her fat teacher tote into a kitchen chair. "Let's get the hell out of here. Let's go out."

"I bought some stuff to make you a curry," I said, holding up the garam masala I'd gone all the way to Fairville to find.

"That's great," Charlotte replied. "That's really sweet of you. You can make it tomorrow. Really, let's go out. I need to feel like a grown-up tonight. The kids were making fart jokes all seventh period. There's this one kid who names his farts after the different school lunches. Today was the Nacho Grande."

"That rules out Mexican, I suppose."

"Oh, I already have a place all picked out," Charlotte told me.

"Okay, well, we can go out," I said, leading her into the living room. "But I think maybe we need to talk for a minute."

"Uh-oh," she said with a sigh. "Sounds serious."

"Maybe," I said, handing her the page from the *Looking Glass* she'd left on the coffee table the first night. "I should've asked you about this earlier. I just didn't know what to make of it. Why did you bring this up?"

"Oh." Charlotte looked at it noncommittally. "I wondered where I'd put that."

"You left it on the coffee table."

"I'm sorry. I'm sort of a slob."

"You were reading this thing to me from an old issue of the *Looking Glass,* Charlotte? Why?"

"I guess I just wanted to see if you'd be willing to talk about it."

"What about it, exactly?"

"Well, I thought those poems might be a sensitive subject. I wasn't sure if you'd *want* to talk about them, frankly. I guess I thought I'd start by letting you know I admired them."

"I don't know what that means."

"Okay. You're right. It was stupid. I felt stupid about it as soon as I did it. I probably should've been more direct. I should've learned my lesson the first time around."

"First time around?"

"I tried to get you to talk about them just after we graduated."

"I don't know what you're talking about. . . . And what exactly did you want to ask me about it?"

"It felt to me like you still had something to say. About Rose, maybe, but maybe not. Maybe the parts connected to Rose were just to get my attention. Either way, it felt like you were trying to send a message to *me* at the time. Am I right?"

"When?" I asked.

Charlotte leaned against the kitchen counter and fiddled with the sugar bowl, turning its white porcelain lid clockwise, then counterclockwise.

"When you wrote those things," she said. "When you dropped them in the *Looking Glass* box."

The confidence in her voice stunned me more than her words. It took a moment for their meaning to sink in.

"*I* didn't write them," I said, after recovering my voice.

"I *liked* them, Nora." Charlotte let go of the sugar bowl's top and looked up at me. "And trust me, I didn't like much that was dropped anonymously into that box at the time. Mostly un-requited-crush confessions and the occasional fakey-sounding poem about incest. You know, the kids *still* use that stupid box as their personal Freudian dumping ground—"

"I didn't write them," I repeated. "This week was the first time I've read them. I went to the Waverly Public Library and found them. I've never seen them before. I never read the *Looking Glass* back then."

"I *know* you wrote them. You put a couple of Rose's dreams in them. It was cool how you worked them in. The one about the clothesline and the one about the gym mats . . ."

"Charlotte . . . *you* wrote them."

"Nora . . ." Charlotte cocked her head, giving me a sympathetic look that made me want to kick her.

"*You* wrote them. I didn't have anything to do with that stupid magazine."

"I know it was a really hard time for you. This is why I was a little worried about bringing it up, kind of pussyfooted about it that first night you were here. But I've just so wanted to ask you about them for so long."

"I didn't write them, Charlotte."

"You know, it was such a rough time. Maybe you just don't really *remember* doing it?"

"That's . . . ridiculous," I sputtered.

"Why? Just last night we were talking about how we all take leave of our senses at some point in high school."

"Well, sure. But I think I'd remember if I sat down and penned five or six avant-garde poems and submitted them to a school literary magazine in which I *never* had any interest."

"*Avant-garde.* That's funny that you'd call it that. That's part of what I liked about them. The quirky tone. Years after we'd stopped talking, but they still *sounded* sort of like you."

So sounding trippy sounded like me. Hmm. A few years ago, I might have been flattered by that, but not so much now.

"They weren't *me*," I insisted. "I would *remember*. I was afraid to raise my hand in *class*, Charlotte. Do you think I would ever've put myself out there like this? And then not remember it? To not remember—that's not a *rough time*. That's, like, psychosis."

"Oh, I disagree. Maybe you just don't—"

"You don't need to say it again. I was messed up, but I wasn't crazy."

"No one is suggesting that you were. Let's get in the car, Nora. We can talk about this over dinner."

I hated how she said this, in that gentle way you talk to someone who just needs to come to her senses.

"Let's go. We'll have a drink, we'll talk about it. It'll be easier like that."

"Okay," I mumbled, grabbing my keys.

I'd make her admit it when we got there.

* * *

I offered to drive, figuring that Charlotte would be having a few drinks. I followed her directions until we were parked in the lot of one of Fairville's strip malls.

"We going to that Chinese take-out place?" I asked.

"No, over there," Charlotte said, pointing to the end of the building, with a large green sign that said JB'S.

"Is that a sports bar?" I could see about three big-screen TVs just from the window.

"Yeah."

I was surprised by the restaurant choice, since Charlotte had billed the outing as a "grown-up" one. I didn't care for these places. It's not so much the tedious drone of a sportscast that bothers me, or the excess of televisions, or the icky fried onion blossoms, or the testosterone, or even the women with orange tans and lip liner. It's just having to deal with all those things at once. But Charlotte had always been more of a "sporty" girl than I was, so maybe she went in for it all.

"There a game on of some kind?" I asked, trying to sound amenable.

Charlotte looked at me funny and then shrugged.

"Sure. There's always a game on, I guess," she said. "I told Porter to meet us here at a quarter till six."

"Oh." That explained things somewhat. So we were entertaining a guy.

But when Porter found our table—early, just after we were seated by an ample-bosomed blond greeter—he didn't look to be the sports-bar sort either. He had unruly black curls, and wore angular, horn-rimmed glasses that overpowered his narrow face. A little more decidedly eccentric than I thought would be to Charlotte's taste, but what did I know? We hadn't talked boys much when we were kids. She'd never told me what her type was.

"How was school?" he asked Charlotte after we'd all made our introductions.

She responded by launching right into a story about some of her sophomore girls. As much as she talked about wanting to get away from the kids, Charlotte seemed to bring them with her everywhere.

"The sophomores are reading short stories," she explained, "in American lit. Today we were reading Joyce Carol Oates. 'Where Are You Going, Where Have You Been?' Read it?"

"Yeah," Porter said. "Actually, I think I have."

Charlotte looked at me. "You probably read it in high school, too. It's about this girl named Connie. She's fifteen, and this sexual predator comes to her door. Slowly convinces her to get in his car."

"Mmm . . . yeah, that rings a bell," I said, scanning the menu.

"And I know it's sort of tasteless of me to have them reading it now," Charlotte continued. "Sort of a gross coincidence, but—"

"Gross?" Porter said. " How . . . ? Oh. Yeah. I see."

"Some girl's mom called me to complain. But really, that was what I was planning to teach this week. And frankly, I thought of skipping it. To be perfectly honest, though, it's so goddamn easy to teach, too. The kids always have a lot to say about poor old Connie. How dumb they think she is.

"So I was watching a group of girls in one of my classes today. They were supposed to be doing these group-discussion questions on the story. But they were goofing off, mostly. There are these pervy lines in the story where Arnold Friend, the creepy older guy, is trying to talk her out of the house, saying stuff like, 'I'm gonna come inside you where it's all secret and you're gonna give it to me,' and the girls were reading each other these lines in funny voices, imitating Barry White, practically falling off their chairs laughing. On some level I think they were just so amazed they'd been assigned something that contained these words. The sad thing is, they think Connie's stupid, but they're *just* like her."

"How's that?" I asked.

"They can't believe what they're hearing. They're so insecure and clueless that they have no idea how to deal with it. They're so insecure and clueless that I usually want to wring their necks, to be honest. But it's that insecurity and cluelessness that, at the same time, makes me so angry when I think of someone taking advantage, hurting one of them. You know what I mean?"

Our goateed waiter took our drink orders: Charlotte's pinot grigio, my soda (I wasn't in the mood to drink), and Porter's gin and tonic. Porter's choice nearly made me giggle. He had such a baby face he could've been eighteen. I knew he had to be at least twenty-three or so, and I hoped he was older than that. Still, Charlotte's whole coiffed-teacher-with-a-cigarette bit—combined with the eagerly boyish way he conversed with her—was starting to give me a Mrs. Robinson vibe.

"So I was thinking that Rose was young, like my girls," Charlotte said after the waiter had left us. "As cool as we thought she was, she was probably just like them. Maybe she *would've* gotten into a car with some creepy older guy. Probably didn't have a clue what she was doing most of the time."

"It's hard for me to think of her that way," I said. "But it makes sense. Hey—you thought any more about Aaron? You sniffed around the teachers' lounge about that?"

"I'm keeping my ear out for that, trust me," Charlotte said, lowering her voice, looking quickly around her for a moment, checking for eavesdroppers. "I heard Philippa mention she thought he and Rose were an odd pair, but I haven't heard any hint of an accusation."

"I see," I said.

Charlotte nodded conspiratorially and sipped her wine. I couldn't tell if she really believed that Aaron could have had something to do with Rose's murder or if it had just been something to talk about late at night—and now something to gab about over dinner.

Porter cleared his throat. "Um, I have some Rose news," he said, then clamped his lips around his cocktail straw.

Charlotte leaned forward. "Why didn't you say so?"

"When I called you, I mentioned I had news." Porter glanced at me. "That's partly why I suggested we meet."

"You're a reporter, hon. You always have news. Out with it, then."

"It'll be in the paper tomorrow. Maybe it's already on the evening news. The state police and the Waverly department got together, put out a short, careful release about the body. I think it's partly saving face, stressing that two thorough searches were done in 1990 and 1991. The remains are many years old, but the receptacle they were in was not. The line they're using is that 'the burial likely occurred more recently than would normally be expected in a case of this nature.'"

Charlotte narrowed her eyes. "So the whole wicker-basket thing is true."

"Well, no one said anything about wicker. I know how badly you want me to blow the lid off this wicker thing, but—"

"So the body hasn't been there sixteen years. We kind of already knew that. Anything else?"

"Yeah," Porter said, glancing at me again. "One other thing."

"Yesssss?" Charlotte said impatiently.

"Ben told me this off the record."

"Noted. What?"

"Some of the bones were broken. They're saying the cause of death, even based on the first forensics, was blunt-force trauma."

Charlotte put down her wine. "To the skull?"

"Well. Yes. But here's the weird thing. Also to the chest."

"The chest?" Charlotte repeated softly. "How . . . ?"

"I don't know," Porter said.

"Maybe someone hit her over the head," Charlotte suggested, "and then, when she fell over, kept beating her?"

I poked at my ice cubes and took a sip of soda, trying to ignore the faint nausea that was just starting to stir in my stomach.

"I really don't know," Porter repeated. "If anyone's conjecturing, I haven't heard."

"Anything else?" Charlotte demanded.

"No. They're expecting the lab results in a couple of days. That'll confirm it's her. Not sure if it will help them with anything else. Not sure how much you can get out of a body that's been around that long."

"Maybe there'd be hairs," Charlotte said. "Of the person who buried her or something like that."

I stared at the menu, suddenly doubtful that I'd be able to eat anything, much less a hamburger dripping with condiments and a side of greasy fries. I don't know why it bothered me that

Charlotte could process and discuss this information so quickly.

"Who's Ben?" I asked.

"The dispatcher," she said with a hint of exasperation. "He and Porter are pretty tight."

We were all quiet for a minute or two.

"You two all right?" Porter asked.

"Of course we are," Charlotte said, studying her own menu.

"You, Nora?" Porter turned to me.

"Yep," I said, then looked up and met his stare for several seconds. I either convinced him or made him uncomfortable, as his gaze darted quickly back to Charlotte.

After we'd ordered, Charlotte excused herself and disappeared into the ladies' room. Porter seemed to relax once she'd gone.

"She left us alone on purpose," he said, grinning at me.

"What makes you say that?"

"In case I wanted to probe you for information, maybe a quote."

"About Rose, you mean?"

"Yeah. Since you're the prime witness and all."

"Nice," I said. *Prime witness.*

"Charlotte's wording, not mine."

"I figured. So did you want a quote? Is that what you're saying?"

"I dunno. You want to give me one?"

"Not particularly," I admitted. "No offense. I just don't have anything to say. Aside from how sorry I am for Rose's family, and that's not something that anyone needs to hear special from me."

"So . . ." Porter shook his gin and tonic and sucked a bit of it through his tiny straw. "This business of your being the last to see her alive . . ."

"Yes?" I was startled to hear him refer to it as "this business." "What about it?"

"I'm sorry. Are you uncomfortable talking about that day?"

"No," I said, deciding not to mention my embarrassing trip to the police station—I didn't want to wind up reading about it in the paper tomorrow. "I just don't have anything to add from when I was a kid. I've never remembered anything un-usual about that day, about her walking me home. I wish I did, if it would help. But I don't."

Porter hesitated. "It might be an interesting story, your coming back here."

"An interesting story? You mean for the newspaper?"

"Yeah. Well, something tasteful. The girl who last saw Rose, coming back. How you remember her and—"

"No thanks."

Porter stirred his ice cubes with his straw, apparently trying to decide whether to let the topic drop. Then he looked around, checking to see if Charlotte was coming. She was taking a while to return.

He took a delicate sip out of his gin and tonic, then cocked his head. "You got any good 'little Charlotte' stories?"

Relieved, I told him about the notes I'd just found in which she'd referred to me as "the subject" and theorized about my capacity for astral projection.

"She mentioned that to me, the investigation," Porter said.

I thought again of the *Looking Glass* poems attached to Rose's dream notes. Annoyingly, this dinner arrangement had delayed my hammering it into Charlotte's head that the writings hadn't been authored by me. She was just so goddamned sure it was me that the matter apparently didn't need any further discussion.

"She liked to figure things out, get results," I said. "She was always taking a lot of notes, making charts and graphs."

"Charts and graphs. Hmph." Porter chuckled.

"And she was bossy. I never saw her as a teacher, though," I admitted. "You really think she's okay teaching?"

"Okay?" Porter said. "Meaning, do I think she likes it?"

"Well, yeah."

"Well . . . it's a job that's nearly impossible to master quickly. She likes to master things quickly."

"I can't say I really understood why she made the switch from journalism. Why she didn't try to go work for another paper."

"Not like she really had that kind of option. There aren't many newspaper jobs to go around anymore, and, at least locally, people knew how she'd been shitcanned. "

The word "shitcanned" gave me pause. That wasn't exactly how Charlotte had told it. I sipped my Coke to prevent my expression from giving away my surprise.

"But that was a dumb thing for them to fire her for, that stuff about the coffee cups," I said.

"It wasn't about the cups. It was a few weeks later, when the town treasurer said Charlotte was messing around in his office."

My straw slipped out of my mouth.

"Oh, shit," Porter said, staring at me. "She didn't tell you about that."

"No."

"It wasn't as bad as it sounds. She was doing an interview with him, he went to the can, she says she saw something on his desk that looked interesting—the police chief's expense report, I guess it was. Just couldn't help herself. Then he came back in. Caught her. Freaked out. Made a big deal out of it with our editor."

"And he fired her?"

"She was already sort of on thin ice. It was harsh, but . . . well, there's maybe more of a future in teaching anyway. I don't know how much longer the *Voice* is gonna be around. And it's kind of a shoddy paper anyhow."

"But that's not really the point, is it?"

"Well, look. I think teaching is actually good for Charlotte. It might not always show, but I think she really cares about the kids. Sometimes the right thing happens the wrong way. Know what I mean?"

Charlotte finally came back to the table, plopping down on her chair with a little smile on her face.

"Yeah," I said.

"What, did you fall in?" Porter asked.

"No," she said. "I was just chatting with someone at the bar."

"Oh?" Porter said, looking down at his drink for a moment, as if the statement reminded him he'd like another.

"You recognize him, Nora?"

"Who?" I asked.

"Look at the bar. Behind the bar, I mean."

We were pretty far from the bar. All I could make out about the bartender was that he was blond, slightly overweight, and wearing a black T-shirt.

"No," I said.

"Maybe you ought to go up and order a drink so you can get a closer look. I'm curious if you'd recognize—"

"Jesus, Charlotte," Porter hissed. "Is that why you had us come to this hole? You figured out where he—"

"Oh, quit your whining." Charlotte swatted her hand in his direction. "Like we're too classy for this place?"

I looked from Porter to Charlotte and back to Porter again, feeling dumb.

"That's Aaron," he said in a low voice. "Aaron Dwyer. Rose's old boyfriend. Charlotte, what did you say to him?"

"Nothing, really. Just went up and ordered a drink to start. Told him he looked familiar. Wanted to see what he'd say, if he'd recognize me from when I was a kid. Didn't seem to. And he's filled out a bit himself. Was pretty friendly, though."

Our waiter arrived with our orders—their burgers and my Caesar salad.

"Well, dig in," Charlotte said cheerfully.

"I'm not going to go bother that guy, if that's what you're thinking," Porter told her.

"Who says this has anything to do with you?" Charlotte said, slicing her burger in half with a butter knife. "*You're* the one who wanted to meet *us* tonight. So we wanted to get a good look at the guy. So what?"

"So you got a good look," Porter said through his teeth. "What've you learned?"

Charlotte ignored his question. I could feel her eyes on me as I picked up my fork.

"You gonna go up there and check him out, too?" she asked.

"Or do you want to wait and just try to chat with him casually when we leave?"

I put a giant piece of lettuce in my mouth and tried not to look at her, the bar, or Porter. Something shut down inside me—the way it always had when Charlotte would push me too far, when my stubborn eleven-year-old self would refuse to reward her, even at the cost of seeming mute and stupid.

"Neither," I managed after I'd swallowed the lettuce.

We all ate in silence for a few minutes.

"What've you learned?" Porter said again.

I packed my duffel bag hurriedly when we arrived back at the Hemsworths'. It was still early—just after eight—when I announced that I'd placed a quick call to my mother and she'd insisted upon an evening visit. When Charlotte eyed my duffel bag, I reasoned that my mother would probably be hurt if I didn't stay the night. Charlotte didn't quite buy it, I could tell, but she seemed worn out and didn't protest. She knew she'd offended me somehow but clearly didn't have the energy to work out why.

After I'd tossed the duffel into my backseat, I drove out of Fox Hill hastily, headed downtown, and parked at the 7-Eleven. I went into the store, bought a large box of Gobstoppers, and then sat in my car for a little while longer, sucking on one after another. I was grateful for my car, for the bright fluorescent light of this convenience store, for the option to escape Waverly. It occurred to me that this was the first time I'd been in Waverly with the benefit of my own mobility. I'd never had a car in high school, and I didn't learn to drive till I was a senior—after sufficient time had passed since my "incident" for me to be trusted behind a wheel. My mother let me borrow hers very occasionally to pick up eggs or milk, but that was it. Waverly, in retrospect, might not have been so bad if I'd wrangled a little more freedom for myself. Waverly was even kind of pleasant tonight, as I sat sucking down artificial cherry and grape, enjoying a little evening breeze coming through my cracked window. But I still wasn't ready to call my mother.

Toby had asked me to the prom in this very parking lot. He'd been giving me a ride home when he stopped for some milk and a few cans of SpaghettiOs, which I assumed would be dinner for himself, his brother, and his dad. This menu made me pretty sad—sadder still to see him struggle to balance all the cans in one arm as he enthusiastically held the 7-Eleven door for the pregnant lady coming in as he came out. I stared at him as he got into the car, tossed the cans into the backseat, and fished his keys out of his jeans pocket.

"Are you going to the prom?" I asked him as he started the car.

He sort of chuckled and said he didn't think so.

"You?" he asked.

I liked how he always drove one-handed, with his left arm draped casually across his open window. I couldn't remember the last time I thought he'd smelled like a monkey. And while the SpaghettiOs made me sad for him, that sadness made me feel closer to him somehow.

"No one's asked," I said with a shrug.

He edged the car up to the road, looked both ways, then looked at me. "That something you're interested in going to?"

"Might be stupid, might be fun," I said.

"You wanna go? With me?" he asked, quite simply, and I agreed.

Now I turned on my car's CD player and listened to a little Neutral Milk Hotel while deciding what to do next. I had a passing impulse to just head back home. I missed Neil, and I was uneasy here in Waverly, despite the comfort of this breeze and these Gobstoppers. It was a little late to head back down 95, but I could stop at a cheap motel on the way home. I was no stranger to cheap hotels—in fact, I liked them. Whenever Neil and I took a road trip, we liked to call the Motel 6s and the Super 8s from their parking lots to negotiate a cheap rate. *Sixty-five?* Neil would say. *I think I've got only about fifty on me. How would that be?* Super 8 was usually willing to bargain. Motel 6 tended to be a little tougher. When we'd get into our fifty-five-dollar room, we'd usually high-five, jump on the bed, shower together, and steal all the little soaps.

But then, those little soaps always make me think of my mother. And I owed my mother a visit at the very least. If she ever heard I'd been up here without going to see her, I'd never hear the end of it, and I'd probably deserve it. I found my cell phone in my purse and dialed her number.

"Hey, Mom," I said, pulling the Gobstopper out of my mouth when she picked up. "Guess what?"

Cosmic Duality:
November 1990

The day after Rose disappeared, we didn't know yet she was gone. We just knew she hadn't shown up at Charlotte's that afternoon.

"Maybe she missed the bus at school," Charlotte said, shrugging as she hit the "power" button of her Nintendo.

The Super Mario jingle filled that endless afternoon. *Ba-DING, ba-DING, ba-DING*, droned the game as Charlotte's mustached little man collected coins.

After about an hour, the ringing of the coins began to numb my ears. I slipped from the room, pulled on my coat, and crept outside. I sat at the Hemsworths' picnic table, pulling my coat tight. Charlotte and I had sat here just this past summer, when Rose had served us sandwiches and lemonade outside. It had felt like a very special occasion, eating outside. But it felt so long ago now in the hard wind of early winter. The table looked gray and splintery, the grass dead.

A few stray leaves rattled in the vegetable garden, stuck to the abandoned tomato stakes and the brown twigs that had once been herbs. Although I couldn't figure why, the sound of those leaves reminded me of Rose's hair blowing sideways into her face—yesterday, in a similar but gentler wind. I remembered how sad I'd been to think of Rose leaving us someday, and suddenly, before I had a chance to hold it back, that feeling was present again. Not just the memory of the sadness but the actual sadness. I wanted to kick myself for remembering it, for letting it in, because once you remember sadness, you can't control feeling it, too.

I got up off the picnic table, walked to the sidewalk, and headed up the street. I passed a house, then another. Mrs. Shepherd was standing in her yard, yelling, *Lucille! Lucille!* Typical old-lady name for an old-lady cat. Too bad for the cat somehow, that she'd been labeled like that, that she'd be Mrs. Shepherd's prissy pet for her whole life and no one would know what kind of cat she really was or really could be.

I stared at Mrs. Shepherd, who continued calling cheerfully

through her cupped hands. She didn't feel how sad this cold air was. I wished I couldn't feel it either. It was the same sort of air that had gently lifted Rose's hair yesterday. It was back, and it was stronger now. I shivered just as Mrs. Shepherd turned and saw me. She began to lift her hand in a wave. I cast my eyes downward and turned, pretending not to see her. I'd probably looked so weird, standing there staring—I didn't want to have to explain myself. I walked back to Charlotte's house.

When the phone rang that night, I jumped but then let my mother get it.

At around the same time the night before, we'd had a strange call just as we were sitting down to dinner. I'd picked it up and heard someone breathing funny on the other end. Whoever it was had sounded scared and had hung up after just a couple of seconds. When my mother asked me who it was, I'd said it was a wrong number.

This time I held my breath as my mother picked up and said hello.

"Oh, hi, Richie," she said. "How are you?"

After a couple of *Uh-huhs* and an *Oh, my God*, she disappeared into her bedroom and closed the door. I knew that *Richie* was Charlotte's dad. And the few bits of conversation I heard through my mother's door made me lose my appetite: *And what are the police doing? Jesus. How is Wanda holding up?*

"That was Mr. Hemsworth," my mother said after she'd emerged from the bedroom.

I nodded.

"He told me Rose didn't come to baby-sit today. Apparently Rose is missing. She's been missing since yesterday."

"I saw her yesterday," I offered. "She came and baby-sat us yesterday."

"I know. Mr. Hemsworth said that. But she didn't come home for dinner last night. She never went home."

"She didn't even go home to sleep?"

"No, Nora. They haven't seen her at all. She just didn't come home."

"Did they call the police?"

"Of course. They called them late last night."

"But I *saw* her go home."

"You did?"

"Yeah. She walked home with me. We walked together."

"And you saw her walk up the hill?"

"Yeah. Well, not *all* the way up the hill. I can't see that far from here. But that's the way she was going."

My mother was silent for a moment, nibbling at her thumbnail.

"Eat your cutlet," she murmured.

I tried to. I cut a small square out of it—one of those tiny, bite-size pieces she used to cut for me when I was a little kid.

"Her parents say she didn't come home," my mother said. "But then they don't get home till fairly late themselves. Maybe she got home and then left again."

"Where would she go?" I asked.

My mother was still biting her nail. When I did stuff like that, she'd slap my hand away from my mouth.

"I don't know, honey. That's what they're hoping the police will find out. It sounds like they're thinking she might have run away."

"I don't think she ran away," I said firmly. I considered mentioning how intensely Rose had been talking about aliens lately, but I decided against it. My mother would think I was trying to make a bad joke.

"We don't know what's happened yet, Nora. We just don't know yet. It's really terrible for her parents."

I cut another tiny square of chicken cutlet and put it in my mouth. I chewed and chewed and chewed but wasn't much in the mood to swallow it.

"She walked you home yesterday? What time was that?" My mother wanted to know.

"Same time as always. When Mr. Hemsworth got home."

"But what *time* was that?"

"I don't know."

"You would tell me, wouldn't you, if anything unusual happened? If someone stopped their car and talked to Rose? If you saw any strangers?"

Strangers. They'd always talked about them in school. I'd always imagined them as gangly, ill-shaven men in black leotards, leaping out from behind trees and shimmying under cars, hissing. Would that I'd ever see anything that interesting on Fox Hill.

"Yeah," I said. "We didn't see anything weird."

"Are you *sure*?"

"Well, *yeah*," I said, a little defensively. How could I not be sure of something like that?

My mother reached across the card table and pushed my bangs out of my eyes. I thought she was going to look at me sharply and tell me not to speak to her in that tone. Or at least tell me I needed a haircut. But she just combed her fingers through my bangs a few times and then stopped, resting her hand on my temple.

"Are you sure?" she said again, softly. She was staring at me now like I was from another planet. Her eyes had grown big, her mouth open and uncertain.

"Yes . . ." I said slowly.

"Oh, my God," she whispered, stroking my head. She wasn't saying it to me. She wasn't saying it to anyone. Not even to God, who I was pretty sure she didn't really believe in. "What Wanda and Lewis must be thinking."

She still wasn't talking to me—otherwise she'd have called them Mr. and Mrs. Banks. She finally took her hand away from my head and stuck her fork into a piece of overcooked broccoli.

She examined it for a moment, then put her fork down and told me that Mrs. Shepherd had agreed to meet Charlotte and me at the bus stop and walk us to Charlotte's after school. She'd keep an eye on us until Mr. Hemsworth got home. At least for tomorrow. After that, my mother said, we'd play it by ear.

I couldn't sleep that night. I lay awake thinking of my mother's question.

Are you sure? *Are you* sure?

Well, yes. I was.

But did confidence have anything to do with the truth? Did confidence in something mean it was real or right? Rose had been sure, in daylight, that no werewolves or vampires existed. And yet something had reached out from those trees along Fox Hill, somewhere between my house and hers, and snatched her away. She wasn't afraid, so she'd let her guard down, forgotten to hurry or hold on to her throat. Whatever it was, it had seen her walking home without a care or a worry and had taken advantage of her confidence.

I shuddered and got up to turn on the bathroom light. But it didn't make me feel any better. Light only covered up fear, I decided. It didn't get rid of it. The dark hid werewolves and ghosts, but light was maybe worse. Light tricked you into thinking you weren't afraid.

I remembered Rose reminding me that my not watching a documentary about aliens wouldn't make aliens any less real. Dark was the same way—it would be there whether I chose to face it or not. I got up and shut off the bathroom light again, feeling my way back to bed. Light couldn't trick me. And I had to remember this tomorrow. I had to remember how scared I was. I wouldn't let the daylight trick me into forgetting.

Ten

May 23, 2006

I spent the half-hour drive to my mother's sucking down Gob-stoppers.

When I arrived at her modest apartment building, I found a spot in its tight parking lot. I decided to eat one more candy before ringing her bell, crunching down the last of it as I contemplated the building's neglected landscaping.

My mother really could afford a nicer place. She simply didn't need one. And my mother rarely wanted things she didn't need. When I was growing up, she was always telling me what we didn't need. I didn't need Fruit Roll-Ups in my lunch box because they were expensive glorified candy. We didn't need cable television because we watched plenty of TV already. So it stood to reason that we didn't have a father around because we didn't need one. I operated on that assumption until I was eight.

But one day—when Charlotte insisted that biologically I must have a father—I started asking questions. So my mother sat me down and told me that she had never been married to my father and that he had died when I was very little. He'd been sick, and the doctor had given him the wrong kind of drugs by mistake, she'd explained. He was living in Florida at the time.

Did I have any questions? she wanted to know.

Of course I had quite a few questions. How come she hadn't told me before that I had a father? Where had he been all these years? Florida? What had he been doing there? All I knew about Florida was Disney World. Why hadn't he ever invited me?

"Did he have leukemia?" I asked after some thought.

It popped into my head because it was one of the few names of diseases I knew. It was what had taken Toby's mother when he was very small, so somehow the word had stuck in my head as the evil sickness that killed kids' parents.

My mother frowned, then reached out and stroked my hair.

"No, honey," she said. "He didn't have leukemia."

"That's good," I replied. I didn't know what else to say. My opening question seemed to make her so sad I thought it best to skip the others. At least for the moment.

After dinner that night, she showed me a picture of him. He was wearing a Red Sox cap, squinting against the sunlight, holding a thermos. He looked way younger than Charlotte's dad.

"We had a picnic that day," she explained. "And did some fishing."

I nodded as if this explained everything. That pretty much closed the subject until I was in high school and my father came up again when I least expected it. If I'd known it would be that long, I'd probably have asked a question or two more.

"Well, I'm glad you're here," my mother said after I'd explained the circumstances of my sudden appearance—that I was visiting Charlotte on a whim. And that I was going to call her tomorrow and set something up, but Charlotte crashed early after work tonight, so I decided to see what she was up to this evening.

"I wish I'd known ahead of time you were going to be around, though." My mother sat next to me on her couch and lifted her cat, Bilbo, into her lap. "Bill would have liked to see you, but he's away till next Tuesday."

Bill was the guy my mom had been dating for about a year. He'd come with her to our last Thanksgiving in Virginia. It had been a surprise, since she'd never, to my knowledge, dated anyone seriously since my father. Very occasionally, when I was growing up, she'd have dinner with someone, but she'd usually come home and tell me what a bore the guy had been or what a poor movie selection he'd made.

"Sorry about that," I said. "It really was a last-minute thing."

My mother nodded, petting down the fluffy hair around Bilbo's neck. He had long gray fur and yellowish eyes and a smudge of dark gray next to his nose. I'd always thought he was incredibly ugly. And now the shape of his skull and the tiny line of his mouth reminded me of the drawings of aliens in Charlotte's books. I've never cared that much for cats anyway. Their daintiness embarrasses me.

"So I guess you've heard about Rose, too," I said.

"Of course," my mother replied, scratching Bilbo's ears.

We couldn't have pets at Mrs. Crowe's, but my mother adopted Bilbo from the shelter after I left for college. She got him fee-free because he was already kind of old and no one had wanted him. He was apparently a day away from euthanasia.

"I wasn't sure if I should call you when I heard," she said now. "I wasn't sure you'd want to be dragging all that out again."

I tipped back my box of Gobstoppers and dropped one of the candies into my mouth. The candy rattled noisily as it slid down the half-empty box.

"Want one?" I asked, even though I knew the answer.

My mother shook her head, making a face.

I hesitated. "Well, I heard anyway. From Charlotte."

"Interesting that Charlotte would call you after all these years. You visiting anyone else? Or just Charlotte?"

"Well, and you."

"That's all?"

"I saw Toby Dean. We had a beer."

"I've always liked Toby. How's he doing?"

"Good. It seems like he knows everyone in town."

"That's what happens when you fix everyone's car."

I nodded. "I guess so."

"He's had it kind of hard. What with his father dying. And that flaky brother of his. Toby's like his father was. Takes care of everyone."

I nodded again.

"Poor Walter," my mother said, referring to Toby's dad. "He really had it rough when Toby's grandmother died. Had never taken care of the boys himself before. He was at his wit's end some days. I think he was drinking some then, and the shop was in trouble. But he really pulled himself together and made it work. Always managed to keep it afloat somehow. And Toby's really done a splendid job taking it over. My understanding's the shop's doing quite well these days."

"I'm glad to hear it," I said.

Maybe my mother heard a bored quality to my voice, because after a moment's pause she said, "Hey—how about we go out for an ice cream or something? Would you be up for that?"

I said sure and told her I'd be happy to drive.

Later I tossed and turned on my mother's couch—the blue one with the navy flecks that she'd bought when I was in third grade. It wasn't quite as comfortable as Paul Hemsworth's old bed. When I curled up against its mushy back, I could smell Mrs. Crowe's place somewhere deep in the velour.

We'd lived thriftily and relatively harmoniously at Mrs. Crowe's for so long. So when I tried to kill myself at the age of sixteen, it was an outrageous indulgence. A desperate bit of frivolity of the kind my mother usually despised. Still, she did all the right things for the first week or so of my hospitalization. She brought me chocolate bars and told me she loved me and chatted with Dr. Petroff and came for the family-therapy sessions but gave me my space, as he likely instructed.

And then, on the eve of my last day there, when my obligatory ten days were up and my release day had been set, they let her take me out of the ward, down to a corner coffee shop for a hot cocoa.

"The doctor asked me about your father," she told me.

I took a big, greedy sip of my cocoa and burned my tongue. I didn't reply.

"I'm going to tell you the truth, Nora."

And that's when she proceeded to tell me that my father had died of a drug overdose. It was clear to her by the time she was pregnant that he had a problem, she said. She'd always thought the drugs might have been self-medication for depression, but she didn't stick around to find out.

She told me that his parents had sent her money the first couple of years after I was born and that they'd met me when I was three but I probably didn't remember it. At the time there was talk of my meeting my father, but it didn't work out. He was still having problems, and her communication with the family faded after that, especially after she got her nursing license. When he'd overdosed on pills a few years later, no one was sure if it was intentional or not.

"They think he killed himself?"

"There was no way to know. He didn't leave a note. I'd like to think it was an accident."

"Now," she said, after giving me a few minutes to let all this sink in. "Dr. Petroff asked me about mental illness or suicide in the family."

I looked into my cocoa. I couldn't enjoy it anymore. It was too sweet for this conversation.

"I didn't tell him about your father."

"You lied?"

"Yes, I lied."

"Why?"

"Because it's nobody else's business."

"God, Mom. You're a *nurse*."

"Yes, I'm a nurse. So I know what kinds of things these doctors pull. They find out about your father and they'll insist on keeping you for a few more weeks. Or send you to one of those adolescent facilities. They'll want to cover their asses. They'll start making assumptions about you. Taking shortcuts. I don't want them putting all that on you when it has nothing to do with you."

"It *doesn't*? I'm not sure if that's true."

"You want to be mentally ill, Nora?" She was now gesturing so wildly with her hands that she practically knocked her coffee cup off the table. "Is that how you want to distinguish yourself? Is that the privilege you want out of your life?"

I looked around the empty coffee shop to see if anyone was listening. The guy behind the counter was sorting tea bags. I wondered if this shop's proximity to a psych ward meant he heard conversations like this all the time.

"No, I just—"

"If you want to claim him," my mother said, taking a breath before she continued carefully, "you go ahead. You want to claim this history that you've known about for only the past ten minutes, you march right back up there and tell Dr. Petroff everything I just told you. That's why I'm telling you. So you can decide for yourself what you think he should know."

I stared at her. I hated everything about her in that moment. I hated the way her gray-streaked hair flipped the wrong way away from her face, always refusing to curl under correctly. I hated the visible pores on her nose and the way her lip twitched when she tried to talk sense into me. Her life's work. And I hated the way those words came out of her mouth, stinking of sour saliva and coffee combined with some foul old-lady smell that was already beginning to develop deep inside her.

"Umm . . . okay," I said skeptically.

"But before you decide, honey—" She said the word "honey" not with affection but contempt, the same way she addressed female drivers who got in her way (*Are you going to turn or not, honey?*). "Before you decide, there's something I want to say to you. I'm sorry you were hurting so badly you felt you had to do this. I'm sorry I didn't see it coming, and I'm sorry if I don't understand it."

She reached for my hand, but I pulled it away, again glancing around the shop for witnesses. She continued anyway.

"If there are some changes we need to make to help you feel better, we'll work on them. But. *But.* I want you to go back in there tonight and look around you. Look at the people there. Look at the people who are paid to care for them. You can have that for the rest of your life, if you want it. The pills and the group therapy. I'm not sure whether your father had a choice, but I believe that you do. And if I turn out to be wrong about that, forgive me."

I started tearing little bits off the rim of my Styrofoam cup, avoiding her eyes. But she stuck out her hand and nudged my chin up with her knuckle.

"You, my dear, have a choice, I'm pretty certain. You can let them tell you that you need them to make you like everyone else. But they've known you for ten days. I've cared for you and watched you carefully your whole life—more carefully than you can imagine, and you may not be the happiest or the most

predictable young woman I know, but I *know* there's nothing
wrong with you."

And I hated her for using the word "woman," as if we had
something biological in common. I hated that she had essentially called me normal without even using the word—as if to
declare that she knew better than the rest of the world what I
was. As if this were a game and she had outsmarted me—outsmarted everybody—and won.

We finished our drinks without another word. I let her walk
me back to the ward and clenched my jaw as she hugged me
before they buzzed me in.

Less than forty-eight hours later, I was out of the ward. Dr.
Petroff never heard a thing about my father. I hated my mother
for putting it on me to tell him, but somehow telling him didn't
seem like the appropriate revenge. After my mother had signed
the last of the papers at the front desk, she walked me toward
the big sliding glass doors.

"What have you got there?" she asked, pointing at the white
plastic bag hanging from my arm. It was full of little soaps and
bottles of shampoo and hand lotion that they gave us in the
ward. I'd always thought it was fun to keep this sort of thing,
on the very rare occasion we stayed in a hotel.

I opened the bag and showed it to her.

"We don't need those," she said.

She grabbed the bag from my hands and shoved it into the
tall silver trash bin just before the doors. The doors slid open,
and she swept her hand out before her, grandly allowing me to
step out first.

But now there was nothing left of those days. I curled up

tight and squeezed my eyes against them. Nothing but a faint scent from these sinking couch cushions that now folded me in like a lumpy blue bosom.

Search for the Soul:
November 1990

After we'd finished drawing our Dogon grid in the dirt, we surrounded it with Whisker Lickin's to encourage Phil to go near it. We'd agreed that putting them in the actual boxes might break his concentration or distract him from his instincts.

Toby carried him out of the house for us, grimacing as the little orange beast swiped at his chest and arms. The struggle worsened as soon as the smell of the outdoors hit Phil.

"Where do you want him? WHERE DO YOU WANT HIM?" Toby screamed as he started to lose his grip on the cat.

"Here. Right at the edge of it," Charlotte said sharply, pointing.

Toby stepped to the edge of the grid. He knelt down.

"Awwww!" He winced as Phil clawed over his left shoulder and leaped out of his arms behind him.

Before we even had a chance to coo Phil toward the Whisker Lickin's, he'd crashed into the brush behind Charlotte's house and bounded out of our view.

"Crap!" Toby yelled.

"Try not to swear in my yard," Charlotte said.

"'Crap' isn't really a swear word," I pointed out.

Charlotte ignored me. "Now what do we do? Do we try and catch him again?"

"That's not gonna be easy," Toby said.

"Maybe we don't need him," I said. "Maybe he's already told us what he knows."

"What's that supposed to mean?" Charlotte challenged.

"Nothing. Maybe he knows nothing."

I didn't bother to try to suggest that maybe Phil sensed that our symbols were inadequate—to imply again that there was at least one symbol missing.

We stood there for a couple of minutes, staring into the Whisker Lickin's–framed grid, silently contemplating what Phil had just done to us. None of us moved or spoke as Mr. Hemsworth's blue minivan rumbled into the driveway.

"What're you kids doing?" he demanded, getting out of the van.

I thought it was odd that he'd yell at us for this, because the day before, when Charlotte and I were drawing it, he'd gotten out of the van and walked right by us with only a "Hi, girls." Maybe it was the presence of Toby that aroused suspicion. Toby's overgrown bangs and smudged T-shirts always seemed to put grown-ups on alert. And now he looked *really* bad, all cut up like he was in a gang or something.

"It's a chart," Charlotte began to explain, "for telling us what—"

"You've ripped up all this grass here. What were you kids thinking? You want to play hopscotch, you draw on the driveway. Charlotte, I know you've got some chalk because I bought it for you a couple of weeks ago. What did you do, lose it somewhere in your room?"

"It's not hopscotch."

Mr. Hemsworth clutched at his belt buckle and pulled his

pants half up his belly. He always did this when he didn't have any change in his pocket to jingle.

"Well, whatever it is, you know better than to tear up the lawn like that. And what are these little things? Candy?"

"I wouldn't have done it if it weren't for a good cause," Charlotte said nobly.

"Charlotte, I don't want to hear it."

"It's for Rose," she continued. "It's to help us find Rose."

Mr. Hemsworth's hand fell from his belt buckle to his side. His lip curled up as he squinted at Charlotte. He claimed he didn't want to hear it, but he couldn't help but wait for more.

"It's not candy, it's cat treats. We got Rose's cat and tried to send him running over it, and whichever boxes he stepped in were supposed to tell us about where she is."

Mr. Hemsworth stared at Charlotte, his mouth and nose twisting up like he'd just smelled something terrible. His gaze shifted to me and then to Toby.

"We weren't making a joke by putting this alien symbol in," Charlotte said, pointing. "We weren't making a joke of her. It's just that she was talking really serious about aliens and stuff, right before she disappeared."

Mr. Hemsworth breathed in and out noisily, like a cartoon bull about to charge. I thought he might ask us which boxes Phil had stepped in, but instead he turned away, without saying anything, and stomped into the garage. Just before he disappeared into the garage, I saw him put his hand on his head and clutch at his wiry, thinning hair.

"Shit!" he yelled.

There was a crash of shovels and rakes falling. Then a clanging I couldn't identify. Maybe a shovel against a wheelbarrow.

First I looked excitedly at Toby. I thought he'd feel vindicated by Mr. Hemsworth's "shit," which was far worse than Toby's "crap." But Toby didn't seem to notice. His head was tipped backward, and he was staring into the sky. I thought for a second he might be praying, but I couldn't figure out why.

"God*damn* it!" Mr. Hemsworth yelled.

I looked at Charlotte. Her face was puzzled but calm. She tapped her foot, as if waiting for the moment to pass.

Mr. Hemsworth finally emerged from the garage. His hair looked messy, his shirt had come half untucked, and he was holding a rake.

I couldn't figure out what he was going to do with the rake, and it didn't seem like he knew either. All the leaves had been raked a couple of weeks ago—I remembered because he let us jump in the piles a few times before he bagged them up. Now he stood and leaned on the rake for a moment, his shoulders sagging. Then he casually raked it once, lightly, over our Dogon grid. He seemed to change his mind, carried the rake over to the back of the yard and started raking out the few leftover leaves that were still tangled in the brown remains of his vegetable garden.

"Let's go inside," Charlotte suggested.

I nodded and followed her. Toby shuffled after us.

Charlotte opened the storm door to her house, kicking it as she entered so I could catch it. I did the same for Toby.

Charlotte called behind her, "Bye, Toby!"

Toby caught the door with his hand and closed it gently. Through the thin pane of glass, I watched him blow his bangs out of his face before he walked away.

* * *

That night, in bed, I still worried about what was missing from our Dogon grid. It wasn't a good sign that Phil had refused to step on any of Charlotte's optimistic symbols. It seemed to me that instead of the scarier symbols I'd thought of the day before, we could at least have added a bird. A bird flying away might be a nice way to put it.

I'd gotten the idea from one of Charlotte's black books—one of the ones we almost never talked about. It was called *Search for the Soul*. Charlotte had explained to me once that it was pretty boring and that it wasn't really about searching for souls. The whole thing was about what the soul *was*, which Charlotte thought was a stupid question. Everybody knew what a soul was. The whole book was about philosophers asking if a soul *thinks* and if a soul *feels* and if the universe has a soul and all kinds of weird questions that made the topic way more complicated than it really needed to be.

I'd had a feeling that Charlotte hadn't actually read the book, so I'd looked at it once to see for myself. I didn't get far, but I'd lingered on the page that said a soul was like a bird, flying away from the body. There was a cool picture of an Egyptian bird with a lady's head. It was supposed to symbolize the soul. But then, a couple of pages later, there was a drawing of shirtless Aztec men having their guts ripped out on an altar. The description next to it explained the belief that the sacrificed men's souls would turn into eagles that would guard the sun. I'd closed the book then and there. It's wasn't just all the blood in the picture that bothered me, but the fact that they didn't show the beautiful eagle souls that were supposed to result from the ritual.

A bird symbol would tell us if Rose had left us for "a better place," as I'd heard Charlotte's mom say of people who died. Maybe Rose was in heaven—if there was a heaven. I had trouble thinking of heaven as anything but the blue-sky-and-clouds place you saw on sitcoms when someone had a light-hearted brush with death. I couldn't imagine Rose in that sort of heaven. What would she do there? Float around all day? And was there sarcasm in heaven? I suspected not. But if not, who exactly would Rose *be* in heaven, and what would be the point of her being there? Would I meet up with her there eventually, when I died as an old lady? What would we talk about? Would she be polite to me because I was old, all sweet and fake the way I was with Mrs. Crowe? Would we have small talk together every couple of days, whenever we met up in heaven, *forever*?

It just didn't sound quite right. But the alternative—that Rose had simply come to an end, her body rotting somewhere, worms licking at her eyeballs—was definitely worse. Or was it? *Never again* was a dull kick in the stomach, but *forever* was a spinning nausea. Which would Rose rather have? Which would I rather have? Not that it really mattered which I preferred, because it wasn't up to me. But maybe I should at least hope for one or the other. Dead and gone. Wait—no. Forever. In heaven forever. Everyone I knew, every day. Until what? Why? Dizzy again. Dead and gone. Never again. Over and done with. But that was so awful and cold and cruel. For Rose and for me and for my mother and everyone.

I couldn't decide which was worse, and the back-and-forth between the two made me feel sick in my bed. I buried my face in my pillow and cried quietly and tried to think of something fun, like categorizing dog breeds or frosting a cake. I thought of waking my mother and telling her how scared I was, but seeing her awakened in the middle of the night, squinting and tired, would only remind me of how old she was. And she was not a person who could answer this question for me, so what was the point? No person could answer this question for me. The fact that my mother was older meant only that she had less time to think about it than I did. It made me feel sorry for her.

I fashioned yellow frosting flowers and green frosting leaves in my head until I fell into a hungry sleep.

Eleven

May 24, 2006

My mother had risen at the crack of dawn to buy me a Boston cream doughnut. When I got up and stumbled into the kitchen, it was perched on a flowered tea saucer on the dining table, along with a cheerful bowl of strawberries. My mother sat at the table reading the paper, her bran muffin untouched beside her on an identical saucer. I wondered how long she'd waited for me like this, sitting patiently by her muffin for her degenerate daughter to roll out of bed.

"Thank you," I said groggily, sitting at the table.

"You remember this?" my mother asked. "Boston cream doughnut and strawberries?"

"Yes," I replied. "This is great."

The night before she'd driven me to college, she'd asked me—casually, while we'd watched television—*What do you consider a perfect breakfast?* Her intention to provide it was obvious, since she never asked questions like that. On the following morning, the appearance of the items I'd mentioned was unsurprising but bizarre—like a last meal before the electric chair. I'd forced them down, smiling. Every couple of years, when we're together, my mother produces these two items together and asks me if I remember.

"Sleep well?"

"Not bad."

I bit into the doughnut. The familiar, comforting doughiness of the standard-issue Dunkin' doughnut. Dripping with an imitation vanilla custard I no longer had much of a taste for.

"Mmm," I said.

"Coffee?"

"Yes, but please. Don't get up. I'll get it."

"Don't be silly." My mother said, already up and pouring.

I put down the doughnut and watched the yellow cream begin to ooze onto its pretty plate.

"Do you remember about Rose's mother and the package of pecan sandies?" I asked, taking the mug from my mother's hands.

"Yes. You mean how she left them on the table for Rose, and Rose hadn't come home and opened them?"

"Yeah."

"That was very sad. Say what you want about Mrs. Banks, she loved her girls."

My mother wrinkled her eyebrows, studying me over her coffee cup, then continued. "You know, I'll always remember this one time—it must have been our first year in Waverly, because you were still little, and Rose must have been eleven or twelve then. I think it was the first time I saw her, actually. I was helping Mrs. Crowe with some of her flowers in the front.

I think it was Memorial Day. The Bankses came driving by. Mr. Banks was driving slow, distracted, I think, because Mrs. Banks was screaming at him. Just the most awful, shrill screaming. Rose and her sister were in the back. And I remember Rose hanging out the window with a badminton racket. Just twirling it around, whooshing it back and forth, looking happy as a clam. They didn't seem to notice that their daughter was hanging halfway out of the car. And she didn't seem to notice them screaming. She was always like that. Casual, I mean."

"You never really did like Rose," I said.

"Why would you say that?"

"I always begged you to have her baby-sit, but you were never into the idea."

"Well, for one, there was no need. I never went out at night. And Mrs. Crowe was always around, always willing to keep an eye on you for an hour here and there. But as I said, Rose was a little on the casual side. I didn't say I didn't like her. She just wasn't what I'd look for in a baby-sitter. Remember that time all of you kids went to Adams Pond and were skating on the ice? And Toby fell through?"

"It wasn't just Rose. Paul and Joe were there. Besides, Toby was fine. He only fell in up to his knees."

"But Rose was the oldest. Rose was about thirteen then. And she knew better." My mother hesitated. "She was the oldest *girl*, I mean."

"And yet you had her baby-sit me once."

"Yes. Well, she was older by then. And just that one time, because you kept begging. It was more like a treat for you than anything else. I don't think I really had a commitment that night. Just went out to give us both a little novelty. Even that one time, I felt a bit odd hiring her. To be honest, it didn't seem to me she much liked baby-sitting. She just seemed to me the sort of girl who'd invite her boyfriend over as soon as the parents left . . . that sort of thing."

"She never did that at the Hemsworths'," I said.

My mother nodded and put her hand at the back of her neck, feeling the bottom of her hairline absently. "Well, true . . ."

"True . . . but?" I prompted.

"Well, after that one time she sat for you, something . . . happened. Something that made me vow never to let her sit for you again. The thing is, she disappeared just a couple of weeks later, so it was never an issue."

"Something happened?"

My mother hesitated. "Well. At the hospital."

"Oh."

This was familiar. Occasionally, as a kid, when I'd mention this or that classmate or teacher, I'd see a passing shadow in my mother's eyes that told me she'd encountered that person at the hospital, that she knew something about him or her that I wasn't allowed to know. I almost never asked.

"What did you see?"

"Well, it's not really fair of me to talk about it. You know that."

"She's dead," I reminded her. "And you brought it up."

My mother shrugged, conceding. "Well. She ended up in the ER one night. She'd gotten so drunk at a party that a couple of the kids who were with her were afraid she'd drink herself to death."

"Oh," I said. "That's weird. I just don't remember her that way at all."

"What? Drunk?"

"Just . . . I don't know. I hate to say it. That kind of kid."

"Well, we can give her the benefit of the doubt if you'd like. Maybe she'd never drunk anything before and didn't know when to stop. Maybe one of the other kids kept feeding it to her. Or maybe her boyfriend. That pretty boyfriend of hers wasn't exactly Mr. Sensitive. She was lucky someone thought enough to bring her in."

"Who brought her in?"

"Paul, actually. Paul Hemsworth."

My mother noticed my surprise.

"I didn't say *he* was drunk," she said, maybe thinking that this information didn't jibe with Paul's squeaky-clean reputation. "It was smart of him to bring her. Conscientious. It was so soon after that other boy's accident—the one who was paralyzed. Maybe the kids were a little more on edge after that, a little more cautious."

I nodded. I remembered the accident she was talking about. Brian Pilkington was the brother of Sally Pilkington, a girl in my grade. He was around Paul's age—in his class or maybe the one below it, like Rose.

"Did anyone ever tell the police about her doing that?" I asked. "How close was it to when she disappeared?"

"A couple of weeks. Her parents picked her up. They knew about it. I'm assuming they told the police anything they could they thought would be useful. That night included."

"Oh."

"It was really terrible, the way those two things happened so close to each other. Rose and, before that, that poor boy—what was his name—Pilkerton?"

"Pilkington," I supplied. "Brian Pilkington."

"Two of the worst tragedies for Waverly, same year, same class. Well, maybe not the *worst*. But the most dramatic. One kid paralyzed, then another disappears. That's a lot for the sheltered little Waverly kids, all in the span of one or two months."

"I wonder if Brian Pilkington still lives around here," I said.

"I don't know. I think his parents do. I think I've heard that name mentioned."

"They still Jehovah's Witnesses?"

"Were they?" my mother asked.

"Yeah. I remember that his sister couldn't dress up on Halloween."

"Huh," my mom said with a shrug.

But I'd surprised myself, remembering that the Pilkingtons were Jehovah's Witnesses. I hadn't thought about the Pilkington family in years. When I was a kid, I'd known nothing about the religion, except that it involved knocking on doors and not getting Christmas presents. And I still didn't know much, but I knew that the common joke about their leaflets was that they always showed people petting lions or leopards and antelopes and people all frolicking together. What startled me was that it immediately brought to mind one of the *Looking Glass* writings—one of the two without a corresponding Rose dream to match it: *You are knocking on his door this time . . . / with fruit trees and sunshine / and pinafored children hugging smiling lions.*

"Were you there the day of his accident?" I asked my mother. "When they brought him in?"

"No," she said. "I'm glad I wasn't. The way Ruth Hemsworth

tells it, it was terrible. He was unconscious for quite a while, his mother was screaming when she first came in—"

"Right," I said, not wanting to hear any more.

I wondered if Mrs. Hemsworth talked about it a lot at the time. It seemed to me Charlotte had brought it up frequently, in that morbidly curious way she had—at least until Rose disappeared.

"Nora? You all right?" my mother asked.

I was trying to go over all those old *Looking Glass* passages in my head. I couldn't remember them word for word. I hesitated just long enough for my mother to repeat the question.

"Yeah," I assured her. "No worries."

After we said our good-byes and my mother left for her shift, I decided to drive back to Waverly and head to the library again. One thing my mother had said stuck out: *So soon after that other boy's accident—the one who was paralyzed.*

I wanted to reread the *Looking Glass* passages and look up Brian Pilkington's accident, if possible. I'd forgotten that the accident was so close to Rose's disappearance. I'd forgotten about it completely once she disappeared.

I went to the *Looking Glass* binders first and turned to the poem I'd thought of while talking to my mother:

> *You are knocking on his door this time—*
> *a perfect cabin on a lush green hill*
> *with fruit trees and sunshine*
> *and pinafored children hugging smiling lions.*
> *When he opens the cabin door,*
> *his face is warm and his eyes forgiving,*

and he touches you softly on the face.
But then his hand moves up your chin and into your
  mouth
and pulls out one of your eyeteeth.
He holds it up for you to see, and you say,
"You can keep it. You can have as many as you want."
He pulls out a front tooth, too,
and drops both teeth on his welcome mat
as if to say
You can keep your stinking teeth,
and slams his bright red door in your face.

I wasn't sure what to make of this one. Rereading it, I felt that the connection to Brian Pilkington was more tenuous than it had been in my memory. Still, I tucked the whole *Looking Glass* binder under my arm and asked the Cone Lady about old issues of the *Valley Voice*.

It didn't take long to find something on Brian's accident. I knew it had been at least a few weeks before Rose's disappearance but sometime that school year, which put it in September or October.

I found it in the issue for September 21, 1990:

WAVERLY TEEN IN CRITICAL CONDITION
AFTER ROUTE 5 CRASH

Brian Pilkington, 16, was traveling east on Route 5 when he swerved to the right and drove off the road. His Datsun sedan crashed into the ravine and struck a tree. Police believe he was traveling at a very high

speed and may have swerved to avoid a deer or a dog.
His condition is listed as critical.

The word "Datsun" made me dizzy. I flipped back in the
Looking Glass till I found this one:

> *You are running through a sunlit field.*
> *A red Datsun is chasing you,*
> *revving its engine, plowing through*
> *grass and wildflowers.*
> *You're breathless and sweaty*
> *as you reach the end of the field,*
> *where a round stone entranceway guards a thick wood.* . . .

Now, could *both* connections be coincidental? Probably not.
I reread all the other *Looking Glass* poems, searching for some
subtle mention of Brian or his accident. I couldn't find anything that stuck out, but my knowledge of both was limited—it
was possible that more references were there and I just wasn't
seeing them.

The connection to the *Looking Glass* and Rose's dreams was
too close to be coincidental. It seemed someone had taken their
basic content and then inserted some embellishments—and, in
at least a couple, embellishments that had to do with Brian
Pilkington and his accident. But who would be thinking and
writing about the accident in 1996—six years after it had happened? Maybe for Charlotte the weight of both tragedies was
jumbled up in some confused adolescent memory. Despite her
denial and her eagerness to blame the passages on me, Charlotte still seemed the likeliest writer. Who else could it be?

Just as I asked myself the question, though, another possibility popped into my head: Sally Pilkington, Brian's sister. Why hadn't I thought of her before? Of course she would still be interested in her brother's accident several years later. It had left him paralyzed from the waist down. (I remembered Charlotte constantly using the word "paraplegic," until I finally had to give in and look it up.) Sally was smart enough to be in honors classes with Charlotte—but for many subjects she was in regular old college-prep classes with me. Maybe she'd been after the easy A's—I was never sure. But I could visualize her clearly even now. She'd always looked the same throughout our school years together: curly brown hair, shoulder-length and frizzy, pulled into a half ponytail at the back of her head. Her face had reminded me of a queen on a playing card—heart-shaped, always serene, with a tiny mouth that was usually pinched into a calmly unreadable expression. She rarely smiled, but when she did, there was a cute, childish-looking gap between her two front teeth.

I checked the editorial box of the *Looking Glass*. Her name wasn't there. No matter. She might have submitted anonymously. But then, she wouldn't have known about Rose's dreams. She didn't even know Rose, as far as I was aware. On the other hand, the one with the smiling lions and the teeth wasn't connected to any of Rose's dreams. Maybe she'd written just that one? That didn't explain its resemblance to the others, or the appearance of a Datsun in one of those others, but it was still possible.

Did the Pilkington kids still live around here? I knew that Brian had eventually gone to college—Sally must have mentioned it. Sally was my lab partner in chemistry class during junior year in high school. We weren't friends, but we were cordial, and I'd probably never have passed the class without her. I did all the grunt work for the labs, and she made all the hypotheses and drew all the conclusions. Normally I'd been okay in science classes, but my brain had been particularly clogged with other shit that year. Thinking back, I realized she'd been very patient with me—probably more than I deserved. She told me before graduation she was looking for a job—not going to college—but I didn't feel I knew her well enough to ask her why or press her on the issue. We'd kindly signed each other's relatively naked yearbooks. Maybe it wasn't such a crazy idea simply to contact her and ask her.

After printing a copy of the article, I parked myself in front of one of the library's Internet-access computers. Cone Lady glanced at me as I did so. I suspected that no one had gotten this much mileage out of the Waverly Public Library's myriad resources in quite a while.

I tried "Sally Pilkington" and "Connecticut" on the online white pages. One came up for Fairville, one for Wilton. Then I Googled her. There was a Sally Pilkington-Moore who was a veterinary technician in Fairville. The vet clinic's Web site didn't have pictures. I tried Sally Pilkington-Moore on Facebook, and there was a profile picture of a brunette woman and a baby. Same delicate little face, smiling with that telltale gap between her front teeth. The baby was smiling, too—one of those wildly happy half-moon baby smiles. Nice picture. Stalking really was so easy these days, I marveled.

I hit "Send Sally a message" and typed a message saying hi, that I was back in Waverly after many years, visiting Charlotte Hemsworth. After some hesitation I typed in that Charlotte and I were having a friendly disagreement about something—something we were trying to remember from high school, and I thought she might be the one to settle it for us. Maybe we could have coffee or something.

When I was done, I read it and reread it. It had that fake bubbly tone one uses on Facebook. Sally had been one of the least bubbly people I'd encountered in high school. If she was still anything like I remembered—and granted, what I remembered was pretty superficial—she'd probably hate it. I fiddled with the sentences for a few minutes, then saw that my allotted twenty minutes on the computer were almost up. I poised the mouse over "send." Go for it? Or reconsider and redraft at Charlotte's? Or not send anything at all? Probably the best choice. A message popped up on the computer saying I had two minutes left. I could renew my session or let it expire. I took a breath and hit "send."

"Shit," I whispered a second after I'd done it. What an idiotic message. Just what the now-mature and matronly Sally Pilkington-Moore needed. Then I read over the *Looking Glass* poems again. After my second reading, it seemed highly unlikely that Sally had written them. The references to a Jehovah's Witness were mocking and superficial, the connection to her brother's accident extremely vague. Sally was a thoughtful person who probably would've written very sensitively about her brother's difficulties—who probably, now that I thought about it some more, wouldn't have written about such things at all. I'd mentioned to Charlotte that I was not, in high school, someone who "put myself out there." Well, Sally wasn't either. Sally had seemed middle-aged by the time we were all thirteen. What had I been thinking?

At least I'd been vague. If she wrote back, I could perhaps dream up some other disagreement Charlotte and I supposedly thought she could settle. Chances are she'd just blow off the message. Batshit old Nora Reed. How embarrassing. Why hadn't I fled Connecticut last night, after the 7-Eleven? What was I still doing here, picking at some crusty old high-school scab? What was it about this stupid old school literary magazine that kept nagging at me, kept pulling me back in?

Mind Over Matter:
November 1990

The police never talked to me directly. There was no reenactment with dolls, no *Nora, do you know the difference between the truth and a lie?* like I'd seen in the court scenes of some of my mother's TV movies. Just my mother and me on Mrs. Crowe's doorstep, explaining that Rose had walked me home as she always did, with nothing out of the ordinary. My mother doing most of the talking and me nodding in agreement.

By then it was common knowledge around Waverly that Rose's parents were convinced she'd never actually arrived home the day of her disappearance. The details were in the papers. When her parents had come home from the restaurant that evening, her jacket and school bag weren't there. And the package of pecan sandies her mother had left for her on the table was unopened—and therefore undiscovered, her mother was certain.

In any case, an unopened package of cookies was not enough to convince the chief investigator that he shouldn't rule out the possibility that she'd run away or that he needed to frighten an eleven-year-old with intense interrogation.

Charlotte believed that I hadn't seen anything unusual, but she also thought the police were making a big mistake.

"Maybe you don't *remember* seeing anything weird," she said to me on the afternoon bus, on the ninth day of Rose's absence. "But that doesn't mean you didn't *see* anything weird."

The black books were making an appearance again, taking on an unexpected second life—but half of them were brown books now. Charlotte had already been told twice this week to put her book away in class, and she'd begun covering the volumes with grocery-store bags to make them blend in with her covered textbooks.

"I know it's not a totally accepted idea—hypnotizing witnesses for information. But you'd think in a big case like this the police would want to use every resource they have. Right?"

I nodded, even though I wasn't sure what resources had to do with it. Resources were what we talked about in social studies, along with capital cities and national languages: lead, gold, maize, sugarcane.

Toby leaned in from the seat behind us. I hadn't known he'd been sitting there.

"The police came to your guys' houses, too?" he asked.

"Yes," Charlotte said. "*Obviously.* They went to everybody's house. They'd be stupid not to."

"Do you think she ran away?"

I glanced at Charlotte, curious how she'd reply.

"Well, I was hoping Phil would help us answer that, but that didn't exactly work out, remember?"

"Awww—" Toby groaned, leaning in closer to us apologetically.

"DON'T STAND UP IN YOUR SEATS!" the bus driver screamed at him. She was a thin, shrill blonde with a talent for making the bus rules seem terrifyingly dire.

Toby flopped back down in his seat behind us.

"Now, I found this little section, and I think it's perfect for us," Charlotte continued. "It gives directions on how to put someone under. Just real simple hypnosis techniques."

"Do you have a pendulum?"

"I'm sure we could find something like a pendulum. Something on a chain. But for a lot of these techniques you don't even need one. The pendulum is kind of an old-fashioned way of putting someone under, you know."

She didn't have to say that the plan was to put *me* under— not her. That was obvious. But to be "put under" sounded scary. Like drowning. And I wasn't confident that this two-page glossy spread—with a small sidebar titled "Do-It-Yourself Hypnosis"—would give Charlotte sufficient expertise to pull me back up once I'd gone under.

"What if I never wake up?"

"Of course you'll wake up. It's not like you're going to be in a coma. It's very simple bringing someone out. Even more so than putting them in."

Toby was now poking just his face over the seat, his chin on his hand.

"You're gonna hypnotize Nora?"

"Yes," Charlotte said, even though I didn't think I'd agreed to it yet.

"Can I watch?"

"No. It's not a show. We're doing it for information."

"What information?" Toby asked, looking skeptical.

"What she remembers about when she last saw Rose."

"Oh. Well, do you have a pendant?"

Charlotte sighed and rolled her eyes. "We don't really *need* a pendant."

Toby considered this, scratching his nose vigorously, squishing it around with his palm. "Would you hypnotize me, too?"

Charlotte bit her lip. "No. *You* can't be hypnotized."

"Why not?"

"You just can't."

It was Toby's turn to roll his eyes.

"Never mind," he said, leaning back in his seat, glaring angrily out the window. "You're so full of it, Charlotte."

When we were left off at the Fox Hill stop, Toby raced on ahead of us as he usually did. He was always running for no apparent reason.

"Have fun, Nora!" he called back. "Don't let her fry your brain!"

"Why can't Toby be hypnotized?" I asked.

Charlotte glanced up ahead before answering, checking Toby's distance from us.

"I didn't want to say it in front of him," she whispered. "But to be hypnotized, you need to have at least average intelligence."

"Oh. I see."

"You're feeling very . . . relaxed. You're feeling very . . . relaxed."

Charlotte's repetition failed to convince me. I struggled to keep the corners of my mouth down.

"Waves of relaxation are coming over . . ." Charlotte took a deep breath. " . . . your body."

Something about the word "body." A giggle escaped my lips.
I didn't open my eyes, because I didn't want to see Charlotte's
stern look of disapproval.

"Very . . . relaxed," Charlotte repeated.

"Say something besides that," I told her, doing my best to
sound sleepy.

"Why?"

"That's actually not very relaxing," I answered, which was
my nice way of saying she sounded stupid.

"You're feeling a little . . . drowsy. Just a little on the sleepy
side. You feel waves of sleepiness coming over you. Waves of
. . . relaxation."

Charlotte seemed to think she'd hit on something good.
"Waves of sleepiness, waves of relaxation. Waves of sleepiness.
Waves of relaxation."

She kept alternating these phrases. My annoyance at her
started to fade into boredom.

Finally she said softly, "Now, what I want you to do, Nora, is
to start counting backward."

I waited for further direction, but none came. "Backward
from what?"

"Ten."

I did as instructed. Charlotte seemed surprised that I finished the task so quickly.

"Um, okay," she said. "Now, slowly, from thirty."

When that was over, she whispered. "Now, Nora. Now that
you're fully relaxed, I want you to take me back to that day. To
that Tuesday. The last day Rose walked you home."

"Okay," I whispered.

"So you're leaving my house. What do you see?"

"I see your yard. I see Rose."

"What's she wearing?"

"Jeans. That jacket around her waist. Purple sweatshirt."

"It was cold, wasn't it? Why wouldn't she have the jacket on?"

"I don't know."

I could hear Charlotte scribbling something on her pad of paper.

"So you're walking away from my house, up Fox Hill. Are you on the sidewalk?"

"Yes."

"Are you talking to each other?"

"Yeah."

"What are you talking about, Nora?"

"Nintendo."

"What about it?"

I could feel myself blushing. "We don't like it."

"Neither of you?"

"No. Rose thinks the music is really annoying."

Charlotte paused, but I didn't hear any scribbling.

"What else are you talking about?"

"Aliens and Druids."

Charlotte sighed deeply—suspecting, perhaps, that I wasn't taking this seriously.

"Rose believes in aliens," I continued without prompting.

"Does Rose believe she's ever seen one?" Charlotte asked, recovering quickly.

"No. I don't think so. But she believes they're real, I think."

More scratching of Charlotte's pencil on her notepad.

"About how long does it take to get to your house?"

"I don't know. A few minutes. We weren't rushing, but we weren't walking real slow either. Just regular speed."

"And while you're walking—think hard about this, Nora—do you see any cars go by?"

"Umm . . . probably one or two. It was garbage day."

"You're not supposed to guess. Just tell me what you remember. Did you see cars or not?"

"Umm. Two went up the hill," I said.

It seemed at least two probably had. Pickup trucks, probably. Townies with pickup trucks who knew the back way to the transfer station.

"Anything suspicious?" Charlotte asked.

"What do you mean?"

"Was either of them, like, a black van with a teardrop window?"

"No."

"Either of them have tinted windows?"

"I don't think so."

"What color were the cars?"

"I don't know. I was looking at Rose most of the time, since we were talking."

"Was there anyone else walking around while you guys were on the sidewalk?"

"No. Definitely not."

"Do you think maybe you were so busy talking to Rose that you might not have seen someone if they were nearby?"

"No," I said. "There was nobody."

"So you guys get to your house . . ."

"Yeah."

"And does she say anything?"

"Well, she says a lot of things. And then she says good-bye."

"Like, what does she say?"

"Just asked me about Druids. I don't remember exactly."

More scribbling. As Charlotte wrote, I realized I'd never asked Rose why she liked aliens best of all of the black-book topics. I wished I hadn't been so caught up in defending my Druids that I'd forgotten to ask.

"Anything else you can remember that she said?"

"Umm, yeah. That when we go to the Bermuda Triangle, you and I, we should bring a good boat. And she's not coming with us."

I could hear Charlotte flipping to a new page on her notepad. "Why not?"

"Because . . . I don't know, because it's unrealistic, I guess."

Charlotte hesitated. "Okay, so you guys finish talking. And you mentioned she said good-bye. Does she seem sad or serious, like it's a real good-bye? Like, forever?"

The question startled me. Thinking back, now, it seemed like maybe it had been that kind of good-bye. But probably I was remembering it wrong. Probably I was just remembering being sad myself—which I still couldn't explain.

"No," I said slowly. "Not exactly."

"And do you say good-bye back?"

"I don't remember." That was the truth. It was terrible to think now that maybe I hadn't.

"And do you go right inside?"

"No."

"Why not? It was cold outside."

I paused. The truth was that I did this often—hung around wasting time outside to shorten the amount of time I'd have to be alone with Mrs. Crowe before my mother got home. It wasn't that I didn't like her. There just wasn't enough to talk about with her. In warmer months I walked down to the bus stop and killed time looking for four-leaf clovers in the big clover patches along the sidewalk. But this wasn't something I would mention to Charlotte.

"I do that sometimes. . . . I just felt like being outside for a little bit. I was collecting a few leaves."

"And you watched Rose walk up the hill."

"Not *all* the way up, of course. I can't see that far. But the first couple of steps away from my house, yes."

"And how long were you in the yard?"

"It felt like a while. Till it was pretty much dark."

"Okay. That's interesting. I didn't know that. Do the police know that?"

When they'd talked to my mother, the police had only been interested in Rose. Not what I'd done after Rose had left me.

"No," I said.

Charlotte sucked in a breath. "Did you hear *anything* coming from farther up the hill? *Anything*?"

"Like what?"

"Like . . . um, a struggle. Or like . . ." Charlotte's voice lowered to a whisper. "Like screaming. Like Rose screaming."

No, I hadn't heard any screaming. As the sky had grown dark, the only noise was from a car or maybe two buzzing up the hill. But the mention of screaming—combined with the memory of talking Druids with Rose—reminded me of something Charlotte had told me once about the Druids. When they captured people in wars, they'd imprison them in hanging baskets that they would set on fire. And then they'd use the shape of the smoke and the sound of the screams as a way to tell the future.

I sat up just slightly, disturbed to remember this information. When Charlotte had first mentioned it months before, it hadn't sounded like much. But now it did. Now that the last thing I'd told Rose was that I'd believed in Druids. If I believed in Druids, I had to believe in everything about them, not only their beautiful, mysterious stones.

"Did you just remember something?" Charlotte demanded. "Did you remember her screaming?"

The cruelty of it was as real as Stonehenge still was. Maybe more. I could feel it. So what was to stop a person from doing such a thing to Rose, or to any of us? And why did Charlotte have to keep mentioning screaming?

"No." I sank back into the pillows. "It was pretty quiet. I picked up a few leaves I liked, and I went inside."

"Are you absolutely positive you didn't hear anything out of the ordinary?"

"Yeah," I said.

But that night, while I was watching TV with my mother, I started to doubt my answer. We were watching *Who's the Boss?* and *Growing Pains*, a lineup that could usually bring me out of any sad funk, despite my mother's clucks at the shows' stupidity. But I just couldn't shake the feeling that I should've heard something. That maybe Rose had screamed and I hadn't heard it. It felt to me like I was always missing things I should have heard.

Just a couple of weeks ago at school, Mrs. Early had told

the whole class we weren't to ask her for a lav pass during the half hour before lunch anymore, and I'd gone up to her a few minutes later and asked her for one. When she freaked and the whole class groaned, I suddenly remembered that she *had* been saying something to the class, scolding us about something, but I'd tuned it out.

Lately I noticed how little I actually listened to people. That's the thing about being the quiet girl. Everyone's talking around you, and eventually, people stop expecting you to participate. So you stop listening, because it has nothing to do with you. It's all other people's noise, other people's business. Sometimes your own quiet starts to drown out everything else. And you get lazy.

You always hear about how crazy people "hear things." But no one ever talked about "not hearing things," which was much closer to my problem. And it worried me sometimes. Now maybe it had kept me from hearing Rose. Maybe Rose had been screaming and I just wasn't listening.

Twelve

May 24, 2006

I resisted checking my e-mail for about a half hour, chopping up vegetables and chicken for the evening's curry. When I stopped and checked it on Charlotte's basement computer, though, Sally had already written back. Sounded like fun, she said. Actually, she was feeling kind of claustrophobic this week with her seven-month-old Max, and it would be nice to have an excuse to get out for coffee. There was a shop called Caffeine's on Bridge Street in Fairville—did I know it? Was that close enough for me? Would Charlotte be joining us?

I don't know why I was so surprised at first. While Sally and I weren't friends, we hadn't anything against each other. And we were both outcasts of the innocuous, invisible type. Did that mean we were more connected than I'd realized? Or was Sally just bored out of her mind?

I wrote back that Caffeine's would be fine and asked for a

time, saying I was free almost anytime before three o'clock to-morrow.

I didn't mention Sally over our curry. Charlotte and I talked mostly about the upcoming weekend. Her mother had called and seemed dismayed that she might be missing me. She'd probably be home by late afternoon Saturday and wanted to know if I'd still be around. Maybe Paul and his kids could come over. Maybe we could have a little cookout. Would I be willing to stay that long? she'd wanted to know. I told Charlotte I'd call Neil and see if that would interfere with any of his plans. I doubted it would. And I was sticking around for at least an extra day to check out the Sally Pilkington situation—what would one or two more be after that?

Charlotte remained at the table after I'd started to clear the dinner dishes.

"There's something I think you should know," she said care-fully. "Something happened yesterday. I didn't find out till after you left. Paul was trying to call while we were out."

"What's that?"

"They questioned my dad a second time. Paul was pretty rattled. We were on the phone for a couple of hours."

"They questioned your dad about . . . Rose?"

"Yeah," Charlotte said, handing her plate to me. "You know, with us always flipping out over you being the last one to see her, I think we often forgot that he was the last *adult* to see her alive. . . . I suppose the police put more stock in that than we did."

"Makes sense," I said, rinsing her dish. "They're really cover-ing all their old bases, I think. With everything that happened yesterday, I forgot to tell you—they called me in to chat with them, too."

Charlotte's eyes widened. "What? *When?*"

"Yesterday."

"What'd they want to know?"

"Just had me go over my spiel about that day. Rose walked me home. Dropped me off. Kept walking. Didn't see anything suspicious."

"That's all?" Charlotte got up, grabbed her purse off the counter, and sat back down in her kitchen chair.

"Yeah. Pretty much."

"How'd they know you were here?" She was pawing through her purse, extracting crumpled tissues, gum wrappers, and several red pens. "Why didn't you tell me?"

"They called me on my cell. They got my number from my voice mail at home. And I told them I was here in Waverly."

I decided to skip the second question. I hadn't told her because she'd already been driving me crazy yesterday. And because I hadn't been sure what she and her cub-reporter boyfriend were up to.

Charlotte pulled a squashed cigarette pack out of her purse and pressed it between her palms, staring at me. I thought she was going to ask me again why I hadn't told her. She didn't.

"The weird thing isn't that they were asking him questions," Charlotte said slowly, drawing out a cigarette. "It's that he wouldn't answer them."

I stopped loading the dishwasher.

"Apparently it started out cordial," she said, thumbing her lighter several times before it sparked. "But there was a point when he stopped. Refused to keep talking to them. Refused until he could talk to a lawyer. That's what upset Paul."

I watched her puffing away for a moment, trying to determine if she was upset herself. It was hard to tell—she wouldn't look at me.

"So it upset Paul . . ." I said. "But how about you?"

Charlotte shook her head. "The thing about Paul is, he's naïve. In a tough situation, my dad has been known, on occasion, to take the hard-ass position. The problem with Paul is that he keeps allowing himself to be surprised by it."

"The hard-ass position? What does that mean?"

She shrugged and blew a slow, elegant stream of smoke over the kitchen table. "Like, being an ass to a cashier who accidentally gives him the wrong change. Or when he has a fender bender, he always gets out of the car screaming. Never apologizing. Never, never apologizing. That sort of thing."

"I see," I said quietly.

"I just thought you should know. So you didn't end up hearing it from someone else."

"It's been a while," I said, "since I've been part of the Waverly grapevine."

"Well. Still."

I hovered over the dishwasher idiotically, wondering what I should say next. It seemed I should ask if she wanted to talk more about her dad, but to ask would imply that there *was* something to talk about. And she seemed to be trying her best to convey that nothing was amiss—only that poor old dainty-hearted Paul had felt that way.

"I wanted to tell you last night," she said, before I had a

chance to decide, "that I'm sorry about the whole *Looking Glass* thing. I don't know if that's why you took off last night. Or if it was because I made you guys go take a look at Aaron."

I wondered if this whole business about Aaron had just been a way for Charlotte to assure herself that the police interest in her father wasn't worrisome.

"Oh, don't worry about it . . ." I said, struggling to sound reassuring.

I wasn't sure I wanted to get into it with her again—about Aaron or the *Looking Glass*. How many more rounds of "You wrote them / No I didn't" did we really need to go through? And what good would it do?

"I'm sorry if I upset you," she said. "It was insensitive how I brought up the *Looking Glass*. I never should have. Or at least once it was clear you didn't want to talk about it . . ."

"I was just thinking today," I said. "I was thinking about how sure you were that I'd written them. And I was thinking about how weird that was, considering how close some of them are to what Rose wrote. So close it's almost as if someone was looking at one while writing the other. And that makes it especially weird that you think it was me. Because you were the one who had access to those little dream notes she'd written when we were kids, not me. Seems a little odd that you think I'd remember that stuff so clearly five years later, in high school, and not consider that *you* were the editor of the magazine and *you* were the one who had Rose's dreams written down and filed away in a box."

Charlotte sighed and drew on her cigarette again. "I brought them up because I wanted to tell you that when I first read them, I felt that way, too. Even then."

"Felt what way?"

"That I'd never forgotten her. That even though we were just kids when she disappeared, I felt we owed her something more. That we weren't ever supposed to give up on her. I couldn't put her out of my mind either. I was glad to see that the feeling was mutual."

I hesitated. Yes, the feeling was mutual. But I'd never written about it.

"Charlotte," I said slowly, "I'm only going to say this once more. And if you can't take it seriously, we're never, ever going to mention it again."

I waited until Charlotte was looking me straight in the eye.

"I didn't write them."

She continued to smoke for a moment. "Okay," she said gently.

"'Okay' meaning you really believe me?"

Charlotte hesitated again. "Yes."

"Did you write them?"

Charlotte stubbed out her cigarette. "No."

"Well, then who did?" I asked.

"I wouldn't have a clue," she said, folding her arms. "Since I always thought it was you. Who do *you* think?"

"Well, I don't know," I admitted. "But I have some thoughts on the matter. Hold on a sec."

I ran to the bedroom and brought back my purse. I showed her the *Looking Glass* excerpts that seemed to be about Brian Pilkington, along with the article about his accident.

"You looked this up today?" she asked after reading the article.

I nodded and decided to leave out the exchange with Sally for the time being. I felt shady enough just admitting I'd looked up Brian's accident.

"Remember his accident and her disappearing were around the same time?" I asked.

"You don't think maybe Sally—"

I struggled to think of the right reply, but Charlotte didn't wait for one.

"Hey," she said. "You know how the rumor was that Rose was seeing someone else and that it pissed off Aaron? Maybe it was Brian. You think? And remember how you said you thought she wasn't herself after the new school year started? Maybe it was because of the accident. Maybe she was upset about what had happened to him. And maybe somehow *Sally* . . ."

I shrugged, unsure if I should add anything.

Charlotte shook her head. "But Sally wouldn't know. . . . Yeah, kind of a long shot." She screwed up her face, thinking.

"Listen," I said, "you want to talk about it on a walk? I just realized, I've been here a few days and haven't even walked around the block yet. Haven't even cruised past my old house."

Charlotte gazed at the article and the *Looking Glass* poems for a moment before answering.

"Oh," she said apologetically. "Jeez. You know, I have a ton of correcting. Maybe you ought to go ahead."

The Psychics:
December 1990

Charlotte wouldn't just let me eat my Oreos for once. She could have Oreos almost whenever she wanted. She didn't understand that for me they were more than a snack. They were an event—an event that didn't need to be combined with conversation.

"There's something I'm sure they haven't tried," she said.

"Huh?" I said, even though I knew she was talking about the police again. The police and Rose and how badly they were screwing everything up. Even with a mouth half full of Oreos, Charlotte couldn't shut up about Rose.

"Psychometry," she said carefully.

I dragged my front teeth into the white cream round, splitting it into two perfect half circles. I knew I didn't need to bother to ask Charlotte what psychometry was. She was going to tell me whether I asked or not.

"You use an *object,*" she continued. "You read the history of an object. Like, something someone used to wear. Or, like, a key or a glove or something."

"Mm-hmm," I said, scraping one of the half circles clean with my teeth. I wondered if anyone had ever used Oreos for a phases-of-the-moon project at school. They were perfect: cream white against a dark round sky.

"I haven't told anyone about this," Charlotte whispered, reaching under her pillow.

My heart flip-flopped as she slid her hand out from under her lilac pillowcase, and I felt oddly relieved when she produced a curved pink plastic object. I'd pictured—for a moment—something more along the lines of a sheep's heart filled with nails.

"It's Rose's banana clip," she announced.

"How'd you get that?"

"She left it in our bathroom."

"When?" I demanded.

"About a week before she vanished. I found it by the sink."

I didn't like how Charlotte seemed to enjoy saying "vanished," like we were in a movie or something.

"Why didn't you give it back?" I asked.

She looked exasperated. "We're lucky to have this."

"We're going to read the banana clip, you're saying?"

"Well, I've been trying to read it already. It's been under my pillow for a few days."

"And has it told you anything?"

"I don't think so. I've had only one dream I could remember, and it was about my overdue library books."

"Oh."

Charlotte pushed the clip across the bed toward me. "I don't think it's going to tell me anything. But you might have better luck."

I tried to enjoy my last bite of Oreo before replying. "You want me to sleep on this thing?"

"Well, actually, we should start with you just trying to read it while you're conscious."

I stared at the banana clip. I didn't like banana clips. They made you look like you had a Mohawk. And I couldn't remember Rose ever wearing one.

"How does it work?"

"I think you get messages from the object by touching it. So you start, I think, just by holding it. Maybe close your eyes, too."

I gazed into the bubble-gum pink teeth of the clip. I tried to imagine Rose's streaky, dirty-blond hair threaded into them. It was the thought of Rose's hair that made me toss the banana clip aside.

"This is stupid," I said.

"No it's not."

"Yes it is. Rose lost this clip before she disappeared. It was in your bathroom before she was even missing, right? It doesn't know anything about what happened to Rose."

"The *clip* doesn't know anything," Charlotte explained, her voice rising. "Nobody said the clip knows something. It doesn't have *thoughts*. The idea is that it was hers, so by reading it, touching it, we can pick up on what's happening with her."

I looked at the clip skeptically. "How come I don't remember her ever wearing a clip like that?"

Charlotte shrugged. "You're not here every time she's here. Like my parents' anniversary."

I looked away from the clip. I hated the Pepto pink of it—it was giving me a stomachache. And I couldn't help but think Charlotte was putting me on, trying to get me to pretend to extract insights from some stupid banana clip she'd maybe dug out of her own jewelry box. So she could expose me for the fraud I was and then laugh.

"I don't think it's hers," I insisted.

"Well, I *know* it's hers. And I think we should try everything we can to find her. Even if it seems stupid."

So I was the bad one. The one who didn't really care about Rose, when I should care the most. Since it was me who had lost her.

I finally gave in and humored Charlotte again. I sat Indian style on the carpet and let her lay the clip gently into my palms. I fingered it for about fifteen minutes, telling her I was picturing Rose looking in a mirror, doing her hair, examining her work from behind with a compact mirror, frowning, putting the mirror down, taking her hair out of the clip, doing it all over again.

"There's someone she really wanted to look pretty for," Charlotte whispered. "Not Aaron, I bet. Someone else. 'Cuz she was looking for a new boyfriend, right? Who was it?"

It had seemed to me Charlotte had wished, before Rose had disappeared, that it was Paul. She never mentioned that anymore.

"Lie down on my bed for a minute," she said, irritated by my silence. "Maybe it will help you relax and concentrate."

She gently balanced the clip over my forehead, then grabbed her notebook from her nightstand.

"Who did she want to look pretty for?" Charlotte demanded.

"I don't know."

"Now, really concentrate. What else are you seeing?"

"Nothing else," I said after a few moments of silence.

"Are you *sure*?"

I pulled the clip off my head and sat up. "Nothing else," I said, and practically threw the clip at Charlotte.

I didn't want to think about Rose's hair anymore. Because when I thought of Rose's hair, I remembered it with a man's hand on it. The hand was Charlotte's dad's. They were sitting together in the garage. His hand had been patting her shoulder just before he'd stood up, and it had gotten tangled, just for a moment, in the dirty-blond ends as it came down from her shoulder. It had been tangled just for a second, before pulling away and disappearing into a pocket to jingle coins. For such a short second, it would've been easy not to see it or remember it.

"I don't want to do this anymore," I declared, getting off the bed.

Charlotte tapped her pen against her lips and scrutinized me like I was a lab rat.

"Okay," she said quietly.

Thirteen

May 24, 2006

I had about a half hour before dark. As I stood at the end of the Hemsworths' driveway, I considered my two possible routes. I could go down Fox Hill, where the road met Main Street, where you could cross over to Adams Road. That road would take me by the old junior-high tennis court, where I'd spent much time as a teenager. Somehow, around age fourteen or fifteen, I'd decided I was fat and needed to start running. I was too embarrassed to jog around the neighborhood, so I would walk down there and then run slow, endless laps around the abandoned courts. Sometime in the 1970s, someone had gotten the brilliant idea that the junior high needed a tennis court. But there wasn't enough room for one right by the old school building. It was built a ten-minute walk from the school, and the result was that no one ever played on it or kept it up. The clay was badly cracked, as if an unlikely earthquake had hit Connecticut. Weeds crept up the cyclone fence. It felt like the end of the world. Its desolation had always made me feel strangely safe—no one would bother me there.

Past the tennis courts, a path went along the back of Mc-Mullen Orchards and then out to Adams Pond. It was a little far, but we hung out there sometimes when we were kids—when we were bored enough to walk all that way. We'd never swum in it—it was too muddy and frog-ridden and gross—but all of us neighborhood kids had gone there to ice-skate a couple of times, against our parents' advice. I remembered the first time, when Charlotte and Toby and I were about eight. Rose ventured out first, imitating an overly theatrical figure skater, making her twirls and hand gestures look deliberately idiotic. And then Paul, not to be outdone by a girl, skated out after her, sliding gingerly on his big blue Adidas. He circled Rose, laughing as she hammed it up. Toby's older brother, Joe, slid out past them, moonwalking nearly to the middle of the pond, making the three of us little kids—Charlotte, Toby, and me—crack up as we stood and watched from the edge. Only Toby eventually joined the older kids on the ice.

The orchard–to–tennis court route was an altogether more pleasant walk than the one up Fox Hill, past all the familiar houses. But I didn't wish to get any closer to the place where Rose's body had been found. Charlotte had told me that part of the pond area was still cordoned off, last she checked.

I headed up Fox Hill instead. I passed Mrs. Shepherd's—a charming light yellow Cape with about a million bearded irises—then a couple of houses owned by people whose names I'd never known. Then I reached Mrs. Crowe's.

It was greener but smaller than I remembered it, and it needed a paint job. I squinted upward at the two windows of the room that had once been my bedroom. The glass looked cloudy, as if it hadn't been washed in a great while. Still the same old heavy, drafty windows, with the rusted locks that always opened and closed with a tiny metal scream. I'd spent years behind those windows. Now it all seemed a blur of math homework, imaginary boyfriends, sad songs played over and over on an ancient pink plastic boom box. I kept walking. How strange it felt to walk right past this boxy green house as the darkness settled and not enter its wood-paneled front hallway, its lukewarm yellow light.

A few more houses as the hill got steeper. I looked only sidelong at Rose's parents' house, although its barnyard red made it difficult to ignore.

Past her house, one or two more modest homes before the road twisted up into the trees and houses got farther apart. Then there was the heavily wooded chunk of land that no one seemed to own or build upon and, farther up, the sharp turn where Fox Hill forked. Fox Hill Road continued up the steep incline, Fox Hill Way shot down to the right, toward a few more houses, Toby's, and then the transfer station.

I decided to go for Fox Hill Way.

Toby's house looked better kept than I'd expected. Even against the darkening sky, the white paint job looked fairly crisp. I got a whiff of freshly mowed lawn as I approached the property.

The smell of cut grass always made me think of Joe Dean, actually. Mrs. Crowe paid Joe to mow her lawn when we were kids. Once, on a ninety-degree day, he'd asked me to bring him a wet cloth to help him cool off. To my delight, he started mowing with his head tipped back slightly, the cloth covering his face. And he had me yell him directions so he'd turn in the right places and avoid hitting any trees or mowing straight into the road. Mrs. Crowe nearly lost her mind when she came outside and saw what we were doing.

Despite the fresh paint on the Dean house, the little outbuildings were looking pretty dumpy. The shed where Joe had once worked was practically falling over. The always-condemned root cellar didn't look like much more than a small pile of lumber sinking into the grass.

"Hey, Nora!" someone yelled.

I squinted at the Deans' stoop. It was Joe Dean, who was sitting on the top step, smoking.

"Hey," I said. "I was just taking a walk."

"You looking for Toby?"

"No . . . but if he's here, I'll say hi, I guess . . ."

Joe led me into the house, through the living room to the kitchen, where Toby was sitting reading the newspaper. He looked startled when we came in.

"You've got a visitor," Joe said.

The kitchen was exactly as I remembered it. It had a reddish brown linoleum floor that was supposed to look like little bricks, and plain white cabinets grubby around the metal handles. On the table there was a loaf pan half full with a crusty dark brown substance and a butter knife sticking out of it.

I was about to ask what it was but thought better of it. I didn't want to be rude. But Toby caught me looking at it.

"It's a meat loaf," he explained. "A failed one."

"Why isn't it in the fridge?"

"Joe decided it was inedible. Was gonna clean the pan out, I think. Gave up halfway through scraping it out, looks like."

"I'll do it tonight," Joe said defensively. "Jeez."

I couldn't stop staring at it. What Toby described had to have occurred several days ago for the meat loaf to achieve its rock-like quality. It made me want to giggle. You could put this pan in a museum and call it *Bachelorhood*.

"We've been trying to be a little better about cooking since Dad died," Toby said, as if to explain.

"That's good," I said stupidly.

"Nora, you want a beer or something?" Joe asked. "An ice-cream sandwich? Both?"

"Umm . . . what're you having?"

"Sandwich," Joe said. He seemed much more lucid than he'd been at the bar.

"Okay. I'll join you, then."

Joe fished the box of treats out of the frost-encrusted cave of their freezer and handed one to me and one to Toby. We all peeled the thin white papers off our ice-cream sandwiches. I licked ice cream off the edges for a moment, then stopped, thinking it might look a bit uncouth.

"So," Joe said. "How're things at the Hemsworth homestead?"

"Yeah," Toby said. "I noticed your car was gone last night. I thought maybe you'd left town."

"I went down to Bristol to hang out with my mother for a little while. It was getting kind of weird with Charlotte, actually."

"Weird how?" Toby asked.

He'd laughed when I'd mentioned the *Looking Glass* at his shop. And it didn't seem like a hot idea to explain about Charlotte's dad—or her sudden investigative interest in Aaron Dwyer either.

"Oh, it's just kind of strange to spend so much time with

someone you used to know . . . a long time ago, when you were a different person. . . ."

I looked at the softening ice-cream sandwich in my hand, trying to decide if I should continue.

Toby sat back in his chair and considered my words for a moment. "Well," he said. "If things are getting weird over there, you can always crash here."

This wasn't the response I was expecting. In fact, it startled me. Toby looked amused by my reaction. Joe, thankfully, didn't seem to notice.

"I wanted to ask you about something," I said to Joe, deliberately changing the subject. "Something you might remember better than Charlotte and I do."

"Yeah?"

"Do you remember Brian Pilkington? And his car accident?"

"Of course. Poor guy. But I hear he's doing fairly well now, considering. He's a professor or something."

"But do you remember very much about his accident?"

"Not really. It was out on Route 5. He drove right off the road."

"I remember that my dad was the one who came in and towed the car," Toby piped up. "Said his Dodge was so wrecked he couldn't believe that the kid even made it out of there alive at all."

"It wasn't a Dodge," I said. "It was a Datsun."

"Oh." Toby looked at me funny. I'm not the sort of girl who remembers car makes and models, but I wasn't about to offer that I'd just looked up the accident earlier that afternoon.

"Well," he said, "either way. I just remember my dad talking about it. I didn't see it myself."

Joe turned to Toby. "Did Dad really clean it up?"

"Yeah," Toby said.

"Huh. I don't even remember that. I remember they thought Brian must've been speeding like a maniac. Wasn't like him. He was kind of a laid-back dude. And wasn't he a Jehovah's Witness? Maybe the Holy Spirit got a hold of him or something?"

Toby sighed, looking embarrassed at Joe's bad joke.

"Speeding is kind of a secret vice," Toby said. "It's not always who you'd expect."

Joe and I nodded at this vehicular wisdom, since Toby knew about these things.

Joe seemed disinterested in the topic of Brian Pilkington.

"You see the latest article about Rose?" he asked, turning to me suddenly.

"No . . . but I heard all about the press release from one of Charlotte's newspaper friends."

"It's scary," he said. "I hope she didn't suffer, or at least suffer for long. Them finding her like this, it makes me think someone could have been keeping her for a while—alive? Something terrible . . . something sick like that."

Toby glanced at me apologetically.

"You need to try not to think like this," Toby said. I got the feeling he'd already said this to Joe many times. "Whatever happened, at least it's over now."

Joe looked to be struggling to keep his face stoic, despite a wobbling chin. I finished the rest of my ice cream and was left with sticky chocolate crumbs on my fingertips. Toby noticed and handed me a napkin.

"Let's show Nora the lighthouse room," Joe suggested.

"If it'll make you feel better," Toby said.

Toby and I remained at the kitchen table for a moment before following Joe to the stairs.

"Lighthouse room?" I whispered.

"This little room up in the attic. I can't remember if you ever went up there. We didn't call it the lighthouse room—Rose did. Do you remember, though, that Charlotte's been up there? You remember the day she came over and went up there to record for ghosts?"

"A little bit," I said.

"Yeah, well, I'm sure Joe will tell you the lighthouse story. We were just talking about it this morning."

Toby and I climbed the stairs together. Toby's room was the first one on the left when you came up the stairs. I remembered that much. I glanced into it before he led me farther down the hall. Still poorly lit. Still covered in gentle floral wallpaper that didn't suit him, now without the Nirvana and Pearl Jam posters that had once masked it.

"You still sleep up here?"

"Nah. Downstairs, usually."

"In your dad's old room?" I asked, proud of myself for remembering the sleeping arrangements.

"No. On the couch, usually. Especially in the summer. It's a lot hotter up here."

"And this is Joe's room, right?" I said as he led me into another bedroom.

"Yup."

Toby led me through Joe's room. More cream-and-lilac floral walls, totally unsuitable for its occupant. Toby turned the knob of what I thought was a closet door. But it opened to a narrow staircase.

"That's weird," I said.

"I know, isn't it? These old farmhouses have some quirks."

The creaky wooden stairs led up to a single room with a small window and pink-rosebud wallpaper. It was crammed with boxes, piles of old magazines, board games in fatigued boxes. Joe was already upstairs when we got there, standing by the room's single small, square window.

"My grandmother said they'd used it as an attic bedroom at one time," Toby explained, "although I can't imagine sleeping up here. It must have gotten really hot and really cold. We've always used it to store crap, mostly. Dad filled almost all the space with his train magazines and fly-fishing equipment. I still don't know what to do with the stuff. I should sell it, I guess."

"Not necessarily," I said. "Not if you want to keep it around."

"Look," Joe said, motioning for me to move closer to the window.

I did. The small, square window gave a decent view of Fox Hill. To the east you could see only trees, where the road twisted off to the transfer station. But to the west was the overgrown grass on that side of the Dean property, and Joe's shed. Beyond that you could see down across a couple of backyards and, below that, Rose's family's house, which was set farther back from the road than the houses before it.

"I didn't realize," I said, "how much you could see from here."

"That's what Rose got such a kick out of. When we were kids and I told her this room was haunted, naturally she wanted to see it. But once she saw it, and the way you can see her house, she didn't care about ghosts. See those two windows on the side of Rose's house? That's the Bankses' living room.

"She and I were about ten, and she'd seen this movie where

these kids who were neighbors would communicate at night from their bedrooms with their flashlights. Of course, in this movie the kids had actual stuff to communicate about on a regular basis, and they had the convenience of their bedrooms facing each other. But Rose wanted to try it. We tried it a couple of nights. She set a time after her parents would be asleep. Didn't even bother to use a flashlight, actually. Just blinked the living-room light on and off. In Morse code. I remember we sat here waiting a couple of hours for her to do it."

"It was kind of scary," Toby added. "Because we never came up here at night."

"That's cute," I said.

"Yeah," Joe agreed. "It's not the whole story, though. She got bored of it pretty fast. But then, a few months later, we were all at the bus stop and she said to us, 'Where were you guys last night? I was SOS'ing you for like two hours.' As if we'd been sitting up there every night, just on the off chance she'd be blinking her lights again."

"That's weird. You think she was in some kind of trouble?"

"Trouble? No. She was a little sad because her parents were fighting, but no real trouble. Rose liked to dramatize sometimes."

You're such a drama queen, Rose. Do you know that? I thought of Aaron and Rose at the fork in the road.

"Well, it's still a nice story," I said.

"Yeah," Joe said, frowning. "I think I need another cigarette."

And with that he turned from the window and started back down the stairs.

"He used to spend a lot of time up here," Toby whispered.

"Right after Rose disappeared. Thinking maybe that light in her living room was going to magically start blinking some night."

"Jesus, Toby. That's really depressing."

Toby gazed out the window for a moment before moving toward the stairs.

"Yup," he said. "It is."

"Toby?" I said, and he turned to me.

I lowered my voice to a whisper. "You think Joe and Rose were ever . . . more than friends?"

Toby stepped closer to me again. "Yeah," he said softly. "Yeah, maybe a little."

"A little?"

"Well. They never dated. That wouldn't have worked, since she was so popular and all. And she was dating that Aaron guy for most of high school, right? But there was a little crush, I think, yeah. A mutual one. It was fairly obvious."

"Huh."

"Why do you ask?"

"It was just a thought. Just the way he talks about her, is all."

Toby's gaze met mine. "Have the police talked to you yet?" he asked.

"Yeah," I said.

"They ask you about my brother and Rose?"

"No. Honestly, they didn't ask me much of anything."

He nodded, slapped me amicably on the shoulder blade, and then headed for the stairs.

I followed him down into Joe's room. Just before we walked out of the room, Toby lifted his hand up instinctively to turn off the light. Finding it already off, he pulled it quickly away.

The way he hovered his hand over the switch made me notice the wallpaper above it. The cream color was blotchy from years of cigarette smoke. Looking closer at the purple-blue bunches that decorated it, I saw that they weren't flowers at all. They were blueberries.

"Blueberry wallpaper," I mumbled, following Toby to the hallway but stopping there.

"Yes," he said. "Someone must've gotten a good deal on it. They used it there, in my room, and in the downstairs bathroom. And inside the linen closet."

I went farther down the hall and peered into his room again. Of course he was right. I glanced over at the bed, where we'd fooled around so many years ago.

"I didn't remember that," I murmured. "That it was you who had blueberry wallpaper."

"Yeah?"

I stepped into the room and touched one of the tiny blueberries. I thought of the blueberry wallpaper in one of the *Looking Glass* poems. The more I thought about it, the less likely it seemed Sally Pilkington could've had anything to do with it.

"I've been in this room. How could I have forgotten that?"

"The one time you were up here," Toby said, "we were a little drunk. And not drunk enough to sit staring at the wallpaper."

"Could I have been that crazy?" I said, looking at Toby. "Could I really have forgotten?"

Toby reached out and touched the top of my hand gently, just for a moment. "What're you asking? Crazy for forgetting the wallpaper?"

"No. Not only that. For everything. Everything I did back

then. High school, I mean. Everything I remember and maybe a bunch I don't."

Toby shook his head again, then gave me his gentle one-and-a-half stare.

"You weren't crazy. You were fucked up. There's a difference."

I struggled to hold Toby's gaze. Just a few minutes after he'd suggested—however innocently—that I could crash at his house, there was maybe more in this gaze than I knew how to handle. I'd wondered a few times what would've happened if I'd chosen to stay with him on prom night. Would anything be different now if I had?

I pulled my hand to my side.

"I know," I said. "Thanks for recognizing the difference. Listen—I ought to get back to Charlotte's."

I needn't have rushed back. When I returned to the Hemsworths', Charlotte's car was gone. She'd left a note for me on the kitchen table:

> *Nora, So sorry. Paul called. Wanted to talk again,*
> *so I'm meeting him for coffee. Hope to be back soon.*
> *Charlotte*

I turned on the TV and watched a couple of reruns. I called her cell phone. No answer.

I fell asleep on the couch waiting up for her. When I awoke after midnight, her bag was back in the kitchen, her car back in the driveway, her bedroom light shut off. She apparently hadn't wanted to wake me.

June 7, 1997

Toby and I weren't invited to any post-prom parties, but we didn't much care. Toby's gearhead friends weren't prom types, and I didn't really have any friends anymore. Toby and I hung out on the swings of the elementary school, getting buzzed on drinks we'd mixed in his dad's Ford pickup: vodka and lemonade in innocent-looking soda bottles that could be dumped quickly if someone caught us on the playground. It was my first taste of alcohol, and I was happy to be experiencing it alone with Toby rather than with a bunch of people throwing up and passing out around me.

When we got tired of the swings, we walked back together to the old Ford. I was carrying my shoes, enjoying the feel of the grass against my feet. I allowed myself to press closer to Toby as we walked to the truck, feeling I was luckier than the girls at those parties. Held tightly against Toby's tuxedoed chest during the last slow song at the prom, I'd peeked around at the other girls and their dates and felt that Toby was actually one of the more attractive guys there. He certainly looked more mature than most of the others anyway, with his muscular physique and dark facial features. I felt older and wiser than the other girls for looking past our stupid primary-school judgments and seeing this about him. I felt freed somehow, noticing this. One month left at Waverly High, but I was already essentially free. And the vodka only accentuated this feeling.

As we'd approached his house, Toby assured me that once his dad was passed out on a Saturday night, he'd never wake up. Our late-night encounter with Joe lessened my giddiness some-

what, weighing me down with embarrassment as we mounted
the stairs to Toby's room. But by the time we were sitting together on the bed, listening to Joe's car pull away, the feeling
started to return. I liked Toby. And I didn't care what anyone
else thought anymore. That was the best part of it.

"Are you going to kiss me?" I asked, letting the buzz say what
it wished.

"It's easier if you don't ask," Toby admitted.

"Uh-huh. I see," I said, laughing. "But I'm not so sure I want
to make it easier."

He tilted his head and touched his lips to mine. I pulled away
for a moment, surprised by the moisture of his mouth and the
wormy feel of the tip of his tongue.

"It's okay," he said, looking alarmed by my reaction.

"I know," I said, mostly to hush him. "Okay" was one of the
least romantic words I could think of, and it was awkward on
his lips.

I turned to him resolutely, and we sank back into the pillows.
We kissed until it didn't feel weird anymore.

"Nora," he said, stopping to brush my hair away from my
face.

"Be careful," I said, giggling. "You'll flatten out the curl."

"You don't need that curl anymore, do you?"

"I'm not sure. Are we all supposed to still have our hair done
when we go for breakfast at Friendly's?" I asked.

"I don't think it matters. Since neither of us is invited."

I laughed as if this statement were hilarious, then kissed him
again, wondering if I was pushing this new vodka personality
beyond its reasonable limits. Was it the vodka talking, or had

I just always wanted to act this way? Maybe, behind the hair and deep down beneath all this thick silence, I was the happy-hooker type.

We rolled around for a while, our hands moving only up and down each other's hair and backs.

Toby stopped again, propping himself up on an elbow.

"So, Nora."

"Yeah?" I replied, trying for a coy smile.

His own smile faded. "Do you think my house smells funny?" he asked. He'd apparently mistaken my expression for wrinkling my nose.

"Well . . . no," I said, unconvincingly.

"It's the dirt cellar that makes it smell that way," he said. "No matter how much you clean the house upstairs, there's all that moisture down there. Big mildew problem."

"Uh-huh," I said. "Well, that's okay. It's an old house, you know?"

He was a little drunk, too. I don't know why I'd assumed he'd have an iron tolerance when I'd never heard of him ever drinking. Maybe because his brother and his dad were both known to pack it away pretty well. But here he was talking about mildew when we were supposed to be kissing. I kissed him again.

"Nora," he said.

"Yup?"

"Why have you been so quiet? I feel like you used to talk more when we were kids. When was it you stopped, exactly?"

"I don't remember now," I said, feeling the happy hooker slip away. "But I'm talking now, aren't I?"

"Yeah," he said, moving closer to me again. I could feel his breath on my face.

"Yeah," I repeated.

"When you don't talk, people start thinking you've got a bunch of secrets."

"No," I said, gazing at his muscular arm and beautiful hand. "They stop thinking about you at all. That's what they do."

"Not me," he said.

"Okay. Not you."

"Can I ask you something?" he said. "I mean, you don't have to answer if you don't want."

"Okay."

"Why did you do it? Last year? When you took those pills?"

My face was already red from the alcohol, so I didn't need to blush. I closed my eyes for a moment, thinking about it. "It's hard to explain."

"Yeah? I'll bet."

I thought for a moment that he was being sarcastic. I sat up.

"I'm sorry," he said, "I didn't mean that like it sounded."

"Don't be sorry," I said, shrugging. "You're actually the only one who's really bothered to ask me straight out."

"Is there some secret?" he wanted to know.

I wasn't sure I understood the question, so I shook my head.

"No," I said. "There's no big secret. I was depressed, I guess. Or . . . that was part of it."

"Depressed why?"

I gazed into his slightly crooked eye and tried to ignore the other one, which was studying me with unaccustomed intensity.

"I don't know if I can explain—"

"Well, there must've been *something*. Something specific that made you do it."

I stared at him, then reached behind his neck and pulled him toward me. I let him kiss my neck, hoping it would help him forget his question.

He tightened his arms across my back. "I wanted to tell you when it happened. I wanted to tell you I get it."

"Get what?"

"I think I get it about sort of half trying it and seeing what happens."

"That's what you think I was doing?"

"You're still here, right?"

"Don't do that," I said, pushing his arms away. "You don't get anything."

"Okay," he said, pulling back from me. "What's the matter?"

"I don't know," I admitted.

We lay facing each other for a few minutes, not touching.

"I do get it, though. I get it that something could eat at you like that. Slowly, till you're not sure how the hell you're going to get away from it."

"*'Eat at you'?*" I said, offended that such prosaic language was being applied to my heretofore very, very serious mental breakdown. Even my mother didn't talk about it like that. "*'EAT at you'?*"

"Umm, yeah," Toby said, shifting his eyes nervously, as if he were dealing with a crazy person. "Umm. That's what I said. 'Eat at you.'"

He put his hand on my back, pulling me close once more. He felt warmer now than he had before. He was starting to sweat a little. "I think we both know. We both know what that's like."

And just as he said it, I thought I caught a familiar odor rising from him, of mothballs or monkeys or both. I pushed his hand away again. This was Toby, I remembered suddenly. Toby with the dumb laugh. Toby whose big, strong hand could pull me back into the muck of my pathetic Waverly youth, from which I was just now barely starting to emerge. With or without his knowledge, that hand wanted to pull me back into a darkness from which I probably couldn't escape twice.

"Aren't you going to ask me what I mean?" he said pleadingly. "I think you would know what I'm talking about."

"No, I wouldn't. I wouldn't understand anything. Everyone thinks if you're quiet, you're sweet and sensitive. Or if you're fucked up, you can understand everyone else's problems. Well, it's not true."

I stood.

He sat up and stared at me. "What's the matter? You're taking off on me?"

"I don't think I want to do this."

"We don't have to do anything. Who said we're doing anything?"

"I think I need to go home now."

"I never asked for anything. . . . You know I wouldn't. I just want to talk."

"I don't like talking about it—the pills, the hospital." This was a lie, as I'd felt oddly relieved when he'd asked me about it. I'd wished for a while now that someone would allow me to explain—*really* explain. But it was the closest thing to a real excuse I could think up for my panic.

"We don't need to talk about that. I'm sorry. Stay, Nora. Please stay."

I shook out both my hands nervously, as if flicking off water. "I can't, Toby. I can't."

As I said it, I realized it was I who was about to start crying, not him. It had been me all along. I started to back out of the room, mortified.

Toby tried to clasp my hands. "It's okay, Nora. I won't touch you. Please stay."

"I can't," I repeated. "Don't make me stay."

"Okay," Toby said, dropping my hands. "I wouldn't. I won't."

"Okay," I said, grabbing my prissy black satin handbag. Stupid prom, stupid formalwear. Why had I decided to do any of this?

I grabbed my shoes and raced down the stairs. I held the black pumps close to my chest as I ran down the hill, then slipped them back on my feet for my approach to Mrs. Crowe's. The lights were off, but I preferred to wake everyone up with the clicking of my heels than continue to feel the desperation that my stocking feet implied.

No one woke up. I ran upstairs and threw myself onto my bed. I stared at the ceiling and willed September—when I'd leave this room and this town forever—to come and come fast. I fell asleep in my prom dress, with the lights on.

Fourteen

May 25, 2006

Sally and I talked about her son, Max, for a good fifteen minutes before anything else was said. He sat on her lap, alternately gumming and conversing with a rubber turtle. I asked her about teething and crawling and sleeping through the night—all the basic questions I could think to ask about babies. I have this problem with my friends who already have kids—I don't know how much or how long we're ever supposed to talk about the baby. I'll keep talking about it forever, so as not to seem the insensitive, childless heathen, but I have trouble listening very intently to the answers.

And Sally and I really didn't have anything else obvious to talk about. That became clear to me with each infant-related question I asked and each thoughtful answer she gave. I watched—rather than heard—her answer. Her face was a bit chubbier than I'd remembered, and she had a more stylish, more angular hair-

cut than the one she'd always had as a kid. She seemed perfectly
at ease with a baby in her lap and smiled more in the span of
our twenty-minute conversation than I'd remembered her ever
smiling in high school. This was a person I no longer knew—or,
more accurately, had never really known.

It wasn't until after she'd come back from nursing Max in
the ladies' room that we started to chat a little about Rose. She
brought it up, which didn't surprise me. Probably it was the
biggest news Waverly had had in recent memory. She admitted
she'd never known much about Rose—she was startled to hear
that Rose had baby-sat Charlotte and me.

"Really?" she said, with genuine surprise.

I explained to her that we'd always had a childish interest in
Rose's life and had been nosy about her boyfriends.

"And actually," I said slowly, "we were wondering if your
brother and Rose ever dated or anything like that."

Sally struggled to swallow her mouthful of caramel latte.

"Rose Banks? And my brother? Are you kidding? What
would make you think that?"

"Oh, well, see . . ." I was unprepared for the question. "She
just . . . uh, hinted about another guy. After she dumped her
first boyfriend, she said some things that one might think—"

"There's no way," Sally interrupted me.

"Why do you say that?" I asked, relieved she hadn't waited
for more of an explanation.

"She was a pretty, relatively popular girl, right? That's what
I gather anyway."

"Yes. As far as I know, that's true."

Sally's little pink mouth remained expressionless, but she
cocked her head slightly. "I don't know if you remember, but no

one in my family was ever popular. A girl like that would never have gone out with my brother."

"Oh, I don't know . . ." I said, feeling I should say something charitably contrarian. Besides, Rose *was* turning out to be less predictable than I'd thought.

"Well, I *do* know," Sally said. "I don't believe they were ever friends. Not that he would have mentioned it to me, actually. But her name never came up. I don't think I ever heard of her until she disappeared."

"Would you have known who all his friends were?"

Sally looked at me patiently, with her little mouth drawn in tightly—as she used to when I couldn't figure out the simplest of chemistry equations.

"There's no reason you'd remember much about my family," she said quietly. "But our parents kept pretty close tabs on our free time. Any friendship that the family didn't know about wouldn't be a significant one."

"Oh," I said, nodding, embarrassed that my question had come across as pushy. "Okay."

Max threw his turtle on the floor and squealed. Sally shifted him onto her left knee and picked it up for him.

"How *are* your parents?" I asked.

Sally sighed and shifted Max back to the middle of her lap.

"Fine, as far as I know. I don't see them much. Brian and I left the church quite a few years ago. Only my sister Laurie stayed. Most of what I hear about them is through her."

"I'm sorry," I said.

"It's okay. We're used to it, I guess. I hope things will be different in a few years. I hope they'll want to get to know this guy at least." Sally indicated Max, then kissed his head.

"Yeah. Hopefully. That sounds hard."

"Is this what you and Charlotte wanted to ask me? When you wrote to me?" Sally asked. "About my brother and that girl Rose?"

"No . . ." I said.

Sally took a careful sip of her latte. "Charlotte doesn't work for the paper anymore, does she?" she asked.

"No."

"I used to read her articles, but I heard she was fired."

"She's teaching high school now. At Waverly, in fact."

"Oh. Now, *that's* interesting. And how is her brother?"

"Oh. Paul? Okay, I guess. I saw him the other day. He's a physical therapist. He's married. Has a couple of kids. A boy and a girl. "

Sally looked thoughtful. "Did *he* say something about my brother and Rose?"

"No. No, I guess we didn't think to ask him."

"Well," she said after a moment, "I'm certain they weren't friends, Rose and my brother. And you probably wouldn't re-member the timeline, but when she disappeared, he was in the hospital. It was a pretty intense period for all of us. The disap-pearance of this girl in his class didn't really register that much, at the time. We were all too busy dealing with Brian and his . . . circumstances."

Sally cleared her throat. "But, you know, if you're just look-ing to talk to people who were in her class, I'm sure he'd be happy to talk to you. I really don't know how much he'd be able to tell you. By the time that girl disappeared . . . he was still in the hospital. He was getting used to being in a wheelchair. And dealing with memory-loss issues from the accident."

She hesitated. "Just a lot of difficult stuff at the time. So as far as Rose—more than anyone at Waverly High back then, I can guarantee you he wasn't paying any attention."

"I understand. And I wouldn't think of bothering him about this."

"Well . . . I wouldn't go that far. He wouldn't want you to avoid talking to him if you're talking to everyone else. He doesn't like to be treated that way."

"Where is he now? What's he up to?"

"He lives in New Haven. Teaches at Southern."

"Teaches what?"

"Political science."

"Oh," I said. "How nice."

"I can give you his e-mail if you want."

Sally's tone seemed to soften when she said this, and I took her up on the offer.

"So . . . that was what you wanted to meet to talk about? It sounded to me like you and Charlotte had a friendly wager going or something."

"Oh. Yeah. Umm . . . no. It wasn't about that. We were actually wondering if you ever wrote for the *Looking Glass*."

"For *what?*" Sally looked distracted. She put her face closer to her son and sniffed.

"The school literary magazine."

"Oh," she said, sitting back up. "No. I didn't do any extracurricular clubs or anything. I tried writing for the school newspaper once or twice, but it didn't work out, because I didn't have anyone to drive me home."

"But kids didn't have to be in the actual club to submit to the magazine. A lot of kids even submitted anonymously."

Sally smiled. "You're asking if I did?"

"It's a long story. When Charlotte was the editor, there were a couple of anonymous poems in there that she thought I'd written. For years she thought it was me, I guess. But it wasn't. It came up during our visit. We were talking about it, about who else it could have been, and your name came up."

"Me? Why?" Sally looked amused. "What were they about?"

"Oh, just these little poems. They were well written. You were one of the better writers in the class, we were remembering."

I actually had no clue if Sally had been a good writer. But she had been an all-around good student, so it was plausible.

"I see."

Her eyes looked dubious, but the corners of her mouth went up a little at the compliment. At that moment I felt ridiculous for bringing her here, for dragging this perfectly nice woman into my lingering high-school neurosis and its accompanying face-saving lies. So we'd both sat next to each other over a Bunsen burner a decade earlier—so what? Almost everyone sits over a Bunsen burner with someone or other. I could have been anybody. She could have been anybody. The randomness of our sitting here together now was particularly embarrassing, because I was the one who had initiated it.

"It was just a silly thing between Charlotte and me," I said. "I'm sorry."

"Don't be sorry," Sally said, cocking her head again, smiling gently. "And no—no, it wasn't me."

"Okay," I said.

"Must've been quite a poem, if you two are still wondering who wrote it. Now, what year did you say it was printed?"

"When we were juniors," I answered. "Long time ago. Really, it was just a lark, just a stupid—"

"Oh, that's okay. But I'm curious now . . . what was it about?"

"Oh . . . it wasn't just one poem, actually. Just a bunch of poems. Kind of abstract poems. Like riddles, almost. All attributed to 'Anonymous.'"

"You gonna contact anyone else?" Sally asked. "Any other ideas? Like, Rob Fishkin was a good writer. You guys asked him?"

"Umm . . . no, not yet. Maybe Charlotte will," I said quickly.

Sally picked up her fancy caramel coffee and took a sip. "Mmm," she said, putting it down. "I'm glad we came here. I love this stuff."

"So . . . how did you meet your husband?" I asked, hoping to bring at least part of this conversation into the current decade.

"He's a vet," Sally said. "Where I work."

I nodded, and she asked me a similar question about my husband. And we were off again.

Spirit Summonings:
December 1990

Charlotte's dad was angry. Charlotte had forgotten to use the bungee cords on the trash cans again when she'd taken out the trash, and now some dog had gotten into it and scattered garbage all around the yard.

"Get on out there and clean that up," he told her when he got home. "Did you just walk right by that mess when you got off the school bus?"

"I don't know," Charlotte said sullenly.

"Well, you'd better go clean it up."

"Okay," she said, and then turned to me. "C'mon."

I started to get up. This would be the second time—Charlotte and me plucking moist tissues and chicken bones out of the grass, our hands growing cold and numb in the wind.

"What do you mean, 'C'mon'?" Mr. Hemsworth asked Charlotte. "The garbage is your responsibility. Nora doesn't have to help you pick it up if she doesn't want to. Right, Nora?"

I hated it when adults did this—put me between respect for them and loyalty to my friends. There was never a right answer. I nodded vaguely but said nothing.

Charlotte rolled her eyes and stalked out of the room. I was actually glad to be rid of her. She'd been talking about psychometry again, this time suggesting that we use the mugs she was pretty sure she'd seen Rose using. Luckily, Charlotte's father had come home early, but I envisioned her making me press a WORLD'S GREATEST DAD mug into my forehead in the near future.

I needed something to distract her—or at least make her see things my way. She had to see that this game wasn't fun anymore. The outcome was probably going to be worse than either of us imagined.

I gazed at the black books fanned out across the carpet. I wanted to talk to her in language she could understand, and maybe one of her books would help me with that. I sorted through the volumes and made a small pile of the ones that had to do with ghosts and dead people: *Phantom Encounters, Hauntings*, and *Spirit Summonings*. The pictures on the covers of the first two were dark and creepy, but the one on *Spirit Summonings* was pretty. The young woman on the cover had her eyes closed, with cloudy blue sparkles swirling around her delicate face. It was sort of a comfort to think of Rose that way—sleeping in the light of blue stars. Maybe this was what Charlotte needed to accept the truth—a comforting way to think of it.

I started to look through the book for something to help me talk to Charlotte. There was a man with a mustache who talked to dolphins in his head. Kind of cool, but not useful to me at the moment. A story about two girls named Kate and Maggie Fox, who started the séance craze in 1848 by tricking their mom into thinking there was a ghost in their house. They did it by tying an apple to a string and knocking it around under their bed. That sounded like fun, but I didn't want to *fool* Charlotte. I just wanted her to see things the way I saw them: Rose was probably dead.

I kept flipping pages. Old-timey pictures of séances. (Could I convince Charlotte to have a séance? Did I want to?) People spitting and oozing something called "ectoplasm." More old photos. Harry Houdini. Arthur Conan Doyle. Boring, boring, unhelpful, boring.

Near the end of the book was a short section on Ouija boards. A Ouija board could certainly be arranged. Robin Greenbaum had one—we'd used it at her birthday sleepover. But everyone had gotten giggly and stupid with it. When we'd all quieted down and begun to take it seriously, Robin's little sister had freaked out and started to cry. After that we decided to communicate only with "future ghosts"—made-up people like "John Zappo from 2095." That had been Charlotte's idea, to calm Robin's sister. I couldn't decide if I was relieved or disappointed by this innovation. Could there really be such thing as "future ghosts," and if so, what, exactly, made them less scary than past ones?

In any case I probably didn't want to involve Rose in a similar giggly, stupid activity. And if she was really dead—not pretend dead or "future dead"—it felt terribly disrespectful somehow to make her the subject of a board game.

I turned a couple more pages sadly. Maybe it was hopeless. Charlotte was interested in experimenting with my head but not so interested in learning what was really inside it. I wanted to tell her what that was, but I was afraid of what she'd think of it. She might hate me for it—just as she'd hated me for a few days when we were in second grade and I admitted I no longer believed in Santa Claus. She'd been so disgusted with me she'd kicked me out of her house for the afternoon. You'd think *I'd* be the one disgusted with *her*, for her babyish belief. But somehow it ended up the other way around, with me home watching a boring soap opera with Mrs. Crowe, straining to believe again.

The thought that Rose had died was the same. To tell Charlotte would be like cutting myself open and showing her my dark, disgusting insides. But to keep it from her was to lie, which made it even uglier, as did pretending alongside her that a mug or a banana clip would help us bring Rose back. I couldn't help but be angry at Charlotte for making me feel even more twisted and rotten each time she talked about it, each time she made me pretend for her.

"What're you doing?" Charlotte asked as she came back into the bedroom.

"Just looking at one of your books."

She slid the book across the carpet to look. I let her. I was interested in what she'd say about this book, which was mostly about dead people. Maybe she'd give me some kind of opening.

She flipped a few pages past where I'd been looking. She

stopped at an article called "Tuning In the Departed," which had a black-and-white picture of an elderly man in front of a few television sets.

"Oh, this guy," Charlotte said, as if seeing an old friend again. "Klaus Schreiber. Thinks he sees dead people in his TV static."

I noticed the word "thinks" and waited for more.

"Sad," Charlotte continued. "See, his daughter died, and I guess that's supposed to be her on the TV screen. Some people think it's real. Some people think it's not a ghost, really, but some psychic connection between what the person *wants* to see and the TV. Like, maybe Klaus's mind is somehow making that picture of his daughter on the screen."

I watched carefully as Charlotte gazed at the picture for a moment more, then closed the book with a soft, undecided "Hmph." Then she turned to her backpack and pulled out her math textbook. We were supposed to be doing homework together, since we both had a lot today. As she opened to a fresh notebook page, I glanced down at *Spirit Summonings* by her knees, and the pretty sleeping girl on its cover caught my eye again. It was comforting to think of Rose that way, if I had to think of her dying.

But, looking at it, I also realized that this gentle picture would be lost on Charlotte. It wasn't comfort that she needed. Charlotte required a complication, a task, and, if possible, high-tech equipment. If I wanted her to understand how I felt, I had to help her—I had to give her what she needed.

Fifteen

May 25–27, 2006

On Thursday evening, Charlotte and I drove to the elementary school after dinner for a walk around the playground. We didn't talk about Rose. Instead we talked playground memories: How Sam Allison used to wear sunglasses at recess and charm all us girls by telling us Helen Keller jokes while he pushed us on the swings. How Amy Priest—now possibly the most famous person in our class, since she'd appeared for a couple of weeks on *The Bachelor*—had cried inconsolably when a bird pooped on her shoulder during a kickball game. And how the kids used to tease Toby, accusing him of wanting to "do it" with Little Debbie, the wholesome gingham-clad girl who appeared on those cheap snack packages he practically lived on.

When we'd exhausted that topic, we'd talked about the cookout that Charlotte's mother seemed to so desire. We'd have Paul and his wife and kids over, maybe a few of the neighbors. I offered to shop for the food on Friday, and Charlotte didn't protest.

* * *

I was slicing up chicken breasts for kebabs when she came home on Friday evening.

She got home late, looking a little disheveled. Her eyes were red, and a big piece of hair was hanging out of the prim knot at the back of her head.

"Rough day?" I said.

She grunted, threw her bags down, and immediately extracted a cigarette from her purse.

"Beyond rough," she murmured.

"Are you okay? The kids crazy today?"

I didn't want to say so, but it looked like she'd been crying.

"The kids are crazy every day. Either that or I am."

Charlotte's gaze met mine again. Her eyes were glassy, with little purple-gray streaks beneath them. She looked exhausted.

"Porter called. The lab results are in. Confirming it's Rose."

A slippery piece of chicken breast fell out of my hand.

"Oh," I said, putting down my knife.

"It'll probably be all over the local news tonight."

"Probably," I said, uncertain of what else to say.

I wasn't sure if either of us really needed to say how sad it was. And it wasn't a surprise. We both already knew—everyone did. But maybe, in spite of all the evidence, part of Charlotte had remained hopeful, as she'd always been when we were kids.

"I'm really sorry, Charlotte," I said softly.

Charlotte nodded, then stared at her cigarette for several minutes without smoking it. I turned to my raw chicken breast, suddenly sickened by its moist pink flesh. I dumped the remaining breast uncut into the marinade and stuck it in the fridge.

"Imagine my surprise," Charlotte said as I sat next to her,

"when I got an e-mail from Sally Pilkington saying she was sorry she missed me for coffee."

"Oh—that," I said.

"Yes. That. What were you doing contacting her? Seeing her?"

"Is it really such a big deal? We just kind of . . . caught up."

"But why *her*? And why didn't you tell me?"

"Well, we'd talked about how maybe she'd know something about . . ." I hesitated. I didn't really wish to bring up the *Looking Glass* again after what had seemed like a truce the last couple of days.

"About what?" Charlotte folded her arms.

"The *Looking Glass*," I said sheepishly.

Charlotte rolled her eyes. "Bullshit, Nora."

"What?"

"Can you explain to me, then, why now she wants us all to have coffee with her brother tomorrow?"

"Really?"

"Yeah," Charlotte said.

I studied Charlotte's sad eyes, confounded. Was she really this upset with me for contacting dorky old Sally Pilkington? Or had the test results thrown her somehow? Maybe Rose's death was, at long last, sinking in.

"Is that a . . . problem?" I asked.

"We'll see, I guess, won't we?"

"You said we'd go?" I asked.

"Yeah." Charlotte finally lit her cigarette, taking an eager drag. "I didn't feel I had much choice. We're on for tomorrow at ten in Fairville."

"What are you not telling me, Charlotte? I don't get it. Doesn't sound like the most fun Saturday morning I've ever had, but you could've made some excuse, and I don't understand why you're so mad at me."

"I'm not mad at you!" Charlotte yelled, mashing the barely smoked cigarette in the tray. "Why is everything about you anyway? Has it occurred to you I'm just having a shitty week?"

She got up and stalked into the living room.

I followed her and found her standing by the goldfish tank, staring into it.

"Nora," Charlotte said, "is there anything you wanted to ask me? Is there maybe something you were asking Sally that you should've been asking me?"

I puzzled over this question for a moment. Should I have asked Charlotte first if Sally might've written the *Looking Glass* poems? Should I have asked Charlotte first if Brian had dated Rose?

"Umm . . . no," I said slowly.

Charlotte picked up the can of fish food and began sprinkling it liberally into the tank.

"Did you have something specific in mind?" I asked.

She stopped sprinkling for a moment, watching as a couple of the fish swam to the surface.

"No," she said, sighing as she continued to pepper the water with fish food.

"You know, those fish are going to explode."

Charlotte slammed the can down next to the tank.

"So *let* them explode. We'll just buy more, like we've always done!"

With that she collapsed on the couch next to me and buried her face in her hands. She didn't speak for several minutes.

"Did you want to talk more about it?" I asked.

Charlotte rubbed her eyes, stood up, and headed back into the kitchen to grab her tote bag.

"There's nothing more to say," she muttered.

And she apparently meant it literally. We barely spoke over dinner, which she suggested we eat in front of the television. A couple of hours later—before the news came on— she excused herself for bed.

Sally and Brian had arrived before us. Brian appeared pretty professorial despite the wheelchair. His face looked even younger than Sally's, but his slightly overgrown hair was just starting to go prematurely gray. A neat little goatee failed to mask the boyish roundness of his cheeks. His baby nephew sat in his lap, pawing at Brian's crisp black polo shirt with his tiny wet hands.

Charlotte seemed stunned at the sight of Brian, and paused before heading to their table. But then she took a breath and approached them, greeting them before ordering her coffee.

After the initial small talk, Brian put one hand carefully on the table.

"I wanted to talk to you two because I thought you could explain something for me. Now, I know we are talking about a few years ago here. Nearly a decade. But would either of you remember sending me something when you were, say, in high school? Does that ring a bell?"

"You're asking if one of us *sent* you something?" Charlotte asked, screwing up her face.

"Yes," Brian said evenly.

"No . . . I can't imagine," she said softly. "Something . . . in particular?"

"I'll put it another way," Brian said, taking in a breath and glancing at Sally, who was nervously tapping the tabletop. "How much do you know about my car accident? About who was involved? Did anyone talk to you about that? Rose? Your brother?"

"Not at the time," Charlotte murmured.

"Not at the time?"

"No. Then when? Around 1996, by any chance?"

"No," Charlotte said, shooting me a confused look. "In 1996? No. Paul didn't tell me what happened till a couple of days ago."

"I see." Brian looked skeptical. "Because of everything with Rose these past few days, I guess?"

"Yeah," Charlotte said, turning red as she turned away from me.

"Would you mind telling me what he told you about it?" Brian asked.

"I think maybe it's best you call him. Probably the two of you should talk. I can call him and have him—"

"No. No, if I'm going to talk to Paul, I think I'd prefer he initiated it."

Charlotte nodded. I could feel Sally's eyes on me, watching me look from Brian to Charlotte and back. She cocked her head. My confusion clearly interested her.

"Do *you* know what happened?" she asked me.

"No," I admitted.

"So when you contacted me, you didn't—"

"No," I repeated. "I really contacted you about the *Looking Glass*."

Brian shifted his gaze from Charlotte to me. "The *Looking Glass*, 1996? Correct?" he said.

"Yeah," I admitted, uneasy that he kept stressing that year.

"But you don't know the full story of my accident? You have no knowledge of that?"

"No," I said. His accident was in 1990. I didn't understand the connection. "And I think I'm the only person at this table who doesn't know what you're talking about."

Charlotte stiffened, and Sally looked very sad. Max the baby hiccupped.

"Would you mind telling me?" I asked Brian.

Brian studied me carefully, moved his nephew into Sally's lap, and took a long, thoughtful sip of coffee before speaking.

"Well," he said, watching me as he began, "I couldn't remember the accident. I knew that I'd been out proselytizing. Everyone said I'd been driving too fast. And I could never imagine that could be right. I never drove fast. I was never in a hurry to get to the next house. I hated having to knock on people's doors. And I certainly wouldn't have been in a hurry to get home. I was never in a hurry to get home.

"On one hand it seemed important to remember. The story that people were telling me couldn't have been true. They said I'd been speeding like a maniac. It was as if I'd awoken in this alternate universe, paralyzed, with a story behind it that I couldn't believe. It was frustrating—no, torture, actually. To have this terrible thing happen and to have to believe this crazy, impossible story about myself speeding home. It seemed important to remember, to prove it wrong. It wouldn't fix the injuries, but it would at least prove I didn't deserve them. The harder I tried to remember, though, the more impossible it seemed. My mind was blank. The memory was gone. And after a while it seemed like trying to remember was a way of avoiding the reality. This was my life now. I had to go forward. Maybe it would come to me someday. But I couldn't focus on it anymore."

"I'm sorry," I said stupidly. I felt ashamed for looking up his accident in the town library, treating his tragedy like a trifling factoid in my relatively mundane quest to figure out a couple of weird poems from our old school lit magazine.

"So you can imagine," he continued, ignoring my interjection, "how disturbed I was in 1996. When I got a letter in the mail, describing—confessing what happened."

"What?" Charlotte said. "Was it from Aaron?"

"Maybe I *was* driving like a maniac," Brian said, ignoring her as well. "Maybe I *was* showing off. But I wasn't the only one. There was a car behind me. Chasing me, you might say. Or just fooling around. Depending on how you look at it."

"And who was in that car?" I asked.

Brian studied me again, perhaps trying to determine if my question was genuine.

"Aaron Dwyer, Rose, and my brother," Charlotte said softly.

"Why?" I asked. "Why would they do that to you?"

Brian glanced at Sally. "Good question. But it's explained in the note I received."

He reached into his pants pocket, pulled out a folded wad of notebook paper, and spoke directly to Charlotte.

"I thought for a while your brother might have sent this. But the postmark was from Waverly, and when I tried to contact him, I was told he was in D.C. for graduate school. Still possible he sent it, but it didn't seem likely somehow.

"Seemed sort of a sick thing, really. I thought maybe Rose's parents? Rose's sister? But again, it didn't fit somehow, and I didn't want to bother her family, under the circumstances. Eventually, though, I thought maybe a *kid*—maybe a kid would do this, thinking it was the right thing. A kid who'd somehow gotten her hands on some information from Rose, or maybe from Aaron or Paul."

Brian watched Charlotte carefully for her reaction.

"Can I see that, please?" Charlotte said, extending her hand.

"I put it out of my mind till just yesterday," Brian said, still gripping the note, "when my sister calls me up and tells me you two have contacted her out of the blue—you two, who not only are close to Paul, of course, but it appears were close to Rose when you were kids, too."

"*And* the *Looking Glass* stuff you wanted to talk about was from 1996," Sally put in, her face tight. "And it turns out, when I went looking, that in spots they seem to be about my brother. We don't care so much about the *Looking Glass*, but sending this kind of thing to my brother, now, that's . . . that's another story."

Charlotte crossed her legs and shifted in her chair, her cheeks still red—with anger, frustration, or embarrassment? I couldn't tell. Brian unfolded the note, which consisted of two yellowed sheets, written on both sides, jagged-edged from being torn out of a notebook.

"So my question to you is whether one of you sent this to me, when you were kids," Brian said, handing the note to Charlotte. She tucked her arm and elbow around the paper as she read it.

"I've never seen this," she said once she'd finished.

"We're all grown-ups now," Brian said with an unconvincing breeziness. "If you sent it, it's okay. I'm not mad. You would've been, what—sixteen? I wouldn't be angry. I simply would like to know. What with their finding Rose, it's just become a little—I don't know—raw, again."

"I'm really sorry," Charlotte said. "I'd tell you if it had been me. Really, I would."

Sally sighed and bounced Max lightly with her leg.

"Then give it to Nora," Brian said. "Because I wanted to ask her, too."

Charlotte hesitated, folding the paper. "I'm sure she didn't—"

"Give it to her, please," Brian said sharply.

Charlotte placed the note on the table and pushed it over to me. I opened it and read the first few lines:

> *This is what happened, for anyone who cares about the truth.*
>
> *Paul and Aaron and I were hanging out at Aaron's. There was going to be a soccer party that night, we were hanging out there early. Paul had given me a ride.*

The blue handwritten words had a familiar roundness to them, with telltale curlicues coming off the *a*'s and the *u*'s.

"It's Rose's handwriting," I said.

"You remember what Rose's handwriting looked like?" Sally asked, sounding skeptical. "After all these years?"

"It's easy to remember, because—"

Charlotte glared at me over her coffee.

"Because we kept some things she wrote," I explained. "Just silly kid things we had her write for us when she baby-sat."

"What makes it hard to believe that it's really Rose Banks's handwriting," Sally said, "is that it was sent in 1996, like Brian said. From Waverly."

I continued reading:

We were thinking of ordering a pizza when the doorbell rang. And who should be at the door but Brian Pilkington and one other guy. I barely recognized him. I hadn't seen him much since the ninth grade, since he started being shuttled half the day to that technical program.

The other guy was older and did most of the talking. We let him talk and talk and talk and took their Watchtower. Brian just kind of stared at us the whole time. Was he embarrassed? I don't know. Probably just hoping nothing bad would happen, that Aaron would keep his mouth shut.

Which he did, miraculously, till they were done talking and the door was shut again.

After we all got over how weird it was, Aaron said something like, "I ought to go to his house and shove my religion down his throat."

He didn't really mean it. Just typical Aaron stuff. But somehow we started laughing about how funny it would be to go knocking on a Jehovah's Witness's door. Not for the reaction or the revenge, but just for the idea of it.

And Paul said, "Yeah, and we can give him this," and he grabbed a TV Guide off the couch. And said something nerdy, like about the Church of Popular Culture or something. Suddenly we were all into it—this idea of following a Jehovah's Witness home and knock-

ing on his door. Probably all for different reasons. Paul
to sound smart. Aaron to be jackass. Me? Well, I don't
know why now. I can't remember. I wish I could.

Brian and his friend were parked up the street. And
just as we were getting into the idea, they were getting
into their car.

We all hopped into Aaron's car. We followed them.
Aaron did a good job at first, keeping his distance.
Brian dropped off the other guy at Stop & Shop. We
talked about not following through at that point. For
some reason we'd been thinking we'd end up at the older
guy's house, not Brian's. The older guy wouldn't know
our names. And we didn't know his name either. To go
to Brian's would be meaner and less funny somehow
than to some nameless Jehovah's Witness's.

But Aaron kept following Brian, and we talked
about who would do the actual knocking and talking.
I offered. Aaron wouldn't do it right, and Paul would
probably chicken out. It was then, as Brian headed out
of downtown toward Route 5, that he seemed to notice
us. He went a lot faster all of a sudden. Aaron sped up.
I was laughing. I'm afraid now that's part of what made
him go so fast. I like speed—my dad never goes above
sixty-five.

Brian was taking some of those curves really fast.
Aaron was right on his tail. It was Datsun versus Dodge,
clunker versus clunker. I liked to think that Brian was
playing along, that for a secret moment he liked being a
regular kid doing something crazy along with us. Not the
Jehovah's Witness, not the smart kid who got shunted

*off to technical school because his parents thought he
should just sit tight and be a plumber till Armageddon,
not the kid who needed to pretend he didn't know us.
Because I remembered him sneaking a cupcake when
Lisa Owen brought them in for her birthday in second
grade—I remembered that about him. I would always
have that on him, and I loved him for it. I promise that
was what I was thinking when we were chasing him at
over sixty miles per hour. It doesn't matter now, but for
the record that's what was in my head.*

*Paul was telling Aaron to stop, to leave Brian alone.
This was a bad idea. We should wait and knock on
the door of a Jehovah's Witness we didn't know, some
other time. He was trying to stay cool, but I could tell
the speed was scaring him. But we kept at it. I think the
very tip of Aaron's car tapped Brian's bumper. That's
when Brian swerved.*

He'd been going so fast. He drove off the road.

*And yes, we kept going. I wish by writing this I could
change the ending, but no matter how I write it, it comes
out the same way. And I am so sorry.*

*Paul spoke first. I think he said "Oh, God." But we
kept driving. Aaron kept saying "Shit" and pounding
the wheel. I didn't say anything. Aaron took Chestnut
Street around the back way to downtown. Paul called
911 from the Dunkin' Donuts parking lot, but we didn't
stay.*

*After that we went back to Aaron's. I don't remember
saying anything for the rest of the night. I feel like I haven't
really said anything since. It's been three weeks now.*

I don't know what should happen.

But I wanted to be able to say it, and I want something to happen.

I won't stay quiet. I won't pretend I wasn't a part of what happened to Brian.

I won't live that way.

And I am sorry.

"You got this in 1996, you said?" Charlotte said, glancing at me.

I tried to quickly process what she was the thinking. The year we were juniors. The year I'd gone crazy. The year Rose's dreams had appeared in the *Looking Glass.*

"Yes," Sally said.

Brian gestured toward the note with his hand. "So the account here. Is that basically what your brother told you, Charlotte?"

"Basically."

"It's essentially what Aaron told me, too," Brian said.

"Aaron?" Charlotte looked stunned. "You talked to Aaron?"

"Yes. Several years ago." Brian stirred his coffee so hard that some of it sloshed over the edge of his mug. "It seems Aaron grew a conscience around the time his first kid was born. That's when he contacted me. I couldn't forgive him, exactly. But I could tell him that my life has certainly improved since then. In some really unexpected ways. Things have happened that wouldn't have under different circumstances, perhaps. And I hadn't hated him—hadn't even thought about him, really—for years. That seemed enough for both of us."

"Did you ask *him* about the note?" Charlotte asked, a little sheepishly.

"Of course. He didn't know what I was talking about. And I hope you'll not take this the wrong way, if he's still a family friend—but I don't imagine him a great bluffer."

"He's not a family friend," Charlotte said quickly. "And yeah, I know what you mean. Look, I'm sorry we couldn't help you figure out where the letter came from. And more so, I'm sorry about my brother."

Sally looked at her. "So—but no idea who this could've been, then?"

"My guess would be someone close to Rose," Charlotte said. "How else would they have gotten this?"

"That's assuming she wrote it," Sally pointed out.

"True," Charlotte said.

After that no one said anything else for a couple of minutes.

I don't know what anyone else was thinking, but I was trying to imagine Rose writing this confession. The handwriting had me pretty convinced it was her. How was she feeling when she wrote it? Who did she give it to? And why? And what happened after that?

We all stared into our laps, and I wondered when this silence would end.

Thankfully, the baby began to babble after a moment, and Brian's face lit up as he turned away from us and babbled back.

Phantom Encounters:
December 1990

Charlotte munched down about six Nilla wafers as I waited for her to finish the article I'd found for her in the books—"The Quest for Ghostly Voices," about people recording ghosts with tape recorders. I held my breath. I knew that Charlotte would be interested. I just wasn't sure she'd be willing to apply it to our current problem.

"I think we should try this," she said finally, reaching into the box for yet another wafer.

I exhaled.

"We can use my tape recorder. The black one," she suggested.

I nodded. "Good idea. So we're going to see if we can hear Rose?"

"No," Charlotte said. "No. We're only going to see what's out there. Record where she walked. Maybe record a little around her yard. Just to see what's out there and what it can tell us."

I nodded again. I didn't really know what this explanation meant. Maybe Charlotte didn't either. I couldn't think of anything or anyone I'd want to hear from besides Rose. But still, this was a step in the right direction for Charlotte. Toward putting Rose to rest.

"You have a blank tape?" I asked.

"No. But there's this one with some stupid Bon Jovi on it that I don't want anymore."

"Great," I said.

It took us forever to get up to the woodsy lot near the top of Fox Hill. Charlotte kept pausing before each house on the way, tiptoeing onto people's front walks, pointing the tape recorder at their doors, and pressing "record."

"You never know," she said, "who or what saw something, knows something. May as well see what we can pick up. Tension. Weird psychic energy. Whatever."

After each house she'd murmur into the recorder, "That was 110 Fox Hill Road," or whatever the address was, in case we heard something on the tape later that might require further recording and study.

"We're now between 114 and 116 Fox Hill," she whispered into the machine when we finally arrived. "We will be recording in the woods until a new address is announced."

"Should we sit down?" I asked. "So we don't make too much noise?"

"Yeah, probably."

Charlotte sat on a rock, and I sat on a root and watched the tape's wheels turn.

"Lots of dog poop around here," Charlotte observed after a few minutes.

"What?" I whispered in disbelief. It seemed unlike Charlotte to break this scientific silence with such a pointless observation.

"Look—there, there—and there. Since this isn't anyone's yard and you can't really see it from the other houses, people just walk their dogs here and don't clean up."

I shrugged. "Well, probably it doesn't hurt anyone. But maybe we shouldn't talk about it right now."

"It's actually okay for us to talk, I think," Charlotte reasoned. "Like, in Jürgenson's recordings there were birds. The ghosts talked *about* the birds, and their voices were different enough from live people's that he could tell. So it's okay to talk. The ghosts need something to talk about."

"I don't think the ghosts want to talk about dog doo, Charlotte," I said.

"Dog *doo*?" Her face twisted in disgust at my babyish word choice. "Dog *DOO*?"

"I think the ghosts have better things to talk about."

"How do *you* know?" Charlotte demanded.

"I just do."

"Whatever, Nora."

We were quiet again. I stared into the dull gray sky. It would be dark soon.

"Isn't this where they found you that time you wandered off and your mom was freaking out?" Charlotte asked. "When we were little? When you were following a squirrel or something, right?"

I didn't reply. I couldn't think of any reason she would bring this up now, except to make me look stupid. Yes, I'd been following a squirrel that evening. But it had looked injured, and I was trying to decide how I could help it. I was afraid that if I lost track of it, it would hobble off somewhere and die.

CRACK!

Charlotte jumped. "What was that?"

"I don't know," I whispered.

CRACK! Another snap of a twig, followed by a shuffle. Charlotte stood up.

"Probably someone walking their dog," I said.

"Shhh," she said.

The tape recorder hummed away, eating up our silence.

Just as Charlotte and I started to relax again, we heard a long, hissing breath coming from behind us. My heart thudded madly for a moment, but then the breath gave itself away.

"Nor-*aaaaaaa*," it whispered, the final part of the vowel falling into a low, clumsy laugh.

I stood up and put my hand on my hip. "Toby?"

"Yeah?" he replied from inside an evergreen about twenty feet behind us.

Charlotte stopped the tape recorder. "I'm going to kill him.

If he's been there the whole time, the whole tape will be inconclusive."

"I've only been here a few minutes," Toby said, emerging from the tree, pine needles hanging from his Patriots sweatshirt.

"Well, that's just great," Charlotte snapped.

"It's okay," I said. "It's something else for the ghosts to talk about."

"Oh, shut up."

"Press 'record,'" I insisted. "If you don't, you might miss something."

"Did I hear right," Toby said, "that you guys are recording ghosts talking about dog crap?"

"No, Toby," Charlotte said. "God! Just get out of here, okay?"

"Can't I watch for a few minutes?"

"There's nothing to watch. You—"

"Sure," I interrupted, raising my eyebrows in an appeal to Charlotte. "You can stay as long as you shut up."

Charlotte seemed satisfied that I'd at least spoken rudely to Toby. I settled back on my root as she hit "record." Toby crouched in the leaf-covered dirt. We were all classroom-quiet. The cassette tape squeaked away, circling round and round, lulling me into a little daydream about my mom letting me get a dog and me walking it here in the trees. The dog would be a beagle, and I'd name him Chester or maybe Charlie.

"IIhhhhhh," a slow, sickly breath jolted me awake.

"*Poooooo*-dle *poooooooop*," it croaked.

I giggled out loud, then slapped my hand over my mouth.

Charlotte stood up. "Get out of here!" she snapped.

"I swear that wasn't me," Toby said, grinning his guilt.

"That wasn't even funny," she said, glaring at me. "Both of you, get out of here if you can't take this seriously."

Toby pulled me gently by the sleeve. "Let's go, then."

"No, Charlotte," I said. "It's almost dark. You can't stay here by yourself."

"A few minutes of quiet here would be more useful than all this . . . all these . . . shenanigans."

Toby and I glanced at each other, and I started giggling again.

Charlotte pushed my shoulder with her fingertips. "Get out of here, then."

"I'm sorry, I didn't mean—"

"Just go. We'll listen to it all tomorrow."

Toby led me out of the trees, and I found I was happy to be away from there. Even if it meant I was alone with Toby with nothing to say.

"What's that all about anyway?" he asked me as we stood by the road. "You guys are ghost hunting?"

"Sort of."

"In the woods? Wouldn't it make more sense to do it in an old house or something? Like mine? There's this one room we've got that's haunted."

"We're not looking for any ghost. We're hoping to get something from Rose—or . . . um, *about* Rose."

Toby said nothing for a while, just breathed heavily, noisily through his nose.

"When Charlotte had me grab Phil, she seemed pretty sure Rose was alive," he said finally. "Now she thinks she's a ghost?"

I gazed up into Toby's slightly crossed eye. Its gentle droop made his face seem always sympathetic.

"*I* think she probably is," I mumbled.

"You do?"

"Yeah."

"You think something happened there in that spot?"

"Well . . . I don't know what happened or where it happened. But I think she's . . ."

"Dead?" Toby said.

"Yeah," I admitted sadly.

Toby nodded solemnly, shoved his hands into the pockets of his jeans, and started walking. I walked alongside him even though we were going in the wrong direction for me—up the hill, toward his house. In spite of our grim topic, I liked the novelty of this—walking on a sidewalk with a boy, talking to him almost as easily as if he were Charlotte. Even if the boy was only Eyeball.

"They say you were the last person to see Rose," Toby said, looking straight ahead.

"Yeah," I replied. "I guess."

"Do you ever wonder if it's really true?"

"Whaddaya mean?"

"Well, that you were the *last*. You're the last person to see her that they *know* about, but that doesn't really mean you're the last."

"That might be true. But it's the last person they know about that matters."

"No," Toby stopped walking for a moment, shaking his head. "It's the one they *don't* know about that matters."

He had a point there. Eyeball really wasn't as stupid as Charlotte liked to think.

"What if someone else came out and said they saw her after that?" he asked. "*After* you?"

I shrugged. "That would be good, I think. Because they could probably give the police more clues."

"But it would be weird, wouldn't it?"

"Because it's been a while," I agreed, "so why would somebody suddenly say they had seen her after me?"

"Yeah," Toby said slowly. "It would seem like they were lying."

"Or like they weren't sure they were remembering right," I said.

"Or they'd been hiding something," Toby added.

"Yeah."

"So you probably were the last person to see her," Toby said. "The last person that matters anyway."

"Yeah, probably," I admitted, hoping it didn't sound too conceited to say so.

We'd reached Toby's house by then. Its dull white paint looked sickly gray against the dusk. Such a big old house—too big, I thought, for just a dad and two boys. It hadn't seemed so when Toby's grandmother was alive. She'd owned the house for a long time and had kept it charming and neat. Now the Dean men seemed like guests in a dead lady's house.

"I should probably go home," I said. It was getting dark fast.

I could barely make out Mr. Dean sitting outside in a lawn chair. It was the chair that Joe usually sat in during the summer, just in front of the shed where he worked on his crazy projects. Now it was smack in the middle of the lawn, between the shed and the root cellar. A small, round orange dot glowed in front of Mr. Dean for a moment, then faded, like a firefly. He was smoking, but I was too far away to smell it. It seemed pretty cold to be lounging outside, but maybe Mr. Dean wanted to keep the smoke smell out of his house. He didn't usually smoke much.

"Hi," I said, waving, feeling bold. Usually I waited for parents to acknowledge me first, but Mr. Dean was so humbly sad sometimes that he motivated an unusual friendliness in me.

"Evening," he replied hoarsely.

"You want me to walk you home, then?" Toby asked.

I shrugged. "If you want."

"Okay," he said.

When we reached Mrs. Crowe's, Toby said, "Maybe tomorrow you and Charlotte can come record at my house."

"Maybe," I said.

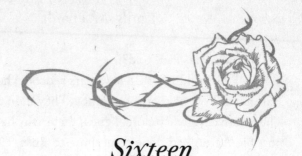

Sixteen

May 27, 2006

Neither Charlotte nor I spoke until we were more than halfway home.

"You really just heard about all of this in this past week?" I asked. "About the accident?"

"Wednesday night," Charlotte admitted. "I showed him the *Looking Glass* things after you showed me the stuff that might be connected to Brian and Sally. I thought he might find it interesting, too. He kind of freaked out when he saw it. Then he told me. Said he was planning on telling me soon anyway, actually. What with the drama about my dad being questioned and all."

"Jesus."

"When we were kids, there was something between Paul and Rose. I really wondered about it. I was afraid . . . well, I don't know what I was afraid of, exactly. Doesn't matter. We know what it was now, I guess."

"Who else has Paul told?"

"Well, he told his wife a few years ago. Said he had no idea if Aaron would've told anyone or not. They didn't stay in touch. They were never very close. I guess that's why he thought it was possible Aaron had done something to Rose. He'd be the one with the most to lose if Rose started telling people what had happened. He was the driver."

Charlotte turned in to the Stop & Shop parking lot.

"We need anything else for this picnic thing?"

"Marshmallows. I forgot marshmallows."

Charlotte's cell phone began to ring. She ignored it.

"I'm sorry I was crazy last night. I wasn't just upset about my dad. On top of that was what Paul told me, and then hearing that you had talked to Sally without telling me. . . . I thought maybe you somehow knew and were going behind my back to find out about it."

"I contacted her because I thought maybe, *maybe* she'd written the *Looking Glass* poems," I explained. "It was just a lark. It wasn't my intention to talk about your brother. I had no idea about this stuff about the accident. I had no idea what it would lead to."

"I understand," Charlotte said, shrugging.

She shifted in her seat, let go of the keys in the ignition, and sighed.

"Speaking of that old *Looking Glass* stuff . . . seems like Brian's letter and those poems are related. Both were in 1996. Probably involve the same person or people."

"That letter really did look like Rose's handwriting," I added.

"I'd have to see it again and hold it up against her dream notes to really be convinced," Charlotte said. "Maybe it's just a good imitation. Rose couldn't send it herself. Rose was dead. So who does that leave?"

"Someone who knew about the accident," I said. "And if Paul didn't tell anyone, that just leaves Aaron, or someone he knew."

Charlotte was quiet for a moment. "Well," she said slowly, "Paul actually told one other person. Back then."

"Yeah?" I studied Charlotte's tired eyes, trying to decide if she wanted me to ask.

"My dad," she said. "He panicked and told my dad."

"Really?" I said uneasily.

"Honestly, Paul just told me this yesterday," Charlotte said quickly. "There was a point when Rose was apparently losing it. Couldn't handle what they'd done. Couldn't handle it being a secret. She wanted to confess. She was threatening to write to the police about it, the newspaper. Even go directly to the Pilkingtons. And I guess my dad was afraid of being sued or something."

"So . . ." I hesitated. "What did your dad do about it?"

"Nothing, as far as Paul knows. Wanted to chat with his lawyer about it before they said anything, I guess. Asked Rose not to say anything till he had a chance to do that. But a couple of weeks later, Rose was gone. . . ." Charlotte frowned. "By then I guess it was sort of like . . . what was the point?"

The space between Charlotte and me was quiet again for a moment. Was I not supposed to make a big deal out of this? Was I supposed to tell her it was all okay? Was I supposed to act like it was perfectly normal for a grown man—a well-respected member of the community, no less—to know that his son was involved in an accident that had paralyzed another kid and to say nothing about it?

Charlotte's phone rang again.

"I'll get this," she said, "While you go get the marshmallows."

As I scanned the Stop & Shop cookie aisle for graham crackers, I thought about how it was Charlotte who'd first introduced me to s'mores. We were about nine, and she'd just come home from a camping trip with her family. They'd had all the ingredients left over, and she'd convinced her dad to let us bake marshmallows in the oven—just one for each of us. I remembered him chuckling as he pulled the two jiggling brown puffs out of the oven, looking small and lonely in the very middle of the large metal cookie sheet where Charlotte had positioned them. And Charlotte had so delighted in watching my reaction when I ate my s'more—far more than in eating her own. *I can't BELIEVE you've never had one before*, she'd repeated proudly. I couldn't quite grasp that this had happened in the very same kitchen where Charlotte and I were headed now. It seemed that afternoon had happened to three different people, in a different dimension.

I paid for the marshmallows, graham crackers, and other treats and headed back out to Charlotte's Saturn.

"Do you remember that time when we made s'mores in your oven?" I asked, reaching for my seat-belt buckle.

Charlotte looked distant and disinterested. "There's been a change in plans," she murmured.

"Hmm?"

"My mother. She's staying in New Jersey. For now."

"What about the cookout?"

Charlotte shrugged. "Says she's sorry about that. Says her sister wants her to stay a little longer, wants her to stay for my cousin's stupid community play or something. I'm guessing, actually, she just doesn't want to come home. I guess she talked to Paul about what's happening. She can't stand his drama sometimes. Always lets me deal with it."

"Well, that sucks," I said, referring to the picnic.

"You're not missing out on much, watching my mother eat half a burger and then doze off in her lawn chair."

"Still would've been nice to see her," I said uncertainly.

"Yeah, well. She can be inconsiderate sometimes. But maybe I'm being cynical. Maybe she's really dying to see that community production of *Brigadoon*."

Charlotte didn't say anything for the last mile home. As she drove, I considered Brian's letter again. The truth about his accident was overwhelming enough—along with Charlotte's father's knowledge of it and, most disturbing, perhaps, that Rose had likely sat down at some point and written a full account of it. And one small detail kept needling me as I tried to absorb all this information: *Datsun versus Dodge, clunker versus clunker* . . . I hadn't thought much about it when I'd read the letter, but it came back to me as we approached Charlotte's house.

When we got home, Charlotte threw her purse down and retreated to her bedroom. I followed her but hesitated by her doorway. Standing in the doorframe, I watched her curl up on her bed.

"You okay?" I said.

"I don't know, Nora. Glad my mom's not coming home, though. I don't have the energy to pretend to be all right this weekend."

"Do you want to talk?" I said.

"I don't know," Charlotte replied, closing her eyes. "It depends on what you want to say."

I leaned against the door, feeling inadequate.

"You can come in, you know," she said. "If you want. Come in and sit down."

I stepped into the room and sat at the swivel chair behind her work desk, which was covered with a pile of multicolored plastic file folders. Each folder had a tab in English-teacher language: *"Mice Men Unit." "Hamlet Unit." "Per 2 Homework Corrected." "Per 5 Homework TB Corrected." "Sophomores—Misc. Crap."* She'd actually written *"Misc. Crap"* on a file folder. Granted, it all looked like misc. crap to me. There was one file folder on the floor, notebook paper spilling out onto the beige carpet.

"Remember that day with the tape recorder?" Charlotte asked, opening her eyes.

"Yeah. Sort of."

And as I said so, it occurred to me that that was the last time I'd been in this room—the last day I'd come over Charlotte's when we were kids. We'd fought that day, and I'd never come over again.

"Sort of?" Charlotte said. "I remember it so well. You were in rare form that day. Don't you remember how you destroyed my tape?"

"Yeah."

"You snapped that day. It was kind of like you decided that afternoon that we weren't gonna be friends anymore."

"I'm not sure if I *decided*. I wasn't that calculating as a kid," I said.

"But after that day it was very clear. You didn't want to come over to my house. You wanted to be alone."

"I was a weird kid. What can I say?"

"I was always confused about what happened. What I'd maybe done to make you feel that way."

I wondered how we were supposed to talk about this—seriously, as Charlotte did? Or with an air of amused distance, as Toby had wanted to talk about prom night? On what terms could any of us really explain how we were when we were kids? And how much could that explanation really mean now?

"After a while, after Rose disappeared, you were different. You got weird. You were really quiet all of a sudden. You didn't—"

"I was weird before that, Charlotte. That's what everybody forgets."

"Not that weird, really." Charlotte pulled herself up on her bed and twirled a lock of hair in her finger. "Nora, were you afraid of my dad?"

"Your dad? No. I was afraid of you."

"I'm serious."

"So am I. I was afraid you'd never stop until . . ."

"Until what, Nora?"

"Until . . . I don't know. I was a dumb kid. I was confused. You kept trying to get me to talk. And I didn't know how to talk about things."

"Like what things? What didn't you know how to talk about?"

"I don't know," I repeated, muttering.

Charlotte looked out the window for a moment. I followed her gaze to the expanse of grass where the Hemsworth trampoline used to be. I wondered when the trampoline had been removed and the hole filled in with dirt and planted over with grass.

" 'The last to see her alive,' " Charlotte whispered. "That

bothered you so much, didn't it? And I used to badger you. I get it. It annoyed you. But that day, that last day, when we fought. What were you afraid I'd make you say?"

As she asked the question, that day came into focus. It was the last time I'd been in this room. Oddly, the room hadn't changed much since then. Sure, Charlotte's frilly lilac bedspread and curtains were gone—replaced by simple wooden blinds and a fluffy mint green duvet. But the furniture was in the same arrangement—bed by the window, desk by the door. The carpet was still beige. Everything still smelled like cigarettes.

"Don't do this, Charlotte," I said.

"Something about my dad? Were you afraid I didn't know my dad could be a dick sometimes? Were you afraid I didn't already know that? Or was it something worse?"

I stared at the wide, empty swath of carpet in the middle of the room. That was where I'd always spread my sleeping bag when I slept over. Where I'd sit cross-legged doing my homework or flip through Charlotte's black books. Where I'd gaze at my favorite picture in all of them—the statues on Easter Island.

"Come on, Nora. You were the last to see her alive. Was it something worse?"

The last to see her alive. This was the spot where I'd lost it on Charlotte, that last day we were friends. *The last to see her alive,* ringing in my ears till I couldn't take it anymore.

"Something worse?" I repeated. *Maybe a kid . . . a kid thinking it was the right thing to do. Datsun versus Dodge, clunker versus clunker.*

"You came all the way back here, after all these years. The last to see her alive. You must have something more to say."

I stood up, my mind racing. *Datsun versus Dodge. The last to see her alive.* The Hemsworths' trampoline—once a deep hole, now filled in.

"Something about my dad? Something about Paul? Did you say something to the police about them, Nora?"

Charlotte was now studying me carefully.

"Nora," she said. "Your face is white."

She stood up and gently clasped my arm.

"You never answered my question," she reminded me. "About Paul. About my dad."

"I never thought anything so terrible, Charlotte. I never allowed myself to articulate what I was so afraid of. But it was never anything like that."

Charlotte gripped my arm tighter.

"But why this look on your face, then? Like death warmed over? Nora, did you say something to the police about my dad?"

"*No*, Charlotte. *Nothing.* I think I stood up too fast," I said, clawing her fingers off my sleeve. "Calm down."

"Oh." Charlotte let her hand drop and sat on her bed again. "Because I can explain about my dad. I'm not sure about now, but back then, when Paul told him about the accident . . . he wasn't trying to shut Rose up. He wanted Paul and Rose to keep quiet till he had a chance to chat with his lawyer about it."

"You mentioned that," I said quietly.

"Maybe he dragged his feet, and when he got around to it, Rose was already gone. Bringing it up after that could get messy."

"Maybe you should talk to him about it," I suggested. "Maybe you should hear it from him instead of Paul. If you're worried about it."

"I didn't say I was worried. I'm just explaining. In case *you* were."

"Okay," I said, sitting on the swivel chair again.

"And the money," Charlotte continued breathlessly. "The money was an entirely different issue. It had nothing to do with the accident. Dad was apparently overpaying her because he felt bad for her family. From his job at the bank, he knew what trouble the Bankses were in with their restaurant. He was just trying to be nice. He started doing that *weeks* before the accident. Paul even knew about it. And Aaron, too, maybe. Probably Aaron mentioned it to the police when they questioned him this time around. That's my guess."

"I see," I said. "Well, that all sounds understandable."

I wasn't entirely sure of what I was saying. I'd remembered something. Something about being in this room with Charlotte, with her picking my brain as she always had. Something I'd somehow forgotten to think about for a very long time.

Charlotte sighed and lowered herself onto her pillows, closing her eyes again. After a few moments, I thought she was sleeping.

As I listened to her breathe, I thought again about the last time I'd been in this room with her. We were eleven. I think I'd been looking at that same stupid picture of Easter Island. I'd thought myself an Easter Island statue. Except I hadn't a clue what secret I was supposed to be keeping. I knew only that if I stayed silent and special, it might keep Rose sleeping soundly— keep us all in the quiet, comforting dark.

"It's too bad," Charlotte piped up—although she didn't open her eyes. "It's too bad you never gave me any credit."

Last to see her alive. Datsun versus Dodge. The words in my head nearly drowned her out.

"Credit?" I repeated, confused by the word. "For what?"

"Well, maybe 'credit' is the wrong word. I mean, it's too bad you never trusted me. You thought I felt nothing of what you were feeling. But I did. Maybe I didn't know how to help you, and trying to get you to talk was all I could think of. You forget that I was only eleven, too."

"Eleven?" I said, barely following her now.

Last to see her alive. Last to see a-liiiiiive. It was a kid's voice singing the words. Teasing, almost.

"I mean after that, too," Charlotte continued. "When we were a little older. The best friend you'd had, and you couldn't trust me. And you never thought I might need someone to talk to as well? But you didn't trust anyone enough to talk. You isolated yourself. You were like a wounded animal half the time, scared of anyone talking to you. Not just about Rose after a while. About anything. It got so pathetic. It was really sad to watch you. But I didn't know what to do."

Last to see her alive. Last to see her alive. It wasn't Charlotte who'd driven me crazy with those words. Of course. It was Toby.

Charlotte blinked at me now, looking concerned. "Nora?"

"Yes?"

"Are you angry?"

"No," I said, just barely.

"I guess I shouldn't have said 'wounded animal.' I shouldn't have said 'pathetic.'" Charlotte's voice was sleepy now. "You're angry."

"Not at all," I said, rising again. "I know exactly how I was."

"I'm sorry."

Her eyes were still closed. She didn't appear aware that I was leaving the room.

"Don't be sorry."

"I'm freaking exhausted, Nora. I'm punchy. I don't even know what I'm saying at this point. I—"

"Charlotte," I interrupted her. "Don't worry about it. But I think I have to go somewhere for a few minutes."

"Good. That works. Because I think I need a nap for even longer than that. If you promise you're not mad."

"I'm not mad," I said softly.

I watched her nuzzle her pillow, then roll away from me, toward the wall. Five minutes later I was in my car, speeding back downtown.

Seventeen

May 27, 2006

I parked in the Dunkin' Donuts lot and crossed over to Deans' Auto Body.

Toby was working with one other guy. Each was tinkering under a different raised car.

"Hi, Toby," I called over the whir of the other guy's drill.

"Hey, Nora," Toby said, poking his head out from under a teal sedan.

"I need to talk to you," I said. "About Brian Pilkington's accident."

Toby let his hand fall to his side, his small wrench tapping the side of his work pants. "What about it?" he said, screwing up his face.

"You know . . . what *really* happened."

Toby glanced back up at the car above him, as if it were listening to us. The other mechanic's drill whirred again.

"Is it really urgent? I've got a customer waiting on this."

"Well . . ." I said reluctantly.

Toby was slapping the wrench so hard against his thigh that it must have hurt. "What's really going on, Nora?"

The drill stopped, and the other guy peered at us.

"You okay, Toby?" he asked.

"Yeah," Toby said, then turned back to me. "Go to the waiting room. I'll get you after I finish this."

Twenty minutes later after he'd rung his customer out, he led me outside and behind the building.

"You're the one who just came in here out of nowhere," he said. "So maybe you ought to talk first."

I took a deep breath. "You knew about Brian's accident, didn't you?"

"What about it?"

"That Rose and Paul and Aaron Dwyer were involved."

Toby tried to narrow his eyes at me—though his weak eye didn't fully cooperate. "How were they involved?" he asked, his voice flat.

"Are you saying you don't know? I think you know. Because you said 'Dodge' when you meant 'Datsun.' You mixed them up because you knew that both types of cars were involved. Which means you knew there were two."

"I'd never mix up a Datsun and a Dodge, Nora."

"You'd never mix them up if you were talking about real cars you'd seen. But you might if they were just cars in a story, or words on a piece of paper. I know you said Dodge when you meant Datsun. Maybe you just didn't remember who was driving which."

Toby folded his arms, clasping both his elbows. "Where is this all coming from?"

"I just saw Brian and Sally," I said. "They explained what happened. And they had this letter—"

"Nora," Toby said, letting go of his elbows. "Is there something specific you want to ask me?"

"Well, to start . . . how did you know? And why didn't you ever tell anyone? Did Rose tell Joe? And Joe told you?"

"No." Toby's mouth straightened into a line, losing its amused expression. "This has nothing to do with Joe. Joe never knew."

"But how could . . . Did Aaron tell?"

"Nora, is that all you wanted to ask me about? Brian's accident?"

"*All?* A kid was paralyzed."

"I don't mean to downplay that. But it was seventeen years ago. And the way I read it, maybe the kids were all just fooling around. I'm not saying it wasn't tragic, that the kids in the other car shouldn't have felt like serious assholes, but— What's the matter?"

"Toby." I lowered my voice. "You just said 'the way I read it.' "

Toby hesitated, considering his own words. "I did, did I?"

"Yeah," I replied, my heart racing now. "You've seen the letter?"

"Isn't it funny," he said icily. "How I keep wanting to tell you things? When you always seemed the least able to handle it?"

"I can handle it," I said defensively. "I'm different now."

Toby took his keys out of his pocket and studied them. "Are you sure about that?"

"Yes," I said.

He shrugged. "Isn't it funny when you get something you always wanted a little after you've stopped wanting it? Just a few days or a few months or a couple of years after you've given up? Don't you hate it when that happens?"

I didn't reply.

"Nora," he said, finally looking up at me. "What do you want from me?"

"Well . . ." I said. "First of all, I'd like to know if you've seen that letter. Where? When? How? If it wasn't through Joe, then—"

"I told you, it has nothing to do with my brother!"

And with that, Toby turned and rushed back into the garage. Before I had a chance to react, he was outside again, trudging to his pickup truck, which was parked alongside the building a few feet away.

He got in, started the engine, and revved it a couple of times. Then he wheeled the car around in a circle so his open driver's window was facing me.

"I'm going home," he said. "I asked Jake to call one of my other guys to come in for me."

"Why?"

"Because I can't talk here."

I hesitated. "So we're talking?"

"If that's what you really want. You can follow me home. But you'd better be sure. Last time I checked, you weren't sure. But you're an adult now, and I assume if you show up and start asking me these kinds of questions, you actually want to hear the answers."

"When we were kids, Toby, I didn't—"

"Shh. I said I can't talk here. You can follow me home if you want. But then, whatever I tell you, you can't decide you don't want to know. On the other hand, you can just get in your car and drive the same way back to Charlotte's and I would never blame you. Think about it, will you?"

"But, Toby," I said. "What do *you* want me to do?"

Toby's good eye looked sad and his bad one tired.

"I stopped wanting you to do anything a long time ago," he said. "You're the one who showed up again after nine years. I wasn't expecting you. So don't ask *me* what you should do."

Then he hit the gas and left me in the parking lot.

Not a minute after his truck had disappeared, I knew I'd be going after him. But I felt that doing so might be a betrayal, unless I did something else first.

I pulled my cell out of my purse and dialed home.

"You sound weird," Neil said after we'd greeted each other. "Is everything okay?"

"No," I admitted.

"What happened? Is it the car?"

"No. It's . . . Waverly. It's this place I'm from."

"You're tired of it, sounds like. Well, if I were you, I'd have just stayed a weekend."

"Tired? No." I walked across the parking lot and got into my car as I talked. "Neil, have you ever wanted to come back here with me? To see where I'm from? Because I'm starting to realize, there was never anything wrong with Waverly. It's actually kind of cute. Perky little neighborhoods. Pretty old town green, town library. Everyone seems nice enough. There's nothing wrong with the place. It could be any nice little town."

"Where is all this coming from, Nora? I thought you hated it there."

"I didn't hate it here," I said. "I didn't ever hate it here. I hated myself here."

"Yeah, well," Neil said after a moment's pause. "I hated myself in high school, too."

"Who said anything about high school?"

"I just figured that's what you were talking about."

"Why's that?"

"Because you've always been weird about high school. Ever since we were in college. Your stories about high school are always kind of vague. Or about other kids, not you. There was one story you told that I'm pretty sure actually came from a John Hughes movie."

"And this has never bothered you?"

"No. Why would it? Who the hell cares about high school? I always hated those girls who were always telling boring stories about their old drama-club friends."

"So what do you think I was like in high school?"

"Based on what I've gathered from your mom, I figured you were kind of goth."

"Shut up. Goth didn't even exist when we were in high school."

"Of course it did."

"Not really. It didn't have a name yet, I don't think."

"So you weren't goth? What are you about to tell me? That everyone hated you?"

"No."

"Because I don't care if they did. They were stupid if they did."

"It wasn't like that anyway. People didn't hate me. No one bothered to hate me. I was nobody."

"Well." Neil sighed. "Everybody's nobody in high school, really."

"No," I said. "No, that's not true. Let's not bullshit here, okay? I mean I really wasn't there. I was silent. I was afraid to speak, till it seemed like there was truly nothing to say. Silent at school, silent at home. I tried to join clubs, but it seemed like you had to talk too much in them all. I'd have friends for a little while, but I could never keep them. It seemed like if I got too close to anyone I'd have to say too much—too much of what, I don't remember."

"Nora, are you crying?"

"No," I said, my voice breaking. "Well, maybe."

I started my car so I could close my window.

"And this went on and on," I continued when I caught my breath, "until it seemed like I might have to say or do really, really stupid things just to know I still existed in some real way. Until I *did* a stupid thing or two. And I wish I could remember how it started. How I came to be so dumb as to make myself so miserable, and how I came to blame this place as if there were something in the water. Because it wasn't that way always. Not when I was a kid. Something happened to me in between that I've never understood. I'd always been quiet, but I just became scared and *silent* all of a sudden, which is something entirely different. Do you understand?"

"I think so," Neil said. "But you turned out okay, so what does it matter now?"

"But, Neil, I didn't just hurt myself doing this. I hurt other people. Because there were things I could've said, things I could've done, people I could've listened to, conversations I could've had, if I'd trusted myself enough. "

Neil hesitated. "I'm not sure I totally understand everything you're saying, but if you're saying there's someone you need to apologize to, then do it. I get that. I've felt that way about those years. If there's someone there you hurt—are you talking about Charlotte?—then all you can do now is say you're sorry. Honestly, people probably don't care anymore nearly as much as you think they do. It's been quite a few years. But you're there now. So if it's important to you, say sorry if there's someone there you think deserves it."

"Yeah, I'm thinking of doing that," I said. "That's kind of what I was hoping you'd say."

"Okay," Neil said, sounding a little perplexed.

"And when I get home," I added, "I'll explain it better."

"Sure. Or you could just tell me a story from *The Breakfast Club*, for old times' sake."

"Right," I said, laughing a little.

It was an appropriate reference, since the story I'd be telling him was mostly a typical one about teen angst. But connected to it was a much sadder and more consequential story—about an older girl whom I'd loved and who'd gone missing and died. Maybe it was just sheer timing that I'd ended up tangling the two in my head, and found myself unable to tell either one for so long.

"But don't let me do that, Neil," I said, sniffling as I put the car into gear.

"Okay. I won't. If you insist."

"I insist. But I have to go now," I said. "I'm driving."

Hauntings:
December 1990

We had to ring twice. Toby's mouth was hanging open when he answered the door.

"We came to record for paranormal activity," Charlotte announced. "May we come in?"

Toby hesitated, wedging his head between the door and the doorframe. "Umm. Right *now*?"

"Is this a bad time?"

He swiveled his head around, looking into the house.

"It's just the girls. Nora and Charlotte," he said, then turned back to us. "You want something to eat?"

"Can we come in, then?" Charlotte asked, nudging the door open farther.

"I guess," Toby said, shrugging, letting go of the door.

Charlotte went in first, and I followed. I wiped my feet on the green Astroturf of the mudroom before entering the Deans' TV room. The warmth of the room brought out the distinctive smell of the Dean house: mildew, mothball, and Hamburger Helper. Joe was on the couch watching *Donahue*, scrunched down so far his neck nearly touched the seat cushions.

"Hello, just the girls," Joe said, without looking away from the television.

I sat on the other end of the couch, figuring that, without any parents around, no permission to sit would be needed or granted. I balanced the black books I'd brought along on the arm of the couch.

"Nora tells me there's a room upstairs you think might have a ghostly presence," Charlotte said, keeping things professional.

"Don't you want something to eat first?" Toby asked.

"I'm fine, thank you," Charlotte replied, shaking her head.

"What've you got?" I asked.

"A few different things. Want me to show you?"

"Okay!" I consented eagerly, suspecting that the Dean family offerings contained several snack items that weren't allowed by my mother's budget or philosophy.

Charlotte tapped her foot on the hardwood floor, her lip twitching disapprovingly for just a second. "If you don't mind, I'm just going to head right on up to the room in question."

"By yourself?" I asked.

"It's the third room on the left upstairs," Joe chimed in. "Then you go through that room to get to the stairs up to it."

"You go through one room to get to the other room?" Charlotte said.

"Yep. That's what makes it a secret room. The people who built this place—you kind of have to wonder what they did with that room. That's what makes us think it might be haunted, see?"

Charlotte wrinkled her nose at Joe for a second, then turned and marched up the stairs.

Toby waved me into the kitchen with him.

"There's these cookies," he said. He opened a cabinet, and a moth flew out. "But I think maybe they're stale. And—oh, look! You like cheese curls?"

He produced a fresh, unopened bag from behind a few tattered cracker boxes.

I didn't much like cheese curls, but since he seemed excited about them, I answered, "Sure."

Toby waved away another moth and produced a blue plastic mixing bowl from another cabinet, then filled it with curls.

"That's a lot," I observed.

"We're four people," he pointed out, then opened the refrigerator. "Do you like root beer?"

"Yup."

Toby pulled a three-quarters-empty bottle of Stop & Shop root beer out of the refrigerator and set up two glasses. Then he filled one glass about halfway.

"It looks flat," he said quietly. "I'm sorry."

"That's okay. I like it flat. It's sweeter that way."

Toby started to hand me the bottle but stopped himself, then poured my root beer for me. I pretended not to notice, but I could feel a sensation of goose bumps traveling up my forearms. Pouring for me. It was just a few steps away from kissing me. Kind of gross.

A moth from the cabinet fluttered by Toby's hands for a moment, and he flicked it away. He did it so naturally that I was pretty sure he was used to having moths around. I wondered if this was what it was to not have a mother around—to have moths in your kitchen. I felt, suddenly, like I understood Toby just a little better. But that probably didn't mean I'd ever want to kiss him.

"I wonder if Charlotte wanted you to go up there with her," he said, leading me back into the TV room.

"What do you mean?"

He shrugged and made a place for the cheese curls on the coffee table in front of Joe, pushing away newspapers, a broken soldering iron, and a pile of empty movie cases.

"I mean she's not afraid?" Toby asked.

"She'll scream if there's any trouble, I guess," I said, sitting on one side of Joe as Toby plopped himself on the other.

Joe stared at the TV and said nothing. Donahue kept talking to the housewife who worked part-time as a stripper. Toby and

I ate cheese curl after cheese curl. I tried to suck the orange cheese dust off my fingers, but that just made it soggy, mashing orange crud into my fingernails.

Toby announced he was going to check on Charlotte. Then he thumped up the stairs, leaving me with his brother.

"Don't you want some?" I asked Joe, offering him the bowl of cheese curls.

Joe turned and gazed at me in that stupid, sad-eyed way that Toby sometimes looked at teachers in class. Like he didn't even know what the question was, much less the answer. Then he plucked a single cheese curl out of the bowl and said, "Thanks," smiling for a split second and then returning his attention to the TV.

I noticed that the cheese curl stayed in his hand. We watched *Donahue* together for a few more minutes. When Toby returned, Joe got up and disappeared into the kitchen, leaving his cheese curl on the couch cushion between Toby and me.

On the TV a husband of one of the housewife-strippers came out and answered Donahue's questions. The subject hadn't felt so embarrassing while Joe was around. Now, watching it with just Toby, it was unbearable. I grabbed one of the black books off the arm of the couch where I'd left them.

"You ever look at these before?" I asked Toby.

"They Charlotte's?"

"Yeah."

"Charlotte's never shared anything with me."

I tossed him *Phantom Encounters*. "Go for it."

On the very first page of my book, *Hauntings*, Charlotte had circled and starred a few sentences in green ink:

The physicist Sir Oliver Lodge, for instance, pro-
posed in 1908 that hauntings were a "ghostly rep-
resentation of some long past tragedy." Lodge and
others believed that violent emotions might somehow imprint themselves on their environment for
later transmission to people sensitive enough to tune
them in.

I wasn't sure why this passage would interest Charlotte. I
didn't totally understand it, except for the phrase "violent emotions." Did Charlotte really know what that meant, somewhere
deep down? Or was it something that just made her curious?
Like almost everything else she circled and underlined?

I flipped past a few dog-eared pictures of haunted English
castles. Charlotte had been heavy into the haunted English
castles for a while, but not so much lately. I skipped a chunk of
pages.

"Hey, look at this," Toby said. "'Reports of naked ghosts are
rare.' Charlotte underlined that, looks like."

I shrugged. "It's probably true, right? Ghosts are usually
wearing clothes when people see them."

But Toby kept laughing, which annoyed me. Weren't we too
old to be laughing just because a word like "naked" or "gas"
came into the conversation? I rolled my eyes, moved farther
down the couch, away from him, and looked out the window.

"Hey, Toby," I exclaimed, "it's snowing."

Toby didn't close his mouth as he looked up. "Cool," he said,
dropping *Phantom Encounters* on the couch.

He grabbed his puffy brown jacket and headed outside.

I followed him. It was coming down pretty fast, in a thick white slant. This was no gentle dusting. This was no-school-tomorrow snow.

"Wow," Toby said, jumping down the stoop, skipping all three steps, sticking out his tongue.

I went after him, feeling the flakes land on my cheeks. I liked that this was a feeling you forgot every year, till winter came around and hit you in the face again and helped you to remember.

Toby tried to skate on the driveway, but there wasn't enough snow built up yet.

"Remember that time at the pond, when we were little?" he asked.

"At least here you know you won't fall in," I said.

"Not as fun this way, though. Part of the fun's knowing the ice could break."

"Uh-huh," I said, even though I wasn't sure I agreed.

Mr. Dean's truck rumbled up the road and into the driveway. He got out of the truck with a gallon of milk hooked on his thumb.

He seemed startled to find Toby and me on the front lawn.

"What're you two doing?" he asked.

"Just tasting the snow," Toby answered.

Mr. Dean handed him the milk. "Put that in the fridge for me, will you, Tobe?"

It seemed odd to me that he'd send Toby back into the house when he was going there himself. Toby grabbed the milk and went inside with it.

"How long've you two been out here?" Mr. Dean asked me.

I tried to look him in the eye to answer him. I'd been trying to do that more with parents. But something about his appearance distracted me. A greasy chunk of bangs was practically in his eye. His face was bony and grayish. His cheekbones and Adam's apple looked sharp and painful. Looking at him now reminded me of when Toby's grandmother was dying, when my mother used to come and help him.

"Since it started snowing," I said, glancing away again.

"Just came out to the yard, just now?"

"Yeah."

Mr. Dean did a 360-degree turn, gazing around the yard, eyeing our footprints in the thin layer of snow.

"Pretty, ain't it?" he said.

Mr. Dean was the sort of guy who knew better than to use a word like "ain't" but used it anyway to make things friendly and fun.

"Yup," I answered.

The front door of the house creaked open, and Toby came bounding down the steps. His dad gave him a quick smile and a nod and then trudged over to the lawn chair between Joe's rickety shed and the condemned root cellar. Without wiping off the snow that had already begun to accumulate in the chair, he collapsed into it with the same satisfied sigh with which one might fall into a living-room recliner.

Toby didn't seem to notice my quizzical gaze. I was supposed to accept it, I guessed, because this was one of the wacky things dads did that I didn't understand. It wasn't much weirder than some of the stuff Mr. Hemsworth did.

"Come here," Toby said, leading me to a hillier area of the yard around the right side of the house. "We could almost sled here."

He positioned his feet in a skateboarding stance and slid a couple of yards down the slick grass. He stumbled at the steepest part and slid into the grass as if it were home plate.

"You okay?" I asked, even though his fall had looked pretty intentional.

"Yeah," he said.

I put my hand out to help him up. He yanked at it, pulling me down next to him. I giggled as I hit the grass but quickly let go of his hand. It felt too weird touching his thick, cold fingers, even for a second. Too close to kissing.

Toby didn't seem to notice. He lay back on the frosted grass and opened his mouth to catch more snowflakes. I felt awkward sitting there watching him, but I didn't want to do the same. I'd never much liked the taste of snowflakes.

Wondering when Charlotte was going to come out of the house, I got up and walked back to the front of the yard. I looked around the yard and noticed Mr. Dean still sitting in the lawn chair. He sat motionless, a soft cap of snow piling on his head.

Toby followed close behind me. "Look at his hair," he said, laughing.

I didn't laugh back. I stood up and stepped closer. Mr. Dean's motionlessness perplexed me. It was almost like he was dead. A chill shot through me. Then Mr. Dean crossed his feet. So he wasn't dead. But the chill remained in my arms and legs. His face was blank. Not goofy blank like Joe's in the house. Blank blank. Dead blank. He didn't seem aware that it was snowing.

No, I reassured myself. Mr. Dean wasn't dead.

But Rose was.

I knew it. I still didn't know how I knew it, but it was as real now as it was in the middle of the night. Rose was dead.

I took another step closer to Mr. Dean.

"He's pretty tired," Toby informed me. "He's been short-handed at the shop. Probably we shouldn't bother him."

"I'm not bothering him," I murmured, staring at Mr. Dean. His cheeks looked especially white, his skin thin and grayish. His eyes were still expressionless, like a dead person's would be.

Mr. Dean blinked, which startled me. You don't expect to see a skeleton blink. Not that Mr. Dean was a skeleton. But Rose was. I just knew that Rose was.

I heard Toby stepping closer to me.

"He's always liked the snow," he said softly. "I wouldn't be surprised if he fell asleep like that."

"Uh-huh," I said, moving just a little closer.

But Rose was. A gust of wind blew by us all, moving the direction of the snow briefly. It hit me cold in the eyes. I squeezed them shut, and when I opened them, Mr. Dean was actually looking at me.

Just for a moment, and then his eyes were blank again. But that moment was enough. The pain in them made me feel like I was alone in my bed in the dark.

"I think my sled's in the shed if you want to—" Toby started to say.

I tried to push by him, but he grabbed my jacket and then stared at me with both his good eye and his crooked one.

"What is it?" he asked.

But his voice was more defeated than surprised. As if he saw what I saw. As if he hadn't wanted me to see it. I stared back at Toby. Even with the one lazy eye, his eyes were warmer, more alive, than his dad's—but just as painful to look at. I saw Charlotte's black books in his eyes. Pictures from Charlotte's awful black books. A screaming captive burning in a Druid's hanging prison cage. A sheep's heart full of nails. A young Aztec warrior with his heart ripped out, but with no bird soul to free him. *Violent emotions.*

I looked away. I wrestled myself from Toby's grasp, and I ran down the lawn to the sidewalk. I raced away from the house.

"Where you goin'?" Toby called after me, his voice sounding almost normal again, but not quite.

I nearly slipped on the snow that was quickly collecting on the sidewalk. But I didn't fall. I ran.

Eighteen

May 27, 2006

Toby opened the door before I knocked.

"I didn't think you'd come. It's been an hour."

"I was thinking, like you asked me to."

"Good," he said, leading me to a cheerful green IKEA couch that seemed completely out of place in the dusty old Dean living room. He'd opened all the windows, and a pleasant spring breeze floated through the room, softening the mildew scent.

"And what were you thinking?" he asked, sitting next to me.

"I was thinking I may not have understood everything I felt when we were kids. I was thinking I want to understand it now."

Toby looked around the living room, his gaze bouncing from the window to the torn leather recliner to the blank television screen and finally back to me.

"You do, do you?" he said, his eyes flat.

"Yes," I said.

"You asked me if I read the letter," he said slowly. "The letter Rose wrote about the accident."

"Yeah."

"I didn't just read it. I sent it."

"In 1996?"

Toby thought about this for a moment, doing the math. "We were in high school. Yeah. That's about right."

"Where the hell did you get it?"

"Out of a notebook of Rose's."

"And how did you get that?"

Toby hesitated. "I found it."

"When we were kids?"

"No. That year—1996."

"Where did you find it?"

"In the attic room. In a pile of junk. In a backpack."

"A backpack? Jesus, Toby. A backpack of Joe's?"

"No." He pressed his fingertips into his hairline, wiping away a droplet of sweat. "Rose's."

"In the attic room?" I repeated, disbelieving.

"Yeah. And I didn't know how it had gotten there. I didn't know what to do with it. But Rose had written a bunch of shit in that notebook, I'll tell you. It was her history notebook. But it didn't seem like she was much interested in history."

"What else was in the backpack?"

"Couple of her textbooks. Couple of pens. Some ancient hard candies. Six-year-old Jolly Ranchers."

"And in the notebook was the letter about the accident."

"Yeah. I didn't know what to do about it. Sent the letter to Brian. Seemed like he should have it if he wanted it. In case he ever wanted to call Aaron and Paul on what they'd done or whatever. Seemed like what Rose might have wanted."

"But—" I said, stopping at one word to try and check the quaver in my voice.

"But what?" Toby stared at me.

"But . . . that wasn't all the notebook had in it."

"No," Toby said, looking away from me and attempting to rub a grease spot off his thumb. "No, it wasn't."

"The *Looking Glass*. Those poems in the *Looking Glass*. Did you write them?"

"No. Rose did. I found them in her notebook. I submitted them."

"Why did you do that?" I asked.

"I was seventeen. I was a kid. When I found it, I wasn't sure what it all meant. I didn't know what to do. I was confused. I think you can understand that, huh, Nora? Not everything you did back then made sense either. At the very least, I thought they'd catch Charlotte's attention. Charlotte who was so desperate to figure out what happened to Rose. And I didn't want to keep it to myself."

"But didn't you wonder how Rose's backpack got into your house?"

"Yes, I wondered!" Toby snapped. "What do you think? Why do you think I did such stupid things, sending her warped scribblings here and there? But who did I have to talk about it with? Who could I have talked to? My brother? My dad? I was afraid of what I might find out. There was only one person who I'd ever considered talking to about Rose, and she was really fucked up that year. She couldn't handle something like this."

"I'm sorry," I whispered.

Toby didn't seem to hear me. He stood and began to lumber up the stairs. A few minutes later, he returned with a tattered notebook in his hands.

"Have you asked your brother about it since?" I asked.

I stared at the notebook as he sat on the couch again. Its purple cover was worn white around the corners, and the paper had brown spots on the edges. It had once been a three-subject notebook, but one of the divider pages had been ripped out, the other tab mashed down. Someone had written *"History"* across the front in black pen. Below that, someone had erased the cover hard to form the word *"HI"* in the purple cardboard.

"No," Toby said, tracing the *"HI"* with his finger. "What she wrote in here was enough. Or at least enough for me to know I didn't want to ask anything else. It said enough to make me afraid to ask."

Toby looked up at me. "Before I show you this, I need to ask you. Did you really come to me because of a Datsun and a Dodge? Was it about sleuthing that one out, or was there something more to it?"

"What do you mean?"

"What I'm asking is . . . was it my imagination that you always kind of knew that something wasn't right?"

"I didn't *know* anything."

"You didn't know any details. But there was something in your face, more than once. . . . You knew you should be scared of something."

"But I swear, Toby, that's *all* I knew."

"That was *something*, though. And sometimes I wonder how you even knew that."

A gentle breeze blew through the Dean living room, lifting its dusty smell into my nostrils for a moment.

"Yeah," I said. "Sometimes I wonder that, too."

"And because you knew that—that's why I never expected you to come back. Nora, what are you doing back here? Don't you see it's too late to come back and ask?"

"How could it be too late?"

Toby flipped the notebook over and stared at the back of it. Someone had scribbled *"He's so gross!!!"* on it in pencil, and someone had agreed *"Yeah"* in black pen. I wanted to yank the notebook out of his hands but knew I could never beat Toby in a wrestling match.

"Do you remember that night, when I asked you why you tried to kill yourself?"

"Yeah. What does that have to do with Rose?"

"A lot. You'll see when you read this."

"Are you going to *let* me read it?"

"Yes. If you answer the question."

"Okay . . ." I said skeptically.

The notebook seemed almost a tease into a conversation that might never end—because this was one question for which I'd never have a satisfactory answer.

"I did it," I said, "to set myself free. I'd been so quiet for so long. No one noticed I was even there anymore. Sometimes I wondered how much there was left of myself. I did it to see what I could make happen."

"Fancy way of saying you did it for attention, then?"

"No. Well, yes—if you're one of those people who needs to call it one thing or the other. Death or attention. The first being noble and tragic, the second being loathsome and pathetic. Then yes, I'm in the loathsome-and-pathetic category. But I think you know it was more complicated than that. You knew me. You remember."

"Yeah." Toby seemed to relax a little, his grip loosening on the notebook. "But that's still not an explanation. To say it was complicated doesn't explain."

"Okay. Well. I felt trapped. I mean, no, I didn't want to die. But I didn't want to feel trapped anymore. And *that* wasn't about anyone else. That was just about me."

"Trapped by what?"

"Trapped in my own sad, small view of myself, I suppose."

"Uh-huh. And did it work?"

"Yes, actually. It did. It was a terrible, pathetic thing to do, but in a twisted way it did work. It made me see how desperate I'd gotten. And that no one was ever going to care how sad I looked or how silent I'd become. That I could take it that far and discover that the world kept turning and everyone mostly just kept about the business of making themselves happy, which of course is exactly what they should be doing. That the best way to stop being desperate is to stop waiting for other people to see it and take care of yourself instead. However the hell you can. Even if that means shutting out old parts of yourself or people who are used to those parts. Even if you have to be a little cold about it. Get the hell out and into a situation where you can have better ambitions for yourself than someone finally caring to ask what's wrong with you."

I caught my breath, surprised at some of the words that had just come out of my mouth.

"Some touchy-feely therapist at the hospital help you figure that out?" Toby asked, sounding skeptical.

"No. It took me years to figure that out. By myself."

"You ever regret it? Regret hurting your mother like that?"

"I regret hurting my mother. But I don't regret figuring that out. So on some level I don't regret it. I hate to say it like that, but it's true."

"So you've made peace with it. That what you're saying?"

"No. I wouldn't go that far. But not everything needs to be made peace with, don't you think?"

Toby rolled his eyes—at me or at the idea of making peace, I couldn't determine. Then he ran his finger along the metal spiral binding of the notebook.

"But what if you had died?" he asked.

"I knew I wouldn't. Even if I didn't admit that to myself. In the back of my mind, I knew I was being way too careful for that ever to happen."

"What if you'd been wrong?" Toby asked, his voice rising.

"I wasn't."

"But what if you *WERE*?"

He threw the notebook at me. It bounced off my shoulder and landed right in my lap.

"Toby . . ." I said, picking it up and holding it tight, in case he changed his mind. "You think Rose killed herself?"

I couldn't read the frustrated look on his face. Immediately after I'd said it, it felt ridiculous. A suicide can't bury herself in a wicker trunk.

"Why don't you read what she wrote?" he said, getting up and taking a step away from the couch.

"Are you going back to work?"

"No. Just outside. Just for some air. I hate the smell of this house."

"Can I—"

"No. Just stay here and read it. The last section was where she wrote all that dream crap. Plus the letter about the accident. She kept writing it over and over, adding stuff. The second section is her journal. Read that part."

Toby went outside. I stayed on the bright green couch and read.

9/4

Tomorrow is the one-year anniversary of Aaron and me. It feels weird for it to have been so long. When it started, I didn't think anything serious would happen. Six months is serious, I guess. It makes me feel owned sometimes, and I don't like it. When other guys talk to me now, it's different. It's like I'm married. I don't like feeling married. Especially when I think we'll break up once he graduates at the end of this year. Do we pretend all year? Do I have to be married all year? I suppose this is my role. To go with him to homecoming and prom. To cry a tear when he leaves for college. To give him some practice so he doesn't make a fool of himself when he meets the love of his life.

9/7

I think I was too hard on Aaron last time I wrote. He really isn't as selfish as I made him sound. I've liked having a boyfriend, having someone to do things with. I'm not saying he uses me—at least any more than I use him—but sometimes it feels like we're going through the motions of the high-school relationship, nothing more. He's nice to me. I just get sick of the role, that's all. That's all I was trying to say. And I guess in the end I am jealous of him—of having only one year to go. What would that feel like? Two years seems so much more than one. This is the year that really matters for col-lege—blah, blah, blah. I don't know. I guess I can try to care about grades—I mean, really care, like Paul does. I could probably do just as well as him if I did.

9/23

Thought I would, but I haven't. Thought I could, but I can't. "Sorry" is a word you say after your par-ents catch you scratching your sister, a word you don't mean. "Apologize" is the word you replace it with when you're old enough to pretend. Neither is ever enough.

10/1

Paul responded pretty much as I expected. He's a good kid, but robotically so. Don't copy off other kids' papers. Listen to the teacher. Say please and thank you. Doesn't know how to figure out his own right and wrong outside of that. Like a kid who knows how to add, multiply, and divide but can't figure out which to do in a word problem. Doesn't know how the rules apply to real life. He knew he shouldn't be doing it at the time. But now that there's a problem with no clear rule or solution, he doesn't have a clue.

10/2

But then, do I have a clue either?

10/9

I can't believe he told. But, more unbelievable, nothing's happened. And they all want me to wait. Not shut up—they don't say that. Just wait. Wait and see. Even Mr. H. Wait till what? Till Paul gets into Tufts? Till Jesus arrives and waves his arms to restore Brian's severed nerves? Maybe we're just waiting for time to pass? Maybe, years and years from now, people will soften because what happened will be past. But I couldn't stand those years in between. Years and years of knowing he can't have what I have and I could have stopped it. Year after year of normal life I don't deserve.

10/11

Starting to wonder if any of these things I've been telling myself are true. If I'm so much braver or

better than Aaron or Paul or Mr. H, why haven't I
said anything yet?

10/13

I went to Joe's late last night. His father was sleeping, and so was Toby. He let me up into his room. I
went to ask him what kind of pills he could get me.
He laughed. What did I think, he was some kind
of candy man? And what did I think this was, the
'70s? And I thought of telling him why. What would
he do if he knew? Not sure, but I think at least
he wouldn't judge me. Joe's already seen and done
some things. But he has never hurt anyone. That's
the thing about Joe, no matter what people think
of him. He'd grow 'shrooms, but he wouldn't hurt
a fly. And I guess that's why I couldn't tell him. He
thinks I like him now, and I guess I do. As much as
I can like someone right now. He at least is honest.
He at least doesn't pretend to be better than he is.
He doesn't pretend his future is sacred.

10/15

So now Mr. H is suddenly paying me even more.
Afraid of me and my mouth? Probably he doesn't
need to worry. I'm just tired now. The first time, I
didn't realize till I got home that it was way more
than it should be. I told him the next day, and he
said not to worry about it. Then this week he did
it again. And I was too tired of all of us to care
anymore.

10/16

Joe kissed me tonight. Kissing Joe is nothing like kissing Aaron. With Aaron the kiss was always a means to an end. Aaron was always trying to move us both efficiently into a frenzy, or like he's driving a car with his lips. I can see how amused Joe is. The girl down the street going through a bad-boy phase. It could end as easily as it started. He'll take what he can get. A kiss or more. It doesn't need to go anywhere.

10/17

Shouldn't be kissing anyone. Remember? What do you deserve?

10/21

Would it kill them to know what I had done? Or would it just kill me to have them know? Why am I so selfish that this is what I care about? What about him? Forget me, what about Brian? He even slips my mind some days now. What's wrong with me?

10/25

How do you let fate decide? Stand far in front of a train and see if it stops? Stand in a river and see if it takes you? But there is no train and no river in Waverly. Where is the nearest train? There's the Metro North out of New Haven. And where does the Amtrak run, from New Haven to Hartford and up through Massachusetts? I know it exists, but I don't

even know where else it runs. Several towns west.
Nowhere near here. I can't imagine hearing the
train coming and standing your ground. All of that
noise and metal coming closer. Maybe it hypnotizes
you. But I can't imagine. Maybe if you didn't know
it was coming, closed your eyes, put on headphones
and played music on the highest volume. Would that
be loud enough that you wouldn't hear it coming?

10/28

Toby saw me. I pretended I didn't see him, because
how to explain? Poor kid. What would I say if he
asked?

10/29

Stood out in the tennis courts last night instead.
With headphones again. But for what? For aliens
to land and claim me? For the werewolves to stalk
me while I obliviously listen to Peter Gabriel, only
to open my eyes just before they rip my heart out?

10/30

Forget pills, forget aliens and all that silly shit.
Quit with the drama. Get serious here. Real sin—
real punishment.

11/2

Kiss 95.7 on my Walkman last night, like I used to
listen to when I was the girls' age. The third song
was Madonna, "True Blue." I knew this song from

*before I was even their age. I'd liked it—it was so
cheesy. I didn't know anything then. Seems like
even Madonna was innocent back then. I had to
stop after that song. Because the song made me
think of my parents and how to them I'm still that
age. For all they know, I could still love such a
song.*

11/3
If not this, what?

11/5
*Simon & Garfunkel tonight. Their first album.
Wednesday Morning, 3 A.M. Over and over. "Bleecker
Street" is my favorite. Sometimes, peace.*

November fifth was the last entry. Rose had disappeared on
the eighth. I read and reread. It did sound as if Rose was sometimes thinking about suicide. It was hard for me to tell if she'd
been at all serious. When I was sixteen, I never would've written about it. Somewhere in the back of my mind, I'd known
that committing my intentions to paper would give away their
fraudulence.

And there were, of course, other interesting aspects to this
journal besides the suicide musings.

There was the stuff about Mr. Hemsworth, for one. I wasn't
entirely confident the extra pay had nothing to do with her
silence about the accident. Charlotte maybe wanted to tell herself that, but Rose certainly *perceived* the money as something
more than generosity.

And kissing Joe? Somehow I wasn't surprised. But was that a big secret to the Dean boys? Had Joe mentioned that to the police? And what had Rose been doing when Toby had seen her? Screwing around with Joe? Smoking herb with Joe? Taking pills from Joe?

The Deans' front door opened, and I jumped.

"Toby—" I said, standing.

But it was Joe at the door.

"I didn't hear your car," I said.

"Hey," Joe said. "Nice to see you. Wasn't sure you'd stick around this long. You come for some BBQ? Tobe and I were talking about getting some ribs."

"No . . ." I said. "Toby still in the yard?"

"Nope. He supposed to be?"

"I thought he went . . . outside."

I realized after I'd done it that I was gesturing with the notebook. Without thinking, I clapped it against my chest, which caught Joe's attention.

"What's that?" he asked, pointing with his chin.

"Nothing," I said.

"Looks old," he said, smiling. "Old love notes from good old WHS?"

"No," I said, clasping my arms around it tighter.

"You don't fool me," Joe said, giving me a playful nudge on the arm. "I know you and Tobe were hot and heavy. Guess that's why you keep showing up here, huh?"

"Joe," someone snapped behind us. I whirled around to see Toby standing there, glaring at both of us. As I did so, Joe yanked the notebook out from under my arms.

"Let me see here," Joe said, opening it.

"No!" Toby yelled, lunging for Joe.

"'Rose Banks,'" Joe read from the inside cover, stepping backward away from him. "'American history.'"

The expression on his face reminded me of Elvis again. This time the young Elvis, the side of his lip pulled up in a good-natured but half-witted smile.

He turned to me. "Wow. Where'd you get this? Rose leave it at Charlotte's house when she was sitting? Anything good?"

Toby snatched it from Joe and handed it back to me.

Joe sincerely had never seen this notebook before. Either that or he was drunk again, but it didn't seem or smell like it.

"Yeah," Toby said to me, recovering his breath. "Anything good?"

"Nothing good," I said. "Just history notes. Toby, you ready for that walk we talked about? To the tennis courts, for old times' sake?"

As we headed out the door, Joe called after us, "We still grilling, Tobe?"

"Yup!" Toby yelled back.

Nineteen

**Psychic Voyages:
December 1990**

I ignored Toby as he shouted after me. Running as fast as I could, I almost slipped in the snow a couple of times but managed to recover and stay on my feet. I forgot to breathe till I was halfway down the hill, then ran right past my house. My mother wasn't due home for a couple of hours. I couldn't imagine sitting with Mrs. Crowe, politely watching her soaps with her, swallowing this feeling over and over until it maybe bubbled out of my stomach and barfed itself all over her imitation Oriental rug. No, I could not go home. I circled Charlotte's house a couple of times, hoping she would get back from Toby's soon. I squinted up the road, relieved to see a figure coming down the hill. But as it came closer, I saw that the figure was wearing a puffy brown coat. It was Toby, not Charlotte.

I crept back into Charlotte's backyard and stared out onto the whitening lawn, vegetable garden, and trampoline. I re-

membered the time Charlotte had dropped one of Paul's soccer
cleats down under the trampoline to drive him crazy looking
for it. I'd wondered how deep the hole was.

Right now I didn't care how deep it went, as long as it got
me out of this snow and away from Toby. I squeezed between
the corner springs and crawled halfway across the width of the
trampoline.

I pulled my knees to my chest and tried not shiver too hard.

I breathed in and out carefully, and after about a minute I
managed to stop shivering altogether.

I'd learned to breathe like that from Charlotte. She taught
me one night in August, when I slept over at her house just a
few days before the start of school. She had been trying to get
me to have an out-of-body experience, which she'd expertly
referred to as an OBE. The list of tips in her black book was
easy enough to understand. She'd stood by the window of her
bedroom, using the remaining evening light to read them as I'd
lain on her bed, eyes closed, imagining, just as she'd instructed,
that I was floating. And concentrating on a single image—I'd
decided on Charlotte's old stuffed unicorn, which had caught
my attention just before I'd closed my eyes.

"'Breathe rhythmically,'" she'd read, "'keeping your mouth
slightly open.'"

Easy enough. But why would you *want* to leave your body?
I'd wanted to ask Charlotte when we'd read the book together
over dinner.

We'd looked at some pictures of the shadow of a man getting
up and leaving his sleeping body. The pictures were dark, and
the man was naked and skinny—and when you looked closely,
you could sort of see the lump between his legs. If that was why

Charlotte kept lingering on those pages, she didn't say so. But I wondered.

When she'd finally turned the page, there was full-page picture drawn by a woman who'd had an OBE. A tunnel of trees and leaves, all drawn in delicate silvery lines. That was what she'd seen when she'd left her body.

I held that image in my head now as I scrunched under the trampoline, breathing carefully in and out. Although I hadn't any wish to leave my body—whatever that meant to Charlotte or anybody else—the spot drawn in that lady's picture seemed a place I wouldn't mind going to. A tunnel, but a gentle one, with little round leaves carpeting the ground. If I could just disappear there for a while, I could forget everything.

"Nora?"

I jumped. Toby's head was poking down between two of the trampoline springs.

"I knocked on Charlotte's door," he said. "Then I followed your footprints in the snow. What're you doing down here?"

I thought about the question. Probably the answer was that I was just hanging out alone. I thought of saying, *I want to be alone*. But I wasn't sure that was true.

"I'm astral-projecting," I said, watching Toby climb into the trampoline pit. He huddled right beneath where he'd appeared and didn't come any closer.

"What's that mean?" he asked.

"It's when you get your mind to float away from your body," I explained.

"Why would you want to do that?"

"I dunno. You can fly above New York City. Or go to another planet."

"Isn't that just, like, using your imagination?"

"*No.*" I scoffed, channeling Charlotte. "You *really* go there. Not just in your head. Your . . . um . . . *soul* really goes."

"What happens to your body while you're gone? Does it die?"

"No. I don't think so."

"Well," Toby said, considering this, "I wouldn't risk it."

I closed my eyes.

"Everything is going to be okay," he said after a moment.

I opened my eyes and stared at him. He was trying to talk like someone on TV. People said that all the time on TV, but it had no place in real life.

"Shut up," I said.

"Why?"

"Because nobody says that."

"But I thought we should—"

"You can stay here," I interrupted, "if you're quiet."

"Okay," Toby said after thinking about it briefly.

I closed my eyes. I breathed in and out carefully. After a few minutes, I could hear Toby doing the same. He was breathing so deeply I started to wonder if he was sleeping.

I decided to shut him out, along with everything else. I made the space in my head white and slowly tried to redraw in that space the tree tunnel I'd seen in Charlotte's book. Arching silver trees forming a delicate wooded tunnel. But however I imagined them, they kept looking, eventually, like the woods between the Cooks' place and Larsons' house. The space that had swallowed up Rose. It seemed just yesterday I'd thought of it like that.

Maybe I couldn't fly away to New York City or another planet. But I could get back to yesterday. I could draw and redraw those trees between the Cooks' and the Larsons' in silver lines till they formed a swirling, leafy tunnel for Rose to wander into and disappear.

I listened to the almost-snoring of Toby's breath and stared down into that beautiful silver-lined, leaf-strewn tunnel. It went on forever. Back to yesterday—way back beyond yesterday, really. Back to when Rose had wandered up into those trees and disappeared. Back to before I'd been afraid of her dying. Before I'd seen Toby's father's face and it made me think of skeletons.

Before all that she'd simply wandered into this endless shining passage of trees and never stopped walking. I just had to take myself out of this space and time and put myself there. I could think back past today and yesterday, the days before, and quiet myself into it. I let my sighing breath match Toby's and let everything behind my eyes go soft silver and white.

Silver branches and leaves curling in on themselves, embracing Rose till I could no longer see her. A nest, really, for her to sleep in. Nothing more. Nothing scary. Just a nest. For us both to sleep in, Rose and me.

Twenty

May 27, 2006

We didn't say anything at first—not till we were a good distance from Toby's house, walking past the wooded area that had seemed so vast when we were kids. The bright green maple leaves seemed to glitter as they fluttered in the breeze.

"What did you see, Toby?" I asked after we'd passed Mrs. Crowe's. "When she says, 'Toby saw me.'"

"You really have no idea?" he asked quietly.

"No."

"Because for a long time, I thought you knew. I thought you knew about Rose somehow, and that was why you were so messed up."

"What? What did you think I knew?"

"I even thought, when you tried to kill yourself, you were trying to be like her."

We were both quiet as we passed the Hemsworths'.

"Except she had a reason," Toby added. "You didn't, really."

"I had a reason," I said once we'd reached the bottom of Fox Hill and began crossing Adams Road toward the tennis courts. "I just explained it to you."

"Didn't sound like a very good one, though."

"I don't recall saying it was a good one. What would be a good one anyway?"

We crossed over the small gravel parking lot for the courts, then down the tree-lined path that led to them. Toby stopped walking for a moment.

"How about knowing you'd helped paralyze someone for life, maybe?"

"But, Toby . . ." I said. "How could she have . . . ?"

Toby just shook his head. "God, sometimes I wished it was you. Everyone thought you had some deep, dark secret. Poor Nora. So scared. So silent. What did she see that was haunting her? If you were the one who got to run from here and never come back, why wasn't it you who had to bear it? It wasn't fair."

We'd reached the courts now. Toby lifted the rusted latch and held the metal gate open for me. As always, there was no one playing tennis, despite the perfect weather for it. The wind picked up as we began to walk around the edge of the court. Waves of green leaves billowed in the space just beyond the court's fence.

"What did you see?" I asked him again. "I really want to know, Toby."

He ran his finger along the cyclone fence as we walked. "I saw her a few nights before . . . I saw her. It was after dinner, it was already dark. My dad had me take the garbage out to the

end of the driveway. And when I got there, I heard this singing, this humming. I followed it. I found her there at that blind
curve, just after Fox Hill Road turns into Fox Hill Way. She had
her eyes closed. She had her arms and palms spread out by her
sides like she was waiting for the Rapture or something. She
was humming that song 'Sweet Dreams Are Made of This.' You
know that song?"

I nodded, shuddering for some reason at this detail.

"When I got closer, I saw she had headphones on. That's why
she didn't hear me coming.

"I couldn't figure out what she was doing. Was she on her way
to see my brother again? Waiting till a little later, when my dad
would probably be zonked out on the couch after a couple more
beers? So she could suck face with Joe some more? But why was
she right the fuck in the middle of the road? I wondered. Well,
not *right* in the middle. If she was right in the middle, someone
would be able to see her before they turned. But no, she was
just a little off to the side, where they wouldn't.

"But it wasn't till I read what she wrote that I understood.
She was playing chicken, like. Playing chicken with herself, 'cuz
she thought she maybe wanted to die. Thinking nothing about
who would hit her, of course. Thinking of nobody but herself
and her own drama. Like someone hitting her would fix Brian.
Like it would fix anything. Who thinks that way? Who's that
selfish? Who's that crazy?"

It wasn't a real question, but I had a real answer. A confused kid, of course. A kid faced with a very adult guilt she'd
been unable to handle. So she'd started doing desperate—although strangely juvenile—things. Practically drinking herself

to death. Asking Joe for pills. Playing pedestrian chicken on a blind curve, willing fate to take her. Like what I'd done, but with a riskier calculation and, apparently a different outcome.

The desperation of it was painful, the stupidity of it familiar. Suddenly I felt weak in the legs. I stopped walking and grabbed onto the cyclone fence to keep myself standing.

"Someone hit her, Toby?"

"Not the night I was out. Not that night. And I didn't know for years. I didn't know exactly what happened. But a couple of days later . . . she must've been doing it again."

"Toby?" I said slowly.

The waves of green leaves were now making me dizzy. They swelled with a particularly strong gust of wind, and I half expected them to wash over us like a tidal wave.

"Yeah?" Toby said.

I felt his arm on my elbow, steadying me.

"Was it Joe?" I managed.

"Joe didn't have a car yet," Toby said, then lowered himself down to the clay, sitting right in the sun. "He walked home from work in the dark most nights, or my dad picked him up, depending."

"Oh," I said, getting to my knees, then sitting next to him.

He squinted at me, waiting for my next question.

"Was it your dad?"

Toby's face was stone. He glanced around at the trees before answering.

"Yeah," he said.

We sat together for several minutes before he spoke again.

"A couple of days later, after I saw her, the day she disappeared—she came to our door when she was done baby-sitting you guys. Asking for Joe. I was the only one home. When I said he was working, she left. And then, an hour later, my dad comes home. It was dark by then. And he comes in the house screaming, *Toby, don't go outside! Don't go outside, Toby!* Then, *Call Mrs. Reed!* And I dialed your number. And then he was like, *No, don't call her! Never mind, Toby! Don't call!* So I hung up. And then he says to call 911, and then he changes his mind before I do it. And then he starts saying, *Don't go outside, Toby.* Says it over and over like a crazy man. But after a half hour, he stops saying it. And a few hours later, he's back to normal again, just staring at the TV like almost any other night.

"And later I asked him what was wrong and why I couldn't go outside. And I let him tell me there was something in his truck for Christmas he didn't want me to see. *Something in his truck for Christmas.* Do you believe that, Nora? Do you believe what a bonehead kid I was? But come Christmas there *was* a new dirt bike for me. A new used dirt bike. So it was possible, wasn't it? It was possible?"

Toby stared at me.

"Yeah," I choked out. "It was possible. And you were only twelve."

"I was so thick I let myself believe it. Somewhere in the back of my mind, I knew that something was wrong, but I managed to put it out of my head. But then, when I was seventeen, I found the backpack with the notebook. Still, though, it was just a notebook. It scared me, but it wasn't enough to condemn anyone. I managed to rationalize it away. She left some shit at our house. So what? She'd been sneaking over and seeing my brother. It was possible. And all that stuff she'd written—I sent some of it to Brian, I put some of it in Charlotte's box. And no one did anything. Nothing happened. It started to feel like I'd been stupid to let it scare me. Who cared? No one, apparently. Maybe it was all in my head.

"But then, right before my father died, he told me the whole story. Just opened his mouth two days before he died—between one morphine haze and another. He needed to clear his conscience before he died. He'd turned that corner coming home from happy hour in the dark. And there she was. He'd hit her, and she'd died instantly. And he panicked."

"Why didn't he call the police? An ambulance?"

"Like I just said. Panic, I guess. Why didn't he leave her there, drive those last few yards home, call 911, and come back? I've asked myself that so many times. But he was drinking in those days, the year or so after his mom had died. Made good use of happy hour. I guess he'd had quite a few that night, wasn't thinking straight. Didn't really know what to do. Maybe thought he'd go to jail and there'd be no one to take care of us. We didn't have a lot going for us. We lived by the dump, and we smelled funny, and we didn't have a mother. Maybe he thought the straw that would break the camel's back would be when we were also the kids whose dad killed that pretty blond girl. Whatever he was thinking, once he hid what happened for a few hours—even if he realized later what a terrible mistake he'd made—it was too late to go back on it. I don't know if all that went through his head when he stuck her in the cab of his truck and drove her that tiny little stretch of road between the corner and our house, but that's what he did. Probably none of that crossed his mind. Probably he was just in total shock at hitting her, total shock from taking that curve and smacking right into a stupid-as-fuck teenager with her eyes closed in the road, not to mention a little fuzzy from a bunch of beers, and did something crazy stupid. For a few minutes, I think, his first thought was saving her. Which is why he was gonna have me call your mom. He'd gotten used to calling her for emergencies with his mother. But then he realized that Rose was already dead. She'd died instantly."

Toby looked at the trees as he talked, refusing to meet my gaze. I held still. I held my breath.

"Maybe she hoped my brother would see her when he was walking home. See her and figure it out and feel bad for her. Ask her what the hell was wrong with her. Because I can't imagine she was thinking there was a good chance if she got hit, it would be by my dad. I can't think she would've been that cruel to us."

I wanted to respond to this, to assure Toby that Rose simply hadn't been thinking at all. That she was too deeply involved in a game with herself to think of anyone else. But a more pressing concern came to mind before I could say so.

"Her body," I whispered. "What did he do with her body?"

Toby watched the wall of leaves as it fluttered in the wind again.

"He'd shoved her in the root cellar for a few months at first. Then he moved her that summer when Joe and I were camping. Buried her deep under one of the dirt mounds of the cellar, wrapped in plastic. And she'd been there since."

"But . . ." I said. "But then how did her body—"

"I'm getting to that."

He stood up and paced a few circles around me before speaking again.

"After he died, I looked. I dug. Even then—despite everything, despite the notebook—I had this tiny hope it was just the raving delusion of a dying man. But there it was. There was a dead body in our house. Someone we knew, for God's sake. Someone we liked. Rose had been there alone all that time. If I moved her someplace where someone would find her, at least her family could know, could bury her. And the pond, at least she'd liked it there. We'd all been happy there once.

"So you see now why you've asked me too late. I was innocent for a long time. You could've helped me, once. Even after I found that notebook, I was innocent. Even prom night, when you were drunk and almost let me tell you what I was afraid of, it wouldn't have been too late. But in the end I panicked. I'd never thought it could be real, and I panicked when I saw that it was. Looks like I have some of my father's stupidity in me. Looks like panic brings it out in the Dean men."

Toby stopped pacing and sat with me on the clay again. He stared at me expectantly, one eye begging me to respond, the other looking noncommittal. I put my hand on my stomach, trying to ignore the bile rising in my throat.

"Toby, you dug her up? You saw her?"

"I didn't see anything. Not really. I couldn't stand it. I knew enough to know what it was. Everything was already all wrapped up in an old sheet of plastic. I just rolled the whole thing into this big basket and brought her somewhere they'd find her."

My hand started to move toward Toby, but something stopped me from touching him. Then he turned away from me and buried his head in his hands.

Phantom Encounters:
December 1990

Charlotte couldn't fool me. I knew she'd probably listened to the whole tape last night by herself. She'd probably already memorized every slight tap or scratch in the ninety minutes of tape hiss and was now ready to watch me listen. She probably knew exactly when to watch for my ears to perk up, my psychic sensitivities to give something away.

"I hope we find something," she said theatrically, setting a bowl of freshly popped popcorn between us and pressing "play." "I hope we can prove old Tom Edison right."

Old Tom Edison. I rolled my eyes. There'd been something in her books about Thomas Edison in his golden years trying to capture ghost voices on recording devices. Kind of interesting, but I didn't appreciate Charlotte's tone. Like we knew Mr. Edison well enough to call him "Tom," like we were all characters in one of my mother's PBS mysteries—jolly and clever even though someone was dead.

Charlotte crammed a handful of popcorn into her mouth, crunching it noisily as we listened to her announcing the first address where we'd done our outdoor recording. As the tape moved steadily to the part where Toby had interrupted us, Charlotte sat at her desk and examined her bottles of nail polish. I expected her to fast-forward through Toby's "shenanigans," but she didn't. I ate some popcorn, pulling the best buttery pieces off the top of the bowl.

The early recording was over fairly quickly. Then there was a break in the tape, then Charlotte announcing, *"We are at the Dean residence, on the top floor. The Deans do not use this space for anything but storage, according to resident Toby Dean. This may be because of fears of . . . possible paranormal activity. I'm positioning the recorder on a box. . . ."*

There was some shuffling, then the sound of Charlotte's footsteps pacing the creaky floorboards, then silence.

Charlotte opened her bottle of pearly-pink nail polish and began painting her left thumbnail with it. Figuring I needn't go through the charade of listening super carefully either, I grabbed *Mysterious Lands and Peoples* out from under her bed. Now that we were investigating nearly full-time, Charlotte kept the black books more readily available than she had before Rose had disappeared. I turned to my favorite Easter Island picture and stared at it as the tape hissed on.

Then there were footsteps on the tape again.

"This is where I went to the bathroom," Charlotte confessed. "I also peeked in Toby's room. He has a poster of Alyssa Milano. Isn't that *gross?*"

I nodded.

Then silence on the tape, then more footsteps. Then a guttural, sighing sound came out of the recorder.

"Rose. Roooooose. Where's ROOOOOOSE?" the voice asked abruptly, startling me for a split second before I realized it was Toby. *"Nobody KNOOOOOOOWS."*

"I'm gonna strangle him," Charlotte said, rather casually.

She was now painting the other fingernails on her left hand.

Toby repeated his words again, then was quiet for a moment, then started humming slowly, deeply, perhaps as he thought a ghost would hum.

Then the ghost voice started singing "Every Rose Has Its Thorn" by Poison.

"God, Toby's so *lame*," Charlotte declared.

The song performance went on for quite a while, with Toby repeating the same lines several times and skipping the ones he couldn't remember. Then he began imitating the song's tinny guitar solo, getting really into it, forgetting he was supposed to be a ghost:

"Neenerneener-neenerneener-neenerneener-NEEEEEEEEEEEEEEEEEE!"

I cringed as Toby screeched right into the microphone.

"What a dork," Charlotte said, looking at me expectantly for agreement.

I agreed somewhat but felt it would be unkind, even disloyal, to say so. I thought about Toby and me below the trampoline the afternoon before. When it was just him and me, he knew how to be normal, how to be quiet. So quiet I could picture that silver forest while he was sitting right next to me. So quiet I could've gone to sleep right there under the trampoline and barely even remembered he was there.

But his singing was so loud and so awful I could barely remember that quiet now. His voice was deep like his brother's and slow like his dad's. And maybe a little sad.

Just when I thought I wouldn't be able to stand it a second longer, his song came to an end. Then I could hear him clucking his tongue, probably trying to think of some other obnoxious thing a ghost could do. It took him about a minute to come up with something.

"*Who . . . Who? Who was the last?*" He spoke in that low, throaty voice that death-metal singers use—that always sounds like a really mean Cookie Monster or a deranged Santa Claus.

"*Who. Was. The Last. To See. Her. A-liiiiiiive?*"

"*To see her ALIIIIIIIIIIIVE?*" the death-metal voice asked again.

"Really in poor taste," Charlotte said in her best imitation-teacher voice.

"*WHO. WAS. THE. LAST,*" he started again, this time more rhythmically.

I clenched my hands into fists and tried to ignore him. I stared at my perfect Easter Island picture. This was the second time Toby was wondering who was really the last to see Rose alive. The stupid death-metal voice didn't scare me—just the question he insisted upon asking again.

"*TO SEE HER AL-IIIIIIIIIVE?*"

I got up from the carpet.

"*WHO—*"

I jumped over to Charlotte's desk and stopped the tape.

"What?" Charlotte said.

"*I* was," I insisted. "I WAS!"

Charlotte wrinkled her forehead, not understanding.

"He's almost done," she said. "After this he goes downstairs again."

I ejected the tape from the player and held it in my hand for a moment. Charlotte could listen to this over and over and never really hear Toby, because she didn't know how to listen the way I did. She didn't know that Toby was trying to say something.

He was a boy, and he didn't have big words like she did—so he could only say it in a stupid boy way. She didn't know how to hear it, and I didn't *want* to hear it—ever again. So this tape was useless.

I pinched a bit of the brown tape out of the rectangular hole in the bottom of the cassette and flung a stream of it sideways.

"NO!" Charlotte screamed, bounding out of her chair and tackling me.

After I'd hit the floor, I kept pulling the tape out, as she grabbed at me, scratching me, getting fresh pink nail polish on my hands, arms, and face.

"What are you *doing*?" she screamed. "Are you crazy, Nora? What's wrong with you?"

She managed to snatch the cassette from me. I grabbed a piece of the tape off the carpet and twisted and pulled and bit at it till it broke in half.

"Oh, GREAT!" Charlotte moaned, falling back on the carpet. "Now we'll never get to listen to it again. All that research!"

"What do you care?" I said. "You've already listened to the whole stupid thing anyway."

"So? So that means you get to ruin my tape?"

"I'll buy you a new blank tape."

"You better."

"I will."

"Fine."

Charlotte sat up and stared at me. "You're mad at Toby? For messing up the tape?"

I didn't reply.

"Did you hear something?" she said, lowering her voice.

I stared back at her. She wasn't all that mad about the tape, really, now that she'd caught her breath. How could I explain to her that I'd heard something terrible in Toby's voice? And that she'd heard it, too—she just didn't feel it the way I did. I didn't understand it, but I felt it, and she clearly didn't.

Maybe that was why I'd been angry at her for so many weeks. She knew things. But sometimes she didn't feel things.

"I heard the same thing you did," I mumbled.

We sat together on the carpet for a minute more, Charlotte looking at me, me looking away. I gazed across the room to where her black book lay open on the floor, still turned to the Easter Island page. I thought of finally asking to borrow the book but decided against it. I didn't think I'd be coming back here tomorrow.

"I don't feel well," I said. "I should probably go home now."

"You gonna throw up or something?" Charlotte wanted to know.

"Maybe," I said, since puke was at least something we both understood.

And then she let me go.

Twenty-one

May 27, 2006

I don't know how long we sat on that tennis court together. The sun was bright, but there was still a breeze. A bird in a nearby maple tweeted cheerily. Toby didn't lift his face from his hands.

"Like I said, I wished it was you," he said into his hands, finally speaking. "Everyone thought maybe you had some dark secret inside you, something you'd seen, something that haunted you. Something about Rose. Too deep and dark to even remember, much less tell. I wished it had been you, not me. Like everyone thought. So how does it feel now, to actually have the kind of secret everyone thought you had?"

I breathed in and out carefully—the way Charlotte had taught me so long ago. Back when I was her subject. Slowly, the trees around the courts began to look like trees again. My heart finally stopped racing.

I didn't answer his question.

"It's not too late, Toby," I said instead.

"It's too late. I moved her. I hid her. Not when I was twelve, or even seventeen. Twenty-eight. I'm twenty-eight years old. It's too late."

I stared at the short, dark hair on the top of his head. So different from his almost-mullet when we were kids. It was a younger look than he'd had as a kid. I reached out and touched his ear so he would look up at me.

"It's not too late for it to be me."

Toby shook his head.

"Say I found that notebook somewhere," I said. "Like the Hemsworths' house. Rose was always leaving crap there. Maybe we just discovered it in Charlotte's box of black books, just this week, when we were skipping down memory lane. But, Jesus, it practically describes how she died. It's almost all there. And when I read it, say it all came tumbling back. What I'd seen, what I'd heard. Rose in the road in the dark, with her Walkman."

Toby's lips twitched as he considered my words.

"What kind of car was your father driving? That old truck?"

"Yes. His old red Ford."

"Surely with all your automobile expertise, you know of a truck with a similar build, a similar height that could have hit her in the same way."

"Well, lots could. Depending on the height of the tires. Chevy Silverado. Toyota, GMC, whatever. Even a minivan could—"

"Okay. So I was wandering around the neighborhood, waiting for my mom to get home. I saw Rose with her headphones, but I didn't understand it. And then, a little while later, I saw a black truck with GMC across the back go up the hill, before I went inside. Listen, Toby. I'm really considered a witness. Not just some bozo walking in off the street with some crazy theory."

"An eleven-year-old girl and you remember GMC? You're crazy."

"I'd say it was a big black truck. The Bankses would at least know what happened. They'd at least know she didn't suffer long."

"But they wouldn't know who did it."

"Does it matter who did it? It was an accident. The hardest part of it is still true. How much does the driver matter, when you know Rose's part of it? So the one who did it was a guy in a black truck, not a red one. Put her in the back and carried her away. Maybe I even saw that part. And apparently he buried her later. They just won't be able to find the guy."

"I don't think you can lead the police into all that, Nora. I don't think they would believe that you would have—"

"Forget what they think of me. Forget what crazy things I'd have to say about myself. A lot of people around here still think I'm a little crazy. Makes it all the more believable, doesn't it? No one could figure out what screwed me up so bad that year I never got over it. It makes twisted sense, doesn't it?"

"No," Toby said. "Not really."

"Well, I don't have to tell all that if you don't want me to. I could just give them the notebook. Or just mention the truck."

"A truck would implicate my dad eventually."

"Maybe," I said slowly. "But would that be so bad?"

"What?" Toby said.

"Your dad's gone now. You don't need to protect him. Maybe

he moved her just before he died. Would he have known how little time he had left? Maybe he moved her to protect you? Maybe at least *you* didn't know anything."

Toby bit his lip, looking thoughtful. "Maybe," he said softly.

"And you've already been punished enough. Do you need to protect your dad anymore? Maybe it was all your dad. Maybe I did see a red truck if you want it that way. But maybe you're as shocked to hear it as anyone else."

"Maybe you ought to think about this a little more." Toby still sounded doubtful. "You wouldn't come off looking very good."

"Who cares how I look? If I saw everything—if I saw your dad—it's all believable. Because it's all true. And there's Rose's own words to back it up. And if they believe that your dad could hide the body, they sure as hell can believe he moved it."

Toby avoided my gaze.

"C'mon," I said. "Just think about it."

"And what about Charlotte?" he asked. "You gonna include her in this plan?"

"I don't know. Does it really matter? I haven't thought about it that far yet. I just came up with it."

"If you're going to say you found that notebook at her house," Toby said, "you'd have to let her in on it. Or risk making her family look suspicious."

"Oh," I said, considering this.

"Why don't you sleep on it? Think about it. Spend a little more time with Charlotte this weekend. Think about that part of it. Because, you know, if you make this confession and she thinks you've been keeping this from her all these years, she's never gonna talk to you again."

"But she'll be happy her dad won't be under suspicion any-more."

"Her dad," Toby said, shaking his head. "That's right. Her dad. I heard. I'd forgotten about that. Might look a little funny that the person coming out of the woodwork with this nutty story is a friend of the daughter of one of the people they've been questioning. Have you thought of that?"

"I'm not a person coming out of the woodwork. I'm the prime witness. I'm the only one anyone ever thought could've seen something."

"Well . . . listen. You've started me thinking. But we should talk more. Way more, before you think of doing anything. Don't do anything stupid, okay? Don't talk to Charlotte yet. How about we talk about this again tomorrow?"

"All right," I said.

"Where does Charlotte think you are anyway?"

"Nowhere in particular. She fell asleep. So I kind of ran off."

"Maybe you ought to get back to her. Can you have coffee tomorrow? How about Denny's?"

"Sounds good," I said, relieved I didn't have to keep trying to sound convincing. I wasn't at all certain I could pull it off. But I was going to have to, somehow. I owed him something. I wasn't sure what that was, exactly, but this was the best I could come up with.

Toby got up and put his hand out. It took me a moment to realize he was helping me up.

"Nine o'clock?" he asked as I stood.

Something about the feel of his callused hand in mine made me hesitate to answer. Something about his loosening grip, or the lukewarm temperature of his palm. I tried to hold on to his hand for an extra second, but then he let go.

"Okay," I agreed hoarsely.

"I've got to go buy some ribs," Toby explained, stepping toward the gates of the court, "take care of my brother. I promised him a little barbecue."

It seemed to me a bit bizarre, after all he'd told me, that the next step would be to go home and grill some meat with his brother.

"All right," I said anyway.

We didn't talk much on the walk back up the hill.

"Nora?" he said when we reached the Hemsworths' place.

"Yes?"

"Whatever happens, and whatever anyone thinks of you—I can tell that you turned out all right. You did what you needed to do, and you turned out all right. Just like you said. You're all right."

He said it wearily, and with a hint of obligation. The way you tell your host the food is delicious or a bride she looks beautiful.

I hesitated, wondering whether I should thank him or tell him he needn't say such things.

"Good-bye, Nora," he said, and continued up the hill.

Mystic Places:
January 1991

By now Charlotte knew not to try to walk home with me when we got off at the bus stop. For weeks I'd been sitting at the very front of the bus so that when it stopped, I could flee out and up the hill, several paces ahead of anyone who got out after me.

But this time Toby was second off the bus, and he ran to catch up with me.

"Hey, Nora," he said.

"Hey."

"Why do you always walk so fast anyway?"

"It's really cold out. I'm just in a hurry to get home."

"How come you don't walk with Charlotte anymore? Did you have a fight?"

"Ask her," I mumbled, staring down at the icy sidewalk, trying to step carefully.

Toby shook his head. "She asked me to ask you, actually."

I didn't have a reply to this. "I just want to get home," I repeated, shrugging.

"Are you guys investigating Rose anymore?" Toby wanted to know.

"Definitely not," I said, quickening my steps to get ahead of him and then slipping on the ice, falling hard on my butt.

"Oh, crap!" Toby said, trying not to laugh. "Are you okay?"

"Yeah," I said, looking away from him.

He put his hand out to help me, but I pretended not to see it.

"Haven't you heard? She just wants us all to leave her alone," said Charlotte, who had now caught up with us. She was walking with Sarah Boswell, the fourth-grade gymnastics prodigy from up the street.

"I'm not bothering her," said Toby. "I'm just helping her up."

Charlotte gazed at me sadly as she passed, then continued to talk to Sarah.

Toby stared down at me, his bad eye seeming particularly

crooked. I hated looking at that stupid droopy eye. Why was Toby taking so much longer to get the point than Charlotte had?

"Just let me help you up, and then I'll leave you alone," he offered. "How about that?"

I looked away from him again, lowering my voice to a growl. "Skip the first part."

"But—"

"Just leave me alone, Eyeball," I snapped, so loudly it surprised even me.

"Oh," he said, startled.

Then he stepped past me gingerly, glancing back at me for a moment before continuing up the hill.

I looked around me before I got to my feet. Everything was January-ugly now. The dull white of the icy sidewalk. The crust of dirt the plow had left on the snow at the roadsides. The gray of the sky and the thin fog that floated from my mouth as I sat there sighing.

I knew that spring was supposed to come someday, but it seemed too far away to be believed. This year was different that way. I just didn't think it would ever come. The snow seemed too high and the ice too thick to ever melt. This year springtime was like Atlantis. I wanted to believe in it, but I couldn't. I'd believe it when I saw it. And I had a feeling it was going to be winter for a while.

Twenty-two

May 28, 2006

I awoke to the sound of Charlotte screaming.

"When? WHEN? Jesus!"

I sat up in bed. What time was it? Charlotte and I had stayed up way too late, drinking Riesling with our burgers and s'mores. I'd collapsed into the bed but found I couldn't sleep, worrying about the details of my plan to help Toby. Could I possibly lie to the police? Would it be obstruction of justice if the death was an accident and the driver was dead? Could I go to jail if someone figured out I was lying, even if the story I was telling was essentially true? Now I had a headache from all the worry and all the wine. But I still planned to meet Toby and get down to business.

"Last night, I guess" was the response Charlotte received from Porter.

He was here at the house, in the living room. Whatever news he'd had, he'd come to give it to Charlotte in person.

"I saw the press conference on Channel Eight, just about an hour ago."

I put one foot out of the bed and stood up. I squinted at my phone. Ten o'clock. As I checked the screen, I saw I had a voice mail.

"They're saying a family member of the person responsible has come forward. A very credible source, apparently. And the story basically checks out with skeletal forensic evidence. Probably a vehicular incident, followed by a cover-up, is what they're saying. A sort of hit-and-run. 'Vehicular incident.' Why they can't just call it a car accident, I don't know—"

With a trembling finger, I hit "play" on the voice mail. It had arrived around eleven the previous night.

"Hey, Nora. It's Toby. I just wanted to say thanks for that thing you offered, but I don't think it's gonna work out. I'm glad you came back here, though. I probably forgot to tell you that."

There was silence and then a shifting noise on the message. I thought Toby was about to hang up, but he continued.

"Isn't it funny how the people you grew up with know what you're really capable of and what you're not? Kind of annoying, actually, isn't it? Anyway. Thanks, Nora. Take care."

The voice-mail lady asked if I wanted to erase, replay, or save the message. I was too stunned to make a choice. I sat on the bed as she asked again.

"Where's Nora?" I heard Porter ask from the living room.

"Still sleeping," Charlotte said.

No. I wasn't. But it *was* late.

I pressed a button to replay Toby's message.

I'd awoken way too late.

Twenty-three

October 15, 2007

Charlotte called me to ask if I'd be attending the ten-year re-union.

By then Toby had been put on probation for moving Rose's body and had since left Waverly. The court had been lenient, in no small part due to the Bankses, who testified that they did not wish to see him punished for a crime his father had committed when he was just a child. But Deans' Auto Body business had declined due to the scandal, and Toby and Joe had put the house up for sale. They'd sold it dirt cheap to a big family desperate to put their kids in the high-scoring Waverly schools. Joe was still around, though, Charlotte assured me—living with a new girlfriend in Fairville. Toby had moved up to Vermont or New Hampshire somewhere and was working in a garage up there, if the intelligence gathered from his brother's occasional visits to Atkins could be trusted.

And as far as I knew, Charlotte herself still hadn't any plans to move from Fox Hill. But she was getting her master's now, thinking of being a reading specialist, and looking into jobs in other districts.

We didn't discuss these things during this particular call, though. The topic of the call was the reunion. Charlotte was helping organize the event herself. She'd even seen Kelly Sawyer on the roster—it was going to be interesting. She knew it was a long shot, she said, but could she coax me to come?

Of course we both knew that the answer was no. I cited the long drive as an excuse, plus an extra class and a particularly busy fair season. The truth was, I hadn't the energy or the inclination to return to Waverly quite so soon—to fret again about a girl lost in the trees at the top of Fox Hill, a girl trapped in silence, a girl I'd probably never understand.

Right before we hung up, Charlotte promised me a full report on the reunion. I almost told her not to bother but stopped myself. I wanted to hear. And I wanted us to have a reason to talk again.

Mysterious Lands and Peoples:
July 1990

The first time I saw those Easter Island statues in the summer, we were sprawled out on Charlotte's trampoline with a few of her books, eating pretzels and drinking Pepsi, trying to get a suntan with Rose. I was so curious about the statues that I stopped looking through the pictures and actually read a bit about them.

The statues weighed as much as fifty tons, I reported to Charlotte and Rose. But no one knew how they got from the quarry to all the different places on the island where they now stood. Some islanders believed that in ancient times the statues had magically walked from the quarry on their own.

"Nobody really believes that," Charlotte said, applying a second layer of 35 SPF sunblock to her arms. Unlike Rose and me, she didn't seem to have any actual interest in making her skin any browner.

"They wouldn't say it if they didn't believe it," I countered.

"Forget believing it," Rose said without opening her eyes. "Maybe it really happened."

"No," Charlotte said confidently. "It didn't."

"How do you know there weren't magic moving statues way back then?" Rose asked. "There's no way you can know that, Charlotte."

"Magic didn't exist then any more then than it does now," Charlotte said with a shrug.

Rose finally sat up and squinted at Charlotte. "And how do you know *that*?"

"Magic was how people explained things they didn't understand," Charlotte informed us both. "They needed to believe in magic because they didn't have science."

"That's just one way of looking it," Rose said, lying back and closing her eyes again, as if dismissing the topic. "Magic could've existed then even though it doesn't now. Just like penicillin exists now but didn't then."

"Penicillin exists now because we *invented* it," Charlotte pointed out.

"'*We*'? Who's this '*we*'?" Rose asked. "Did you have some hand in it?"

Charlotte glared at Rose and murmured something under her breath.

"Penicillin exists because we need it," Rose reasoned. "And maybe we need it because there's not magic anymore, like they had then."

"They had magic then because they had nothing better to believe in," Charlotte insisted.

"Did it ever occur to you that it was easier to believe in it because they *had* it?"

"No," Charlotte said, grabbing a pretzel and crunching on it with angry vigor.

Rose let the conversation drop there. Neither of them asked me what I thought. But it seemed to me Rose could be right. I wondered about the people who lived on Easter Island in ancient times, back when magic maybe existed. Was their magic there one day and gone the next? Were they upset and confused the day it left them? Or did it fade gradually?

Either way, it could be true. Magic had existed in the past. But it had left the earth at some point, and there was no way for us to pull back the years and see it and feel it again—or even to prove that it had once been real. It felt true because Rose had said it. It probably wouldn't feel true always, but it did for that moment, that hour, the whole rest of that afternoon.

Acknowledgments

First, I would like to extend a huge thank you to my awesome agent, Laura Langlie, for believing in this book from the very beginning and working so hard on my behalf.

I would also like to thank my wonderful editor, Carrie Feron, as well as Tessa Woodward and the whole Avon/HarperCollins team.

And, of course, thank you for everything, dear Ross—but especially for your patient multiple readings despite my stubborn refusal to add explosions, cowboys, or rescue dogs.

I also owe many thanks to my gracious early readers: Cari Strand, Mason Rabinowitz, Nicole Moore, Megan Gregory, Jessica Bundschuh, Emily MacFadyen, and Eric Kaye.

Also, thanks to my family for their support, Leigh Anne Keichline for her encouragement, D. T. for her spirit, and Kristen Kertesz Patterson for the good old days.

Ross Grant

EMILY ARSENAULT has worked as a lexicographer, an English teacher, and a Peace Corps volunteer in rural South Africa. Her first novel, *The Broken Teaglass*, was selected by the *New York Times* as a Notable Crime Book of 2009. She grew up in Connecticut and now lives in Shelburne Falls, Massachusetts.

Emily Arsenault